SOMETHING TO ANSWER FOR

Something to Answer For

by

P. H. NEWBY

faber and faber

This edition first published in 2008
by Faber and Faber Ltd
3 Queen Square, London WC1N 3AU

Printed by CPI Antony Rowe, Eastbourne

A CIP record for this book is available from the British Library

ISBN 978-0-571-24325-9

CHAPTER ONE

The Take-over

The old girl kept writing and complaining about the police. It was enough to start Townrow on a sequence of dreams. Night after night he floated in the sunset-flushed, marine city. He could smell the salt and the jasmine. He dreamed that Mrs Khoury, Mr Khoury and he were all sailing out of the harbour in a boat that slowly filled with water. He dreamed he was in a hot, dark room with a lot of men who argued and shouted. It must have been in the Greek Sailing Club because when a door opened there were oars and polished skiffs; and opposite, high over Simon Artz's, on the other side of the Canal, was Johnnie Walker with his cane and top hat setting off for Suez. Or was it the Med.?

By this time, Mrs Khoury was writing to say he was the only friend she had left in the world and she wanted to buy him a ticket on a jet so that he could see for himself what a mess Elie had left his affairs in; and he could make the police track down the murderers because in spite of the Revolution and the troops leaving the Canal Zone these Egyptians still took notice of an Englishman. She was an old woman. She was at her wits end. In spite of her Lebanese passport she was Townrow's fellow-countrywoman and, really, she had nobody else to turn to.

Naturally, he had to laugh. He wrote and explained she wouldn't be able to send him the money because of the currency control; he had next to no money of his own, though now that Jean had married again he didn't have to pay any more alimony, thank God. He had never actually married Liz so there was no financial liability there. Even so, times were hard. It was the height of summer, too, and in Port Said they'd be stewing. It would not be nice. He couldn't bring himself actually to make this last point in writing. It might have seemed selfish.

No, it was a lie times were hard. He was flush now he'd started milking the Fund. That was between him and his shadow.

He had a letter from the London office of United Arab Airlines to say a first-class ticket had been paid for in Cairo. When did he want to use it? There was the usual literature with pictures of the Pyramids and boats on the Nile. Yes, but once he was there he was stuck. He'd be completely at the old girl's mercy.

Nevertheless, he was tempted. He fished out the back letters. She was a lot younger than Elie but even so she'd be a good sixty. Twenty-five years in that climate couldn't have done her a lot of good. She couldn't live for ever. She was the sort of stupid old cow who didn't make a will. This was a pity when you thought how much money Elie must have picked up one way and another. He owned the block of flats they lived in. He was a director of the Phoenician Shipping Line and for about fifty years had shipped cotton and onions out of Port Said, coffee and whisky in. What Mrs K meant by saying his affairs were in a mess probably amounted to no more than the discovery he had banking accounts in Lebanon, Switzerland and the United States; and a couple of dozen gold bars under the floor boards. She was naive. It was all hers now, even the gold and platinum dentures. If he really was the only friend she had left in the world he ought to be advising her about her will. In fact, he began to see himself as sole beneficiary.

The actual teeth were gold but the plate was platinum alloy. The set had been made in Beirut by a deaf and dumb Armenian mechanic who had learned his trade in Naples. Townrow remembered that Elie had told him all this within minutes of their first meeting on the beach at Port Said in 1946. This, the only time in his life he had been on horseback, Townrow was thrown on his head in front of the Khoury's beach hut and Elie brushed him down with his own hands, seated him in a canvas chair, gave him some iced mango-flavoured syrup to drink, threatened the man who hired out the horses, said he was glad to make the acquaintance of an Englishman because his wife was English too, and finally hooked his dentures out for Townrow's inspection. Townrow was still dazed and, thinking the old chap wanted to make him a present of the teeth, would have shaken his head if it hadn't hurt so much. Elie said they were the most remarkable teeth in the world. But for the Revolution the man who had made them would have gone to St Petersburg and worked in the Fabergé workshop. But now he was dead and these teeth were his masterpiece.

"My wife," Elie had said, pointing happily to the back of the hut where Townrow noticed, for the first time, a grey-haired woman sitting in a deck chair reading. Her blue and white striped dress was so long it hid her feet. She took no notice of her husband or Townrow. What with her rather grim little mouth and somewhat bleached cleanliness she looked like Whistler's Mother on holiday. Elie, on the other hand, might have been an old jockey, gone to fat.

They had taken him back to their flat for supper and even now Townrow could remember the strangeness of Mrs K not saying a word until they were actually seated at table. With a real Cockney twang she then said she had been born and brought up in Stepney and she didn't care who knew it. Townrow replied that although he was only a sergeant in the Service Corps (that was because he had been sent down from Oxford) he was one of the Lincolnshire Townrows and his old man was heartily ashamed of him; a lie, but it established a social relationship and that was all Mrs K who cared a hell of a lot that she came from Stepney, really wanted. If Townrow wondered why she'd married

9

this foreigner she had a reason for that too. She had been a First War Widow.

Her father was captain of a cargo ship that made regular runs between Europe and the Far East. She took to sailing with him to get used to being a First War Widow. Four times a year they went through the Suez Canal and after the first two trips there was Elie Khoury regularly waiting for her at Port Said or Suez as the case might be to make the journey through the canal with them and try to persuade her to marry him. He was a widower, nearly as old as her father, and violently in love. He gave her a silver photo frame, a little watch set in diamonds, pearl earrings, a silk stole, a gold-plated pen, an alligator-hide suitcase, ropes of Turkish Delight stuffed with nuts and cream, bottles of perfume and a pair of German field-glasses. And she was in her mid-thirties. They were married in 1922. What do you expect, she had seemed to demand, after a war in which all the better men had died?

Elie had listened to all this with a grin.

"Even so, I'd never've married him if he'd been a Jew or an Arab no matter how much money he'd got, but Lebanese is different, they're almost European in a way and Elie is Christian, of course, which makes a difference even though he's R.C. My mother was strong Baptist and she would not have liked me marrying an R.C. His English is as good as mine, if not better."

She was a shrewd, practical, hard old trot. Townrow thought of her when his father was dying and they sent for him after all those years. It was an invitation to the death of a stranger. Anyway, the ward sister lifted Dad's eyelid and said, "You see, no reaction! He's not conscious of anything," then pulled her finger away to watch the lid close over the sightless white as though it was a blind over the window opposite. She was no more than idly interested. That would have been Mrs K all over. She had done a bit of Red Cross nursing in, of all places, Montenegro in 1918. She must have slipped into the basilisk eye and tight lip routine like a pro. All the more surprising, then, that the death of Elie should set her shouting for help in this girlish way. If Townrow had been asked he would have said she wanted little more from life than a permanent farewell to Port Said. She hated the place. Now was her chance. She might have to cut a few losses. The Nasser government could scarcely be expected to make life easy for an absentee *rentière* but if she really wanted to live in Tunbridge Wells Townrow was sure Elie had fixed his estate so that she could do just that, and in style. Instead, there was all this screaming about murder. If there really was some question of foul play Mrs K herself was as much of a suspect in Townrow's eyes as anybody else in Port Said.

Until he fell on his head outside the Khoury beach hut in 1946 Townrow had no special feelings about the place. He was a sergeant in the military Embarkation Office waiting to be demobbed and if you were in that line of business, putting troops on or off ships, Port Said was the sort of place you were likely to be. But when he had this accident he saw it differently.

For one moment he balanced on his right ear and shoulder, his legs straight up in the air. As he so balanced he saw, upside down, a girl in a bathing costume. She stood with her legs slightly apart and was so relaxed and contented inside her big, glossy thighs and pouting breasts that Townrow thought she must be one of the happiest people alive. Beyond her was a cloud ribbed evening sky and one of the red-brick cathedral towers. The stiffening went out of him, he crumpled and lay on his back looking into Elie's anxious eyes.

Either the girl then went off to another part of the beach or she was a vision because Townrow saw no more of her. Of the two possibilities the vision, he thought, was the likelier. The city quivered in her after-glow. The sun was low enough for those clouds to be red. Beyond the black palm trees the Casino Palace Hotel lost its colour, thinned and broke apart over the night rising quickly out of Asia.

11

Concrete, steel, glass, sand and salt water belched a warm sexuality into his face. He could smell all Egypt, from the mud of the Nile to the roasting corn cobs on the De Lesseps breakwater. No ordinary girl could have done that to him.

As he shaved a muscle twitched at the corner of his left eye and he put down his razor to look out at the north London roof tops. It was a grey day. Perhaps it would be no bad thing to be out of England for a couple of months.

At Rome there was a sixty-minute wait and Townrow spent it in the airport waiting room and the bar. A big man in an expensive-looking panama came over to him and said, "You English?"

Townrow realised the man was younger than he looked. In spite of the weight, the stoop, and the quivering blue cheeks he was probably in his late twenties. He had a good vocabulary but a thick accent. "I am from Israel. I am a journalist. I've been in the States on a trip."

In addition to Townrow there was already one man sitting at the table. Over the tarmac there was a view of the control tower. Because of the heat the air rippled over the tarmac like water and the main buildings and the base of the control tower rippled too. This other man had been complaining to Townrow about the heat and saying it would be even worse in Athens. He was a Greek who worked for a travel agency in Paris.

"What can I do for you?" Townrow said to the Israeli. He did not ask the man to sit down and as he himself remained seated the atmosphere was not friendly. The Israeli seemed to be in a rage. Perhaps he was drunk. But no, it wasn't that.

"In March, 1942," said the Israeli, "I was living in Budapest with my father and my uncle. Now we listened to the B.B.C. of course. Why did your government not warn us about going on those trains?"

"What trains?"

"You know what I'm talking about, don't you?" said the

Israeli to the Greek who nodded pleasantly and indicated the vacant chair. Even so he did not offer to buy the Israeli a drink. He was smoking a cheroot and drinking whisky.

The Israeli sat down and the chair creaked. He must have been twenty stone. He looked into Townrow's eyes. "Whenever I see an Englishman I ask him this question. Never is there a good answer. I have vowed to put this question to every Englishman. It is what I owe to the dead."

"You'll have to spell this out a bit."

"The Final Solution," said the Greek, nodding his head rhythmically, as though in time with music audible to him alone. "If the Allies had agreed to exchange lorries millions of Jews would still be alive. I know this. I was in the Resistance. I was in touch with G.H.Q. Middle East, Cairo."

"I was in Budapest," said the Israeli.

"I may even have helped you to escape, no?"

"No."

"I helped many Jews," said the Greek.

The Israeli was impatient. His eyes had not left Townrow's face. "The question I put is this. We listened every night to the B.B.C. Very good. You know what would happen if we were caught listening to the B.B.C.? Death. We all listen. We sit in the dark, and so I sat in the dark with my father and my uncle. At no time, I tell you, did the B.B.C. warn us about those trains. It is useless to deny it. Why was there no warning? We Jews did not know. We were told the men went to Germany to work in factories and on the land. Why did the British not say,' Stay away from those trains. Do not go on those trains. They are death trains. They will take you to the extermination camps.'? If the British had said this my father and my uncle, do you think they would have gone? They would have killed themselves first. They would have gone across the river into Yugoslavia."

"So that is how you escaped," said the Greek. "Through Yugoslavia."

"I was there when the war ended. I went to Israel when the war ended. Do you know what I think," the Israeli said to Townrow. "This was British Government policy. What other explanation could there be? The British Government connived. What are the Jews of Europe to the British? They connived with the Nazis. It was part of their anti-Zionist policy."

"What date are you talking about?"

"In March, 1942, my father and my uncle went on a death train."

"Maybe at this time the British Government didn't know."

The Israeli laughed savagely and gestured with his open hand. "Yes they knew."

March 1942 was a time Townrow could remember because it was in the Easter of that year he was slung out of college and went into the army. But he just could not remember what was generally known about the concentration camps at that time. If there were stories in the papers people might have written them off as propaganda.

"They didn't know. Or if they did know they did broadcast these warnings and you didn't hear them."

The Israeli laughed again.

"Every time I meet an Englishman I rub his face in this connivance. When you are in England, ask about: why did the government not warn the Jews in Europe? I myself would never visit England because of this responsibility your government shares for the death of my father and my uncle and—— "

"I'm not listening to this."

"Why should I lie? Tell me that!"

"No British Government would do this. You're crazy. Look, I'm bloody sorry about your father and that, but you mustn't *say* things like this. It's mad."

"The British Government knew and said nothing. You think the British Government never do anything disgraceful?"

"You're bloody mad."

"I'm not talking about you and the English people. I'm talking about the government."

"No British Government is like that."

They were attracting attention from neighbouring tables. Why should this Jew have pounced on him in this way? Perhaps it was the English clothes. Thank God, being an Israeli he couldn't possibly be on the Cairo flight. Speaking for himself he'd always been pro-Jewish, especially pro-Jewish women, and it was maddening to have this fanatic come up and spit in his face. He could not get up and just walk away. For one thing, he suspected the Israeli would run after him, shouting; for another, he wanted to stay and ram the stupid accusation down the fellow's throat.

"The English," said the Greek travel agent, "are not a grateful people. In spite of my services I myself was suspected. Can you imagine that? I didn't expect too many decorations." He shrugged. "I am a Greek. But I was sent for, to Cairo. I was accused of being a double agent. Can you imagine all this?"

"When there's a war on—— " Townrow began.

"That's exactly what the British Government said in 1942," the Israeli shouted. "This is our opportunity to get rid of the Jews."

"Aw, you're just sick. No British Government—— "

"How do you know?" The Israeli seemed really amused now, as though Townrow had made a good joke. He dropped his voice to a conversational level. "You don't know what goes on at government level in times of crisis."

"He is English," said the Greek, "so he thinks he does."

"No British Government could do anything too obviously nasty. The system won't let it."

"The system!" said the Israeli, sneering.

The Greek snapped his fingers for a waiter and tried to order drinks all round but Townrow and the Israeli declined. So he ordered scotch for himself and lit another cheroot.

"I was two years at school in England. I understand the English. You sir, and I," he said to the Israeli, "know that all governments are bad. In Greece, we have a corrupt government. I say this openly, here in Rome. I would say it in Athens. The French have a corrupt government. Any Frenchman will tell you. Americans, Russians, Venezuelans —I have been in Venezuela—will say they have crooked government. This is how it is. The Englishman is not like this. He thinks he is good and sincere himself and he believes he has a government that is good and sincere too. I don't care whether it's a Labour Government or a Conservative Government. He may disagree with it but he does not thing it is corrupt. This is what he understands about life. Every Englishman, when he is abroad, feels he can speak authoritatively for Whitehall. An illusion. They think, in Britain, that private life and public policy is one seamless garment. Every country has its special illusion. This is the British illusion."

"I don't know Greece," said Townrow. "Maybe you have got crooked government there. Maybe the French have too. And all the others. I don't think they're all honest men in Westminster, either."

"When our friend accused the British Government of being partly responsible for the death of his father you rejected the possibility. An American would have considered the possibility. And I as a Greek, would have considered the possibility. Here is the great difference between the English and the rest of the world. You live very smug."

"Snug?"

"Smug. You are smug, like owls."

"Owls?"

"Or missionaries."

"I tell you," said the Israeli, "the British Government carry responsibility for the death of my father."

"Crap."

"Don't say that."

Townrow thought the fellow was going to punch him. So

he stood up with the intention of clearing off before a fight started.

"You're sick," he said. "But everybody's not sick. You want to remember that. We're not all like you."

This amounted to a claim that he, personally, lived in a glow of spiritual well-being. He had not always. Until he got used to the idea of being a snake he used to punish himself. Those binges, those long walks, all that talking about himself whenever he found somebody who would listen! He liked to explain he had a misfortune in his life. A little, vital spring was broken. He was a mal-functioning machine and he liked kicking himself to see whether that made him go any better.

It was a phase. He had been able to snap out of it. So far from punishing himself, most people would say he did himself rather well these days. He liked nice things: food, clothes, drink, women. The main thing was to be honest about yourself, *be* yourself, accept yourself as a crook, if that's what you were, *enjoy* yourself.

Townrow became aware that he and the Israeli had been standing and looking into each other's eyes for some time now.

Unexpectedly the Israeli put a hand on Townrow's shoulder and said, "Just because you're a nice guy yourself, it doesn't mean you've got a nice government." He even smiled.

The Immigration Officer was asking him questions in the airless heat of a summer night. Why was he visiting the United Arab Republic? How long did he plan to stay?

"A friend of mine died and I'm here to marry his rich widow."

Townrow was at once marched off by a couple of soldiers to a small room furnished only with a couple of canvas seated chairs and a trestle table. There was a small barred window high up against the ceiling. Half an hour later one of the soldiers brought him coffee but refused to talk. Light had faded from the small window and a single electric bulb had been switched on before the door opened again and Townrow was escorted down the corridor by the same two soldiers. He stepped into an office and saw two civilians sitting behind a table with his passport open before them.

"What was the name of the friend who died?" They were the leanest Egyptians Townrow had ever seen inside good suits and he assumed they were the New Men of the country, army officers. They were not smoking and they did not ask him to sit down.

"I was making a joke. She's sixty at least. She's got a moustache."

"But if she is very rich?"

"Colonel," said Townrow to the man who had spoke, "if you were thirty-two next birthday would you marry a woman of sixty-odd?"

"What is a Fund Distributor?" asked the other man who was now studying the passport.

Townrow had thought this a real joke when he had filled in the application for his new passport; but now he was not so sure.

"I distribute a fund which cannot be spent for the charitable purpose it was collected."

"Is this a profession, a Fund Distributor?"

"Certainly."

"For what was the money collected?"

"A lot of people were drowned. It is a complicated legal issue."

"Where does this rich woman live you are going to marry?"

"I am not going to marry her."

"Why not, if she's really rich? If I were not married already, I would marry a rich old woman," said the Colonel, "but I have a good wife already, thank God. This widow lives in Cairo?"

"Port Said."

"Ah!" The two officers spoke together. They were silent.

"So, you wish to visit the Canal Zone." The younger of the two had sorted this out for himself and the elder became excited. He threw a lot of questions. Was the widow still living in the house of the deceased? If Mr Townrow was not offering marriage to her what was the purpose of his visit? How did he come to meet the Khoury family in the first place?

"So you are a soldier! You were stationed how long at Port Said?"

He was marched back to his cell and spent another hour, in darkness this time, listening to the breathing of the soldier on the other side of the door. The interrogation had made him sweat. He slackened his tie, undid his collar and was trying to find a dry bit of handkerchief to dab his face with when the light went on, the door opened and the Colonel walked in with his passport.

"O.K. Mr Townrow," he said, "You can go and I hope you have a pleasant stay in the U.A.R."

"Go? Where to, now I've missed my train?"

"There'll be a train in the morning. There are plenty of hotels."

"I've no money for hotel bills."

The Colonel shrugged. They had already left the Immigration block and were walking over to the Customs where Townrow's luggage presumably still was.

"This fund," said the Colonel, "when you have distributed it will you distribute another? If not, it does not seem to me a real career."

"There were anonymous contributions and collections and the papers were lost. It's a big Fund. This is a life work."

"The money can't be spent on the families of all these drowned persons?"

"No."

"This is the law in England?"

"Yes."

The Colonel thought about this. His mouth was bunched

so that his moustache stood out aggressively. "There must be opportunities to put some of this money in your own pocket, then. After a time people get tired. They forget."

"What are you accusing me of?"

"I should be very tempted if I were a Fund Distributor." The Colonel shrugged. "It is human nature. When everybody has forgotten about this fund who would miss a thousand pounds, two thousand pounds? But I expect you are a very honest man."

"Do I have to answer that question?"

"Good luck with the old woman," said the Colonel when finally he handed Townrow over to a Customs officer. He marched off, probably thinking of rich old women and large charitable funds having no legal outlet. Patches of sweat that looked quite black in the arclights sprouted from the armpits of his silvery jacket.

Townrow's only plan, once arrived in Port Said, was to go straight to Mrs K's but the heat and smells of early afternoon struck him as soon as he walked out of the station. Foreign parts. These were foreign and stinking and overlaid with his own private military recollections. The army was all right. He'd never been very regimental but he'd enjoyed it. Better than life in the suburbs fiddling the accounts. He knew how to stalk and shoot a man. There must be some way of using skills like that. In a bar off the Edgware Road a man who said he was Major Bray tried to recruit him to guard a pipeline in South America for a hundred quid a week all found. He told Major Bray this sounded too soft and respectable. Bray said there were plenty of jobs for trained soldiers. Why couldn't they keep in touch? Nothing had come of it but from time to time Townrow had fancied himself as a mercenary shooting it out in a tropical forest. He was fancying himself now but the only fight he found himself in was with a couple of porters. They wanted his two bags.

A hot wind blew from the west, straight out of Arab

Town. Townrow put on his dark glasses, fought off the two porters and climbed into a Ford cab of the early nineteen-thirties, with seats of cracked leather, smelling of hay and goat and petrol and jasmine. He decided he would not go straight to the old girl's. She'd be asleep anyway. He would go to one of those places out of bounds to other ranks when last he had been in town. He would check in at the Eastern Exchange and show he was independent. Whatever happened Mrs K was to understand he was independent.

While his bags were being taken up he had a double scotch in the bar. Off duty he used to come into this place in his civvies in spite of the "officers only" rule and it hadn't changed. The three great fans twirled against the dun ceiling. The bar-tender was new but Townrow recognised the grey-headed man with one eye who had his gallabieh tucked up around his waist and walked around with a mop and pail of water. He almost greeted him. The room was up on the third floor, overlooking a courtyard. He took a shower and stretched out naked on the bed. The phone might be ringing for him at that very minute in the Hampstead flat but on the whole he thought it pretty unlikely. Liz wouldn't ring him. The bloody office wouldn't ring him because they thought he was on holiday. Well, he *was* on holiday, wasn't he? He was on a month's holiday. It wouldn't matter if he took five weeks, six weeks. One good thing about the office, they let him run the fund how he liked. After a couple of months they might start something. It wasn't exactly a nice feeling that was brought on by the realisation that even when he'd been away three months the only people to care would be the office. It was enough to make him think of Major Bray and wonder whether he was in the telephone book. What was wrong with being hired to kill? There was a chance of getting bumped off yourself, and that was good too, wasn't it?

He woke in the dark to find the mosquitoes biting him. The office didn't know where he was, neither did Bray, and neither did Mrs K for that matter. He had not told her he was on his way. She might at that very moment be sitting down to write another letter to him. She might have deteriorated to the point she was actually handing in a cable. Or phoning.

Somewhere at the back of the Eastern Exchange was a little park with rough grass and palm trees. You took the street leading north out of the north-east corner, once left into a much narrower street where the houses had huge wooden doors, grilles on the downstairs windows and verandahs on the first floor with a lot of fancy ironwork. Townrow put on his linen suit and made off in this direction.

During the war-time black-out the only sure way of locating the Cyprus Bar was by remembering it was opposite the great white-washed portico of what looked like some religious institution, a convent maybe. It stood out in moonlight, starlight, or even the mild phosphorescence that seemed to hang in even the darkest summer night. If Christou still ran the place he might not remember Townrow after all that time.

But he did. Townrow parted the fish-netting and stepped into the familiar den, lined with barrels, lit by a 50-watt electric bulb that swung inside a protecting cage. The light was so bad the place seemed larger than it was. The corners were pocked with deep shadows. There was the peculiar pickled-walnut reek of vatted alcohol. Christou rated friendliness pretty high so there was no bar-counter to separate him from his customers. They stood, or sat around on chairs, Maltese, Cypriots and Greeks mainly, drinking arrack or ouzo or Cyprus brandy, talking, smoking and spitting into a great china pot decorated with a green dragon that swallowed its own tail. Christou was drawing a measure from one of the sherry casks when Townrow came in. He looked up.

The man had aged. His thin white hair looked almost lemon in that light. The rather heavy face had dropped. Instead of being hidden behind a lot of fat his eyes stood out like a bull's. He had real dewlaps. Perhaps he'd been ill. He'd lost a good couple of stone but he looked as smart as ever in his white silk shirt and blue slacks.

"You got any Greek brandy?"

Christou spoke English with a good accent. Townrow remembered that he'd been a schoolmaster in Limassol before knocking somebody off ("It was a feud. Nothing dishonourable,") and having to run for it. "I've got Greek brandy, certainly. But it's just scented piss."

"Double Camba."

"Have this Cyprus brandy. It's on me. British and best."

He drew a quarter of a pint into a tumbler, handed it to Townrow and disappeared through a door to come back a few moments later smoking a little cigar and carrying a garland of jasmine which he hung round Townrow's neck. "The last Englishman I served with Cyprus brandy dropped dead in the street and I'd like you to have your flowers now." He was busy for some time serving and wise-cracking, in Greek mainly but a certain amount of English for Townrow's benefit. From time to time he took a swig from a blue jug. Men ducked through the fish-netting and asked for arrack or wine and a glass of water.

"You ought to have a fan," said Townrow. "Either that or take the roof off."

Christou stopped and looked at him. "I know you." Sweat dropped from the end of his nose and collected like oil on the point of his chin. "I knew you the moment you came in. You're Sergeant Townrow."

"My name's Bray, Major Bray. Have one yourself."

"No thanks, major. I got a liver and two kidneys to support." He took another swig out of his blue jug. "The last time I thought of you was when the British Army sailed out."

"But that was nine whole months ago!"

"Well, I thought you'd abandoned me, sergeant. No letters, no perfume, no flowers. I had to exercise a real effort of will. I looked at all those Gyppo brass bands and said my farewell to Sergeant Townrow and the British

Empire. You heard about the bands? They had the Salvation Army, the fifes and drums of the Camel Corps and the Zagazig Zither Band lined up to give the big musical raspberry as the troop ships sailed out. But for once the British got their information right. They'd sailed the night before. I looked at those frustrated Gyppo mugs and felt proud to be a British Protected citizen with permission to enter the U.K. without let or hindrance. What brings you back to Port Said, sergeant? It can't be a cruise. You'd never have the money, you soak. So you're either one of the advance party or spying."

"My name's Bray," said Townrow. "Major Bray."

By this time there were only three customers left and Christou was enjoying himself so much he told them to help themselves. He sat with Townrow in a corner drinking out of his blue jug. He rolled about in the English language like a colt in a dust bowl, legs in the air, so to speak, and whinnying. "All these men are spies. They don't come in here for drink. They are trying to trap me. I tell them I have suffered under British imperialism. I am an exile from my country, and I poison British troops daily. Or did when there were any about. Sergeant Townrow!" He fetched another tumbler of brandy. "When I have poisoned you and presented them with the corpse maybe they'll leave me alone."

"How did Elie Khoury die?" said Townrow.

Christou put down his jug and began shouting at his customers in Greek and kitchen Arabic. He allowed them time to drink up, refused to take their money and when the last of them had gone, shut and bolted the door behind him.

"Now we're here," he said to Townrow, "just the two of us with all this drink." He produced a bottle of Votris out of a crate and set it on the table between them. "I had completely forgotten, dear sergeant, that Elie was a friend of yours. Well, here's to him." And they drank a couple of inches of Votris each.

"This is all right," said Townrow.

"Specially imported from Athens." The sweat stood out on Christou's forehead like little pearly blisters. "Poor Elie. I'd have gone to his funeral if he'd had one. I could have gone too." His eyebrows shot up. He spread out his hands. "What an Odyssey. That woman must have some Greek blood in her."

"Why didn't Elie have a funeral?"

"He did. It was in Beirut. I couldn't go. Did you know there was a law against taking bodies out of Egypt? Neither did I. Neither did anyone else. Maybe so many mummies got exported the Gyppos became neurotic about it. No, when your corpse is carried out of here, sergeant, they'll bury you in the Protestant cemetery, down beyond the sewage farm. They told Madame her husband would have to be buried in Egypt. They were after his bones for ivory. You know what she did? She put the coffin in one of these little fishing boats and sailed out into the Med. In the middle of the day. The Harbour-Master saw her, and the Captain of the Coastguards saw her, and the Port Medical Officer, and the Inspector of Customs and the Garrison Commander and the Naval Officer-in-Charge and the Captain of the ferryboat. They all saw her. She was wearing a sheet tied round her head like a nurse. And she had big rubber boots. There were blankets and a crate of food and bottles. The coffin was in the bottom of the boat with nothing over it. The lieutenant in charge of the ack-ack battery near the De Lesseps statue saw the sun flashing on the handles of the coffin as she sailed past. I went on to the breakwater and waved. Maybe everybody thought she was going to drop him overboard once she got outside the harbour. That would be in territorial waters. It could be held the law was not mocked. But she sailed to Beirut. Alone! She took a week. Nearly three hundred miles! Then they wouldn't let her ashore! There's a law in Lebanon against bringing bodies *into* the country!"

Townrow guessed this was all lies. "You said he had a funeral."

Christou put the empty bottle back in the crate and pulled out a full one. "If I spoke harshly about Greek brandy I want you to remember it's just a matter of style. Sergeant! I am a Greek and I have never been to Athens. We Cypriots are purer Greeks than the Greeks of Athens. All this makes one bitter. You can pay for this bottle. I'll pay for the next one. Elie had his funeral. But first of all I have to tell you that Madame was intercepted by the Israeli navy! They made her open the coffin. Can you imagine it? The deep, rolling, blue water all around them, a Jew gunboat, and this mad old English woman with the skin peeling off her nose. You can see the coffin with the lid off and Elie's face and crossed hands in the midday sun. The Jews took their hats off while Madame swore at them. They all bobbed up and down. There was a dolphin. They even asked her how she knew her course. She had the salt dried on her face and hands, so much white powder. Her father was a sailor. By night she kept the North Star well on her port. By day she'd recognise any landfall. She'd know Carmel. Beyond that Naqura. The truth is, the set of the wind this time of year you wouldn't go far wrong if you just sailed with it. There's a dolphin I know, goes that way too in the middle of June. He may have had something to do with it. Thirty miles out at sea you can see snow on Lebanon. She came back by air. I asked her what she did with the boat. She said she'd burned it on the shore."

Townrow tried to stand up. "You're a liar. How did she get him through the Lebanese customs? Tell me that."

"If you were a customs officer and a flaming red stringy woman in a white hood sails out of the sunset with a corpse in an open coffin and a bag of Maria Theresa dollars and another bag of gold sovereigns what would you do? You'd see the plain wooden cross stitched to his shroud and know him for a fellow-Christian. And even if you were a Moslem customs officer you'd reflect he was no mere heathen, but a man of the Book like yourself, with discs of gold on his closed eyelids and silver on his mouth. Elie was buried under an umbrella pine in the cemetery on the road to Beit Meri. You have to cut the rock there. The soil is thin."

Townrow fell sideways off his chair and struck his head against a cask. Christou tried to help him up but Townrow said No, he'd like to lie there for a bit with his cheek against the cool concrete, thinking.

"You've given me a lot to think about," he said in a slow, deep voice, like a High Court judge on a hot afternoon. "Dolphin is an intelligent beast."

"One mustn't exaggerate. It's child's play sailing one of those little boats. You wedge yourself against the tiller and hang on to the main sheet. At night you can tie it."

Christou turned Townrow over on to his back.

"What are you calling yourself Major Bray for?" he asked, and dashed a jug of water into his face.

"Dolphins are almost human," said Townrow. "She'd talk to it as they swam along together. And it'd talk back. It's wet in here, Christou. It's coming through the ceiling," he said. "Bray? Because I'm a hired killer. I'm shooting it out in a tropical forest."

Christou filled his pipe and sat on the floor at Townrow's side with his back against a crate. "So now you know why Nasser took over the Suez Canal."

"Nasser couldn't take over a—— " Townrow cast about. "He couldn't take over a—— "

"Didn't you know? You're not in a tropical forest now, son. As soon as Nasser knew Madame had sailed out of the Suez Canal with her husband's body, the Maria Theresa dollars, the sovereigns and who knows what-else bullion, art treasures, antiques, the finest Arabian Myrrh for the corpse, bees-wax candles and incense, he got up in the largest square in Alex, Colonel Nasser did, and proclaimed he no longer recognised the international status of the Canal and Egypt was taking it for its own."

Townrow tried to lift his head. "You mean, just because that crazy woman—— "

"'She would never have dared,' Nasser said, 'if she'd known the Canal was Egyptian property.'"

Townrow struggled to understand. "But she wasn't *in* the Canal. She just sailed out of the harbour."

"Nasser said that before the Canal there was nothing here but a sandbank. Every brick and camel dropping in the twin cities of Port Said and Port Fouad is Canal. I am Canal. This boozer is Canal. You are Canal. The harbour is Canal. We've been nationalised."

"Major Bray wouldn't have liked that," said Townrow. Christou had to bring an ear down to catch the words because Townrow was speaking without moving his jaw. "She was only doing her duty as a wife."

"Being a Moslem country they'd have different ideas ideas what constituted wifely behaviour. It struck Nasser as imperialistic ruthlessness." Christou breathed smoke out of his nostrils and sighed. "Anyway, you can understand why I thought you were one of the advance party, Major."

Townrow was awakened by the warmth of the sun. He could not move. He was lying on treasure. All this gold dazzled painfully and he had to shut his eyes again. He was able to move the fingers of his left hand. They dabbled in sand.

He could tell he was quite naked and that the top of his head had been smashed in. Even with his eyes shut he could not keep out the dazzle and this set off dull explosions to one side of his skull. He rolled over on to his face and felt the sun on his buttocks. A long time later he struggled to his knees and found it was quite true, he'd been stripped. Even his socks were gone. He put a hand to his head and found it was still covered with hair. The light amazed him.

Because it hurt so much he had to squint about cautiously. Where was he? This wasn't home. He was kneeling in a desert of fine sand. Straight ahead was a huge lake of straw-coloured water with islands in it that were little more than sandbanks though some of them had trees on. He could see sailing boats and white birds. The sun was still very low. The water, the sand, the boats, the trees, looked so fragile he fancied he could put his hand through it all, as though it were a painting on silk not a couple of feet from his nose.

Not the place he remembered, not the Irish countryside. One minute he had been riding along in the back of the open car, gazing over the rocky walls and the stony hillside and wondering about that grove of trees. Why trees in this rock? Perhaps a stream had washed down soil from the hills and these trees had somehow got themselves planted, real wild trees, not Forestry softwoods.

He knelt with his back to the sun and turned his head to the right. Here was more sand and, in the distance, a city made of small pieces of white and pink, with windows flashing in the sun. Townrow looked at his wrist but his watch was not there. He could see an ocean-going steamer with a red funnel propped up on the sand about five miles away, so he knew he wasn't at home. There were a lot of flies about too. They made for his eyes.

Hearing a regular, dry, clopping sound he set his teeth and slowly rose to his feet. The blood thudded about inside his skull. He saw a man on a donkey coming along a little metalled road and tried to shout. He had no idea whether he'd succeeded. His mouth felt as though it had been scoured out with quicklime.

"AAh!" He found he was screaming. He ran over the sand and stood in the path of the donkey, waving. The rider had a nut-brown, cheerful, bearded face. He was wearing a grey gown tucked up to his waist, so that Townrow could see his white-pantalooned legs. But he appeared not to have noticed Townrow at all until at the very last minute he twitched the donkey's head on one side, produced a heavy stick from nowhere at all and gave Townrow an almighty crack on the side of the head as he sailed past.

Townrow had blood in his mouth and it was less disagreeable than he might have expected. He was in some foreign country and he could not remember how he had got there. After a while he was able to stand up again and talk in something like his normal voice. He spoke to the flies. They seemed to be settling all over him.

He could see another grey donkey. Irish donkeys were brown. This one was pulling a little flat-topped cart on which there were two men in dirty drawers and rust-coloured jackets. At the sight of Townrow they shouted. One of them had a whip with which he gave Townrow a cut across the shoulders as they rattled past. They had a load of baskets and as one of them fell off about fifty yards up the track they had to stop and pick it up. Townrow was so crazy with pain and anger he tried to catch them up, but they were away again, jeering and cracking the whip before he could get anywhere near. Now he was set in that direction he thought he might as well keep on.

He knew by the length of his shadow it was still early. Most of what he saw was empty, pale sky. The sand, the city and the sky were all bleached. It was the sort of morning you expected to see a good drenching of dew and, sure enough, when he turned and looked back towards the lake to discover whether any more traffic was on its way, he saw his own wet footsteps. He crouched. He touched his feet. He had cut them on the stones and they were bleeding. What stones? he thought. There was just sand and this tarmac. Perhaps he had walked on a tin or broken glass. He had blood on his feet. He was much too tired to stand up. He crouched in the middle of the road, watching the little khaki-coloured closed van bear down on him from the direction of town.

A couple of men wearing tarbooshes and old army uniforms jumped out and grabbed him. He knew superior force when he saw it and made no resistance. He supposed the man on the donkey and the two men on the cart had lodged a complaint.

"I am Irish," Townrow said as soon as he was inside the van. "I've been robbed and beaten up. I want to go straight to my Consul."

For by this time he knew damn well he was not in Ireland. He tried to remember why not.

The policemen did not speak English. They produced a pair of pale blue cotton trousers, convict's garb by the look of it. Townrow had just put them on when the van stopped. The door opened and he was levered out into a courtyard from where he could glimpse blue water through an archway. With one hand he had to hold up his pants. The other was grasped by one of the policemen who led him out of the sunlight down a white passage and into a cell where the door was immediately locked on him. An iron bedstead with wooden slats occupied one wall of the cell. He lay on this for some hours, watching the shaft of light from the one high, barred window, move across the floor. He shouted now and again but there was such a row going on, a radio being played very loud, bells ringing, orders shouted, women crying, men screaming, boots tramping on bare boards, the ferry and other canal traffic sounding sirens and hooters, that Townrow had to choose his moment carefully. He was in Port Said. He knew that. He could even remember the journey down from Cairo. The intellectual effort was so exhausting that he fell asleep.

"Sir!" He woke to find a man with large, sad Pharaonic eyes bending over him and touching his shoulder.

Townrow stared up at him, saying nothing, not because he did not want to. The sounds would not come. The man produced a glass of water and held it in front of Townrow's face. At this Townrow found his jaw slackening and sounds emerging from some point very far down in his throat. Another man now lifted him into a sitting position.

"You are English?" said the man with the big eyes. Townrow could now see his uniform. He was an officer of some sort.

"I've been murdered," said Townrow. He had drunk the glass of water and now asked for another. "They must have taken me out of town and dumped me."

"It's not so bad," said the officer who had been quietly

looking him over. "You'll need half a dozen stitches in that cheek. The officers say you were running about naked."

"They stripped me."

Townrow could hear somebody laughing. He could see now that the cell was full of policemen, so full he could not make out who was laughing. It must have been somebody at the back.

"And when I tried to stop a man he hit me with a bloody great cudgel."

Even the officer began to smile at this. Townrow looked at him carefully. His mind was functioning more clearly. He knew these gentle, big-eyed, well-spoken Egyptians, from his Army days. One had been in charge of dock labour. Another used to give Arabic lessons. But it was the first time he had seen one, a Christian that is, dressed up as a policeman in Egypt. He was reconciled to being in Egypt now. He had come there for some purpose. But what?

"What's so funny?"

"I expect this man hit you with the cudgel because he was frightened of you."

"Frightened? A naked man? Covered with blood? A couple of swine came along on a cart and they had a go at me with a whip!"

Whoever was laughing must have understood English. Perhaps the intellectual cream of the Port Said police force was gathered to hear Townrow's statement; at any rate they understood enough, after a certain amount of muttering between themselves, to crow with laughter. The officer drew a handkerchief out of his sleeve to wipe his eyes. Townrow could see he was trying not to laugh.

"They were fishermen," he explained. "They bring up baskets of prawns every morning."

"British Consul," said Townrow. "Get me to the Consul."

"But if *you* were riding along," the officer insisted, "and a wild man, all naked, jumped out at you, wouldn't you hit him with your whip? Of course you would.'

"I did not jump out. You a Cop?"

"Yes. I am the Legal Officer, Lieutenant Amin."

"If you're a Christian you must know the story of the Good Samaritan."

"But in your case," said Lieutenant Amin, more amused than ever, "the Levite did not pass by on the other side. He hit you with a cudgel. Don't misunderstand us. We are not laughing because we are cruel men, or even because you are English and because you have been beaten. We are laughing because you were reduced to the essential human condition. You were naked and hurt. You were as any one of us might be if God decided. And then, in this, the classic situation, if I might put it so, you naturally and hopefully turn to a fellow human being for aid. And what does he do? He hits you. That's what we find so funny."

The lieutenant shook with a suppressed laughing, or could it have been sneezing? He blew his nose and straightened his shoulders. "I daresay you were very drunk last night if the truth is known."

"What of it?"

The Legal Officer gave an order and the mob tramped out of the cell, leaving a sergeant with a ball-point and sheet of paper clipped to a board.

"Give all your particulars to the sergeant," said the Legal Officer, "then we'll run you down to the hospital."

That evening Townrow was talking to Mrs K on the telephone. She did not know he had even left London.

"Where are you?" She sounded cross.

"I wanted to warn you I've got a damn great bandage round my head. I've had four stitches just under my left eye. No, it's nothing. I just didn't want you to be surprised."

The police had picked up the rest of his gear from the hotel and by the time Townrow had put it on in a cubicle in the Casualty ward his only reserves were three pairs of socks, two pairs of underpants and three vests, two shirts, three ties, handkerchiefs and a plastic raincoat. He had travelled light. This worsted grey suit and the brown shoes he now stepped out in were all he had in that line. Oh, there were the two pairs of pyjamas but he wasn't wearing pyjamas in the street. Men did, of course, in Port Said but they were a special cut, with no flies. He hadn't a piastre. Luckily, his passport was in the hotel office where they had been using it to fill in forms. No, he wasn't reporting to the British Consul. That would mean more forms.

The Khoury flat was the top floor of a building looking south over the Midan el Zaher. Townrow made it after five minutes hesitant walk. With only one eye functioning he could not judge distances. He seemed, if not actually floating, at least not quite in touch. There seemed altogether too much excitement, too many lights, too many big unshaven men in double-breasted suits rushing about and shouting. The cafés were full. Twangling music and throaty, rhythmical singing came from the loud-speakers slung up at all the corners. When the eye surgeon asked him what he thought the British Government would do about the nationalisation of the Canal Townrow had not answered immediately. The question, or it might have been the bright light, or the smell of anaesthetic, or the way his cheek had gone numb, made his stomach tremble. This question had been put to him before. He couldn't remember where.

"Get very nasty, I shouldn't wonder," he had said. "When did all this happen? Why don't people tell me these things?"

The surgeon had been surprised. "You did not know?" he said in the slightly W. C. Fields accent he had picked up at the American University, Beirut.

Townrow did and he didn't. He would have liked to see a newspaper to discover whether there was any mention of him in connection with the grab. He felt guilty about it.

Townrow thought it was hard that when for once he had decided to do the decent thing and help this old trot settle her late husband's estate, make a sensible will and see that no piastres fell through the grating, he should feel this check to his confidence. It was not true he did not know about the nationalisation of the Canal. Somebody had told him. Somebody had told him it was entirely his fault. He wished he could remember where he had been last night.

The front door was opened by a Berber servant wearing a little round hat covered with glass beads that caught the light and made Townrow's one eye ache. The lad had lips that reached very nearly from his nose to his chin. At the sight of Townrow's bandaged head the rest of his face became eyes.

Mrs K's voice could be heard. "Is that you, Jack? Come on through, for God's sake, and Hassan will get you some coffee. We shall all be dead in a fortnight."

She had been sitting in a basket chair on the verandah. Behind her the sepia fronds of the palm trees caught the light of the street market below. This door to the verandah must have been open all day because there was dust everywhere, quite grey on the dining table, and the smell of unrained-on streets hung in the air. In spite of the heat she had hanging from her shoulders what looked like a stole of white silk lace. She must have lost a lot of weight. It seemed a long way from the high, bony forehead to the sharp, prominent chin. And he had remembered it as a round face. The only roundness was now supplied by the small-lensed steel-rimmed spectacles. She looked at his bandage and said, "They've been after you already. How did they know you'd arrived? That's what I find so frightening. Even I didn't know you were in Port Said. But they discovered it."

"Who's they?"

"They murdered Elie, you know that surely? Your life isn't worth fifty piastres."

The boy brought the coffee and they sat side by side on the huge, damask-covered Knole settee which Townrow remembered Elie telling him had been sent out from the Army and Navy Stores as a birthday present for his wife. He had to explain that he knew very little about what had happened. When he came to early that morning he was out in the desert, naked.

"No clothes on at all? You couldn't have brought a lot of stuff with you, so your wardrobe must be depleted."

Her Cockney accent and starched vocabulary would have served her well as some Labour councillor in an East End borough; and that, by God, was where she ought to be instead of inheriting all this money in a Levantine port and tying herself into knots about it. He would tell her she had a duty to relax and enjoy herself. That's what the old man would have liked.

"Elie wasn't quite so tall as you and I expect you remember him as a well-built man but the last two or three years he lost stones and there must be clothes of different sizes because he was always buying new and he never threw any away." She took Townrow into a bedroom and began pulling underclothes out of drawers and suits out of wardrobes, flinging them on the bed and telling him to take what he wanted.

Townrow stood in front of a mirror, holding a silk shirt to his chest. It was broad enough across the shoulders but the sleeves came only half way down his forearm. Townrow remembered this oddity about Khoury, that he had arms that seemed about six inches shorter than they ought to be, though they were very thick and hairy. He used to joke about it. With hair on his arms like that he ought to be able to walk bolt Upright supporting himself on the ground with his knuckles but the truth was he had to reach down sideways even to undo a fly button. Townrow looked at the maker's tab inside the collar. "Doucet, Rue de la Paix, Paris." Made to measure and worth every bit of fifteen quid.

He had white socks, white ties, white suits. Mrs K measured a pair of trousers against his leg and it didn't look too impossible so she made him go into another room and change out of his London worsted. Townrow didn't object to the shirts but there was something about wearing a dead man's trousers that made him argue. She would have none of it. She pushed him through the door with the trousers, a complete change of underclothes, a shirt, a curious yellow silk waistcoat, and a snakeskin belt. He reflected that it was, from any sensible point of view, an emergency. He could not wear any of the jackets. The sleeves were too short. So if he fell in with her wishes that night he was not committed to inheriting Elie's complete wardrobe to the exclusion of the properly fitting suits she would in all fairness have to buy him. Even so, he wished the clothes didn't stink of camphor.

"That looks very well," she said, on his return. "What size shoes do you take?" She produced a tie-pin with an enormous pinkish pearl and said, "There, you might as well have that too. What would I be doing with a tie pin? Elie'd have been glad to know you were wearing it. He bought it in India." And, without actually crying, and without, indeed, ceasing to talk about the cuff links and the gold cigarette lighter and the Rolex Oyster, she nevertheless produced tears that slid from under the little steel-rimmed spectacles and made her somewhat pinched cheeks and pointed chin glisten. "It's so good of you to come all the way from England, just for an old woman."

"Did Elie have any Canal Company shares?"

"Why do you ask?"

"If Nasser's taken the Canal over they won't be worth anything."

"He'll never get away with it. And even if he did he'd have to pay compensation. This country is propped up by the Americans, you understand that?"

"As a matter of interest," said Townrow, "how much did Elie leave?"

"About fifty thousand Egyptian pounds."

Townrow could not see her eyes because her spectacles were catching the light but he guessed she was watching him as closely as he was watching her. "You mean in stock and cash?"

"The estate. He wasn't a rich man. He was too lazy. There's some gold in the bank in Beirut."

"Gold?"

"A few bars."

"He was always going to Switzerland."

"He didn't have any money in Switzerland."

"How many bars of gold?"

"Four. Why?"

"That's a lot of money."

Mrs K said she had never been worried about money. When her father died he left her some slum property in Whitechapel and a house at Rickmansworth which was let, furnished. She sold the slum property to a development company and now there was a bank and a supermarket and a block of flats on the site. And what, legally, could she do with bullion? There it lay in the vaults of the bank. She was a British national, she had retained her nationality in spite of her marriage, and it was illegal for a Britisher—she used the word—to hold bullion. Elie was like her. He had never really been interested in money either. It was not having children.

Townrow wanted a drink but he remembered that the old girl had been dead against it. Elie did all his drinking off the premises. She never allowed so much as a bottle of the stuff in the place. The left side of his face seemed even more numb than when he arrived so he said perhaps, now he had made his presence known, they had better put off any more serious talk until the morning. If she could lend him a few quid to be getting on with he would be trotting back to the Eastern Exchange for an early night.

"It's time for my evening walk anyway," she said and sent Hassan for a white umbrella which had, as she pointed out to Townrow, an unusually long steel ferrule. This ferrule was no more than an eighth of an inch across at the tip. She said an attack was always possible. You could give an attacker a really nasty wound if you drove this umbrella at him with enough force. Elie had been found dead in the

38

street at 9.30 in the evening. In spite of all the confusing rubbish talked by the police and the doctors and the lawyers she made a point of going to the spot every night at about 9.15 and hanging about. One night she would see his murderers, and, by a sign that had so far not been revealed, recognise them. "It'll be on your way. If we walk together I can show you where Elie was found."

She gave Townrow a five pound note. She said that she would call at the Eastern Exchange the following morning to pay his bill. Hassan would transfer his belongings to the spare room where he would be comfortable and properly looked after. She would want to look at those stitches to see that the flesh was healing. Remember, she had been a nurse. Besides, there was no point in running up hotel bills.

He saw he was not going to shake her off easily. She might accompany him back to the hotel and supervise his going to bed. This he would not stand for. He remembered a bar between the Eastern Exchange and the Hotel de la Poste where you could buy bourbon even in 1946 and this was what he felt he needed to combat the double vision that was now afflicting his one exposed eye. Two ghostly and overlapping women drew two stoles together over the breast with two cameo brooches showing the head of Queen Victoria. They put on white gloves, picked up the umbrellas and turned towards the door.

In the square Townrow could smell the sea air. They were crossing one of those long, straight streets running due north and south. A clammy brininess swilled down the canyon from a remote tree with coloured lights on it standing against the blackness of sky over the Mediterranean. He could see better in the salt air. Maybe it was what his eye needed. He saw just this one tree and the red, blue and green lights slightly moving a quarter of a mile away. Except for the street market, and here there were gas flares and people shopping for vegetables, and pots of yoghourt kept warm under sacking, this was not a part of the town to draw the crowds. When Mrs K and Townrow turned west into an even worse-lit thoroughfare it was so quiet they could hear the siren on the Port Fouad ferry.

"Do you know where you are?"

Townrow recognised it from years back. There was the great white gateway and the row of low buildings opposite, a bit like the out-houses of a farm, where at one time he used to go drinking in a den called the Cyprus Bar. He wondered if it still existed. From where he stood the place seemed to be boarded up. There were no lights.

"Elie was found in this gateway. Why they didn't kill you too I can't imagine."

"They want me to turn up in the rest of my clothes some time," said Townrow.

He was wearing the dead man's silk underclothes, and his white silk shirt and his white cotton trousers. It occurred to Townrow that if anyone knowing how Elie Khoury came to pass on his equipment should emerge from the Cyprus Bar in some way that caused the light from the open door to fall on Mrs K's face he might well think, this being the scene of the crime, that the dim figure at her side was Elie's ghost. But the bar probably closed down when the British troops left. Christou was the man's name. Perhaps he was dead too.

"How was Elie attacked? I mean, what was it? A knife?"

"There was not a mark on his body."

"I've been having dreams," said Townrow. "Sometimes I think I'm home. My brain's bent. I keep thinking my name is Bray."

She said she would walk him back to the hotel and he agreed on condition she went home in a taxi, but as luck had it there were no taxis free once they reached the main Sharia; they were charging about full of singing, cheering youths, some sitting on the roofs, waving flags. In one of the side streets leading to the Canal a public meeting seemed to be going on. A mounted police officer in a steel helmet was reaching down for a glass of water from a waiter at one of the pavement cafés.

Townrow said they had better wait until the excitement died down and edged her into Jack's Bar where they still had the tartan-covered stools and sold a good bourbon. Mrs K took a pineapple juice.

"My grandmother was a Miss Bray," she said.

The only other customers were a couple of German sailors drinking bottle beer. Townrow had another bourbon and still Mrs K did not complain so he reckoned she needed him too badly to run the risk of offending him; and, sure enough, she opened her handbag and produced a gold chain with a slim, handsome gold watch at the end of it, with Lemoine, Genève, inscribed in tiny black copperplate on its ivory face.

"This was Elie's. I know he'd have liked you to have it."

The watch was not going. Townrow wound it up, set it by the bar clock to 10.10, and held it to his ear. Either the night air or the bourbon had worked on his optic nerves because he could see everything clearly now and, what was more, his throat was cool and he could have sung if he'd thought the Huns would join in. But he did not know any German songs.

He held the watch in his right hand and patted Mrs K's arm with his left. "This is a fine watch and I'm proud to be its owner and in these circumstances. You know, I liked Elie. Do you dream much?"

"I never dream."

"Do you ever dream the same dream twice?"

"I don't dream."

"There are dreams I have come again and again, like this one of Elie lying in his coffin at the bottom of a boat and me sitting there at the stern with the sail smacking. Never believe that you can't dream in colour. This water is real blue. When the water breaks along the line of a wave it's not just white, it's dazzling. The coffin is open. You can see the little bird face."

Mrs K sat upright with her pineapple juice untasted before her. She began stabbing the floor with her umbrella.

Townrow thought she might be annoyed, but he was only describing a dream and that is what the little bony mask had looked like.

"There's a boatload of Jews coming out to take a look at us. On the way out I had a row with an Israeli who said we didn't warn the Jews."

"Dreams bore me." Mrs K was preparing to leave. Townrow swallowed his drink and followed her out on to the pavement.

"You've got to make allowances," he said.

The town was noisier than ever. An armoured car was being eased through a mob up from Arab Town, all excited and shouting. He wanted to walk all the way home with her but she said no, he could call at eleven in the morning. She would have something important to tell him.

"You've got to make allowances for Jews," he said. "It's natural for them to be suspicious."

Mrs K was using her umbrella to clear a way. "In this town it's everybody for himself. There's no real law."

"If you say the British Government just doesn't behave in that way, they ask,' How do you know?' We just know they don't." Townrow stopped Mrs K by putting a hand on her shoulder. "I ought to have taken his name and address so that I could write. I could let him know the facts. Dates and that."

She had to remove his hand from her shoulder. "Go to bed and get some sleep. You need a good sleep and then you'll be better in the morning. Remember, I've got things to tell you."

Townrow just could not get through to her. Perhaps he had not explained very well. Governments made mistakes, O.K., but you had to feel they were doing their best.

"It was in 1942," he said. "Nobody knew about the gassing in 1942. There couldn't have been any warnings."

"Goodnight, Jack," said Mrs K. "I do make allowances. You had this bang. But you've changed, and that's a fact, and not for the better."

Townrow watched her go. After a while he wanted to run after her. In the U.K. you trusted people. In the main you took it for granted people acted decently. You made an assumption about the man who sat next to you in the Tube. You didn't know for sure. You just assumed. Well, if you didn't make assumptions like that how could you trust the government? Townrow wanted to tell Mrs K that trust in big things started with personal relations, he didn't see why she should rough him up, but she was lost in the crowd. If he started running he might trip and fall. If he fell he might find it difficult to get up again and if he lay on the ground this mob would trample him flat. So he just stood there, waiting.

CHAPTER TWO

A Fall from the Balcony

In the English language paper was a picture showing Nasser standing up in a car and waving what looked like a huge white handkerchief, or it could have been a sheet of paper. Townrow counted the number of faces in this photograph. Excluding the people on the balconies and in the smudged distance there were thirteen. They looked healthy. In the right foreground was a handsome, smiling officer with a moustache, obviously a squash-playing tee-totaller, and in the left foreground, was a thinner, more intellectual type who might have been straight from the polo field. They wore British-style berets at a British angle and this made Townrow think they must be pretty good. Real pros. Nasser himself had the kind of well-fed radiance that would have looked good in an ad for vitamin pills. His teeth shone, his eyes shone, his cheeks had a glow on them and his neat, well-brushed hair was free from dandruff and every hair follicle was undoubtedly fat with the appropriate nourishing oil. Townrow could not remember seeing Egyptians with faces like these. He remembered pear-shaped faces, hollow faces with big eyes, ferret faces, nose-less faces, faces that were a bit unreal in their studied reserve, like masks. Perhaps these new faces were what appeared after the masks had been whipped off. It must have been a real Revolution after all.

The report said the Egyptian Government had requisitioned the staff of the Canal Company and that traffic through the Canal would continue without interruption.

Townrow went down to the waterfront and watched a French oil tanker and a Dutch passenger ship, the *Oranje*, slide out towards the Mediterranean.

Townrow could see out of his one eye without distortion. The double vision had gone. Perhaps he did not feel so fit as Colonel Nasser looked, but he would cope. He did not take the bandage off to shave. He thought he would never get it on again without help; so he shaved half his face and could now feel the unshaven bristles tickling under the wrappings. This was unimportant. What worried him was his mind. It had skidded. It might skid again. He remembered, as a child, seeing his mother put her hand into a coal fire and draw it out again, blazing like dry wood. He knew *that* was a dream. But you couldn't pin everything down, everything ridiculous that is, as a dream.

Five years time and he would be really middle-aged. That was when you needed a bit of give in your character. If you had no give you might snap in two. A bridge that was rigid would snap if it carried too much traffic and maybe the way he remembered ridiculous things that had not happened was a sign of too much traffic. Elie in his coffin was a sign of too much traffic. He had seen the wooden cross in the sun. There were other signs. International politics. He had never been too exercised about politics of any sort, he was more the religious type in spite of being flung out of that college, but he had been really worried by what that Jew said in Rome. Wasn't that ridiculous? Perhaps he just had a weakness for Jews. Perhaps he was just getting old and confused.

He put a hand up to the bandage. You deserved that, you snake! You know you wanted it. You enjoyed it. But, by God, if ever he laid hands on the bloke who did it he'd kill him.

"Mr Townrow?"

He turned and saw a woman sitting in one of those miniature Fiats with the engine at the back. This one was putty coloured. All the windows were down and it had stolen right up to the kerb behind his back without his noticing. He paid more attention to the car and what was going on in the immediate neighbourhood than he did to the woman. So far as he could tell it was just an ordinary car. It was a couple of years old, perhaps, and it looked as though it had not been cherished. There were dents. The front bumper was tied up at one end with string. She was parked immediately opposite Simon Artz's store and nothing in any way remarkable seemed to be going on. A Chrysler was parked outside the cable office. A long way down to the left cars were queueing for the ferry. A small group of what, judging by their little hats and wide shoulders, might be German tourists with a ship's officer in attendance were away up towards the front looking at the Anzac memorial. It was only ten o'clock but the sun had a bite. Townrow now looked at the woman and saw that she had fine teeth, a long dark face and the kind of smoky-red hair that was naturally black.

"Yes?"

"They told me at the hotel you'd gone out for a walk. You're the only man I've seen so far with a bandage round his head." Her accent was faintly American. "My name's Leah Strauss."

He held his head on one side and stared at her. She was in her thirties and smiling. This was not unreasonable. He assumed he looked absurd in Elie's cotton trousers. They were too big for him. There were big folds on each hip where he had tucked them into the snakeskin belt. And they were short of a length. As he wore sandals and no socks he must have showed quite a lot of naked, hairy foot.

"My father is David Abravanel. He's Mrs Khoury's lawyer."

"Where d'you get your American accent?"

"I married a soldier." She patted the seat at her side. "You're meeting my father at eleven. Why don't you let me take you round town for a bit?"

46

"You let me do the driving."

"O.K.," she said and moved over. "If it makes you happy."

He had to sit with his knees up to his elbows and was glad of all the room his trousers gave him. Mrs Strauss had to sit with her knees up too and this gave Townrow an opportunity to admire them and the long calves in slick, transparent stockings and the little feet in their square-toed olive Italian shoes. Townrow liked her voice. It was throaty.

"How did your accident happen?" she asked.

"Wish I knew."

At the Casino Palace he turned left and drove slowly along the front until he found one of the parking lots that served the bathing huts. This time of day it was practically empty. As he nosed towards the shelter of some trees the dust came up like brown fire.

"What's this all about?" He switched off the engine and the green back of Ferdinand de Lesseps, the purple shadow under the breakwater, the huts and the empty sea floated brilliantly up through the murk. The heat was worse than he had remembered. It was only just after ten in the morning and already the air was being cut off. So he did not smoke. She did. It was an English cigarette.

"Only to say I hope you'll take Mme Khoury back to England. Will you?"

"If your father's her lawyer he'll know I won't. Why do you want to get rid of her?"

"My mother is dead. Because of my marriage I have an American passport. My father has an Egyptian passport. He is an Egyptian national. We are, of course, Jewish."

"So?"

"So he's liable to be jailed and if he's jailed he'd die because he has a bad heart. Anyway, he's an old man and it is not nice to be jailed."

Townrow realised he was not after all being abducted with a view to his being beaten up, stripped and left naked in the desert once more. He did not even think this woman

47

was going to start threatening him. Her story was too complicated, and she herself was too female and responsive. It was a fight not to touch her.

"My father is loyal. He would not abandon Mme Khoury even though she has been sending gold into Israel. This is the rumour. Is it true? It makes her a dangerous woman for an Egyptian Jew to have as a friend."

"She told me she hadn't got any friends."

Townrow had driven into this parking lot and stopped as far as possible from any other car or building so that no one could creep up unobserved. He had not planned this splendid view of the blue water. They might have been easing out into it. Beyond the horizon the sky was white and scrubbed but for two pencillings of smoke from remote steamers. But overhead it had turned to as heavy a blue as the water itself and in his mind's eye Townrow could see sailors emerging from it, bearded like prophets.

"You've got to remember that Egypt is at war with Israel. From the Egyptian point of view this smuggling is—"

"What smuggling?"

"You were with her, weren't you? There was an Englishman on that boat."

"An Englishman on what boat?" asked Townrow. "And what makes you think I'm an Englishman?"

"If you don't want to tell me."

"She hasn't smuggled any gold. It's ridiculous. You can forget it."

He couldn't remember Mrs K in the boat, just Elie and himself. He opened the door of the car and struggled to put his feet to the ground. One way of checking on the passage of time would be to look at the date stamped in his passport by the Immigration Officer at Cairo Airport and comparing it with the date in that day's paper. But he still hadn't recovered his passport. He would have to collect it from the hotel reception before leaving, if he did leave.

"Where are you going?" The woman's voice was nearly

lost in the hiss of the palm fronds and breaking waves. "I just think you ought to take Mme Khoury to England if you are her friend."

"Did you ever see a soldier fall off a horse hereabouts some years back?"

"A soldier fall off a—— "

She was luscious in the same sort of way, but silly with it. Maybe if he'd been a Port Said Jewess he'd be silly with listening to rumours too. A slice of melon lay in the sun coated with flies. Townrow gave it a kick and walked off towards the breakwater. He stuck his hands in his trouser pockets and kicked the ridged sand. A boat with a black funnel and a yellow ring near the top was sliding north on the other side of the breakwater and by the time he reached the top it was a quarter of a mile or so out to sea, sitting on a white scut of water.

He wanted to point his mind at something.

Looking south, he could see the main basin with its shipping, an anchored P. and O. liner, a French gunboat, a low-lying freighter flying the Turkish flag and swinging on a chain to turn into the Canal Company Workshops (presumably Nasser's Workshops now) on the other side of the Canal. He could see down to the islands and to Port Fouad where he used to go swimming at the Club and eat bacon and eggs afterwards. Close at hand was the fishermen's quay and half a dozen single-sailed clumsy boats. There was no other place the voyage to Lebanon could have started from.

Townrow descended the stone steps. These boats had eyes painted on their prows. In the first boat a boy was asleep on a heap of nets. A boy was three-quarters of the way up the mast of the second, drawing the sail in with his heels and lashing it. There were baskets and a couple of rotten mullet in the third. Nobody recognised Townrow, nobody spoke to him, although a brown, knotted old man, wearing nothing but his white drawers and a turn of cloth round his head watched every move he made.

A FALL FROM THE BALCONY

A light flashed at the end of the east breakwater. It was too far away to make out the details with his one eye, but activity of some sort or other was going on at the gun emplacement. There was another battery at the end of the west breakwater. Townrow pointed his mind at the international situation. What happened when the British Mediterranean Fleet sailed in? He saw he stood a chance of being hit over the head again for two quite separate and unrelated reasons. The first of them, the Canal, he had no strong feelings about. If he had been an Egyptian he would not have wanted to take it over. He would have wanted it filled in. Israel, though, pulled at him because he liked Jewish women. If he was picked up for trading with Israel and if they interrogated him non-stop for three days and nights he would say that he liked Jewish women and to that extent had to admit being involved.

Now, this woman was Jewish.

"You are not involved," he could imagine that Coptic policeman saying. "You are deeply implicated. Do you not think it strange you wanted to ferry Mr Elie Khoury out of the country with as much of his personal treasure as you could lay hands on? Is it possible you killed Mr Khoury? Can it be that you are an Israeli agent? Perhaps you are Jewish yourself?"

If she had not talked about the boat he would have been sitting in the car with her still.

Townrow climbed back to the street. It was twenty to eleven by the clock in the window of Cox and King's Office. An armoured car followed by three truckloads of troops in steel helmets rattled down towards the Customs House. There was no time to return to the hotel before going to Mrs K's. It was on the cards men were waiting to arrest him at either place, at the Eastern Exchange for being an Englishman who had helped provoke the Egyptian Government into assuming control of the Canal; and at Mrs Khoury's flat because he was Jewish.

He wondered if that Jewish woman was still waiting.

A FALL FROM THE BALCONY

If arrested he would want to know if the police had ever seen a Jew with a foreskin and they would reply there was no end to Israeli ingenuity. Townrow would not mind. He'd settle for being Jewish. The women alone made it worthwhile. The hard case over his heart melted at the thought of the types he had known: fair haired, frosty and fleshy Jewesses with grandparents in Russia, an unusual straw-coloured woman from Ferrara, a dark-haired, little-mouthed, small-voiced harvest mouse of a woman whose family came from Lithuania when it still had forests. He could not even remember their names. By them he wanted to be thought well of as they emerged breast-high, and what breasts, from their alien corn.

He was pro-Semitic. You had to be pro-Semitic when you remembered what the Nazis had done. But, to be honest, his attitude had as much to do with a girl as it did with politics. She worked at the Reception Desk at the Union Jack Club in the Waterloo Road and turned out to be Jewish, a very lively girl with a little round head and a lot of curly brown hair in a style that didn't come naturally to it. They went dancing once or twice. He put his fingers through her hair and said there was so much of it, bunched up on her neck, some people might think it was a wig. She gave Townrow the feeling they had always known each other. She was very gay. She told him about her family. He told her things about his family he had never told anyone else, about his father being such a drunk, for example, and even when he tried to put his hand up her skirt she wasn't outraged or frigid, she was just physically very strong and pushed him right back against the door of the cab they happened to be riding in. She told him he was a man and he wasn't to be ashamed of his sexuality, it was perfectly natural. She also said she could not understand how it was possible to believe another human being came back from the dead and you had to worship him as God. He couldn't remember her name. This happened on leave in, it must have been '44.

Not the sort of thing he would have wanted to tell that Israeli in Rome Airport, not during the row they had. Another time he might. He could quite easily see himself marrying one of these women, and you couldn't say fairer than that. You couldn't be anti-Semitic and want to marry a Jewish woman. It could happen to any Englishman. It could happen to anybody in the Government. There were Jews in the Government, weren't there? That was what that Israeli, never having been in Britain, (at least, only in transit, that was for sure) would not understand. There were Jews in the B.B.C. Must be. You couldn't see *them* being party to keeping quiet about those trains.

There was nothing to be party to. You couldn't see Churchill and Attlee and Eden and Macmillan and that lot turning a blind eye to the Jews being massacred. All governments stink a bit. The Greek had been right about that. There were some dirty deals, no doubt. But the British system was too open for anything really shameful. They shot the Irish martyrs but the ghosts walked. Ireland was the exception. It was the dark stain, forty years ago, but the British had no stomach for it now.

The Israeli in Rome couldn't have made a bigger mistake, picking him, of all people, for this sick talk. He could have been a Jew himself and worn a little cap and a shawl. What was an Irishman but a sort of Jew?

If Townrow ever ran into that Israeli again he would have to say that even he, an Irishman, knew the British would have warned the Hungarian Jews in '42. Frankly, he reckoned they did. They must have.

Townrow walked on, not thinking about what he wanted to think about.

He was ten minutes late and had the feeling he was interrupting a row. Mrs K did not even look round. She was sitting at a writing table in the corner with a business ledger open in front of her. A reading lamp was switched on because although the windows and door to the balcony were wide open to admit air the shutters were closed to keep out the sun.

She examined a piece of paper and began writing in the ledger. "This is Mr Abravanel. He's a lawyer. Mr Townrow, from England, the only friend I have."

Abravanel stood so close to the shutters that slivers of horizontal brightness jumped up and down on his dark suit as he moved. They seemed to break like spray. He was old. He had grey coconut matting hair, dark glasses and narrow, shrugging shoulders. Abravanel, too, did not look at Townrow, but went on talking to Mrs K rather sadly, each sentence ending with a lulling cadence and a sigh. "You have become a silly old woman, Hah! Illusions are for the young. Aah! People of our age should look at life for what it is. Hmm! Elie was old and died. Nobody attacked him. Nobody murdered him. Can't a man die of natural causes any more? Hhh! There is enough malice in the world without inventing it. But there!" For the first time he looked at Townrow. He extended his right hand and came some paces across the room, tut-tutting at the sight of Townrow's bandage. At close quarters he revealed too much skin about his cheeks and throat, as though at one time he had been much fatter. "I suppose we need enemies as plants need the light," he said.

To grasp his hand was like holding a bundle of pencils. "I trust you are not suffering. Mrs Khoury told me of your—— "

"I just met your daughter."

"Elie often spoke of you. Surprising we never met when you were here before. He was fond of you. He admired you. Strange. I mean it was strange because it was French culture that interested him. I was the Anglophile. And yet Elie it was who married an English wife and had an English friend. My wife was of very good family but she never spoke a word of English, only Arabic, Italian and French. So you have met Leah. You know what? She married an American with father and mother in Livorno, a good Jewish family, but now he has gone depressive in Cleveland and he has drugs and shock treatment and douches. She told you all this? They spent all their money. She was not eating."

"Where are the deeds to the island?" Mrs K called out. She had turned in her chair and was jabbing her fountain pen in Abravanel's direction.

"They don't exist." Abravanel went on looking into Townrow's face and talking gently. "It wasn't Elie's island."

"That's how he talked about it."

"In any case it is worth very little. It was a place to shoot duck. All that part of the lake belongs to the Antiquities Department. You know that? There is a pillar lying in the mud."

"Elie was always talking of sinking a well. Would he have talked like that if he didn't own it?"

"Certainly. He was very romantic. Only a romantic would talk of sinking a well in a marsh."

"Before we go any farther," Mrs K said to Townrow, "I want you to lie down on that settee with your head on a cushion. I must look at that eye of yours."

The little Berber had brought coffee and glasses of water but Mrs K told him to take the tray away again and bring a bowl and some hot water. From a drawer in her desk she produced a pack of cotton wool and a bottle.

"I was going back to the clinic this evening," said Townrow.

"In this climate I've seen wounds go gangrenous in minutes."

Townrow realised the blood was pumping harder than usual on that side of his face anyway. Why shouldn't he take the weight off his neck? The blood pumped so hard he could almost hear it forcing the stitching apart. The pain went right round to the other side of his head, to a point just over his right ear. He lay down on the settee, putting his head on the pillow. Mrs K switched on a reading lamp some three feet from his eyes and he had to close them. He could feel the heat playing on his face. Normally he would not have been sensitive to it. Of that he felt sure.

While she unwound the bandage she supported the back of his head. But for the stabs of pain he might have fallen asleep. He gazed dreamily through the blood of his closed lids as she stripped off the plaster and removed the dressing. He fell through the warm, red silence that followed.

"What's that?' His cheek had chilled.

"Alcohol." She was cleaning the wound. He heard the snip of scissors.

"Tch! Tch! Tch!" Mr Abravanel made sympathetic clucks.

"It's clean. It will heal." Mrs K sounded disappointed. "There!" He could hear the opening of a tin box and the rustle of paper. "You remember the island, don't you, Jack?"

She must be talking about that place out in Lake Manzala. Elie picked him up in a taxi, just the once, at the dock gates and they went straight down past the Municipal Nursery Gardens to the Manzala Canal basin with a couple of straw paniers containing flaps of bread, goat cheese, cold roast chicken, grapes and beer. Two hours later the motor-boat landed them on a sandy atoll with a single palm tree. A mile or so away you could see the lake steamer following the channel to Matarieh. Elie said that if you followed the channel you could get right through to Damietta. But the lake was mostly marsh. There were a lot of ibis and duck. Flies came up from the mud in clouds. Elie showed him a block of granite covered with hieroglyphs. They sat in the shadow of a mud wall which was all that remained of a building. Their pilot slept with one naked foot resting on the gunwale. Every half hour or so a duck whirred up from the reed beds.

"It was a real rest cure out there," he said, "or it would have been if it wasn't for the flies." He really could not remember Elie saying anything about the island being his. It would have seemed unlikely. If the lake was lower than the Mediterranean as some people said the sea would flow in one day. Perhaps you could have built the island up. Now Townrow came to think of it they had passed other, bigger islands with houses on them.

"Don't know what you mean," Mrs K scolded, "saying Elie died naturally. There was a bruise on the back of his neck. It was broken just as if he'd been hanged. This bruise went down to his shoulder blades."

She applied the new dressing. She fixed it in place with plaster, using the same bandage because it was reasonably clean and she hadn't a fresh one anyway.

Abravanel sighed. "No, no, no. It was a simple cardiac failure."

"Was there a post mortem?" Townrow asked. "Was there an inquest?"

"No need. A simple doctor's certificate."

"Kesab didn't so much as lay eyes on Elie to write that certificate," said Mrs K. "Elie's heart was sounder than mine and I run upstairs if I want to. You're the one with the bad heart, Mr Abravanel."

Townrow guessed he must have shown he had not enjoyed the trip because Elie never took him out to the island again. Another thing he remembered now was that he had had to wear civvies because Arab Town was out of bounds to troops. From that day to this he had forgotten the island. He liked forgetting. You had to forget all manner of things just to survive. Until he heard Mrs K talking he had forgotten what Elie looked like, lying on his face against the white wall, with his coat and shirt torn open down the centre seam.

"Thanks." He sat up and opened his one eye. He could see nothing but parallel bands of sunlight on the shutters. He patted the bandage and said, "I'd like some water."

"When Jack is better," said Mrs K, "he and I are going to come along to your office, Mr Abravanel and check the list of boxes. There's no hurry. It won't bring Elie back. But I'm determined not to be swindled, just because I'm a simple minded old woman who's never understood the wickedness people are capable of."

"I'm all right." Townrow drank and the sweat ran off him.

About a mile out of the basin the motor broke down. He and the pilot took it in turns to row while Elie sat in the stern and watched them. He could see that sunset across the lake as though it was yesterday. Posts, trees, birds, sail, stood black in the golden flux. Elie was black.

"What's that noise?" He stood with the towel in his hands, his head on one side.

"A demonstration?" said Mr Abravanel. "A visit. What else?"

"I hope the British Navy lines up off the coast and blows them all to hell." Mrs K came in from the passage where the Berber had been whispering in her ear. "There are men trying to force their way into this building."

Townrow opened the shutters and stepped on to the balcony. The sun beat down well-nigh vertically. There was no shadow in the street. The brilliance had a sour stink. There were a hundred, perhaps two hundred heads and upturned faces and sticks and tarbooshes and banners gathered in the street. They were streaming into the building. A man in red pyjamas was looking down from a balcony opposite, apparently enjoying the fun because he was laughing, pointing and talking, presumably to someone in the room behind. The chanting turned to a steady roar.

Abravanel stood calmly at Townrow's side acting as interpreter. "Death to the British and the Jews. Death to the enemies of the nation."

"What makes them pick on this building? That's what I'd like to know."

Townrow seized a small flower-pot with a dusty plant in it, balanced if for a moment in his right hand and hurled it across the street. It exploded against the shutter behind the head of the man in pyjamas who gave a startled look in Townrow's direction and shot into the apartment.

"I don't suppose they will kill us," said Abravanel. "They will throw the furniture into the street, perhaps. Somebody tipped them off. Mrs Khoury's servant, perhaps, or the porter."

Mrs K was already on the telephone. "Is that the police? Put someone on who can speak English. Do you understand? You fool, I want to talk to someone who speaks English."

Abravanel took the phone from her, settled himself comfortably in a chair, put his right ankle on his right knee, smiled as though preparing to share a joke with an old friend; and indeed, he might have been doing just that for all the scared, angry old woman and Townrow knew, because he was murmuring, his lips close to the mouthpiece, in Arabic.

Townrow asked Mrs K if there were any weapons in the flat. Elie went duck shooting, didn't he? Where were his guns? With a shot gun he was prepared to have a go at blasting the lot of them back down the stairs. He did not think they would come up in the lift. And if they did? He'd blast them anyway. They would be reduced to setting fire to the building.

"No, no guns," Mr Abravanel called out when Mrs K returned from Elie's room with a couple of cases. "These men will not hurt us. They are harmless. They will simply smash everything." He was still at the telephone. He was on to the Military Governor of the city; or, rather, he explained, to his office. But so far he had not got past the switchboard.

Townrow opened one of the cases and took out a Browning over-and-under that must have cost Elie a packet. Where was the ammunition? He followed Mrs K back into a shuttered room where all the lights, a standard lamp, two reading lamps, wall lights, were all switched on. There was a desk, books, corded boxes and a huge, faded, photographic portrait which Townrow surprisingly remembered was of Elie's uncle, a Maronite bishop who when he wrote, Elie used to say, supported the paper on the palm of his left hand, never on any wooden surface. But there were no cartridges. Townrow gave up the search when he heard hammering on the front door. He threw the gun down and went off to the kitchen for a meat cleaver.

Abravanel was there to put out a restraining hand. "It will be the worse for all of us. We can't stop them getting in. They will have the master key from the porter downstairs."

Townrow had a feeling the mob were after him personally. He was their man. They had had one go at him. They were coming back. He was the enemy and he was glad of it. A great bag of pus would be slit. He grinned at Mrs K.

"They're coming in for me now," he said.

Mrs K went into the kitchen and turned the key behind her. The door shook as she pushed some heavy object, the table or the ice box, thumping against it. The Berber had evaporated. Only Abravanel and Townrow were left in this main room giving on to the hall and Townrow could see by the way the old chap was settling himself on a chair in the corner he was not going to excite himself. He sat quietly with his knees together and his hands resting on them. He shut his eyes. Maybe he hoped the gang would think he was dead.

If they had the master key they did not bother to use it. Judging by the row they were just beating on the door with their fists and kicking it. Townrow noticed there was a bolt not pushed over and was about to spring on it when the door, creaking and whining under some enormous pressure tore open at the side of the hinges, carrying the frame with it. A youngish, bearded man with a cloth round his head forced his way through the gap. Townrow punched him in the face but the fellow scarcely seemed to notice. He made for the first object he clapped eyes on, a glass cabinet containing Mrs K's collection of china animals; Townrow kicked him on the left ankle. He yelled, tripped and

59

sprawled forward on his face with a few of his followers, a boy wearing a scarf, a gallabieh and bright yellow boots, another youth wearing a tarboosh and bleeding from his nose, an emaciated man dressed in what looked like a winding sheet: fists, hairy forearms, a green eye-shield as though for billiards, an eye that was all white and no retina, and with yells and a stink of sweat, bad breath and chewed nuts, they piled on top.

A lad in a candy-striped pyjama top and khaki shorts picked up a chair with a red plush seat and hurled it over the balcony. A couple of other youths prised a gold-painted console table, all cherub faces and wings, from the wall and, staggering under the weight of its marble top moved to the balcony. They balanced it on the rail, shouted to the crowd below and gave it a heave. Abravanel, still with his eyes closed and his clasped hands resting on his knees, was lifted up in his chair and borne off like a god in a Hindu procession. The first arrivals had now picked themselves up off the floor and were taking it out of their friends who had walked over them. Townrow came in for a certain amount of the face-clawing and spitting himself. Glass shattered, pictures were torn from walls, wood splintered. Mrs K could be heard screaming behind her closed door.

Even if Abravanel was dead Townrow did not see why the body of a man who had been the father of such a fetching woman should be thrown into the street sixty feet below. He charged one of the chair bearers and came away with him. The fellow struggled and turned. Townrow saw it was the very man who had first burst into the flat with a cloth round his head and this encouraged him to take a tighter grip of the throat, forcing the fellow back to the balcony while Abravanel, still silent and smiling, tumbled out of his chair and crouched on the floor with his buttocks in the air, his hands over his ears.

Townrow wasn't strong enough to strangle his opponent with one hand, so he had to use the other as well. This left the other man's hands and legs free. As he was now pulling a knife the question was which came first: throttling or paunching? To wnrow let go of the throat with one hand and grapped the knife wrist. By pushing the chap violently against the verandah rail he thought he might break something.

In fact it was the verandah rail. Townrow was surprised Elie hadn't maintained his property better. The wood must have been rotten, the ironwork rusted. The man with the knife went straight through, still clutching his knife, with an expression of wide astonishment on his face. He hung in the sunshine and floated down to the street. Faces scattered. They made room for a clean landing. Townrow thought he could hear the tinkle of the knife when it was jerked from the man's hand and fell on the asphalt. After a moment's hesitation, the man turned on his side.

He had screamed all the way down Townrow now realised. This was what calmed everyone. Abravanel was still on the floor but he had lifted his head and opened his eyes. There was an expression of strained, quizzical expectancy on his face as though he was trying to catch a joke being whispered in the other corner. Nobody tried to stop Townrow from leaving the flat. By the time he reached the street the crowd had gathered closely round the fallen man and he had to shove his way through. He had moved again. Now he was lying on his face. Townrow kneeled and put his hand to the back of the neck. The movement was so familiar to him it might have been a ritual. He knew what to expect. He had been through this before. He felt the sudden recess in the vertebrae and remembered that the size of the black bruise depended on how long the man lived after receiving the injury. In this case, it might be only quite a small one.

At the first opportunity Leah Strauss said, "I don't know what you mean when you say you don't know if it was an accident. You couldn't mean to kill him. But you tossed him over the balcony, or through it. For God's sake, you knew what you were doing, didn't you?" She was amazed.

He shrugged. "How important would you say all that was?"

"The police will think it important."

"I'm a good liar."

"I suppose I ought to admire the way you keep cool."

"I'm not cool. I'm so scared I spend half my time in the loo. Don't build me up into anything. Probably it was an accident. You need more resolution than I possess to see a man off at the sort of party we had in this place. I've seen men off, you know. I've been a soldier."

"It's awful. It's terrible. It's made my father ill. Everybody will be arrested now. What I can't understand is the way you talk about it. Anybody would think it was a joke. Don't you realise how serious it is?"

"On the whole," he said, "I am not the sort of man I'd like to be seen about with. Look, I've admitted to shitting myself. What more d'you want?"

"Another thing, what did I say to offend you?"

"When?"

"In the car. You got out and walked off."

"You called me English. No Irishman likes that."

"Are you Irish?"

He frowned. He wished he could be sure.

Judging by his red tabs, it had been the Military Governor himself who turned up to inspect the damage. What Townrow remembered was the way Mrs K pinned this chap in the corner and demanded government compensation, She had got over her fright. The place was uninhabitable, she said. She would have to move out. The Egyptian Government would have to pay her hotel bill. They would also have to pay the hotel bill of her guest from England. An ambulance picked up the dead man, an army truck collected about thirty of the rioters, and eventually Townrow himself was taken to an office overlooking the ferry where he dictated and signed an affidavit. He hoped to see his friend, the Legal Officer, but he gathered that a suspected spy who got mixed up in a riot and then murdered an innocent by-stander was regarded as more of a military than a civil problem. The room was full of officers in shiny brown boots.

Surprisingly, Townrow was then told he could go. An unshaved captain with a paper clipped to a board said an inquiry into the disturbance would be held the next day, or maybe the day after, or perhaps next week. He was to hold himself in readiness and certainly he was not to leave the city. He assumed they were letting him loose for the fun of it. With a bit of luck somebody else would beat him up. And if they didn't, well, there wasn't much chance of his getting away. Port Said was as near as dammit an island. Perhaps they wanted to practice their surveillance techniques on him.

In the bar of the Hotel de la Poste, a man with oddly prominent eyes came over to Townrow's table and said he hadn't been sure at first because of the bandage but if it wasn't Captain Ferris! He stuck out his hand.

Townrow took it and gestured the man to sit down. But he said nothing. Ferris? Did he know anyone by that name? It seemed familiar. After what he had been through, Townrow was slightly rocked at being accosted by this Englishman with the horribly bulging eyes. They stuck out so much the pupils were surrounded by half an inch of white. Unusually prominent eyes like this indicated some disease. Either that or the man was an Armenian (because all Armenians had bulging eyes). Yet again, it might be a sign the man was good at languages. Townrow had heard somewhere that good linguists often had bulging eyes. It revealed a physical type normally possessed of certain intellectual characteristics. Armenians were good at languages, so he understood. Townrow would have preferred not to go into all this. He was very tired and had been drinking scotch on an empty stomach.

"My name's not Ferris," he said.

Those protuberant eyes could not look sly. The man went about just staggered by whatever happened to fall within his field of vision. That was the impression given; continuous amazement. But when he leaned forward and Townrow was able to see the red net in the sclerotic the amazement was touched with an obvious knowingness. He didn't actually lay a finger along his nose.

"Whatever you say, old chap, but I never forget a face." He said it was a small world and he'd never regretted the switch out of china clay into oil. Shunting back between St Austell Bay and Le Havre was no lark for the winter months even if at one end of the trip was the Café-Bar de la Republique with Mme Ferris and her coffee rum. As snug a refuge as you could wish for. But you had no idea the luxury on these oil tankers. He was captain's steward. He had his own private bathroom and two kinds of toilet paper, soft and crisp. The weather was better, too.

"We're tied up in the Roads waiting to go through the Canal empty. Some row about the toll. Captain's waiting for Shell to tell him who to pay it to. With these wogs running it the Canal will be back to duck marsh in a year or two." He brought Townrow another couple of inches of scotch from the bar. "I just sat in the corner looking at you. Knew it was a familiar face. But I couldn't be sure because of the bandage. You had an accident?"

Townrow remembered driving through a tiny Cornish port handling china clay. The trucks and the railway stock, the sheds, the cranes, the derricks, were covered with the stuff. The ground was white and the dockers went about like millers. Out in the Channel the water might be turquoise. It was easy to think of some battered coaster, looking as though it had been dipped in flour and breadcrumbs, swimming into that turquoise water and making for the French coast with this gooseberry-eye soak in the galley.

They smoked real Havana cigars which Faint, that was his name, had bought in Bahrein and talked about the old days when Captain Ferris, ex-infantry, once of the War Graves Commission, stood behind the counter of the Café-Bar de la Republique, the property of his French wife, Andrée, serving dockers, sailors, locals, railway men, troops: the real hard stuff, most of the time, rum, brandy, pernod.

"If you'll forgive the familiarity," said Faint, "Madame was a good bit older'n you."

"It was a love match," said Townrow. "I punched a chap who said I'd done it for the drink."

"Where is she now?"

The tanker run was cushier but Faint contradicted himself and said he'd never been so happy as when carrying china clay. It got in the food and scoured the great gut. His health had been good. It neutralised acids. It absorbed the bodily poisons into itself and thus discharged them from the body. Now, he sat in a deck chair most of the time putting on weight and eating rough oats for breakfast to supply roughage. With china clay you didn't need roughage.

"But for the difference in age," said Faint, "you seemed ideally suited. It all seems a long time ago. What I liked about the Le Havre run was going into this French bar and finding a Britisher behind the counter. It was nice, somehow."

Faint said once he'd had something to eat he would have to think about getting back on board.

"I know a place to eat," said Townrow.

He took Faint by the arm so as not to lose him on the way to the Midan el Zaher, not saying a great deal because he was thinking of all those bottles in the Café-Bar de la Republique. In spite of his bug-eyes Faint seemed less surprised to come across his old acquaintance than he might have been. Townrow was still grappling. The shock had sent him straight back to that cobbled quay. Faint was right to ask about Andrée. What the hell *had* happened to her?

A couple of carpenters, stripped to the waist and wearing army plimsolls and white cotton drawers were working on the smashed doorway. Townrow was able to walk straight in, drawing Faint after him. Faint said nothing. The lift was not working and they had climbed a lot of stairs. For the moment he was just concentrating on breathing. He stood quite still, studying the wreckage. Townrow supposed that with eyes like his he could see all round, like a horse, without moving his head.

Mrs K was sitting at a table, writing, and Townrow went up to her. "You ought to cut your losses. Why don't you go back to England? This town is no longer any place for an English woman."

"This was Elie's home," she said. "That's what hurts. Smashed. They smashed his home. They smashed his easel. Hassan brought the empty paint box up from the street. All the paints had gone."

Townrow introduced Faint who finally looked round, swinging his head in such a way that Townrow noticed for the first time what a long scraggy neck he had: he swung his head like a camel.

"Jesus, you had the bums in?"

"Abravanel's ill. His daughter's been round." Mrs K stared at Faint resentfully. "What d'you mean, bums. I'm not in debt. Don't judge people by your own modest circumstances, Mr Faint. You off a boat? What d'you do? Stoker?"

"Stoker? No, there are no stokers these days, lady, not on my sort of boat. I'm captain's steward. Captain Ferris is an old friend of mine."

"My father was captain in the Ellerman Line and he never allowed any familiarities from his steward."

"On second thoughts," said Townrow, "you go down and wait in the hall. The old lady's had a shock. We'll find some place we can eat."

"Didn't mean any offence," said Faint and he picked his way through the doorway.

"Captain Ferris is what he calls me," Townrow explained after Faint had gone. "Says he knew me in Le Havre."

"When were you in Le Havre?"

"Never been near the place."

He had to raise his voice to make himself heard over the hammering of the carpenters. "This town's hostile. I know what you're going to say. If you leave Egypt you won't be able to realise on your capital that's tied up here. And if they confiscate the Suez Canal why shouldn't they confiscate the property and possessions of absentee British subjects? As they will do. Do you think it'll stop at the Canal? Now, let me tell you something. You think that because you've got a Lebanese passport they wouldn't touch your block of flats and your holdings and your island in the lake. But you never gave up your British passport, did you? When you go to the U.K. you enter on your British passport. That right? You've got your name registered at the British Consulate. Right? These Egyptians are not fools. Did you know I was an Irish citizen?"

Mrs K was watching him closely with her little mouth pursed up and lines like hairs radiating from it. "I'm Irish on my mother's side. Her mother was a Miss O'Connor."

"You see what I mean!" Townrow was delighted. "I'm neutral. All you've got to do is make over your Egyptian holdings in my name and they wouldn't dare touch them. I could send you an allowance."

"That would be generous of you, all things considered."

"The Egyptians and the Irish have a fellow feeling. They are both victims of British imperialism and once your estate is in my name they'd no more think of sequestrating it than the Rock of Cashel itself, assuming it was on Egyptian territory and occupied by the Irish Ambassador. It makes no difference at all that there is no Irish Embassy in Cairo. A citizen of the Irish Republic always gets a welcome at the American Embassy, you know."

"I didn't know you were an Irishman," she said. "You don't look Irish. You don't talk like one. I don't believe you are one."

"I'll show you my passport the moment I find it. But we

can't waste time. If Abravanel is too sick to get out the documents we shall just have to find somebody else. These Egyptians are in a state of high excitement. This time next week they'll have everything that's British, French or Jewish in their pockets and the sooner you get your goods and chattels into the guardianship of a citizen of the Irish Republic the better. Abravanel can make everything he's got over to his daughter. She's got a U.S. passport. It's not worth as much as it was since Dulles said no to the High Dam. But it's better than being a Jew with Egyptian citizenship. What's Abravanel's number? I'll ring him up."

It was night. He had not noticed this before. The last time he had been aware of the time of day a man had been falling away from him with his mouth open through a harsh light. Now there were moths and mosquitoes pinging round the electric light bulb. The loudspeakers were bellowing in the street. The cobalt sky on the other side of the balcony pulsed. The lighthouse, he thought. The Mediterranean and the Red Sea must be full of boats wondering whether to turn back. He guessed the captains would be listening to the short wave news bulletins. Or they'd sit, waiting for the message from the owners. Observed from high enough the American Seventh Fleet would be seen to leave its tracks like a hundred snails on the black water between Cyprus and Lebanon.

A twinge of pain made him turn his head and the picture changed. It was the road again, with the bleached broken wall running off at an angle to climb the mountain. The group of children with fair hair and naked feet were standing at a turning of this road and they were shouting, "Captain Ferris! Captain Ferris!" as he drove past, throwing money to them, on the way to some sullen, landlocked water, it might have been Galway. Somebody travelled with him but he could never make out who it was, male or female, but probably female, he thought.

He did not ring Abravanel. He walked up to the roof

and stood in the starlight. Every forty-five seconds his part of the town was blanched by the lighthouse and in between he could look south to the lights slung from the top of the cranes in the basin. A plane with a red, winking light dropped westward, to the airport. Townrow looked around him. There were cabins on the flat roof where servants like Hassan lived and in one of them an elderly, bearded man was writing in the light of a hurricane lamp. His steel-rimmed glasses flashed when he moved his head. Washing was pegged out on lines. At Townrow's cough the man looked up but he went on writing almost immediately and Townrow turned to lean over the parapet.

He knew perfectly well where he was, what he was doing and why he was doing it. What he had not established was the appropriate attitude. Was he amused, frightened, on the make, altruistic? He had no view of himself. One reason for this was, every time he started a conversation, somebody tried to cast him for some role he could never assume with the conviction he would have liked. You would have thought that talking to Mrs K he would at once be the genial, concerned friend of the family she judged him to be. But did she? She puzzled him. She might be playing some cunning low game and he could not be at all sure she really thought he *was* a friend. He was still struggling out of some sleep, some dream, and the figures who stood round and about did not convince. They were not convinced about him either. Could they even hear his voice? It seemed to have very little resonance. When he raised it there was no response or, at least, not one he could recognise. That old man writing in his shack probably thought he was a Greek grocer on the look-out for an uncurtained bedroom window. Or, perhaps, in the darkness he had taken the bandage for a turban and thought him a Sikh sailor?

The hell of being among strangers was that nobody formed any expectation of how you would behave; therefore you did not know how to behave. You had no notion of what your appropriate conduct would be. You did not know whether you were good, bad or indifferent, not until some-body began to react in a way that told you. When there was an Empire the white man in foreign parts suffered from none of these uncertainties. At 7 p.m. he put on his tails, stepped into the dug-out canoe, and was paddled through the crocodile and hippopotami-infested waters to the formal party where decorations were worn and bridge played until two in the morning. That role had gone out at roughly the time the heroine was strapped to the railroad track. A convincing new one had not been assigned. But history did not let up. You had to keep meeting people and doing things. It was vertiginous.

"I've been thinking," Townrow said when he had returned to Mrs K. "You can't stay here. There is no guarantee that the mob won't come back, or the police, or the military. You can have my hotel room. Get a good night's sleep. I'll move in here. In the morning we can get Abravanel started on those documents. You needn't stay to get everything cut and dried. There's such a thing as air-mail and papers can be signed and witnessed in London as well as here."

"This is my home," said Mrs K. "I'm not abandoning my home. Anyway, you're not Irish."

"Of course you're not abandoning your home. I'm looking after it for you, aren't I? What I've got on my mind is the thought they'll pinch it like they've pinched the Canal."

They argued. By now the carpenters had rigged up a makeshift door that actually locked but they stayed on to listen to the row. Several times Townrow pretended to concede defeat and said he had this friend off a boat waiting for him in the hall below; he had a damn great cabin all to himself with a spare bunk in it and if Mrs K really thought she could manage the Egyptians by herself Town-row had this line of retreat. Before the sun came up he would be in the spare bunk and well out into the Med. Or half way down the Canal. He didn't know which way the boat was pointing. It was immaterial, if Mrs K had no further use for him. Of course he was Irish.

Eventually Mrs K said she would go to the Eastern Exchange, just for that night, so long as he promised to admit nobody to the flat in her absence and to telephone immediately in case of trouble. She took an hour and a half to pack a couple of suitcases. He carried them down to the street and found a taxi for her.

Townrow was not at his best talking to Mrs K. He was not at his best talking to any woman. There were too many unsaid things to remember. Nowadays people talked a lot of cant about the equality of men and women. The fact was, though, that Mrs K had been dispossessed of her flat because she was a woman and he was a man. He was wide awake. Sleep was impossible. He removed his bandage, dipped it in water, and put it on again, fixing it with a gilt safety pin he found on Mrs K's dressing table. As the water evaporated his face was cooled. He sat between the open window and the open door to benefit from the moving air. The gun rested on his knees but nobody came.

"O.K. You can come out now," he called. "You can come out, Elie. She's gone."

But of course Elie didn't come out from anywhere and Townrow never expected that he would. He opened the wardrobes, though. He looked inside that big chest in the kitchen. One door was locked and as Townrow could not find the key anywhere he took it into his head to blow it open, the way they did in movies, both barrels, up and down. There was an explosion that seemed to shake the whole building and Townrow took a blow on his right shoulder. After the smoke cleared the lock still held. Indeed, it seemed quite undamaged. Maybe, the cartridge was blank. He looked at the cartridges left in the box. 12-gauge shot. Now the room stank of sulphur. No reaction to the shot from the rest of the block. No hurrying foot-steps, no shouts, no whistle. Townrow switched the light out and watched the fumes silver in the starlight.

"You must have got the key in your pocket, Elie. Just try it in the lock and see if it still works. You can come out now. The coast is clear."

Townrow took the handle of the door and shook it. "I tell you there's nobody else here, Elie."

He was just normally sexed, not too much, not too little. Before he'd had any it didn't worry him. Now there had been twenty years of it he wouldn't have regarded it as any kind of obstacle to entering a monastery which was what he might well do even now if he continued in this inno- cence about the behaviour expected of him. That way you accepted your innocence, or did he mean ignorance? There you were, alone in your cell confronting the fact of exist- ence. That would be soothing. It would be nice. It would be unalarming. If, on the other hand, it turned out he was defrauding the old bitch he might finish up in a cell of a different sort and grow embittered. If there was anything he hated it was embitterment, particularly in women. Leah was a nice name. Her husband being that way she must have been put to it for sex. It must be on her mind.

Captain Ferris? Who was Captain Ferris? Where was the maniac with the bulging eyes who had invented Captain Ferris? Townrow even went to the trouble of trotting down the eight flights of stairs to see whether he was still waiting. "I'm sorry, old chap, but you've made a mistake," he would say to him. "You've been deceived by some sort of likeness but in point of fact I've never been in Le Havre in my life." Naturally the man had gone, hours ago probably, and Townrow climbed the eight flights again, thinking it was the mention of china clay that had caught his imagination. On the other side of the Canal, way beyond Port Fouad, were the evaporation beds and hills and peaks and pyra- mids of salt which, when the Ities dropped their flares in a raid during the war, looked not unlike tents; a plain of marquees and bell tents. Perhaps it was of these salt hills that he was thinking, and not the white mountains of Cornwall, when Faint spoke of the rough channel crossings and the coffee rum in the Café-Bar de la Republique. Perhaps in some other port, Naples or Rangoon, the real Captain Ferris was crossing a crowded floor to a cow-eyed lonely sailor, saying, "Faint, It is Faint, isn't it?"

The gun was where he had put it, lying across the chair. Stupid to leave it like that. In spite of trotting up and down those stairs he was not short of breath and his heart beat no faster. He was in better condition than he thought.

"Irish?" a voice could be heard saying, or rather pronouncing, on the other side of that locked door. "Townrow is not an Irish name."

"Neither's De Valera. You can't argue from names. There's lots of Protestant Irish from Cromwellian times."

"You never told me you were an Irishman."

"Elie, you were never an easy man to lie to." Townrow rapped on the door with his knuckles. "Open up there, you old fraud."

This was followed by complete silence so Townrow began battering the lock with the stock. He never had a conscience about lying to women. It was part of sex.

Of all the eight, nine, ten doors in the flat this was the only one locked and although Mrs K had not actually forbidden him to enter it was enough to try a man's curiosity. This, when he came to think of it, was one way of reading his relations with women. They were the great shutters-out. They shut him out from themselves, they shut him out from some state. He could not have put it any clearer. The word was "state", in all its meanings; situation, condition, country, kingdom, empire, splendour, glory and transfiguration.

"If you don't come out I shall fire through the panels."

He could hear a cock crowing. This was an astonishing sound in the middle of a city in the small hours. Perhaps time had passed more quickly than he thought. There were, of course, birds and animals everywhere on these rooftops. In addition to chickens some people even kept goats and sheep. For the milk.

But what chiefly astonished him was that he should be standing there in a wrecked flat, holding a gun, listening to the crow of a Port Said cock and thinking, years and years after the event, of the little blue-smocked girl who had seduced him. What her name was he could not remember. He did remember going to the principal who immediately kicked him out of college. "I'm grieved but I have to tell you this means you cannot go on with your training for the ministry." If only he had kept his silly mouth shut. It was a false alarm. She wasn't pregnant.

He switched the light on and immediately saw that built into the lock was a little bolt you could slip the end of your finger into. He pushed it up and the door swung open. He fumbled around for the light switch and saw the room was used just for lumber and storage. There were boxes, leather and tin trunks, piles of books and old newspapers, a plaster bust of Socrates and a stepladder. In one corner was a heap of shavings. But no sign of Elie.

CHAPTER THREE

A Sort of Patriot

"Mr Townrow, I am sorry, but every time I think of you I have to laugh."Lieutenant Amin sat down on the Knole settee, spreading his knees wide apart." You were naked and these men hit you with whips and cudgels. How is your face? You have not yet had the stitches out? Mr Mansoury, the surgeon, is a friend of mine. He is expecting to be transferred to Cairo. But now there is to be a war he will be requested to remain, I have no doubt. Here, in Port Said, we shall be in the front line."

"What war?"

"We have nationalised the Canal. This the British will not be able to tolerate. I am a realist. There will most certainly be a war."

What particularly annoyed Townrow was that he, an Irishman, would now have to quarrel with Amin's simple-minded view of the English.

"I don't mean," said Amin, "to condemn the British Government for attacking us. If I were in Mr Eden's position that is what I should do myself, without doubt. The British national interest calls for an attempt to take the Canal back again. The Egyptian national interest is to resist. I shall be killed in this resistance, quite possibly. I strike no moral attitude. Perhaps you will be the one to kill me. Perhaps I shall kill you. We are not free to decide. England and the United Arab Republic are not free to decide. But this is not," he said, smiling again, "what I have come for, which is to ask how you are, and then to make certain enquiries."

He took out his notebook and asked Townrow if he could borrow a pen or a pencil, something to write with.

This defence of the British that Townrow now found himself launched upon came hard to a man who had stormed a barricade of horsehair sofas, dustbins and old carts (in the spirit, that is to say) to get at the flat-capped British in the Dublin streets. He could not be as old as that. The fighting was in 1916 and he could tell, by looking at the backs of his hands, that they hadn't the skin of a man that old. The fighting must have been before he was born.

"They wouldn't do it," he said, "because next to the Americans there's nobody likes so much to be well thought of as the English. They all know the Kaiser started the 1914 War and that Hitler started the 1939 War. People who start wars and invasions and commit acts of aggression are just Bad Men. The English have become very priggish about this."

Amin shrugged. "Tell me candidly, Mr Townrow, why are you in the United Arab Republic? Europeans don't come to Egypt in July usually."

"They know they've no real power left in the world, and all they've got left is their priggishness."

"Please— "

This assumption the British were nasty enough to start a war was what annoyed Townrow. Anybody would think Amin and that Israeli at Rome Airport had been putting their heads together. He was particularly annoyed because Amin was so free from rancour; to do that Israeli journalist justice he'd been pretty berserk. Amin did not seem to know right from wrong. If he thought the British were bandits why the hell didn't he resent it. The Israeli had spewed hate. He had values. But Amin had not even mentioned the United Nations Charter. He was amoral. Perhaps he had decided life was so harsh he could not afford to have principles. But why should he assume the rest of the world was the same?

"Don't be polite with me," said Townrow. "There's no need. This country is lucky the European power it's had most to do with is England and not Germany, or Russia, or even France. They are fine people. I say that as an Irishman. They are fine people, except when they're in Ireland. I'd say the devil had gone out of them nowadays."

"I don't know if you realise the extent of my authority," said Amin. "I am the Legal Officer. There is no such officer in the British police system. I am very like the juge d'instruction in France. In order to make my enquiries I have great powers under the law. I can interrogate witnesses."

"Witnesses to what? Are you accusing me of something?"

"In a way yet to be determined you were concerned with the violent death of an Egyptian citizen. What I'm immediately interested in is the reason for your being in Egypt at the hottest time of the year. I called at your hotel. You were not there. I was given this address. As a foreigner you are under an obligation to keep the police informed of your movements. Is this to be your address while staying in the Republic?"

No doubt those Immigration officers had been in touch with the Port Said police and Amin knew perfectly well he'd fairly recently been a soldier in the Canal Zone. The kind of paranoia these chaps suffered from they probably thought he was there with plans to assassinate the Military Governor. If the truth were known the men who had set upon him and stripped him were members of the kind of incompetent counter-intelligence service you'd expect the Egyptians to have; so incompetent they forgot to cut his throat. It came home to Townrow that not only did Amin think the British were getting ready to mount an attack on his country but that he, Townrow, was probably part of it.

The lift gate clanged and there was Leah on the landing

in a biscuit-coloured linen suit. Townrow had the front door open and all the windows so that the air could circulate.

"Come right in. This is Lieutenant Amin who thinks I'm a spy or saboteur or something. Now he can go straight back to Headquarters and say the well-known Israeli agent, Leah Strauss has blown in from the States and, what do you know, she's made contact with the British already!"

Amin stood up, smiled, and said he hoped to see Townrow later on when he was calmer. Townrow said he was in Port Said for a long time. Maybe he'd take up permanent residence. Amin and he ought to have plenty of opportunity for getting together in the years to come and if ever Amin found him calmer than he was at present it would be because Amin had conceded the major point, that this belief in the bloodymindedness of the British was necessary to him, and any other Egyptian who though as he did, in the same way that corsets had been necessary to King Farouk, to stop him from falling apart.

"It's quite all right to hate people for what they've done in the past," Townrow yelled, "but not when it confuses you about the real world you live in."

Amin had already gone while Townrow, who was unshaved and still wearing a pair of Elie's pjyamas, orange with silver piping, stood in the middle of the floor, shouting and gesturing.

"You're a nasty swine, I think," said Leah as soon as he stopped.

"Eh?"

"You talk about justice and decency and all the time you're busy swindling an old woman out of her property. If my father wasn't sick he'd—— "

"But he is sick and he can't! Listen, I'm not swindling the old girl. I'm a neutral citizen and if your old man was in his right mind he'd be putting his money and real estate in my name too. Didn't you hear that madman who was here? All these Egyptians talk like that. This week it's the

Canal, next its British property and Jewish property. They're driven by their own sense of guilt."

"You're a crook. My father says you're not Irish."

"That's because I'm not walking about with a pig on the end of a bit of string. He should see me at home. Excuse me!"

He went off to the bathroom, locked the door behind him, and prepared to take a shower. He had to hold his head at an angle to avoid getting his bandage wet; under a shower a man was alone without being lonely. The tepid spray set the blood running just that little bit faster and Townrow responded by thinking, Abravanel could be right at that! The thing to do was take a peep at the passport if it was still in the manager's office at the Eastern Exchange. What sort of a man had he become that he could remember a conversation at Rome Airport but couldn't be sure he was an Irish citizen?

"Are you still there?" he shouted through the door. "I don't see what a man's private life has got to do with his political judgement. It's a well-known fact that some very decent people, abstainers, non-smokers, pious men, have been politically very aggressive. Don't forget that Gladstone bombarded Alexandria. I'm not sure whether Gladstone drank. But he was obviously O.K. in a way I'm not. Compared with me Bismarck, to take another example, no doubt at all, was O.K. I don't agree I'm a crook but I do have spasms of dishonesty, lechery and disloyalty. I've had a hard life. This doesn't mean I'm not entitled to speak out for a bit of international decency. You must try and understand the kind of patriot I am."

Forgetting where he was, he drew his head in like a tortoise and got it, bandage and all, soaked. He swore and threw over the lever that stopped the shower. He took off the bandage and looked at his purple, blanket-stitched face in the mirror. It looked like a carefully repaired plum.

"What's your father's infallible test for an Irishman?" he asked after he had thrown open the door and marched

79

out to confront her. "The poor man has never had a chance. He's never seen me anything but sober."

"I suppose you realise you've no clothes on," said Leah.

"I like to stand in a draught when I'm still wet this kind of weather. As the water evaporates it cools the body. I'm not unpleasant to look at. You'll admit my belly is flat. I have dark and curly hair in all the appropriate places. The hips are narrower than the shoulders. What you see is a hundred and seventy two pounds of masculinity. Does it surprise or appal you? Have you learned anything you did not know before? Don't go!" he shouted. "Don't walk out like this. People might think I'd done something to annoy you."

"Let me get by will you?"

"Not until you tell me what I've got to apologise for?"

"Just apologise," she said. "People like you should be apologising all the time. They need justifying, perhaps as some obscenity that nature's gone in for experimentally. What are you offering me? Rape?"

"It's an idea." Townrow sat down and planted a hand on each knee. "Now that you come to mention it. But I thought we were discussing on a more theoretical basis. Your father says I'm not Irish. Well, that's his opinion. But what do *you* think?"

"Only an Englishman could rob an old woman with your show of high-mindedness."

"So you think I'm English." Townrow scratched his right calf where he had preserved a patch of dry skin since childhood. "The truth of the matter is that you know all Irishmen are as ugly as sin and it puzzles you I'm so handsome. Look at my long Irish skull." He turned his head sideways. "And every Irishman has an upper lip as long as the width of two fingers." He put two fingers under his nose. "My pubic hair is darker than the hair of my head and if you see the sun catching the hair of my chest, my calves or my forearms, you'll know it is golden. I am golden, Celtic, or should it be Gaelic, man. Look at my buttocks!" He stood up and turned round. "Kicked flat by the British. Look at the whiteness of my skin where the sun doesn't get at it. White as a summer cloud from rinsing in the acid bog water. Men like me have been dug up entire after a thousand years from the acid peat bog, their flesh white as a chicken. Don't be deceived by my Kensington English. It started as a cunning disguise. Now it has become inescapable habit. Anyway, I left Ireland when I was very young."

"I still don't like you," she said, "and frankly it doesn't matter to me what you are. You're obviously on the make, in more ways than one."

The tip of her nose had an odd way of going white when she was excited. The lobes of her ears, though, were weighed down with rich blood. Why did he always like women best when they were showing how much they hated him?

"Anyway," he said, "what are you doing away from your husband?"

He was so excited that if, at this stage, she had said something extraordinary, such as, "Are you out of your mind? What are you raving like this for? Do you want to go back home? Is that what all this fuss is about? You know damn well *you're* my husband!"

If she had said this he would have grinned and put his clothes on.

Instead, she suddenly looked like an exhausted child. "They said that if he didn't respond to the drugs in a couple of weeks then he probably wouldn't respond."

"How long ago was that?"

"Too long."

He stood with his hands on his hips, watching her. "I'm really sorry about your husband," he said, and hunted around until he found a pair of shorts which he was able to slip on as a way of demonstrating the depths of his concern and sympathy.

"Leah," he said. She made him feel they had known each other for years. It might have had something to do with the way she hadn't batted an eyelid when he was prancing about naked. He had observed in her certain manifestations of boredom, a tired frown, for example, when she wasn't demonstrating irritation. The way he had stood there, calling attention to certain of his physical characteristics, had been unnecessary. She knew all about him, no doubt of it at all. She probably even knew about that patch of dry skin on his right calf. He pushed his right foot out and pointed to it. "That was where I had a very bad boil, when I was a child," he said, "and that is how it left me. No hair grows on that patch. I used to tell the other boys it was leprosy."

She gave no sign of remembering. That was not the point. What other adult had he ever told about his dry patch? Nobody, so far as he could remember, none of his women. He was easier with her than he'd been with any other women he had ever met, in spite of the way she was angry with him and the cool, contemptuous look she'd given his prick. They understood one another. He put this understanding to the test by suggesting she drove him down to the hospital to have his stitches taken out. Sure enough, she just said, "They're not ready to come out yet. But if you put a shirt on I'll drive you down there so they can give you a check-up."

Once she started talking about her husband Townrow could not stop her. He could not make out whether this was because she loved her husband a lot, hated him or was just inventing him. For the first few years everything was fine. Rob had this good job in the automobile plant. She liked the States. People were polite. They were really nice to each other. The old and blind were helped across the street, not like here. She did not know what it was like in other parts but where she was neighbours helped you out when you were in trouble. When Rob went into hospital people in the next apartment called. This would never have happened in Egypt. Mind you, they could tell by her accent she wasn't American. Everybody thought she was French. Once, she was with Rob in a shoe store and the clerk paid her compliments. Although Rob was standing there right by her side this clerk said she was beautiful and what about a date. They just took it for granted foreign women were immoral.

Rob was depressed. He went to some clinic where they gave him a course of drugs. This cost eight hundred dollars but he seemed better for a time. In the plant there was an inter-com system and Rob came home one day, saying statements about him were being put through this system. What sort of statements, she had asked, and he had been vague about this. She'd asked whether they were statements about being Jewish. Rob had been angry when she said this. He said didn't she know they were in the States now, not in Europe. There was no anti-semitism in the States. Anyway, he was Jewish only on his father's side. She ought to watch herself. That was the way delusions started, thinking there was anti-Jewish feeling when there wasn't.

Cooking was quite one of her interests. She used to do grills and ragouts and special omelettes. Rob was particularly fond of the way she roasted duck with grated lemon peel, wild rice and sweet chestnuts all mixed up together. But he went off his food. That was when he started not sleeping. He used to be up half the night, listening to the radio. He had one of those radios you could hear the police and the taxis on. When she asked him what was interesting about this he said you never knew when you might hear something about yourself.

"Are you married?" she asked Townrow.

"No, I used to be."

This story about her husband made Townrow wonder if she was in Port Said to get away from him; otherwise she would have waited until after the hot season. She needed cheering up a bit. There had been no call to give him all this stuff. If she wanted to tell anyone about it at all, there was her father and, Port Said being her home town, there must have been friends. Perhaps she had given them as much as they could take. Perhaps she bored them to hell. Perhaps she just wanted an audience. It was hard to see what other reason she had for putting up with his company, considering she had called him a nasty swine, and all that. He wasn't bored. He had no interest in her husband as such, of course. Rob Strauss? It didn't sound particularly Italian to him.

It occurred to him that if it had cost eight hundred dollars for a course of drugs in a clinic Rob must be running up quite a bill in whatever hospital he now was. Leah agreed that it had taken all their savings. Townrow wanted to know how much the hospital charged. Treatment for any kind of mental illness took a long time and no matter how big your savings were there must be limits to what you could afford. Leah was vague about this. She said he was in the Jewish Hospital for Mental Ailments. She felt sure there would be no money trouble from this particular hospital. Anyway, Rob had a big insurance.

"I'm a failure," she said. "D'you know how old I am? I'm thirty-eight, and what have I done with my life, nothing. I used to play the piano. I was a very good pianist, d'you know that? I could have been a concert pianist. But I never even had any children. D'you ever get this feeling of complete uselessness and waste? I was brought up to want to do something with my life. What? I could have been a writer. I've got talent. I was smart enough at school."

He said something about it being difficult for a Jewish girl to carve out a career in Egypt.

"I could have gone to Israel. I could have gone to Europe. My father never made any trouble. No, there's a real failure of will. It's my will. I tell you it's the most awful thing to know you've got all these potentialities and yet you've done nothing about them, and you can't do anything about them."

They had been to the hospital where a surgeon in Casualty had examined Townrow's face and told him the stitches were not ready to come out. Leah waited outside. She said her father wanted to talk to him about Mrs K making over her property, but they went to a cafe instead and sat under an awning drinking out of tall glasses of half-frozen yoghourt whipped up with apricot juice. Townrow even put some of it on his wound.

She had an attractive way of sitting with her knees together and her ankles wide apart so that her flimsy little white shoes fell away from her heels. The awning put a shadow across the upper part of her face. Here the skin was a smooth, greeny dusk and the eyes glittered like metal. In the sun her chin was bone white. He felt he'd known her since the beginning. He felt they'd been married, divorced and married again. They were, both of them, lying about this paranoic schizophrenic mate of hers and enjoying every minute of it.

"I'd like you to come and see my father. I want you to be nice to him."

"When you said you were a failure, that's all hooey, isn't it? Your old man can't live for ever. He's an old man and he looks very ill, if you ask me. And if your husband's as bad as you say they'll never let him out of that hospital he's in. You can divorce him. That's grounds for divorce, isn't it? Insanity? In the States? Well, if it isn't it ought to be. Then you'll be as free as a bird. What's thirty-eight? You've got all your life in front of you."

Her face rocked back into the shadow and there was no white chin and white teeth, all natural he'd take a bet, to look at. She was so angry she began to get up but Townrow caught her wrist.

"But it's true. You've got to face facts."

"You're cruel and — and rough!"

"You've got your own life to live. The first time we met it was because you were worried about the effect Mrs K being here might have on your father's safety. You've got to look forward and see what your own real interests are. You could marry me, for example."

85

He was able to let her go at this because she had relaxed back in her chair.

"When your divorce came through you'd still be an American citizen. Or would you? Anyway, you're American at the moment. Know what you want to do? Get your father to put everything he's got into your name, because the Egyptians wouldn't touch American property, even if it was Jewish. See what I mean? You and I could be very well off, living in Port Said, as citizens of the Irish Republic."

After a pause she said, "I love my husband, you know that?"

"Nobody loves a nut. And if he's started the way you say he has he's going to get a lot worse. But it's all a lot of balls, isn't it? Your husband, if you've got one, is as sane as I am, isn't he?"

"Yes, yes," she said. "Yes," and stood up, this time too quickly for Townrow to grab her. He thought it was too hot to do any chasing. Anyway, he had called her bluff and was sure she'd be back.

He thought the piece of paper was a bill, so he did not pick it up for quite a long time. When he did he saw that it carried some smudged purple writing, as though it had been done with a ball-point not built for the climate.

"We could quite easily shoot here and we shall shoot if you are in the city tomorrow."

Townrow looked around. The two waiters were inside the restaurant proper and sitting at these tables in the open air was only one other customer, a long-faced, bare-headed man with sideburns who was reading a Greek newspaper. Townrow went over to him and asked if he had seen anyone leave a note at his table.

Without lifting his eyes from the newspaper the man started to pick his way through the English language. "Yes, a gentleman, very correctly dressed. I have seen him about. You did not look up."

"It was a threat."

Still reading his paper, the man shrugged.

"Which way did he go?"

Again the man shrugged. "He went to the ferry. He walked up towards the front. He is on his way to the station. He took a taxi for the airport."

"O.K." Before going on Townrow turned and snapped his fingers at one of the waiters. He paid his bill—and all this time the Greek went on reading—before saying, "You put the note there yourself, didn't you?"

"I?"

"That note gave me twenty-four hours to get out of Port Said. The police, on the other hand, have different views. They say I'm to be on hand."

"It is difficult for you."

"So I'm taking you along to police headquarters with me."

The man closed his newspaper, folded it and placed it on the table. Now that he lifted his head Townrow could see he had the eyes of a tired old hound who had taken a beating or two. "I am equipped with a revolver. It is here under my left shoulder. If you should try to seize me I should shoot you through the stomach."

"You think there's no law in this place?"

"Not for an Englishman. You are just a man in a foreign city where nobody is afraid of you and nobody likes you. Law is just power. You have no power, so the law won't work for you."

"You a Cypriot?"

"I am Greek."

The man was tipping his chair back and was altogether too relaxed to be dangerous, Townrow thought, if he went for him suddenly. But no doubt he had a mate watching from some corner. Perhaps that was the idea, to provoke him and then shoot him down. Why?

"What's all this about?" Townrow did not put the question at all aggressively. He actually went off without waiting for an answer. He had some notion of coming back when he could think more clearly. He was shaken. That was cold truth. It was one thing to be in the army, in uniform, and all that dirt coming at you from one direction, and officially, so to speak. Quite different to be talking quietly with a man who was ready to do you in under a café awning. Once Townrow had pulled himself together he was coming back to ask this man what the hell it was all about? If he wasn't still at this particular café he wouldn't be far away. Port Said was not one of those big, sprawling places.

"Look," he would say, "I don't know who you think I am. Who is this chap you want out of town? Can't be me. I'm not English. If it's money you want, give me a little time, I can slip you a few hundred."

From the end of the street he looked back at the terrace and sure enough the man was still there, reading his paper.

Being Irish, Townrow thought, or probably so, I'm as much in favour of strong patriotic feeling and free-thinking as most people, but this man is carrying it far. How would it be if I collected my passport from the hotel and took it straight back to the man? But he had an ignorant, fanatical look about him and the significance of Townrow's being Irish would be wasted on him. What would a man like that know of history?

There was no Lebanese Consul in Port Said and the British Consul was on holiday so Mrs K spent some time talking on the telephone to Cairo. They had no record of her at the British Consulate. So far as they were concerned she was not a British subject. Mrs K told the clerk not to be impertinent. She had a British passport to prove her nationality. The fact that she had been married to a citizen of the Lebanon and travelled on a Lebanese passport had been purely a matter of convenience. She had never re-nounced her British nationality and what she wanted to know was whether there was any danger of British property being confiscated, though she hoped that if these Egyptians went as far as that the R.A.F. would bomb Cairo. The clerk said there was not the remotest possibility of the Egyptian Government appropriating British property. So far as he could make out, though, the property in question was not British. If she had a Lebanese passport she was technically a sister Arab and sitting pretty whatever happened. As a matter of interest, what was the date on her British passport? Mrs Khoury said she could not actually put her hand on it at that moment. Could she remember when it was taken out? 1922. That was the year she married Khoury. Before that she had been on her father's boat and they didn't need all these documents. The marriage to Khoury had taken place in the British Embassy in Damascus and she had needed a British passport first of all to get into Lebanon and secondly to get into Syria. Her husband came from an old Damascus family but they had been driven out by the religious riots in 1868. In fact, her father-in-law had been born in an open wagon drawn by a couple of mules on the road to Beirut. It had been a matter of pride to Mr Khoury that he should marry a European woman in the very city from which his grandparents had been driven by religious fanaticism. The ceremony had been witnessed by her father and the military attaché, Major Ratcliffe who some years later called on them *en route* from India and they had a champagne supper at the Casino Palace. She didn't care if that 1922 passport had expired years ago. She was still a British subject. Did the consul know her flat had been wrecked? Why had it been wrecked? Because she was British. Everybody knew she was British. That is why she had been attacked by this mob. Would they have attacked a sister Arab? She didn't speak a word of Arabic. If her husband had died a natural death and not been murdered in the street she would have left the country long ago, as quickly as she could have settled her affairs. But she couldn't turn her back on a crime like that. No, she was not claiming to be a Distressed British subject. She wasn't afraid of anybody. She just wanted to know whether Nasser would pinch her property. Yes, she would most certainly put it all in writing. Not to the Consulate. She would write to the Ambassador himself.

The Lebanese Ambassador was in Europe, the First Secretary was engaged and there was no one in the Legal Department who could speak English. Mrs K spoke to a woman who, it was claimed, happened to be passing the switchboard at the time the operator was trying to be helpful. She said that she herself was an Armenian with a Turkish passport who worked part time at the Embassy because she spoke Russian and German. There were many Russians and Germans to be spoken to in Egypt, she said, by way of explaining her existence, and if she could be of any use to madame she would be quite delighted. Mrs K said she would write.

This was the story she told Townrow when they next met.

"It is all right," she said. "At the British Consulate they tell me I'm officially an Arab, so Nasser won't touch me."

"Makes it much worse," said Townrow, "if they can treat you as one of themselves. There's only one thing these bastards understand, and that's the big stick. If the British Government has washed its hands of you, then it's God help you. An Englishwoman with an Arab passport is defence-less. I tell you there's only one way to protect your property and that's to have it put in the name of a neutral. As I'd have to live in the town there'd be my expenses. But the capital would remain yours. What's more I'm quite pre-paired to make a will in favour of you or anyone or any institution you care to nominate."

"You'll live a long time."

"There was a man offering to kill me only this morning."

"Then it's no use trying to put anything in your name, is it?" said Mrs K. "It takes years to prepare any legal docu-ment in this country. You couldn't post a parcel in twenty-four hours, let alone transfer property. Who was this man anyway?"

"He was reading a Greek newspaper. I recognised the funny print."

"Was he sober?"

"Tell me," said Townrow, "and I'd like you to think carefully. Did Elie have any special Greek friends? I mean Greeks from Cyprus?"

Mrs K shut her eyes, her little chin came up, the lines tightened on each side of her mouth. What with her sharp, yellow nose, she looked like a dead hen. Townrow leaned towards her and said, "I want you to think carefully because I've flown all the way here from London where I wasn't harming anybody. And before I know where I am there's one lot telling me to stay put and there's another lot telling me to move on. What I really want to know is why you asked me to come to Port Said, and then, if you feel strong enough, you might tell me where Elie is buried because I'd like to put some flowers on his grave."

She opened her eyes abruptly. He noticed for the first time what a positive blue they were. They were like enamel. Assuming they had lightened with the years Townrow guessed that when Elie was riding her father's boat up and down the canal they were a deep-sea irresistible, stained-glass window, bluebell blue; and they had a lot to do with his being just where he was. Who did he mean? Elie or he himself, Townrow? He was exhausted by the heat. There was no oxygen in the steaming atmosphere. The sweat trickled down his neck.

"Did Elie have Greek friends?" Townrow repeated.

"He wasn't like that. He didn't care whether they were Greek or British or German. He was just a businessman."

Townrow clicked his fingers. "Now, you know what I mean."

"He always used to say he didn't understand belonging to different nations and countries. He was an internationalist. He used to say he was born in the Ottoman Empire and this made him a real cosmopolitan. He used to laugh about his Lebanese passport. Arabs, Jews, Turks, Armenians, Greeks, Syrians, Egyptians. He didn't care. He would do business with anybody."

"But if he sold coals to the Devil to stoke the fires of Hell he'd *know* it was the Devil. You haven't answered my question."

They were finishing a restaurant meal on a verandah overhanging a street. Mrs K had a long line of grape pips lined up on the side of her plate. She was flicking them over the rail. "Look, I'll be candid. I'm fed up with all these Egyptians and Greeks and Turks and Italians and what not. So far as I'm concerned they're interchangeable. Elie would agree with my point of view on this, but of course he couldn't express it like I do. After all, he was one of these foreigners himself."

"I don't get it."

"He was a very sharp man but he was simple-minded about some things. He saw the world as just a lot of people buying and selling. You never heard him say Greeks are like this and French are like that. That's what I mean. He'd never admit you could generalise. But you can, can't you? I must say I was sorry to hear you were Irish. I don't understand that. You look English. You talk English. Of course, Elie wouldn't have cared if you were English or Irish. But I do. I never liked the Irish."

"Why not?"

"They are untrustworthy and they tell lies and they drink. My grandfather lived at Aylesbury and he used to talk about the Irish labourers who built the railway there. They lived in tents. They lived like animals and they'd fight. There were two Irish in my father's boat. One jumped overboard as we were coming up the Red Sea and the other followed suit two nights later. You being Irish makes a big difference to me. I'm not making anything over into your name. I'm not giving you control of my Egyptian assets."

"I'll be shot this time tomorrow anyway," said Townrow.

"You could always get out on a fishing boat."

"You want me to clear out?"

"No."

Townrow finished his beer and looked at her. "Sometimes I feel Irish and sometimes I don't. If I could get hold of my passport it would help. The police have collected it from the hotel. I can't very well ask Amin what *kind* of passport it is, can I?"

"What did this man look like who said he'd shoot you?" She listened to his description. "That must have been Aristides."

"You know him?"

"He organises the supply of arms to the Greek Cypriots."

Townrow looked at her with his one eye and she looked back without blinking and without seeing him for her eyes were focused on some spot remote, not so much in space as in time. Her thin lips were twisted. It might well have been a smile.

"Was Elie mixed up in that?" he asked.

"Perhaps."

"What do you mean, perhaps?"

Townrow was aware that his face had been brought into focus and the thin lips had straightened and parted. She opened her handbag and produced a purse. "Let's get out of this place and go and check up on your passport."

As they emerged into the glare and dust he said, "I'm sorry I can't agree to you going back to the flat yet awhile, not to sleep that is."

"Why not?"

"I'm comfortable there. I feel I can defend myself with Elie's gun. Short of putting a petrol bomb into the building and machine-gunning me as I jump from one of the windows there is little Aristides can do about it. I expect he's on the phone. I'd like to talk with him."

He could tell by her little tight face and the stiff way she was walking that she was under strain. Either she was angry with him or she was frightened. They were just crossing to the Eastern Exchange when he saw, in fact, that tears were running out of her eyes. She was grizzling quietly with her mouth turned up at the ends so that her upper lip was puckered and the few light, thin hairs of her moustache caught the light. It made him think of all those presents she had given him. He was wearing the Rolex Oyster at that moment. She had cried then, giving his these presents. He thought it had something to do with the sadness brought on by giving away Elie's personal possessions. What she was crying for now, he could not imagine. Strain? These tears could not be for Elie himself. She'd always made it clear how much she despised the man.

He might have telephoned his mother. He loved his mother. He rang directory enquiries with the idea of asking whether they could tell him the number of a newsagent and tobacconist called Pullen, or Pulling or Pooling in a cathedral city near London, St Albans, very likely. He remembered his mother having a flat over this shop. If you telephoned you could hear them shouting up the stairs. The time was just after nine-thirty. That meant it was just after six-thirty in the evening in England. In St Albans, or Rochester or Canterbury, they'd be selling the last edition of the evening papers. Suez headlines. Menzies. Canal Users' association. Commuters who hadn't bought them in town picked up copies for the latest cricket scores stamped in the Stop Press column. It was a time of day when you could expect her to be at home. They would be stunned, in that little shop, to hear the operator say, "Call coming through from Egypt." Mr Pulling or Pullen or whatever would be incredulous. If the line was bad Townrow could imagine himself yelling, "Could I speak to Mrs Townrow. She lives in the flat upstairs?" He would have to put it that way. He could not say, "This is her son speaking. Is she still there?"

She had been a school teacher once. He could even remember being one of the class she taught. He said to the boy sitting next to him, "She's my mother." She was standing with her back to a window through which you could see a red brick wall, angry in the sun, with wistaria blossom blue as the teats of a gas on a low-burning ring. They had a funny little upright Morris which she used to drive because Dad couldn't. It was part of his general ineffectiveness. The time Mumsy actually ordered him out of the car Dad was drunk. It was a summer day. The canvas hood was down; he climbed out of the back seat and walked off down an unfenced unmetalled road with enormous pea-green fields stretching on either side to a horizon made up of great groves of black trees. That couldn't have been Ireland, not with all those trees. He wanted to cry because the wood pigeons, whirring and sobbing, seemed to be claiming his Mumsy's attention. She wouldn't look at him or talk to him. She listened to the wood pigeons.

She might consider he was taking after his father. Telephoning three thousand miles to ask what was his nationality, that was exactly the sort of extravagant, absurd, frightening sort of behaviour the old man was capable of. The fact is it was easier to ask Mumsy about his passport than it was to ask the police. If she was still alive she would tell him like a shot.

The Port Said exchange put him through to Foreign Enquiries who said all calls to Europe were subject to considerable delay. Townrow said he would still like this number and would they ring him back as soon as they had found it. They had the British directories, didn't they? They knew what a cathedral city was. Canterbury for example. The operator said there was so little chance of getting a private call through he wasn't disposed to work too hard at this little problem. Why not write a letter or cable? It might be different if the caller had some kind of priority. Townrow asked what that meant. Well, a journalist or a diplomat had priority. Townrow said he just wanted to talk to his mother, that's all. It was years since he had last seen her. She might be ill. He wanted to give her a pleasant surprise. Norwich was too far out, said Townrow. So was Winchester. St Albans was a good bet. Try Pool, or Poole with an "e". Pulling, maybe. He wasn't very well himself, either, and when a man felt ill it was only natural he should want to talk to his sick mother.

The phone rang. He was stretched out in the basket chair with the instrument at his elbow and the lights from the square below spraying through the open, curtainless window, on to the ceiling of his darkened room. He had only to stretch out his hand. But it was not the exchange with the St Albans number. It was a choked voice he did not recognise, saying "I saw him," and then a long silence followed, or rather, a wordlessness filled with a kind of snarled breathing.

"Who's that?" he asked.

"Mrs Khoury. Who do you think?"

"Is there anything the matter?"

"I saw Elie. He was lying on the ground."

Elie was not in question. He saw Elie in his open coffin on the blue water. Mumsy was the one he wanted to know about. He could not understand why Elie should come into the conversation. Elie was an irrelevancy.

"I want you to come round. I want you to meet me at the front of the hotel. That's where I'm speaking from."

"I can't do that," said Townrow. "I'm waiting for a call to come through. If I miss this call it will be very inconvenient."

"He ran away."

"Who ran away?"

"Elie. I bent over him. I was going to ring the bell of the convent but as soon as I turned my back he jumped up and ran. Me, his wife. He ran."

Then Elie was not dead either.

"I'd like to put the phone down. I'm expecting a call."

"If you come back with me we might find him."

"When did this happen?"

"Ten minutes ago. I came straight here."

At half-past nine every night Mrs K went to that strip of pavement in front of the convent door and at last somebody had decided to take a rise out of her.

"Must have been a joke. Somebody was playing a joke," said Townrow. "You've got to face facts. Elie died."

He listened to the rattle of Mrs K putting the phone down. The line had gone dead. How rude could you get? He hadn't travelled three thousand miles to have a phone put down on him, particularly at a moment when he was engaged on the task of proving that he was an Irish citizen and peculiarly well-fitted to taking possession of every scrap of Egyptian property she had. She ought to be weeping with gratitude.

At ten-fifteen he tried to get through to the Irish Ambassador but the exchange told him there was a two hour delay on calls to Cairo. Townrow asked for his name and number to be put on the waiting list. He undid the knot that secured the bandage behind his head, tied it more tightly, and set off for the Eastern Exchange hotel, locking the door of the flat securely behind him, not taking the lift but walking down the stairs, pausing in the hall, looking keenly around before stepping into the clear moonlight. If he had known where Abravanel lived he would have called and instructed the old chap to draw up his will. "I, Jack Townrow, being a citizen of the Irish Republic and in full health and the possession of my wits do hereby bequeath." It would be a bit premature before having word with Mumsy. She might insist he was born in Liverpool.

While he was waiting for Mrs K to come down from her room he had a couple of drinks in the bar. There were a lot of French people off a cruise liner, all drinking whisky and talking quietly among themselves. Townrow tried to get into conversation with a middle-aged couple but they took only one look at his bandaged head and ill-fitting suit before giving him the brush-off. This prompted Townrow to shout, "De Lesseps was a cuckold and I am the grandson of one of Disraeli's bastards. Yet I held not one share in the Suez Canal Company. I'm proud of it. Can you claim as much? How many of you can deny you've got shares?"

By the time Mrs K joined him he was ready to apologise.

"You caught me at a difficult moment," he said to justify himself, "I was putting in motion certain enquiries. But I shouldn't have spoken to you the way I did."

"What enquiries?" Her dress might have been an extra tall man's vest gathered at the waist by a thin red belt. She wore black cotton gloves up to her elbows and carried a twelve inch electric torch cased in black rubber, holding it like a club.

"You tell me you saw Elie. O.K. You saw Elie. The fact that he got up and ran away doesn't mean somebody was playing a joke. He may have been ashamed."

"Ashamed?"

"I sometimes think the dead are ashamed. I mean, you think worse of a man for dying, and Elie was a proud man."

"He had no pride. I treated him badly."

They came to the end of the street where Mrs K paraded every evening at nine-thirty and the moonlight was so strong on the convent side you could have seen a mouse stirring at twenty yards. With her torch Mrs K pointed to the pavement in front of the gates and even switched it on. It made a faint amber stain on the stones, as it might be where someone had patiently washed away a patch of blood.

"I've got over the shock," said Mrs K.

"How was he lying? Like this?"

Townrow stretched himself, stomach down, on paving stones that smoked dust into his face; and he had to turn his head on one side, resting it on his forearm, in a way that caused him to look straight across the street into a door that suddenly opened and a man stood silhouetted against a background of barrels.

"You don't suppose you imagined it all?" said Townrow to Mrs K's square-toed shoes.

"No. What are you lying down there for?"

"Reconstructing your experience. How near were you when he disappeared?"

Townrow stood up and beat the dust out of his shirt and trousers. "You ought to stop coming here of nights. Go to

Europe and have yourself a holiday. I'll look after things. Abravanel can draw up a document giving me power of attorney."

Mrs K hesitated. "It wasn't you lying down there at nine-thirty? You weren't making a fool of me?"

"No, I've thought of that too. There would never have been time for me to get to the flat before you rang."

"Yes, there would."

"Why should I want to do that to you? You want caring for, imagining things like this. You'd better go back to England. You could call on my mother, if she's still living."

"Don't you know if she's still alive?"

"That's what I was telling you. I tried to phone her. You'll have to excuse me. When you're dead how do you know it? I might have died from that crack on the head. And how do I know I didn't? Some people say the dead see each other. Last time I came this way that bar over there was boarded up and they told me Christou was dead years ago. I knew him. I came and drank in his bar when I was in the army. Then he was gone, he was dead and his bar was boarded up. Well, you can see the lights."

"I've got it wrong," said Mrs K. "I bent over him. I can't remember whether he jumped up and ran away. He seemed just to disappear."

Townrow patted her arm. "You've had a nasty experience and that's the truth of the matter. A snifter of brandy won't do the slightest harm."

A ship gave three hiccupping shrieks on its siren and the ferry roared back. Trouble about right of way in the channel. Wog music on the radios behind bead curtains. They were ringing a bell in the convent and behind all the roof tops there was a white dancing glow that thinned as it went up the black sky to the great stars and moon. There were no lights in this street. Townrow stood in the moon-light like a man on a stage peering into the darkness on the other side, as it might be trying to see to the back of the hall. One of these fine days the house lights would go up.

The scene shifters would come out and pack up everything in sight. The Canal was a great blue strip rising to the flies. Houses fell down. Ocean-going steamers folded stem to stern and were packed away in baskets. The whole damn world was a set of painted flats and when they fell down, by God, and the real people rushed out from behind, laughing their heads off you had to be sure you could adjust to the realisation of the bloody great deception that had been practised on you. You had to pretend you'd never been taken in. You had to let them think you knew all along how phoney the game had been. Elie would be one of the first to rush out. And Mumsy. You had to be ready with a bit of composed behaviour to meet their insane laughter. Not clinically insane. Not like Leah's husband. It was just the insane laughter of people who were laughing because they had the advantage of you. They had seen you taking with the utmost seriousness situations mocked up only to deceive.

When he saw Elie or Mumsy he would play it wryly, pityingly. He'd make them sorry they held out on him. He had no time for people who just watched. You had to give. So long as you put up with existence you had to give. You had to love.

Christou was standing just inside the door when Townrow and Mrs K entered.

"Any French brandy?" said Townrow.

"Greek or Cyprus," said Christou.

"Give this lady a Votris." She did not object in spite of her rules about strong drink. It showed how demoralised she was.

Townrow drew a couple of chairs up to a table. Only two other customers. Business must be bad. Christou brought two glasses on a tray and Townrow watched Mrs K touching her Votris with the tip of her tongue before saying to Christou, "You've lost weight."

Christou rubbed one side of his face and then the other. "We know each other, then? Difficult to recognise you with that bandage. You got a bad eye? You got an infected eye, eh?"

"I used to come in when I was stationed here with the army. We had a pan of brandy on fire in the back room. You remember that? We burned the curtains. Remember?"

"No," said Christou. "It's a long time ago and there've been many soldiers. The light is bad in here." The light bulb hung on such a long flex he could reach up and move it a couple of yards nearer Townrow's face. He shook his head. "No, if you took the bandage off I might remember your face. You British, eh?"

Townrow let that pass because Christou was standing so close that his knee actually pressed against Townrow's elbow. There seemed no reason for this. Unless these little nudges Christou was giving him were a message. Christou remembered him very well and wanted to talk to him privately, perhaps, out of earshot of the other customers. Townrow looked at them, middle-aged, unshaven men with shirts open to the waist. Christou was putting so much pressure on him with his knee that Townrow moved his chair abruptly, Christou laughed and went off to the back of the shop. He brought a half bottle of Votris and said, "Go on, you are my guests."

Judging by the grin on his face and the way he patted Townrow on the shoulder there might have been some private joke between them. Another customer came in, this time for a glass of wine, and all the time Christou was serving him he kept his eyes on Townrow, smiling and winking whenever Townrow looked back.

"I can't drink this," said Mrs K. "I want to go." Christou brought her a glass of water but she said her objection was to taking anything at all in this establishment. If she had been more herself she might have realised where Townrow was bringing her.

"You've got real colour in your cheeks again," said Townrow. "You're looking a lot better."

"It's no accident Elie should have died just across the street."

Christou clapped his hands. "It's Mme Khoury. This is a pleasure and a privilege."

"I know all about you," she said. "You rat."

"Sit down," said Townrow. "He's an old friend. I don't know where this rumour came from, you were dead. Somebody said the whole place was boarded up."

"I am not dead. The years have passed their rough hands over me. We shall never have those days again. Fifty men in here drinking before the place was put out of bounds. Do you remember Staff-Sergeant Wetherby? There's a photo of his wedding group." Christou pointed and, sure enough, there was a yellow photograph pinned high up on the wall. "Greeks and English will always be friends, in spite of everything. We are happy together. We are good for one another."

"As an Irishman, not even English, I don't know why you Greeks should want to kill me."

Christou dropped his hands in astonishment. "Kill you? Who did you say you were? Sergeant Townrow? You did not marry that Copt girl from Ismailia? No. Don't tell me. Townrow!" He brought the light over again. Actually he was shaking with laughter. It had such a grip on him he slobbered. "I know! You had a sister in the Camel Corps! Ten years is a long time but I remember your dear sister reaching down from her saddle and grabbing some Aussie sergeant by the hair. That's what I call love. No? Never mind."

"Why does Aristides threaten me?"

"Aristides!" Christou went over to the two open-shirted men and spoke to them in Greek. He stood to attention to laugh like one of those jocular, sneering sergeant-majors and shouted, "Aristides has been threatening him! Aristides!"

The two men laughed too. Christou seized a bottle and filled up their glasses. "To Aristides!" He shot out his left arm and extended a finger in Townrow's direction. Townrow lifted his half empty glass of Votris, the two men swallowed wine and Ghristou himself drank out of the bottle. "To Aristides!"

Mrs K was the only one who did not drink the toast and she was not laughing either. "If it wasn't for the British you wouldn't be sitting here at all, drinking and swearing and—and spitting."

"Hear! Hear!" said Townrow.

"You're a lot of animals," she said with a sob.

Townrow still had the scrap of paper in his pocket. He passed it to Christou who read it aloud, "We could quite easily shoot here and we shall shoot if you are in the city tomorrow." He translated it into Greek for the benefit of the two men who listened intently and then threw themselves back violently in their chairs, screaming with laughter. Tears of laughter ran down Christou's cheeks. "Aristides always talks like that," he said. "I shall speak to him. He is my friend."

"He's not going to kill me, eh?"

"Wouldn't go as far as to say that. A great man. While the rest of us talks he acts."

"Look—— "

"No, I quite agree. He should not give you such notes. It is not nice."

Mrs K had already left and when Townrow found he could get no more out of these men than free drink and laughter he went too. He heard the door locked behind him. He stood in the darkness listening to the sneezing laughter going on and on, the scraping of chairs, a clock chiming, whistles, muted, remote sirens, radios playing some kind of old-fashioned Balkan jazz. Mrs K was walking down the middle of the street, where shadow and moonlight met, swinging her torch and moving fast.

It was still dark when Townrow was awakened from heavy sleep by banging on the door of the flat. He opened the door and found he had soldiers. With only a dressing gown thrown over his pyjamas and his feet thrust into a pair of Elie's slippers he was rushed off to H. Q. in a car with the sliding roof open. The legs of a soldier sitting on the roof dangled in front of Townrow's face. Another soldier drove and an officer sat in the back seat, humming to himself, belching now and again, reeking of the roast ground nuts he had been chewing, and holding a revolver to the back of Townrow's neck.

The same red-tabbed officer who had turned up to inspect the damage at the flat sat in a large room where all the windows were boarded up and one of the two neon tube lights on the ceiling flickered neurotically. This colonel said they had decided to deport Townrow straight away. He would be put on a plane at Port Said, flown to Cairo and transferred to the first jet out.

"Where to?" asked Townrow.

"New York."

Townrow hesitated, then asked for his passport.

"Sure," said the colonel and spoke to a clerk who immediately began rummaging in a drawer. Time passed without anything to show for it and the colonel began to shout. Townrow was waiting to see his passport before asking why they were sending him to the States. If he turned out to be an American he would have to revise some of his basic ideas. He might even turn out to be Leah's husband.

The colonel began emptying drawers on the floor. Soldiers jumped up and down. Officers came in and out. Within minutes there were papers and files all over the floor. The colonel began hitting the top of his desk with a swagger stick. Dust rose. The colonel sneezed. Townrow thought there was no knowing whose passport they would provide him with eventually.

He was exhausted. With his one eye he saw two of everything. He just wanted to get the British, Irish and American consuls together and tell them about his life so far, as he understood it.

Townrow realised that the colonel and he were alone in

the room. Through the wall came sounds of heavy furniture being moved.

"We shall be contacting you," said the colonel, "as soon as we have all your papers in order."

Townrow did not like to ask him why he was so sure it was an American passport they'd been looking for and was driven back to the flat in the same car with the open sliding roof just as the sun came up. It came up tangerine-coloured at the end of long, deserted streets.

CHAPTER FOUR

Talk on a Hot Morning

B y the time his cheek had sufficiently healed for the
stitches to come out, the excitement over the Canal
had died down. But for the hordes of Egyptians
bathing at the *Plage des Enfants* you would not have known
there had been a take-over. It was the beginning of August.
The *Plage* was Canal Company property in Port Fouad.
Egyptians were never seen there. Townrow knew it from
his army days. There was a glittering, eyebrow-shaped
beach, changing rooms and sweetwater showers. You could
swim out to brightly coloured floats with diving boards.
The porpoises were friendly. They snorted out of the blue
water, played around, rollicked. Jelly fish sometimes floated
just below the surface of the water like great lilac-coloured
poached eggs and if you hit one coming down a chute your
skin turned to blisters. A lot of naked little boys, youths in
loosely tied white drawers, big men with black, matted
hair on their chest who stood in the sea wearing sun glasses
and smoking, these now commandeered the place and after
one look Townrow took Leah back over the ferry. She had
given up being in a rage over what he had said about her
husband. They hired a sailing boat and went swimming in
the outer harbour. The water was still and clear. With the
sail down they could both dive off the boat and swim
around in the knowledge they could get back whenever
they liked. It might drift a few yards, no more.

They were sitting in the boat near enough one of the
concrete moles to hear the clatter of the sentry's boots. He

was an Egyptian soldier with a khaki-coloured flap hanging down from the back of his Foreign-Legion style hat. For some time he was content to stand and watch them. Then he took it into his head to start shouting. Leah said he was telling them to clear off. The air over the mole wobbled, the sun was so hot. The legs and the lower part of the sentry trembled. He might have been standing in very clear running water. Behind him the sky was colourless and a long way off. If he toppled backwards he would fall across Asia. But he didn't. He lifted his rifle and fired. The bullet entered the water about a foot from where Townrow was dangling his hand. The crack of the rifle and the abrupt gobble of the water were simultaneous. Townrow was so surprised he did not move.

"He says it's disgusting for a woman to show herself naked like I'm doing," said Leah.

"You mean he doesn't think we're spies?"

"What's biting him isn't national defence. It's sex."

"Me too," said Townrow. They had changed in the boat. She was wearing an old-fashioned black swim suit so tight her thighs escaped with slight, raised circles of flesh. She had a very little waist and no belly to speak of but at any moment her breasts would break through and stick out, he judged, as firm as marrows. She wore no cap. Her hair was tied at the back with a strip of black nylon.

Before coming out Townrow had taken his temperature and found it was 102. His cheek had healed. There was no infection and it was marvellous to be free of that bandage. But he ought to be in bed nursing his virus. When Leah said she wanted to talk to him he had felt too ill even to listen and he was not much better now. He seemed to be in a never-ending daze.

He slipped over the stern more to get his white body out of the sting of the sun than anything else. At the same time Leah was pulling on a rope to hoist sail. He watched the boat veer off towards the main channel. She wasn't exactly brown, he thought, but she wasn't pink and bleached white like him either. When her skin was wet it was golden. The salt water had crystallised across her back and shoulders.

Townrow swam under water towards the mole. Twenty feet or so down tin cans lay on the white sand. He was a good swimmer. He'd won medals. At Kantara you could swim the Suez Canal and claim you'd swum from Africa to Asia. It was a race he used to win. Townrow first, Staff-Sergeant Andrews second. But he tried to keep his mind off the past. In the cool water his brain was handling memory a damn sight better than of late. With a bit of concentration he could have cleared up the question of his nationality. He needed his energy to reach the mole, though, and grab that soldier by the ankle. Being shot at casually, contemptuously, made him choke. He was so enraged he felt any other shot would bounce off him. Not that he was afraid of being hit. He was a couple of feet below the surface, but what the hell, he was going to get that soldier and his gun in the water with him, the dirty sex-starved rat. Townrow was so mad that although he knew the sentry had him at his mercy he nevertheless went on. He saw himself rearing out of the water and howling with temper.

He surfaced and shook the water out of his eyes. The sentry was gone, though. The mole was enormously high, six feet or so of smooth concrete, and you would have needed a kick like a salmon to get that high.

"Hey!" He was aware, in the same moment that Leah had so manœuvred the boat that she was able to grab him by the hair, and that the sentry had reappeared, about eight yards tall. Townrow floated on his back, thrashing with his legs. He was trying to soak the sentry and he certainly raised a lot of iridescent water. Through these tinted veils he could see the fellow with his rifle up to his cheek. Leah was screaming and dragging on his hair. More soldiers appeared on the mole. One of them was an officer in a peaked cap and white gloves like a traffic policeman.

Perhaps it was this officer who calmed everybody down.

No more shots were fired though Leah went on shouting at the soldiers in Arabic. Later she told Townrow she had made a great fuss about being an American citizen but it was touch and go because they could see she was Jewish (the Egyptians never make a mistake about that kind of identification) and they might have shot her on the chance of her being an Israeli agent. They would have had to shoot her, she said, because it was easier than trying to jump into the boat. They had been very shocked indeed to learn that Townrow was not her husband. No doubt the unpleasant whiteness of his body made the shock all the greater. He looked abnormal and it could fairly be supposed, Leah said, that he went in for unnatural practices. The soldiers were left on the mole struggling with their suppressions.

Townrow lay in the bottom of the boat watching her steer. He felt he had swallowed a pint of iced water and even the hot sun could not warm him. It burned his skin but left him cold inside. Leah thought the escapade had been hilarious and Townrow too tried to look at it in her way. This was not difficult. As he lay there watching her through half-closed eyes he was even ready to think her old man was a dear who needed protecting. Townrow recognised this feeling and took the recognition as further evidence of the better functioning of his brain. The moment he saw the world through any woman's eyes he knew he was falling in love with her and there would be no limit to the crazy, contemptible notions he'd have to take over. If she was in love with her husband he'd have to fall in love with him too. The salt, the sun, the rage, the chill in the belly let him know pretty clearly there was no chance he would turn out to be her husband himself; and now, because she was distressed about the guy he'd get distressed as well. Townrow wasn't content with loving people. He wanted to be them. It was why he always ended up trying to marry the women he fell in love with, instead of just having a good time.

"We'll tie up at the Greek club. I'll send a boy round to pick the boat up later."

"The Harbour Police will do that," said Townrow. "You don't think those squaddies are going to take that lark lying down."

He was able to put out his hand and seize her ankle, to find that when she ignored the gesture he was extraordinarily happy. She could easily have kicked his hand away. He was as ready to laugh as she was now. He seemed to drift up on a great thermal of happiness, shouting about the sentry with the gun and how the concrete had been so high he could not get at him. The brute might have shot him, and he would have gone down in the water like that corporal off Sicily with blood spraying out into the clear water. Perks was the name. If he could remember Perks he could remember anything and he began to shout with laughter and rub his stomach with his free hand, hoping to move the chill.

"My father is ready to tell you something. That is if you promise never to pass it on to anyone."

"That's a big promise."

She shrugged. "I don't suppose it's too extraordinary, what he has to tell you. He's got to imagining things."

"Is this what you wanted to say to me?"

"That's it. You'd have to promise to me not to pass on what he tells you."

"Then what does he want to tell me for? Is it something for my own good, as the saying goes? Meaning, something you don't *want* to know."

"He's mad," she said. "He's crazy. Do I know what goes on in his mind? Let go of my foot, will you? If the Harbour Police come round it's me they'll pick up, you know that? For promiscuity. Hey, I don't like the prospect of that. Let's get off at the Greek Club and change. I'm a sort of member and we can get one of the stewards swear we've been here all afternoon, or something. Or I've not been here at all and you have."

TALK ON A HOT MORNING

The concrete landing-stage rasped them with heat and light. Townrow followed Leah towards the boatshed trying to walk on the sides of his feet, hopping and moaning. Other humans, mainly in swim suits and dark glasses were to be detected through the white flames. But once inside the boatshed he was washed in gloom and the smell of linseed. All around were racing skiffs, polished like violins, dinghies, oars, coils of rope, a brass bell, a miniature cannon and a couple of red marker buoys. Townrow rubbed at his forearms and the salt came off in scales. He was going to rub the salt off Leah's shoulders but when he touched her she cried out and he grabbed her. He held her from behind, one arm across her belly, kissing the nape of her cool neck. She was extraordinarily cool. She was even shivering and he pressed against her for coolness.

A rattle of wood and metal came from the other end of the shed. A man was watching them from a work-bench. Leah freed herself by bending Townrow's fingers back and said she was going to take a shower and change before the Harbour Police arrived. He had better do the same. Townrow was dazed and elated. Just letting Leah's firm, cool, rounded body recede into the darkness was pleasant torture. He supposed he could not rush after her. There was no knowing the lengths these Egyptian police were prepared to go. He guessed his presence in the women's showers would irritate them a sight more than flinging somebody off a sixth-floor balcony had done, and they would have the man at the work-bench to give evidence.

The state he was in though, with his temperature and jumpy memory, there was no knowing the damage she had done. Her buttocks had deliberately thrust back at him. As the realisation bubbled up from Townrow's loins and belly he had to rush out into the furnace where all those mad, strange, staring creatures in human form trembled like salamanders in the flames, and plunge into the water again.

Compared with the Outer Harbour the water was dirty.

He tried to fight his way down to the bottom but he could not so much as see it. He exploded into the sunlight and floated on his back with his eyes shut, thinking, "She attacked me for wanting to take over Mrs K's property, then she came swimming with me and stuck her buttocks out. And she didn't like that bluff about her husband being called." He guessed she was infatuated with him, and that meant, probably, she would go along with him and persuade her old man to use his influence over Mrs K too. If Abravanel said it was a good idea to put everything in Townrow's name the old woman would probably give way, even if it meant a lot of argument. Abravanel and his daughter and he would keep on at the old girl and wear her down.

Leah had taken a fancy to him but he was not vain about it. Newly hatched ducks attached themselves to the first living creature they saw; there was this bearded bird expert whose ducks thought he was their mother. Leah might not have looked at him in London or Baltimore, or wherever it was she lived, but at the precise moment she was coming out of some sort of shell, her eye had caught movement in the undergrowth and there he was, Townrow, for her to fix on. She might have done worse. He was well built and not frightened of anything in particular.

Compared with the European boats moored at the jetty, the local built craft Townrow had hired looked as though it had been cut out of orange boxes with a chopper. A Berber youth with a white headcloth stepped into it and began hoisting the sail. He moved off south of the island and Townrow guessed Leah had given him instructions. Sure enough, a few minutes later a blue and white police launch turned up with a couple of officers in cream-coloured caps like ice-cream salesmen. They cruised along studying the moored craft in a bored sort of way and made off in the direction of the ferry. Townrow swam to the jetty steps and crawled up into the sun.

He took a shower, dressed, and roamed around looking

for Leah but there was no sign of her. He sat on a bench outside the partition masking the entrance to the women's showers. He could hear none of the showers in action and no splashing about. He shouted her name. If she was there she would certainly have answered. No woman he could ask. No attendant. He would have gone into the showers himself and looked round, just in case she was having a fit or had passed out, but he felt dizzy himself. He lay, belly and cheek against the bench, hanging on to it like a plank in a rough sea.

Even after the shower there was enough salt on his skin for him to taste it when he licked his wrist. Or perhaps his tongue was so dry it drew the salt blood. The air was as hot as his blood, no more, no less. He saw himself lying on an immense strand, half in and half out of the water. Instead of legs he had scaly flippers. The white waterfall hung in the air, collapsed and ran up the beach to cover his flippers. The air dazzled.

All this time a plane had been hissing over clean wood and Townrow realised that the man was still at his workbench. He had enough crude Arabic to ask where the lady was. The workman grinned and pretended not to understand. Townrow sat up, put his feet to the ground and unsteadily walked the length of the boat house and out into the sun.

"Anybody speak English?" he said to the men playing cards under the trees.

"Sure," said the one with the rolls of fat bursting out of blue swimming trunks. He was a fiery, coppery, brown, with beads of sweat on his forehead and his skin glistening everywhere, on his chest and arms, it wasn't covered with black hair. He took the cigar out of his mouth and examined Townrow. "Can I help, please?"

"I am looking for someone. You seen a lady?"

"No, no. All ladies go to sleep in the afternoon. There is no lady. We have seen no lady." He spoke to the three other men in Greek. They laughed and looked at Townrow over their cards. They were all sweating like seals with little medallions gleaming against their naked chests. On the table were glasses and beer bottles.

"You must have seen us come ashore."

The fat man shrugged and turned his attention to the cards. The Greek Club had quite a garden. Townrow noticed that his body went exploring. It was as though he remained where he was and his body disappeared behind the great banana tree. It went out to the car park and back to the landing stage without finding any sign of her. So he returned to the boat house. He supported himself by hanging on to a trestle or upturned skiff. To cross the clear spaces he had to let go and hope for the best. He was still on his feet by the time he reached the entrance to the women's showers.

"Hey! Leah! Are you there?"

No answer. He floated inside. The three shower cubicles, the three lavatories, and the changing room with its rows of lockers and a cracked mirror, were empty.

Townrow was too preoccupied with the way his body was behaving to be puzzled by Leah's disappearance. At any moment he might go slithering to the floor. At the same time he was not too sure he was not already lying down somewhere in the hot sun with salt water rushing up now and again to splash over him. Perhaps he was dead. Some soldier had taken a shot at him with a rifle. Well, maybe that soldier hadn't missed. Townrow certainly saw a man tumbling under water with blood coming out of him in a spray. This preoccupation with the body was the most you could expect to know about a death like that. Perhaps it was all very sad. Perhaps he ought to be crying.

The men were still playing cards under the tree.

"Hey!" said Townrow, standing in the shade of the boat shed. "I'm looking for a lady. Do you speak English? Anyone understand me? Have you seen a lady? Can you hear me? Hey!" Because the men went on playing and talk-ing exactly as though they could neither hear nor see him.

There was one empty chair and Townrow went over and sat in it. In the ice bucket were bottles of beer. He helped himself, prised the cap off with an opener one of the men silently handed him, and put the bottle to his lips. He drank enough of the cold beer to start the sweat running down his face and throat. Already he had been there for hours watching them play this incomprehensible game. It wasn't one he recognised. He could not understand what they were saying. It was some sort of gambling game, of course, but there was no money about. Nobody kept the score but the fat man was obviously winning. Townrow got the mad idea he was the prize they were playing for.

"Look, you saw me get out of a boat with a woman some time back?"

The fat man was about to put down a card. At the last moment he changed it for another. "You're an Englishman, eh?"

"I'm Irish."

"You're British, then?"

"What the hell's that got to do with it? Did you see this woman?"

"No," said the fat man. "We saw you step ashore. You were alone. One thing I must tell you. You are not a member of this club. Not one of us has seen you before but you look British to us so we don't sling you in the water. You are our guest. O.K. It is a privilege. But there was no woman."

"She came on ahead of me. She went in to have a shower."

"No woman." The fat man must have won another round because he had dropped his cards and was leaning back. One of his cronies picked the cards up and shuffled. "You look a pretty sick crazy sort of man to me. There was no woman. See for yourself. Where is she now? You off boat? One of these men row you back."

The men went on playing and by this time Townrow knew it was his body they were playing for. He saw it help-lessly stretched on the ground and nationalised. These men

could not run his body though. They hadn't the know-how.
The United Arab Republic was a primitive country that
lacked the technical knowledge to run his body efficiently
for more than ten minutes.

He thanked them for the beer, got up and said he would
walk to the ferry.

If you were accustomed to seeing a man wearing a complete set of dentures in real gold and one day you saw him
with ordinary white ones you might not recognise him.
Townrow walked down Republic Street and saw this man
sitting in Gianola's. He had to stop for a second look. But
for the teeth, Elie looked much as he did when he was
alive. He was sitting at a table under the green and red
awning drinking tea and looking about in a knowing sort
of way. No, though, it was not Elie. Townrow felt exhausted
by the efforts of hanging on to the real world. He had to
relax only for one moment and he was caught up in dreams
and fantasies. This man was all in white. Even his tie was
white. This time of day most of the other customers were
women, some of them young and pretty, eating cream
cakes. The old man's pleasure came, it seemed, from
watching them, because the moment Townrow spoke and
he lifted his head his expression hardened when he saw
who it was. He waved a hand defensively in front of his
face. He looked surprised. He shrugged. He looked up at
the awning. This was the way you might behave to one of
those hawkers with postcards and fly-whisks. Townrow
could not be sure it was Elie. He was like Elie after a long
illness, or raised from the dead. They'd kept his teeth in
Hell and given him new ones. Or restored the originals.

This man in white jumped up and disappeared inside
the restaurant. Because of the children running about
Townrow could not move quickly and by the time he
reached the street on the other side the old man was twenty
yards away. Townrow caught him up and spoke quietly.

"Elie, Elie, for God's sake, Elie." Townrow could have

grabbed him but he was not sure enough of himself for that. He wanted to follow the man and see where he went. At the same time he wanted to be near enough to talk. Plenty of folk lived and enjoyed themselves their relations thought dead. Of course, you had to fake it. You had to set a car on fire, or a house. Nothing left but your charred notebook and your teeth. You could easily get yourself a set of new teeth. But this was different. Elie had been found dead in the street. There were witnesses. Townrow wasn't sure he hadn't seen him himself. He'd seen him lying dead in an open coffin. He could see him in the bright sun, thin as a wafer, with sailors looking down from the rail of a destroyer.

They went north at about four miles an hour. The old man couldn't walk faster. He gave out birdlike croaks and squawks. He arched his body away whenever Townrow came particularly close. After a while Townrow gave up demanding what the hell the game was. He received no answer, not even when it struck him the old man had not recognised him. He said, "You remember me, Townrow. I fell off that horse."

They left the European section and walked into Arab Town where the battered, fragile buildings were taller and every balcony had clothes hung to dry. Sea air did not penetrate. There was a smell of roast meat, latrines and incense. A man clashed a couple of cymbals and tried to sell them glasses of sherbert. There were hundreds of people about, sitting, walking in the middle of the street so that what traffic there was got through by hooting incessantly. Shouting children shot out of side alleys, playing some game.

By the time they emerged into the late afternoon light on the far side Townrow was reviling the old man. "If you're so bloody clever," he said, "tell me whether I've got a British or an Irish passport."

On this open ground there were lots of trotting donkeys sending up clouds of yellow dust. The old fool has taken a room in this quarter, Townrow thought, because this is where the Lake Menzalla steamer starts from and he can get out to his island.

He was in a lather of sweat and his thighs ached. "Everything in this filthy town is a racket. What did you want to get me mixed up in it for? Was I doing anybody any harm? What goes on? Tell me that! We were on a boat. You remember that? What happened? I'm fed up with being beaten up and exploited. What do you take me for? You think I'll crack up, or something? Is that what you're after? You want me to crack up?"

The old man just disappeared at this. He was obscured by the dust and Townrow, out of exhaustion, lost sight of him. He searched round the nearest block but there was no sign. Townrow thought that if he found him he'd do him in anyway, if that was the only way of keeping a dead man down and making sure an Irish citizen got what was due to him. Even a lawyer couldn't claim you'd done a man who was dead already. It was all too crazy. He would not have felt easy in his mind, taking over the property from the old woman if Elie himself was liable to pop up at any minute and dispossess him. At his time of life he needed a bit of security. The time had come to cut his losses. The town had beaten him. To hell with the police and anyone else who told him what to do. He'd take the evening steamer across the lake.

Half way across or thereabouts it ran hard aground and the hundred or so passengers began screaming and shouting. They would have run about if there had been room to move on the now sloping decks. It was night and moonless. Smoke and sparks belched from the funnel. A bell rang on the bridge and judging by the threshing of the screw the captain had put the steamer full astern. She did not budge. For a couple of hours Townrow had been smelling human bodies but now he could smell mud and brine. The lake bed churned to the surface.

It took some time for Townrow to make his way to the stern. He just wanted to get off this boat. He wanted to get away from the screaming women in black cotton drapes. He wanted to get away from the smell of sweat and the conversation of that man who had latched on to him soon after sailing and told him in tortuous English how you could see cities under the water. Corn fields, pastures of green berseem, the date palms lying in the mud, statues, blocks of stone; all these things were in the lake. A soldier in golden armour had been dragged up in a net. Townrow was glad to lose this talkative fool. The stern was actually under water. Here was a long drawn out phosphorescent explosion. The screw dug earth and flung it, flecked with fire, over the black water. There was a cloud of pale vapour. A long way off were still patches of water catching starlight.

Townrow pulled on a rope and the little boat he had spotted soon after leaving Port Said swam up. The steamer must have turned before running aground because this cockleshell emerged on the starboard side, well clear of the stern. Townrow was able to step into it, cast off and shove violently away with his foot before anybody else knew what was happening. Anyway, it was too dark and there was too much confusion for Townrow to be noticed. Except for the navigation lights and those on the bridge the steamer was in darkness. You could tell there were a lot of excited people on board only by the row they were making. Townrow found himself wobbling back to the side of the steamer and had to fend off with an oar. The water seemed to be only three or four feet deep and he was finally able to get away from the side of the steamer by using an oar like a punt pole. He found the other oar and began to row. When he was about fifty yards away he began to sweat again and realised how cooling the churned water had been. Where he now lay the water was stagnant.

The steamer began sending out blasts on its siren. They were probably safe enough. The vessel was broad as a frying-pan and could no more capsize than it could fly. If her stern began to slip back under water and the engine-room got flooded there would be an explosion but the survivors could get out and wade. Townrow turned his attention to the stern of his own little craft; he was delighted to discover that his power of recall was efficient over the really limited period. He thought he'd seen an outboard motor. He had.

Elie's island could not be so very far off. He remembered how they used to lie there and watch the steamers following the channel between Port Said and Matarieh. Even if he wanted to locate the spot there was no point in trying before sun-up. But he had not come to find Elie's island. He was going to lie in the bottom of this boat and snooze and when there was enough light he would see about trying to start that motor. He had no plans. If he came across Elie's place by chance he would certainly go ashore. But he would not waste time looking for it. He rowed for another ten minutes. Pale green water slid from the blades of his oars, glowing and scattering backwards across the surface. The lake broke into wings and the air went into pale scorings and sepia splashes. Wild duck! Hundreds of wild duck! He had rowed into a great settling of them and they burst off the water with honks and croaks. He was startled. Then he began to laugh.

The steamer was still blasting away. All he could see of it now were the sparks and the fire-flushed smoke from the funnel. A voice was booming out so maybe the captain was addressing the passengers with a loud-hailer. Townrow guessed he was telling them to calm down, etc. Townrow knew the stars. Straight overhead was Orion. Over there hung Cassiopeia. Long after he had recovered from being startled by the ducks he still went on chuckling to himself. He was an atheist. His non-belief had hardened soon after they kicked him out of that Bible College. Even in his believing days he had thought life after death a ridiculous idea. But if you did survive this was the first you would know of it, floating in a boat on a great dark, bitter lake. Or something of the sort. The waters of Lethe.

It was a lie to say he was running away. But he was on the move. That was what he liked. Pressing forward. He liked new scenes, new faces, new experiences. A man who stayed put was in decay. You stepped on a plane or a boat and before you knew where you were some new game was being explored. You fell into some new relationship and you became a different person. Someone said to him a man needs an enemy as an abscess needs a poultice, to draw the poison out. He needed no enemy. Provided he kept on the move there would be no time for the poison to gather. That was what he really meant about the man who stayed put; he wasn't so much decaying as accumulating poison. Townrow stuck the oars into the water and rowed hard. The night was hot. Sweat rolled off him and he thought of it as poison excreted.

Sitting in this dinghy as the sun came up he knew he would remember this night and dawn whatever else might slip away. He had kept awake. He sat with a straight back talking to himself now and again. As the stars went, the surface of the lake put on a cold glow and he could see the islands emerge. All this was real. He knew he was there and the sun coming up hot. This was real and certain but nothing else was.

The motor had to be started by pulling on a piece of cord. As Townrow stood up the boat wobbled and sent circles out across the still water. A dozen or so duck took off and rushed clamorously overhead, so near they trailed their droppings of water across him. He could not help tasting it. He passed his tongue across his lips, and the salt tang was enough to make him realise how thirsty he was. Thirst would do for him if he was not careful.

The little motor coughed. The morning was so quiet the splutter startled him. The dinghy moved. He grabbed at the tiller, sat down and set a course due west towards a point where he could see a white building catching the early sunlight in a grove of palm trees. He was not even sure he could break through to the open sea. Hadn't they built a road along the coast between Port Said and Damietta? The boat was light enough for him to lug it across any road. The main thing was not to be seen. Once he had picked up food and water he would head north and see if he could break through to the open sea and hail some boat bound for Europe.

The night of September 14th a man with untidy hair on his cheeks and chin asked the porter of a block in Rue Chérif which floor the lawyer Abravanel lived on. The porter took him up to the fourth and left him looking at a glass door covered with so much ornamental ironwork he could not have pushed two fingers through. Because all the light was coming from inside the flat he could see the servant silhouetted against the glass as he asked, very quietly and without opening the door, "*Min?*"

But the shadow of a woman appeared almost immediately, the door opened and there was Leah, ready to go out, it seemed, with glittering earrings and a white dress and a white wrap and her face alive with expectancy. At the sight of the man on the landing she gasped and drew her little embroidered evening bag protectively up to her chest.

"Expecting somebody?" the man asked.

She looked at his beard and peeling face. Every time he touched it a layer of skin flaked off. He wore a bush shirt, cotton slacks and open sandals. He had a strip of some kind of striped material wound round his head like a turban.

"Who are you?"

"Townrow. I suppose it's because of this beard—— "

"Where have you been?" The words were a long time coming because she was staring at him. She was still shaken. She licked her lips and was still backing away when he said, "Your father in?"

"He's asleep. You can't see him. It's gone eleven."

Down the stair well the lift gate clanked.

Townrow said, "Here's your visitor. Your husband wouldn't like this, you know."

The lift rose from the depths, whining and rattling, to produce a fresh-faced, blue-eyed man of about forty who stepped out and said, "Hallo," to Leah before looking at Townrow and saying, "What's wrong? Anything up?"

Townrow grinned back into the blue eyes while Leah did the introductions. Apparently his name was Stokes and he was a Canal pilot. Like Leah, he seemed set for a night out. He wore an expensive-looking suit that glistened when he moved. His tie was a dark blue bow with white spots and for cuff links he had what looked like gold sovereigns held on little chains. The manner was self-assured. Gaiety had been planned. What the hell was holding it up?

"We've got to be in the office by midnight, Leah. You know I can't be late. Everybody will be there." The voice came from the back of the nose with no resonance.

Leah was still passing the tip of her tongue backwards and forwards between her lips. "God, I could do with a drink." She could not take her eyes off Townrow. "We all thought you were dead. Where have you been?"

"Are you asking me? Who walked out, eh? Who cleared out of the Greek Club without so much as a word? Then you ask me where I've been."

"The Greek Club?"

"Yes, when I went to look for you you'd gone. You said your father wanted to see me. Here I am."

"But not at this time of night."

"Leah—— " The pilot was impatient.

"The police have been looking for you. Mrs Khoury has been out of her mind."

"I've been travelling," said Townrow. "You're not going out with this fellow, are you? He doesn't look straight to me. Does he know you're a married woman?"

"Straight? You talk of being straight?"

Townrow tried to turn up the point of his beard. "When I use the word straight I'm talking about sex. I can see you

123

give it a wider application. I've no strong views on the moral life."

Leah shut the door of the flat behind her. Stokes held the door of the lift open.

"You're not really going out with this twit, are you?" Townrow asked.

"Leonard," she said, "is going down to the Canal Company Offices together with all the other British and French pilots to hand in his written resignation. You don't seem to realise the Egyptian Government may put them all in jail. They're all resigning."

"Is that what you're dressed up for?"

"We're going over to the Yacht Club afterwards to see what happens to the first convoy. It's due in at nine in the morning."

"You mean the convoy will be coming up with Egyptian pilots?"

"For the first and last time," said Stokes. "They'll be screaming for help at two in the morning by my reckoning."

"I'll come with you," said Townrow.

"Go round to Mrs Khoury's flat. She's been worried. She'll be pleased." Leah put a hand on Townrow's arm. "We all thought you were dead. It was just like seeing a ghost, you standing there. I just thought I was seeing things. You go round to Mrs Khoury's flat. Leonard and I will drop you off there."

"The old girl can wait. Sounds as though there'll be some drink going at the Yacht Club."

"Mr Townrow was a friend of Elie Khoury," Leah explained to Stokes, "and then Elie Khoury died and Mr Townrow came out from England because the widow— you see they were clients of my father."

"Mr Townrow, is it?" said Townrow. "Anyway, who said Elie was dead? Can you show me his grave?"

"If we don't go," said the pilot, "we won't be there by midnight."

"You a married man?" said Townrow. "There, what did I tell you? He's married. With kids."

They rode in an open gharry, Leah in the middle, under a full, blazing moon. Every window in town seemed to have a light in it. There were crowds in the cafes. The loudspeakers at the corners were playing music most of the time but now and again a voice broke in and the little crowd gathered before each one cheered and waved Egyptian flags. Townrow thought the pilot must be grinding his teeth over the way he had tagged along; but if he was he smiled at the same time and even talked. He was the sort slow to take offence.

So they all thought he was dead! Leah thought he was dead. But it did not stop her going out with this jerk and having a good time. His corpse might have been lying on a mudbank but she'd be drinking and dancing and laughing.

"You heard from your husband, Leah? How's he responding to the shock treatment?"

He wanted to be sure this pilot knew about Leah's psychotic husband. Leah said no, she hadn't heard, in a casual, flat sort of way out of the side of her mouth and then went back to listening to Stokes talking about the Gyppo pilots and how, if you didn't keep an eye on them, they had the ships climbing up the banks of the Canal. They panicked easily. There was an Egyptian pilot with double vision who always thought there was twice as much shipping about as in fact there was."

"You going back to England when you sign off?" asked Townrow.

"We're staying on. Within twelve hours Nasser will be on his knees begging us to go back."

Townrow would have liked to go into the Canal Company Offices to see these pilots signing their chits but he calculated that if he stayed outside in the gharry with Leah he might persuade her to come round to the Eastern Exchange once Stokes's back was turned. The thought may have passed through Stokes's mind too.

"Leah, would you like to come in and see this panto-mime?" he asked. "I'm sorry I can't invite you too," he said to Townrow, "but numbers are strictly limited."

"I've played the trick myself. You go straight through the building, out the other side and you're away and me left to pay the bloody driver."

Townrow put himself in such a rage that Leah said she wanted to be taken home. She would not go into the Canal Company Offices. She would not go to the Yacht Club. She was upset and confused by what had happened.

"But it's midnight," said Stokes. "Let me just go in and sign."

"I'll just stay with her and look after her," said Town-row. "Now you run along like a good boy."

Stokes twisted his face in a noiseless snarl at this. It was the first time he had shown a human reaction that evening and as he stood there hesitating, his eyes two great black sockets under some harsh electric light, Townrow thought he was going to make more of a fight of it. But instead he shouted to Leah, "I shan't be five minutes," and hurried into the building.

Townrow and Leah were still sitting in the carriage. Townrow tapped the driver on the shoulder, "O.K. Jock. Rue Chérif, and make it snappy."

Leah cried, "No, no, Leonard's taking me home."

"Myself, I don't like Leonard. If he tried to see you home I'll create such hell they'll think the British have landed."

"I'll call the police. I'll have you arrested."

"You would, would you?" He grabbed her round the shoulders with his right arm and used his left hand to hold her chin firm. Before she could scream he was kissing her on the mouth, or her teeth, rather, because her mouth was open half an inch. She hit at him with her free hand but he took no notice. He pushed her head back against the cracked leather upholstery and began caressing her lips with his. She drew her tongue back. He was dizzy with excitement. It was as though he had been hauled out of his own body. He lost contact with it and so with hers. This was how he had been living for the past few weeks. Water, dates, bread and the savage sun. When it was not gold it was purple. The evolutionary process brought creatures out of the water to crawl on the land. But he had put that into reverse. In the heat of the day he had lain covered but for face in the stagnant water, and the frond from a banana tree over his eyes, half fish and half man. A lot of this time he had spent talking to Leah and making love to her so was it any wonder he was jealous? Dead, as he might be, and she out dancing!

He found she was kissing him back. She drew him back down into his body with her lips. "O.K., O.K." she said, as soon as he allowed her to start breathing again. "When Leonard comes back we'll all go across to the Yacht Club."

"Tonight of all nights," he said, "the blasted pilots chuck their hands in. Why can't we go and get ourselves a drink somewhere quiet?"

Three men with arms linked tried to leave the Canal Company building together and found the door was not wide enough, so they came down the steps sideways, laughing and trying to kick their legs up like can-can dancers. They were followed by policemen wearing enormously wide leather belts. A truck, full of soldiers in steel helmets, drew up, and Townrow stood up in the gharry, shouting, "Long live King Farouk!" because he was excited at the way Leah had kissed him back and wanted to hit out at anyone who seemed to be in authority. He reckoned anybody shouting Farouk's name would be dropped on by these brave revolutionary soldiers. But they took no notice and Townrow thought it must be his accent. Leah grabbed him by the shirt and pulled him down.

Stokes appeared out of the crowd.

"It's all done," he said.

Three Frenchmen singing *La Marseillaise* climbed into the gharry too and they trundled away into the darkness at about two miles an hour, soldiers and policemen straggling fore and aft, singing pilots in other gharries, as first one siren in the harbour sounded and then another, and then, it seemed every ship in port was blasting off and the hot, black air wobbled with what sounded like an obscene chord struck and held on some home-made giant organ. They were not letting any cars on to the ferry boat that night, which was just as well because such a mob wanted to cross to Port Fouad and they were able to stand in the tracks where the vehicle would have gone.

"These bloody Gyppos," said Stokes, "they've got it coming to them."

On the other side, the Yacht Club was five minutes from the ferry and Leah said she was going to walk between the two men, holding each of them by the arm, so that they would not get split up. Townrow was telling them about how he had survived in the lake.

"I died," he said. "When my body was cast up on the shore they could see it belonged to some pig of a foreigner so they put me on a pile of old boxwood and set fire to it."

"You certainly lost a lot of weight," said Leah.

"Streaming dysentery."

"You off a ship, or something?" said Stokes, trying to take an intelligent interest.

"I rose from my ashes. There was a whitewashed tomb. It was just an enormous egg with a little door at one side and a lot of writing. And it was all under a sort of canopy made of mud bricks and coloured over in white. There were pigeons and some goats and an old man who came out and gave me Entero-Vioform. Who'd have guessed that, eh? I lay on a mud-brick bench by the side of this tomb and this old chap with nothing on but a tarboosh and gallabieh came around. He'd got long legs like some marsh bird. He'd Entero-Vioform tablets in an old tobacco tin, Three Nuns."

"Mrs Khoury told the police you'd been murdered, like her husband. She was round at the British Consulate the moment they opened because she'd established that even if you were an Irishman the British Consul was charged to look after your interest."

"Was there no enquiry from Europe?" asked Townrow.

"Nothing at all. You ought to see Mrs Khoury. She's grieved."

"He's out of his bloody mind," Stokes said very quietly to Leah but Townrow heard and thought he could be right at that. "He's either tight or sunstruck, or something. They'll give 'im the old heave-ho out of the Yacht Club. I can't say he's my guest. I don't know him from McGinty's goat and they chucked out a steward off a P. and O. boat the other day because he wasn't wearing a tie. This is a great night, you know. We don't want to spoil it, do we?"

Townrow was not crazy. He'd died and risen again, that's all, in a temperature of 105 degrees Fahrenheit in the shade approximately (but there'd been damn little shade) and humidity 95, say, and so much light coming down from the great, cavernous, empty sky that it flooded his closed eyes with blood. He could see the blood washing through the lids of his closed eyes. He never found Elie's island but there were villages with palm trees, dark shops run by Greeks with barrels of pickles, earthenware jars of water he could pick up when he pleased and take a swig. He lived on this bench before the saint's tomb.

"Sheikh," said the man with heron legs and the Three Nuns tin.

"Shay-chch!" Townrow said back to him, trying to imitate the whine and the guttural.

He was out there for years. It made a good man of him. It made him want to give and to sacrifice himself and to love everybody. That was what being a saint amounted to, wasn't it? The old man with the Entero-Vioform opened the door in the side of the white egg and showed Townrow a hole in some masonry. Townrow was made to understand he ought to put his hand through this hole and seize whatever lay beyond. He clasped some dry twigs.

When he ran out of gas he was able to buy a supply from

a one-eyed man who ran a taxi service to Matarieh, or it might have been Damietta. Townrow liked to sleep by day and whine about the lake at night. There were plenty of fishing boats. But you forgot the fishing boats and the dark lake because at night everything was sky. Three quarters of what you saw was a cascade of stars, nebulae, constellations rushing through furry blueness. There were no people up there. Townrow saw no faces. In fact, it had pretty well nothing to do with him, he thought, but night after night he went out and gazed about him. That was what he meant by beauty. There were blue lights and green lights and red lights. On either side of the Milky Way the lights shone out like from some fantastic shunting yard, airport, seaport, some universal, mechanical, signalling haven.

The twigs were a dead man's fingers. Townrow was never going to forget what they felt like. They crackled. He thought a stain might have been left on his own fingers, but he could see no sign of it even in full sunlight. The sheikh held him by the hand through all his bouts of diarrhoea. When the villagers, headed by his friend, the tall man, carried him out to the pyre the saint was there clutching at him. Townrow was upset by this dead man he could not shake off. He thought that if he could forgive his friend, the tall man with the Entero-Vioform, for playing such a dirty trick on him he could forgive anyone for anything. He could forgive Elie for being still in the land of the living. He could forgive this woman, Leah Strauss, with her dyed hair and crazy husband, for the way she just evaporated in the heat. He could forgive his old Dad for the way he climbed out of that car, jumped over the farm gate and walked across that green field, never to come back.

Make no mistake about it, he could have cleared out of the stinking country. He could have lugged this dinghy out into the Med and he wouldn't have needed to head very far north to be in the shipping line. It was like Oxford Street out there. He could have picked any boat he liked. But he talked himself into not going. He had to find out what was happening in Port Said, and what the hell was going on inside himself when he was in Port Said. He had a notion that once back in England Port Said would seem a pretty normal place and letters would start arriving again from old Mrs K saying Elie was dead and she did not know which way to turn. Lies! And that Jewish woman! He'd know for sure he wasn't her husband.

Townrow wanted to lean right across Leah and scream in Stokes's face, "No, I'm not out of my mind. I just forgive and love everybody, Christ knows, even you with your hen's arse for a mouth and your Hairy He-Man's perfume (Yes, I can smell it!) because if I can forgive my old pal with the tobacco tin of Entero-Vioform for playing such a stinking trick on me, I reckon I can forgive even you. Forgive you for what? Well, you exist, don't you?"

He had lain at the bottom of his dinghy watching the half-moon slip west when the dead saint's fingers suddenly ceased to press against his, and Townrow thought, "I'm a good man now. I've been born again. I'm saved, and my friends won't recognise me."

But instead of talking about his state of mind he said he'd always understood the Canal pilots were well paid.

"Money isn't everything," said Stokes.

"As they used to say in my theological college, don't you wish it was?"

"We're not packing in because of the money, if that's what you're driving at."

"I said, 'Don't you wish it was?'"

"We know what we're doing, all right."

"I've been trying to give money away for years," said Townrow. "Thousands of pounds."

They turned into a garden where lights were hanging in the trees and climbed wooden steps to a verandah. Leah said she would rather stay outside. Judging by the roar of conversation the Club House was pretty full and anyway she was fed up with politics, she didn't want to be where she had to listen to people talking about bombing and invasion and the Egyptians putting the Canal out of action. She just wanted to sit where it was cool. She would sit there all night if they wanted her to but she'd rather dance or get tight or play cards, anything but talk politics.

"We can go through to the grass on the other side," said Stokes. "There'll be a breeze off the water."

At the bar Townrow found himself next to an Englishman of about sixty with a fresh, well-scrubbed slightly wobbly face and a silky little yellow moustache.

"Christ," said this man to him. "You smell! You know that?"

"Guest of Captain Stokes."

"Mud, you smell of mud. Where've you blown in from then? Haven't seen you before. Still, this is a time when we shouldn't ask questions, I suppose. If you're a guest you can't buy drinks. What'll you have, Mr—— ?"

"Townrow. I've been travelling. What's the latest?"

"Name of Thompson," said the well-scrubbed man. "But if I don't ask questions I don't answer any. Fair enough?"

"Fair enough," said Townrow, taking his whisky neat.

"Anyway, these French paratroops. You knew that? Cyprus. Landed today. But I'm against it. It's crazy. You can't occupy the Canal Zone. You've got to occupy Cairo. Nasser would set up a government in Khartoum. I understand Arabic. I've an ear for languages. You know, I once travelled passenger on a boat from Bombay to Tilbury, varicose veins, and by the time we docked I was speaking Malay. Lascar crew. I could talk to them. On the radio just now I heard General Hakim Amer say 'The Egyptian Army is prepared to the smallest detail.' Don't misunderstand me. I don't like the Egyptians any more than you do. They're a crazy, treacherous people. Have another."

"It's my turn."

"No, you're a guest. And this conference in Lancaster House fixing to run the Canal by committee! I wouldn't have gone to that if I'd been Nasser. Would you?"

"Did he?"

Thompson stared at Townrow fixedly and seemed to realise for the first time he not only stank but looked a bit of a tramp. He lifted his eyes to the headcloth. "Say, you just blown in from the desert or something? Of course Nasser didn't go to London. Everybody knows that."

Townrow went off with a John Collins for Leah and a double scotch for Stokes but he could not find them anywhere and settled in a chair. He was feeling tired all of a sudden. He ought not to feel tired. Hadn't he had enough sleep during the past few weeks? He did not know how long he had been away. But he had slept at least half the time. He thought that perhaps he'd established a habit. He was at one end of the verandah, near the steps, so that he could see anyone coming in from the garden. As the pilots and their women prepared to mount the three shallow steps they looked up and the verandah light caught their faces. Tables were set about the grass, each under its light and nimbus of moths. Waiters in white gowns and red sashes glided with trays. For all his fatigue Townrow thought something extraordinary was about to happen. These Yacht Club lawns were on the very edge of the last big basin before shipping entered the Canal proper. It was like a stage setting. Nothing moved on the water. There were lights on the big cranes on the other side of the water but none moving between them and the Yacht Club. The sky was as black as the water.

Leah woke him up. She touched his shoulder.

"So that's where you were."

The temperature was about blood heat and the chair so comfortable that Townrow dipped in and out of sleep easily.

"If it's to be a long night I thought I'd better get ready for it. Where's Stokes?"

"He's on the telephone half the time. They're getting reports from stations down the Canal. Or they're trying to. I don't know."

"Do you *mean*," said Townrow, "all these pilots have

133

asked for their cards? It's bluff. They get a hundred quid a week. I don't believe they'd walk out. Or it's done on orders of the British and French as a deliberate bit of wrecking. I've got a drink for you there."

She sat down and picked up the glass.

"You're different."

"Different?"

"You've changed. You haven't been round to see Mrs Khoury? You know she's moved back into the flat."

"I came straight to your place. What does your father want to tell me?"

"Something about Mrs Khoury. They hate each other. You knew that, didn't you? They've always hated each other."

He wanted to possess this woman. He wanted to do it openly so that everyone knew about it. And he didn't want her to give him any trouble about it. He hadn't the strength or the patience for a lot of stalking. And he wanted her to accept him without thinking particularly well of him. Love? He'd rub her nose in it if he had half the chance. He unwound the striped cloth from his head. He began playing with it and noticed how intently she was watching his hands. Her eyes seemed to be made up of lots of little facets, reflecting the overhead light one facet at a time as she moved her eyes to watch his hands. Suddenly he threw the cloth over her head and shoulder and drew her towards him over the table. She screamed, but not too strongly.

"There! Look what you've done." It was her glass. It had smashed on the floor.

"Did you ever send money to the Lydney disaster fund in 1949?" he demanded.

A waiter picked up the broken pieces of glass and Townrow told him to bring another John Collins and a treble whisky. All the time his eyes were fixed on Leah's. Her face was no more than six inches from his. He could see she thought he was up to some game and that in a moment he would kiss her. She had never heard of the Lydney disaster fund. Why should she? She was a Port Said Jewess and Lydney was in Gloucestershire.

"I just wanted to tell you how I earned my living, that's all," he said. He didn't just want to kiss her with the table dividing them. The way she was laughing at him dazed him. He could see her teeth and the tip of her tongue. What was extraordinary was that she didn't think he was crazy. He knew he wasn't crazy but how did *she* know. She wasn't afraid of him at all. She just laughed.

"You're different from the way you were. Do you know what I think? You're an agent. You're here for the British Government. But don't talk about it. Even if you could. I don't want to know."

"You're sure I'm not your husband?"

"No, of course you're not my husband. You're almost a stranger to me," she said in the playful way she might have spoken if he *was* her husband. "We scarcely know each other, do we, Mr—— ?She was so arch it pained him.

The waiter came back with the drinks and Townrow released Leah from his strip of cloth but not before he wondered how the waiter would have reacted if he'd found them making love. It could have been. There was nobody else at this end of the verandah and there were deep shadows.

"Tell me about—what did you say? Lydney?"

The waiter was holding out his tray and Townrow had to ask Leah to lend him a pound.

"Twenty-five scouts got drowned on a boating trip and the public raised £30,000. But the fishermen and the undertakers and the taxi drivers, they didn't want any money, so it all went begging. The trustees of this fund wanted it to go to some scout good cause but the Charity Commissioners said no, and the High Court said no because, they said, the object of the fund had failed and the money would have to go back to the people who'd given it. Can you imagine it? A lot of this money came in five bob postal orders. There were collections at football matches. And some of the donors were dead, anyway. So, that's how I live."

"What do you mean, that's how you live?"

"I work for the trustees, paying the money back. But I tell you it's impossible to find these people. All the trustees want is for the money to go. All the solicitors want is for the money to go. The same applies to the Charity Commissioners and the High Court itself. So I have it, most of it, and they thank me with tears in their eyes for the devotion to duty I'm showing. They said they'd never believe anybody could be so zealous, particularly on the £1200 a year which is what I was getting. I forge the receipts. It's easy. Do they know? Of course they know. They turn a blind eye. They're busy men."

"Aren't you afraid of getting caught?"

"I'm not afraid of anything."

He told the waiter to keep the change. He could see by her grin that either she had not understood what he'd been talking about or she did not believe him. He was too tired to insist. Indeed, he went to sleep again as he watched her face. With his right hand clutching a glass, sitting upright in his chair, he felt the lids of his eyes pressed down and a great blanket of sleep cast over him. He woke up to find her still sitting there. It might have been hours later. She had not moved.

"My right hand," he said, "is still cold from touching the hand in that tomb."

"Must have been a Copt. The Moslems don't go in for that sort of thing."

"I wonder if I've caught something." He lifted his hand and looked at it. "Warm it, Leah." He thrust it towards her abruptly. She took it without hesitation between both of hers and leaned forward so that she could press it to her breast. He was able to curl his fingers slightly and take a slight grip on the soft flesh above the top of her dress. "Some people would call me a crook. But they don't understand. You see, what would happen to that money anyway?

I'm doing the administration a good turn. You know that? But anyway, you're only a crook if you feel crooked. I don't think I've ever done anything wrong. I always feel good, you know. I've got a clear conscience. I've got a perfectly clear conscience."

"There's Leonard," she said, and released his hand.

"Hallo," said Stokes, coming up at a trot, "there's a boat on fire at Kantara. That's thirty kilometres down the Canal," he added for Townrow's benefit.

"The conventional thing would be to say I was a crook," Townrow went on, ignoring Stokes completely, "but as long as you don't hurt anybody, all the rest is red tape, technicalities. Jobs for the lawyers. Take Mrs K's property. If she doesn't give it to me the Egyptians are going to confiscate it, aren't they? There are two kinds of law, book law and real law. Breaking book law is like blood sports. What annoys people is not that you're breaking it but that you're doing a bit of good for yourself, enjoying yourself if you like. I never broke any real law. I was training to be a minister and gave it up. As a matter of fact they made me. But I know enough of the matter to know that the real law is God's law. I'd never break that. I don't think I could. It isn't in my nature, except when I lose my temper."

"Feeling peckish?" Stokes was saying to Leah.

"Bugger off, will you," said Townrow. "Can't you see I'm talking. I was just explaining that although I'm a crook I'm untouched by sin. Second thoughts, though. I'm your guest. If you know where there's food lead me to it."

"When were you in a theological college?" Leah asked. He could tell he was surprising her.

"I was expelled."

"Expelled?"

"A girl reckoned she was pregnant and I believed her. The Baptists said they wouldn't have that sort of thing and I'd better go. She wasn't pregnant, though. She was a liar. I need never have said anything about her. Cut me off from my vocation, she did, the bitch. But you never know what is going to turn out for the best, do you? I still have dreams the bloody Baptists come and drag me back."

"They're serving ham and eggs in the restaurant," said Stokes.

Townrow was following them along a passage when he saw a door with the word Coiffeur painted on it. It was unlikely the fellow would be on hand that time of night but he tried the handle and found the door opening. He put his hand up for the light switch. If he could find a razor he would give himself a shave. But heavy snoring told him someone was on hand and when he looked behind a screen he found a man with long, black greasy hair asleep on a truckle bed. He had to shake him to wake him up.

"You the barber?" he demanded.

The man looked straight up at the ceiling. His tongue was busy inside his open mouth and Townrow looked around. An earthenware pitcher sweated in one corner. He carried it over to the bed and poured a jet of water into the man's open mouth. It filled up and Townrow went on pouring.

"Wake up! I want a haircut and shave," he said. "Here!" He held a bank note in front of the man's face.

When the barber sat up and reached for a towel to wipe his face Townrow could see he was not much more than a boy. He was wide-awake now. For an Egyptian he had delicate features and a clear skin. He had big eyes like a woman. After staring at Townrow for a while he stood up and said in a thick voice, "Sit down in my chair, sir. I'll boil water."

The floor trembled because at the other end of this sprawling wooden building they were dancing to a record player. Any minute you expected to hear the whistle and pop of exploding fireworks. To judge by the thumping of feet and the screams of laughter the pilots and their women were celebrating a victory. Townrow closed his eyes when the barber tucked a sheet under his chin.

The barber was pressing an open razor against his throat.

"I sleep. Why you wake me? No work in the night."

Townrow could have tried to grab his wrist but before he succeeded the barber would have cut his throat. He had only to press a little harder. Townrow knew that blood was already beginning to flow from a point about three inches below his left ear.

"Get on with it, Sweeney Todd."

Townrow relaxed. He settled back more comfortably in the chair and lifted his chin. "Go on! Slice away," he said. The barber was in a foul temper. Even now he might not be properly awake. He was crazy enough to gouge Townrow's neck apart and to hell with the consequences. He was shaking with rage and excitement. Townrow knew this but went on taunting the man. He stretched out his legs and said, "You cut off my head mate and I'll haunt you for the rest of your days." This was more than the barber could understand but the defiance was obvious enough.

The truth was, Townrow felt nobody could hurt him. Defiance was the word. He defied the barber, he defied Leah, Stokes, Port Said, the Canal and the planets.

The barber hesitated, put down the razor and picked up his comb and scissors.

"That's better," said Townrow. "I like the sideburns down to the lobe of the ear. But keep it clean round the neck, will you? And thin it out on top."

When the kettle boiled on the primus stove the barber lathered his face and gave him a cool, refreshing shave. In the mirror Townrow could see his neck bleeding where the barber had pressed the razor ino his flesh. He kept dashing the blood away with cold water but it did not stem the flow, so he went to work with some cotton wool. He touched the wound up with a block of alum.

"That'll do." Townrow stood up and took the towel out of the barber's hand. "Now, clear out will you?" He pushed the man out and locked the door behind him. Within a matter of minutes he was asleep in the barber's bed in spite of the noise of celebrations and when he woke the sun was shining through the uncurtained window.

The Egyptians had managed to line up the convoy due to sail south through the Canal that morning. By going to the edge of the lawn the crowd at the Yacht Club could see the first tanker in line flying the Norwegian flag and behind her a couple of Panamanian vessels. Everything was in order. But there was no movement. The sun was already very hot and the light off the water, when they looked south, unbearably brilliant. North, where the convoy lay it was so calm as to be invisible. The tankers balanced on their own reflections and not much else, it seemed.

The French and the British were not impressed by this. Any fool could line up a convoy. The test would come at nine o'clock when the first convoy from the south was due. This would be the first run by the Egyptians themselves. On the other side of the water from the Yacht Club —the harbour was about two hundred wards wide at that point—was the resthouse where the Egyptians were. Townrow heard a man with some binoculars say he could see old Mahmoud Bakri sitting in the resthouse drinking tea.

Thompson came up to Townrow and said, "That's a nasty cut on your face there. Lucky not to lose your eye. You a member? With Stokes? D'you know, there was an extraordinary chap here during the night, said he was with Stokes. D'you know him? Beard. Smell of swamp. Wore a turban. No time to ask questions, of course. I have no wish to unmask one of Her Majesty's intelligence agents. Have one of these cigarettes? Syrian tobacco. I don't go along with all this talk about the Egyptians necessarily making a balls of running the Canal. What's difficult about it anyway? You're not supposed to say it but half these merchant skippers could take their own boats through if they were allowed to. I'm not claiming the Gyppos could do it straight away. It's a matter of health. They're all sick men. You ever notice their eyes? Defective vision. Once they've got a real health service going things'll be better. But that'll take years. I don't believe in the natural inferiority of one race to another. It's a matter of physical well-being. Statistically, every inhabitant of the Nile valley has three chronic diseases. They didn't have schistosomiasis in Ancient Egypt. Nor bilharzia. Nor malaria. They had a different irrigation system and it just used to sweep all the bugs away. Take the Pyramids. Wonderful edifices. The Great Pyramid was built before the discovery of the wheel. But it's laid down so accurately you can use it to check true north against the magnetic north of your compass. I've done it. After all, I understand navigation. You can use the orientation of the Great Pyramid to check a modern compass."

There were up to fifty people in the Club, men mostly, some in the bar drinking but the majority out on the lawn, looking south. They had sunglasses but they still needed to shade their eyes. Townrow had not seen Leah for some time. He could not see Stokes either. Wherever they were they were probably together and Townrow wondered why he did not feel more jealous.

"They haven't sent for you?" Townrow said to Thompson.

"What d'you mean?"

"The Egyptians haven't sent you an S.O.S.?"

"They will, all right. Bad coordination of hand and eye. Funny thing, though, they make very good squash-players."

"So there you are! You've had a shave." Townrow looked up to see it was Leah, rather faded in the morning light. Her evening get-up looked vulgar. She was amazed by what the shave had done for him. "We couldn't find you so we went round to Leonard's house. He's been showing me pictures of his family."

"Yes," said Townrow, "but he's English. It's pretty much what I'd expect of him. Don't get any false confidence. I'm Irish, remember. Now what's going on?" he asked as a little burst of cheering was heard. She had blue on her eyelids and he hated it.

"It's nine o'clock," said Thompson.

"You look thin," said Leah. "You look very thin and yellow and ill."

Townrow got up and went down to the edge of the water. Some of the pilots were so delighted they were hopping about like fleas. They ought to know. They were the experts. If the convoy did not show up by nine o'clock that must mean it was not coming at all. If that was not a safe assumption these men would not be celebrating. They could not afford to look silly. Some of them were waving across the water and shouting, trying to attract the attention of the Egyptians in the resthouse. Townrow could see these Egypians very clearly. They were not waving or dancing. They were just looking into the sun.

Leah followed Townrow and said, "It looks as though something's gone wrong."

This maddened Townrow. Perhaps he had been more jealous than he supposed. "I'd like to see those bloody boats come up. I'd like to see the grins turn glassy on those faces. Self-satisfied bastards!"

Leah shrugged. "Nobody likes to think just anybody can do his job."

"Particularly when he's been paid a hundred quid a week for it. Shows him up for the fraud he is."

"How can you talk of fraud?"

"I know what it feels like, all right. I know it from the inside. This is different. Fraud on this scale makes me want to throw up. This is international fraud. This is politics."

"I don't see the difference."

"It's O.K. to lie and cheat in a good cause, isn't it? That's what I say. But if it's a bad cause you're fighting for, it's sod-all in the reckoning you've got some of the minor virtues, like being kind to animals."

"You've got to do both, I think. You've got to have a good cause and you've got to be good in yourself."

"It's not that easy," said Townrow. "At least, not to me it isn't. But I start out with a low opinion of what I'm capable of."

Stokes had approached without being noticed. "These Egyptian pilots must have been on duty for sixteen hours. They'd have come aboard at Port Tewfik about four yesterday afternoon. When they got to Ismailia there was nobody to take over, so they came on. No wonder they grounded 'em."

"That definite?" asked Townrow. "You've got that definite? They've run 'em aground?"

"Look for yourself. They've been running the Canal for nine hours and they've made a mess of it already."

"They seem to be stunned," said the man with the binoculars trained on the Egyptians in the resthouse. "Not a flicker of movement."

Townrow looked around for a boat. He had the idea of going across to the resthouse and shaking these incompetent Egyptians by the hand. There were no small craft in sight. If he tried to get into one of the sailing craft no doubt he would be stopped before he got very far. Yet it would take half an hour to travel round via the ferry. He wanted to stop the Egyptians telephoning for help from these gloating pilots. The phone began ringing indoors and he had already turned to rush and intercept the call when a strange, protracted gasp, a sigh almost, went up from the crowd on the lawn and Townrow looked south to see a tanker coming out of the Canal. Behind was another tanker. And another. They came out of the brilliant morning like dummies, a line of stage props wheeled forward with no sort of up and down motion, just a steady, unbelievable glide. Townrow began to laugh and this was the only sound except for the telephone which went on ringing.

"Qu'est-ce qu'ils vont faire pour le voyage de re tour? C'est un question, non? Us doivent être rendus." The speaker was a little moustachioed man with pink, moist lips.

The pilots cheered up at the thought this was only the beginning of the Egyptians' troubles. On the balcony of the resthouse there was no obvious rejoicing. The man with the binoculars said Mahmoud Bakri was patting his face as though to wake himself up. People were coming and going. So much was obvious without the help of glasses. No doubt they were pleased the convoy was so nearly on time. Ten minutes late was nothing. The Egyptians knew it. The French and British knew it.

Townrow first realised something odd was happening to him when he found he could not focus his eyes properly. They were still fixed on a point a mile away. He could see quite clearly the particular tanker that happened to be coming out of the Canal but when he tried to look at the leaders of the convoy they were vague shapes. At the same time he could feel his excitement growing. Leah was standing near enough for him to grab her by the hand. At first he thought it was sexual excitement. He knew how that particular rage of happiness could begin. 'O.K.' a voice would seem to say, 'Let's drop the pretence for a while. Your silly, boring life isn't the real thing. This is the real thing.' When he had kissed Leah in the gharry there had been just a little take-off. But this was tremendous. It almost had him screaming.

"What is it?" said Leah.

He could not say a word. His jaw was set. He was grinning into the sun like an idiot. She put an arm around his waist and steered him towards an empty chair. His legs must have functioned because he made the chair and sat down, still looking fixedly south and grinning. His scorched and pitted face erupted sweat.

"You feel sick?" said Leah.

He sat, hands on the arms of his chair, heels together, unable to move or talk but crackling with happiness. This was the way to live. By God, this was truth. If he stayed there for ever, that was all right by him. The sun would roar over him by day and the moon baste him at night. He remembered a number of naked men with long tubes in their mouths. That was the glass factory in Arab Town years ago, when he was in the army, where the workers kept going on hashish and water. Townrow had one of the pellets and a swig of water before going home and this was why he now thought of the naked glassblowers, because he had the same joy and excitement now as then. There was the same clear awareness of the possibility he could run about inside his own body. He could course between feet, bowels, breast and brain, singing, laughing, making great speeches. The difference was this time he had taken nothing. All that had happened was the arrival of the convoy more or less on the dot.

Attracted by Leah's cries a group of men, including Stokes and Thompson, gathered round and Townrow could tell opinion was pretty evenly divided between those who thought he was tight and those who thought he was having a fit. A man in a grey jacket, apparently a doctor, lifted his wrist and allowed it to drop back on to the arm of the chair. He pursed his lips and looked at Townrow for some moments.

"*Clochard, uh?*" The doctor went off, seeming to think somebody was trying to pull his leg.

Leah was trying to force some whisky into his mouth. It burned on his tongue but he could not swallow. He could not shake his head. He could not move a finger. But he was so relaxed the doctor could lift his hand and let it drop back again; and it did this fairly gently. No wonder the fellow thought this was the beginning of some horse-play. Townrow knew that part of him was laughing like hell but he was too much taken up with other splendours for fun of this kind. The greatest of these splendours was an assurance that everything would be all right. It was in order to be an optimist. He, personally, was O.K. Most things were O.K. If you watched long enough you saw that justice was done. Admittedly it might have to be a really long time. Even he, though, sitting in the sun as the convoy steamed north was there long enough to feel he'd had time to glance into the way the Universe was organised and see that some good principle operated.

Stokes made the doctor come back. This time the Frenchman pulled down the lid of Townrow's left eye and said, "You hear me? You get up?" He put his face so close to Townrow's that Townrow could smell the coffee. He was manipulating the jaw and looking inside the mouth. He shrugged. Townrow knew perfectly well that all the time he was sitting there looking like an idiot or a ventriloquist's dummy. Twelve ships had come out of the Canal by now. He had counted them. It must have been the complete convoy.

A couple of servants arrived with a stretcher and Townrow, still feeling marvellous, was lifted on to it. He was pliable like rope.

"*Il ne cligne pas,*" said the doctor thoughtfully. "*Qui est? Il n'est pas de la Compagnie, non?*"

"Ah!" said Townrow, and began to shiver. The stretcher bearers stopped and Leah, who was holding him by the hand, said, "What is it?"

"Justice," he answered. "Can't you see for yourself?"

The stretcher bearers carried Townrow into a room behind the bar where he was followed by Leah, Stokes and the club secretary who said he had phoned for an ambulance. The main Canal Company hospital was at Ismailia but there was a reception station here in Port Fouad. He could be transferred to the British Hospital later on if that was justified.

"What is it?" said Stokes. "Sort of fit?"

Townrow began to chuckle in a very natural sort of way at this remark. The bearers were preparing to lift him off the stretcher on to a bed, but he said no and sat up. He swung his legs over the side of the stretcher.

"Let me get out. I'm all right." He stood on his feet, swaying a little. "All those resignations, there must be some jobs going. As a citizen of Ireland I could take one of those boats through. You've got to point it down the middle. That's right, isn't it?"

This woman with the dark, red-tinted hair and the evening get up, the mock-diamonds, the big shawl, and all that, looked out of place. Her make-up seemed to have slipped. Like some bad bit of printing the colour shapes did not quite fit her mouth, or her eyelids, or her cheeks for that matter. She wanted some sleep. He could see that his manner frightened her, and that pleased him too.

"We've got an appointment," he said to her and began steering her through the crowd. Stokes tried to stop them but Townrow pushed him violently out of the way.

All Stokes said was, "You couldn't be a pilot. You haven't got the qualifications." Once again he tried to stop Leah leaving, but she said, "It's all right, Leonard. He knows my father. He wants to see my father."

What interested Townrow was that she even dressed the part: the nurse with the white smock and the long white sleeves and the hair done up in a white cap. He wondered where she could have found this gear in such a short time. It was possible that she had gone out and bought it while he was taking a bath, getting into the pyjamas, slippers and dressing gown (these were her father's) and generally failing to resist orders. She had been giving these orders rather more sharply than was necessary, like a big girl playing hospitals. The fuss, the discipline, the concern, were all excessive. Old Abravanel was there but he was brushed aside. He had discarded his dark glasses and Townrow could see anxious, round, darting brown eyes like a chimpanzee's. Leah made him go off and eat in the kitchen. The room Townrow was given had a view of the sea in one direction and the harbour in the other and since he absolutely refused to go to bed in spite of her bullying he was able to relax in a wicker *chaise longue* and look out at the shipping. This was where Dr Catafago examined him. Catafago was a bearded, kingly looking man, but with a shrill voice in which he said he was a graduate of the American University of Beirut and was paid by the visit, at the visit, to avoid misunderstanding.

He rested his head against Townrow's chest, presumably to listen to his heart ('Do not believe in the stethoscope. I use the unaided ear.'), looked deeply into his eyes, tested various mechanical reflexes, prescribed a certain ointment for the sunburned and peeling skin. Again he put his cheek to Townrow's chest. His beard scraped like a loofah. All this time Leah was standing at the foot of the *chaise longue*, holding a large silver pocket watch and a clinical thermometer. Catafago was giving orders now. She produced a notebook from a sort of pouch in her apron and began making notes. She said, 'Yes, doctor. No, doctor,' and did not so much look at Townrow as observe him.

The next day he realised he was not only her patient but her prisoner, too.

"Catafago is a fool. I must get an American doctor," she said.

It was a big flat, with large, lofty rooms and to keep it functioning there was a male cook, a Berber, and two Sudanese servants whose main duties seemed to have been switched to looking after Townrow. Or watching him, perhaps. They brought him toast and coffee, cold, cooked meats, fruit, cheese but no alcohol. Townrow appealed to Leah but she said he was on barley water and artichoke juice. It must have been the small hours of the morning when he woke up to find someone standing by his bed and reached out his hand to switch on the bedside lamp. She really did look like Matron.

"I want you to know," she said, "that I shall never allow anyone to take you away from here against your wishes. You are quite safe here."

Old Abravanel came in one afternoon. Leah ordered him out. He was as amazed by his daughter's behaviour as Townrow was. What is this man to you? Why is he in my apartment? By the way he was switching his eyes from

Townrow to his daughter and back again these questions were to be detected running through his mind. He looked at the clothes she was wearing. He was completely at a loss. He shrugged.

"There is business to discuss."

"Not now."

"Do you not know," said Abravanel trying to assert himself, "it is very likely the French and the British will invade this country?"

"Out of the question," said Townrow from his *chaise longue* where he was lying and looking at his naked feet.

After her father had gone Leah came back and said there was a very good French doctor who ran the St. Francis de Sales hospital at Ismailia. She was trying to get him to come up because he was a specialist.

"What in?" said Townrow.

"He is a specialist," she said.

"I want to talk to your father."

"I can't allow it."

"Look he has things to tell me, see?"

"I can't have you getting excited."

He climbed out of his chair and made for the door but she reached it first and put her back against it. "Just until this French doctor comes," she said. "I don't think you are at all seriously ill, but you are not to leave this room except to go to the lavatory. Are you not satisfied with your meals? The food is very good."

He fell back. "I've no complaints."

"Fine." She led him back to the chair. "You want some books to read?" She produced from her apron pocket a copy of Victor Hugo's *Toilers of the Sea* in an English translation and offered it to him. "My father prefers to read French books in English. This one was written by Victor Hugo when he was in exile."

Townrow opened the volume and found a drawing of a man with terrified eyes in a boat on a wild sea. "What's

149

the matter with you?" he said. "I've not read a book in years. What are you trying to do to me?"

"I'm not trying to do anything. I'm trying to help you. I don't want you to suppose that anyone is doing things to you. We are your friends."

"You're treating me as though I was crazy."

"That's absurd," she said and went out. Townrow was looking once more at the picture in the book when he heard the key turn in the lock.

The first reasonable opportunity he grabbed her round the waist and managed to kiss her on the lips. He was not passionate. He was curious. As he had guessed, her lips were hard to begin with but, as he had not guessed, they softened and parted. He kissed her on the closed eyelids. She had given way at the knees so badly that he was even able to kiss her on the throat.

"Why do you dress like this?" he asked. "It doesn't suit you."

"You were away all that time. We didn't know where you were. You might even be dead."

"What's that got to do with it?"

"You are getting better," she said. "I always said there was nothing much the matter with you."

"Why do you lock me in?"

"It's for your own good."

"You've taken all my clothes away too. Listen, my darling. If you don't bring me some clothes back. Or some better ones. Do you know what? I shall strip naked and use a knotted sheet to lower myself to the next balcony down."

He could see her hesitating over this. Had he really wanted to he could have broken out long ago. He knew, though, that it was not the locked door, really, that prevented him from taking Abravanel by the beard and saying, "I saw Elie. I know he is alive." It was the knowledge that this woman was his jailer. She hypnotised him. Now that he looked at her eyes more closely he saw she had her father's worried expression: the brows a little lifted at the inner extremities, the mouth smiling, the eyes not.

The afternoon Mrs K called Townrow was watching what he could see of the sea through narrowed eyelids and thinking that so much blue and brightness ought to be worrying him more than in fact it was. If he had been a painter he would have needed to do something about the way that heavy cobalt seemed to run on behind the light-house, as though the lighthouse were not quite opaque; and even if he had been just a writer he might have been searching round for words. Maybe he *was* a painter, or a writer, or a photographer. Well, he could have had the aptitude. Some such explanation seemed to be required for the way he knew the glare and the way the colours now seemed heavy, now washed out, all this, ought to be troubling him. A small voice was saying, You've got to deserve a view like that. What have you ever done to earn yourself a place in this great and glorious world? Well, nothing. The fact was it didn't bother him in the slightest. He just relaxed and enjoyed himself.

He heard Mrs K's voice. She and Leah were outside in the hall, talking. Surprisingly Townrow did not get to his feet, go over and bang on the door, demanding to be let out.

"He's resting," he heard Leah say.

Mrs K seemed angry. He could not make out what she was saying but he formed the idea she wanted to accuse him of some failure to do what she had asked. The women's voices became fainter. Townrow scratched some more skin off his forearm and yawned. He was ashamed Mrs K should discover he was locked in. That was why he had not gone over and banged on the door, not even to tell her that Elie was alive and living down in Arab Town, whoever had been buried outside Beirut or at sea. Sooner or later he would climb out of the window. Until then he just owed it to himself not to let Mrs K know he was a prisoner. She would despise him for it.

He could hear breathing on the other side of the door. He turned his head in time to see a folded piece of white paper appear underneath and, apparently in response to some final tap, slide eighteen inches over the polished block floor. Townrow padded over on bare feet and picked it up.

> Dear Mr Townrow, [the writing was a debased copper-plate in purple ink, like a menu in a French restaurant] The Egyptian Government will soon nationalise all property of British and French nationals and it is to her advantage for Mrs Khoury to transfer all her property to an Egyptian national, namely myself. She will not listen to me. Will you please persuade her?
>
> David Abravanel
> *avocat notaire*

"Are you there, Mr Abravanel?"

No reply. Townrow could hear the catarrhal breathing on the other side of the door. He could not be sure it was old Abravanel himself. Possibly it was one of the servants, but Townrow felt in his bones it *was* Abravanel.

"Who is it?" He tried Arabic. Silence.

The room had a writing table, ink and some steel nibbed pens.

> Certainly not, [Townrow wrote on the same sheet of paper] I am an Irish citizen and neutral. Property in my name would not be touched. You are Jewish. Mrs K seems to know a thing or two. How do you know you won't be stripped as an Israeli sympathiser? Worse things have happened.
>
> J.T.

He folded the sheet and pushed it under the door. Within a matter of seconds, it seemed, it had reappeared with some more of the purple writing on it.

> I have never been a Zionist and my famille has been in

152

this country since the seventeenth century. We have always been good Egyptians.

D. Abravanel
avocat notaire

So it *was* Abravanel on the other side of the door. What was he afraid of? That Leah would hear any spoken conversation and come to investigate?

"Listen," said Townrow. "You'd be well advised to transfer all your property into my name if the truth was know. I'll give it back to you in ten years' time. One way or another the Israel question will be settled by then."

Abravanel was sighing and clearing his throat preparatory to speech. What was the matter with the man? Townrow thought. Did he not think he could live ten years?

"I am an Egyptian subject." Townrow could tell by the fierce way he was whispering that he was angry. "There is not the slightest danger of my not being treated like any other Egyptian. You are British."

"I'm Irish I tell you."

"Is there an Irish Ambassador? No. Is there an Irish Legation? No. I don't believe you are Irish but even if you were Irish the Egyptians would not know the difference. You were in the British Army. That would be enough for them."

Townrow turned the handle and pushed in the vain hope Leah had forgotten to lock it.

"What makes you so sure I'm English?"

"This does not *matter*." The old man had worked himself into such a rage Townrow wondered about his heart. If he dropped dead on the other side of the door Leah would blame him for that too. Instead of keeping him prisoner up here she might transfer him to the basement. Those three servants could overpower him, and down there he could be kept years without anybody noticing.

"I wonder you stay in this country. There's no future

for Jews here. Now look, you're Jewish, you don't believe the British could have done more than they did to save European Jews during the war, do you?"

"How should I know, Mr Townrow?" Abravanel was amazed by this irrelevancy.

"Your own common sense should tell you, shouldn't it? There are a lot of Jews in England. You don't think they'd have stood for it if they thought the government wasn't doing everything. Don't you agree?"

"How should I know? The British Government was in the war. Perhaps they had other things to think about than Jews."

"This was different. They would have done everything to warn Jews against going in those trains to Germany. You didn't have to do much thinking to broadcast warnings. They did. Some people said they didn't."

"Who say they didn't?"

"A man I met."

"Forget about it."

"The point is," said Townrow, "it brings up this question of what you believe is possible, like bombing Cairo. You believe the British would bomb Cairo?"

Abravanel seemed uninterested in this line of talk and he was silent until Townrow said, "Can't you find the key and get me out of here? I want to talk to you. I saw Elie walking along the street. How do you explain that? He lives in Arab Town."

"Would I be asking Mme K to transfer property into my name if her husband was still alive?"

"You're a bigger rogue than I am, that's all I know."

"Then you're a simple-minded fool," Abravanel broke out sharply. "You find it easier to suspect me of bad faith than you do to believe in the wickedness of your own government. On top of this you ask me how I know you are English."

"The world's a great deal better for this kind of simple-mindedness. I wish you could get that into your skull.

154

You've just got to believe there are limits. You'd go out of your mind. Perhaps I have and that's why Leah's got me pegged down."

"No, no, it is a way of making up for not helping her husband. She is trying to compensate, poor girl. It is pitiable."

Abravanel could be heard slithering away, probably in his slippers, and Townrow shouted after him, "If you think there's going to be a British invasion why worry about Elie's property being nationalised? It would only be for about a fortnight."

Abravanel shouted back, "Elie was my friend."

It became an exaggeration to say he was a prisoner. He did not want to get out. He was tired. He was waiting for this French doctor from Ismailia, though as the days went by it seemed less and less likely that he would come. Leah no longer mentioned him. It was one more uncertainty to add to the list. Townrow's face creased as he thought of them. No doubt it was a grin. What underlay everything was the basic uncertainty about Elie. Everything else, his own nationality and what had happened to Leah in the Greek Sailing Club that he had been unable to find her, this all seemed to spring from not knowing the truth about Elie. He wondered why he took the confusion so calmly. Serene. The word was one you could use. He would have liked everybody else to share his serenity.

Particularly Leah. One evening she began talking about her husband again. Apparently the first sign of his illness had been his complaint that the phone was being tapped. He worked in an automobile plant—he was an electrician —and he became convinced the company were tapping his phone to make sure he didn't talk about this new process they were developing. He had never been a good sleeper. She used to put out sandwiches and a vacuum flask of coffee in case he went down to the kitchen in the middle of the night. After a meal he could sometimes drop off again. But one night she heard him banging the utensils about. He had one of the kitchen knives, she discovered, and was hacking away at the bread board as though it were a sabre. He pointed it at her when she went into the kitchen, so she went straight back out into the hall and phoned a friend whose husband came round about half an hour later bringing with him, of all people, a Roman Catholic priest. You see, this friend was Catholic and in the excitement the husband had assumed Leah's husband was Catholic too, though they knew Leah was not, and so the priest came, very sleepy and putting up his hand all the time to hide the yawns. He was very kind, though. It had been snowing and the men had snow on their shoulders.

"What happened?" said Townrow.

"We all went back to bed after a bit. The following week he started being a voluntary patient."

"So you came home."

"After a bit. There was nothing I could do. I like the States, though. People're friendly. But if you're a foreign girl they're funny sometimes."

"When did you hear from him?"

"He's not voluntary now."

"What you want is an affair."

"With you?"

"Yes."

"Oh no."

"You've got to learn to be positive about life."

"I don't call it positive to be unfaithful to my husband."

"Could be, you know. You've got to get on some sort of wave and ride it. Or you go under."

The French doctor from Ismailia had the name of Duchâteau and turned out to speak excellent English. He was in his fifties, clean-shaven, very black hair shot with white, big black eyebrows that would have made an oblique angle had they met, energetic, quick. He was an old friend of the family. He gave Townrow a perfunctory examination and shrugged. "Your face has healed. You've had bad burns, Judging by what Leah tells me you've no symptoms of dysentery, but I expect they'll come back. I would have come before but I'm sending my family home. I put them on a boat for Marseilles this morning."

"She didn't say I was crazy?"

"Everybody is, more or less."

"Her husband is."

"So it seems. What's the next move?"

"The police are holding me on a sort of suspended murder charge. They also suspect me of espionage. When they know I'm actually living in the flat of a woman married to an American and she's Jewish they'll think it's an Israeli conspiracy."

"And it isn't?"

Townrow stared at him. "What sort of a specialist are you, anyway? You a psychiatrist? No? Well, I don't know why Leah called you in. I wonder you didn't bugger off back to France with your family. You getting jumpy or something?"

Duchâteau refused to lose his temper. "I have an official position so naturally I will stay. There is bound to be fighting. But you know this probably better than I do. My belief is the French Government is quite delighted over the nationalisation of the Canal. It is just the excuse to knock Nasser out. If it weren't for Nasser the Algerian rebellion would fizzle out next week. The French are more realist in this than the British. Naturally I am concerned about all this. My family have been settled in Algeria since 1871."

He produced some American cigarettes and both men smoked. Duchâteau lectured. "It's got to stop somewhere. There was 1940. There was Indo-China. Now Algeria. Why is it absurd you and Leah are not agents in some Israeli conspiracy? What could be more likely? There is no need to answer or comment. I am discreet. I have known Leah since her childhood. This story of your being out on the lake. I ask you! And she looks after you! In her own flat! She has tremendous spirit, I tell you. She's not the usual Levantine Jewess. Clearly, there is nothing seriously the matter with you physically. What else could I do but assume I was being summoned to be of service? Until Friday I shall be here, staying at the Hotel de la Poste. You can have complete confidence."

He stood to attention, saluted, and would have walked out if Townrow had not grabbed him by the arm, and said, "You can take it from the old master-spy himself there'll be no invasion."

Duchâteau looked disappointed. "What is the plan to be, then?"

"The Egyptians are entitled to nationalise the Canal in a few years anyway. If the convoys keep going through—— "

"I can see you do not trust me. I am sorry," Duchâteau said stiffly, "but in the circumstances perhaps I do not blame you. Always find me at the Hôtel de la Poste. After that Leah has my phone number."

This time he managed to escape, contriving an impression of respectful eagerness. Leah came in some time later, looking a bit puzzled, to ask what Townrow had said to him.

"He wants one of our spare plastic bombs to blow up the Egyptian Army H.Q. He's ready to disguise himself as a Bedouin and take messages to the Israeli army. And he wants to borrow the transmitter so that he can talk to the American Seventh Fleet. I thought he'd come to give me a stool test. I was amazed."

"Why are you so strange? You are laughing at me."

"I wouldn't know whether I was an agent or wasn't an agent. Don't tell me. I just don't want to know. I don't want you to talk to me. Keep that bloody old fool, your father, out of this place, you hear? I don't want explanations."

The words were savage but he spoke gently, with his hand on her arm. He had come up from the depths and was standing high. Not standing. Rushing forward swiftly through blue air. His flight was effortless. This was how you made use of uncertainty and confusion: fuel to lift you from the launching pad. They were driving him in a marvellous trajectory of hope and love.

CHAPTER FIVE

Under Inspection

By the time they were arrested they had given up playing the nurse and patient game. Leah grabbed Townrow and said, "Stop them! You must get in touch with your consul." Townrow had moved into the bedroom the week before. Leah had time to wrap a gown round herself but Townrow was naked except for his pyjama trousers.

He stood up and she pressed her body squarely and flatly against his. He put his arms round her and looked over her head, first at Amin in a smart blue uniform with silver pips, registering that the fellow had not bothered even to remove his cap; then at a curiously pale and puffy woman dressed in a buff-coloured cotton suit with a little badge in each of her mannish lapels. They were accompanied by a couple of amazed-looking police sergeants, each with a Sten gun. Townrow stared at these weapons. All the time he was gripping Leah. She trembled. She was really frightened. Townrow looked at these Sten guns and marvelled, partly that this bunch of policemen should have forced their way right into the bedroom. They must have known they stood a real chance of being scandalised, prudes that they were. Maybe they were not prudes. Maybe they enjoyed exposing themselves to all this psychological tension. Mainly, though, Townrow marvelled at the realisation something had happened to make him love this woman so much he would have been ready to stand there holding her to all eternity. He kissed her on the top of the head.

"Sweetie! Sweetie! God but you're sweet," he said, knowing this was trite, but suddenly ready to produce real tears at the thought of being separated from her. They pricked his eyes.

"I should've thought a time the Israelis were invading you'd be too busy for this kind of bloody nonsense," he said to Amin.

"Your Air Force was bombing Cairo this morning," said Amin.

"Come again."

"The Royal Air Force has bombed Cairo."

"Aw, no." There was no point in Amin lying about this and Townrow had to believe him because yesterday he had heard a B.B.C. broadcast saying Eden had demanded the Egyptian Army retired ten miles west of the Canal. He said to Leah. "He's been looking at the wrong map." He didn't care how much success the Israelis had had in the Sinai peninsula they certainly hadn't reached the Canal and there was no kind of justice in expecting the Egyptians to fall back as though they had. If an ultimatum like that was possible where did things begin to get absurd?

"Get dressed, both of you," said Amin. "We're taking you off for questioning."

"Since when has this been a job for a Legal Officer?"

"These are unusual times."

The policewoman touched Leah on the shoulder and Townrow had to restrain himself from hitting out at her back-handed. If they took her away they'd tear him in half. They would be stripping the living flesh off him. His face and neck ran with sweat. His hands were so wet they slipped on Leah's shoulders and he said to Amin, "Go on, get out of this room, all of you. We'll get dressed and come out. What d'you think this is? A zoo?"

Amin spoke to one of the policemen who began picking up Townrow's clothes from the chair where they had been thrown. The other came round and rapped Townrow in the kidneys with the butt of his gun.

"You can get dressed as we go along," said Amin. "I must warn you not to resist."

"I'm going to phone the British Consul." Leah would have run out of the room but the policewoman grabbed her. A spare policeman, appearing from the hall, put an arm lock on her.

"The Consul is under house arrest. You do not understand." Amin was so remote as to sound absent-minded. "This bombing of Cairo. We are in a state of war. Now the British will bomb Port Said and Alexandria. What can we do?" He shrugged. "Mrs Strauss will dress and accompany this lady."

"Mrs Strauss!" Townrow had forgotten this was Leah's name. "She's an American citizen. You can't touch her."

He tried to hook himself on to the frame of the bed, wrapping his legs round one of the massive Victorian wooden legs, but this only led to the bed being dragged away from the wall. The lead of a reading lamp snapped. A stack of old, yellow newspapers which had apparently been stored under the bed—they were copies of the *Journal d'Egypte* —came to pieces and spilled round the room to be churned up by the feet, two naked pairs, three booted, Amin's in brown shoes and the policewoman's in black, until Mr Abravanel, standing in the doorway, dressed neatly and formally in a dark suit, stiff collar and grey silk tie, was heard to shout, "I warned them. I said the law would punish them if they lived together. It is immoral. It is disgraceful. But everything can be arranged. They will marry. I give you my word."

"This is not a question of sexual morality," said the policewoman, speaking for the first time. She had both arms wrapped round Leah. Her voice was surprisingly deep and masculine. "Under the Revolution we shall have high standards, in public life, private life, everywhere. But first we have to destroy the imperialist aggressors."

Townrow had lost his pyjama trousers. He was carried naked into the hall where, one by one, Amin handed him his vest, his pants, his socks, his shirt, and Townrow put them on while Amin asked if an enemy would get such good treatment in Britain when Britain was being attacked and invaded and Mr Abravanel walked up and down saying, "She had a good religious upbringing. It is the century we live in."

"I'm not an enemy. What is that woman doing to Mrs Strauss in there?" Townrow nodded at the closed bedroom door.

"Dressing. She too is to be questioned. You will be questioned. Everything will be written out. The two accounts will be put side by side. Then they will shoot you."

"For God's sake!"

"I am speaking unofficially. In Egypt we rarely execute people for political reasons, but spying—— "

"When you say the British have bombed Cairo you don't mean they've bombed residential parts?"

"Obviously they've tried to knock out the Egyptian air force. They've bombed the air fields."

"You know I don't believe this."

"If you shoot this man," said Mr Abravanel, stopping and speaking to Amin fiercely, "You know what that will mean? This bombing. Of course there has been bombing. Next week the British will be here. If you shoot this man they will shoot you."

"I have no doubt of it," said Amin calmly.

From the bedroom nothing but silence.

"I want to see Mrs Strauss before I go."

"No."

Two policemen had to hand their guns to a third so that they could carry Townrow out to the lift. The moment he was convinced Amin was not lying about the bombing attack he felt dizzy. His body was too big for him. He lacked the strength to move it. Back at the Yacht Club, when the Egyptians brought their first convoy up the Canal, he had this same feeling of being able to race about inside his head and guts. That had been a gay occasion. But now he was just amazed how people put up with the fact of being human. This sad-faced Copt who spoke scarcely above a whisper, he was obviously no great hero but he went on breathing and talking as though it meant something. And Abravanel and these policemen: Townrow marvelled they didn't break down, cry and say they couldn't carry on.

Amin said the official car had packed up so they were taking him to jail in an ordinary taxi. This permitted Townrow to see where they were going. He sat in the back seat, propped up between a couple of policemen, saying nothing but trying to concentrate on the fact that everybody had minds and knew they had to die: these men, and everybody in sight, Amin in the front seat by the driver with a comfortable fold in the back of his neck, the men and women on the pavements, the boys riding donkeys, the children, all with the infernal sun falling steeply out of the gritty air, they all knew they would be dragged off; but they went on as though it didn't matter. He tried to concentrate on this extraordinary indifference, or forgetfulness, as the taxi drove down past the railway station. They hit the Kantara road and were making for the first bridge when the taxi turned right and Townrow saw the mud-coloured walls of the prison in front of him.

A few minutes later he was in a clean cell with a large, barred window looking on to a courtyard with a big banana tree and the curving trunks of a half a dozen palms, so tall he could not see the foliage at the tops. The window just cut off these trunks. They were gnarled and naked pipes.

"You've got to tell me everything now," said Amin. "Carefully and from the beginning."

Townrow looked up and saw there was a third man in the cell. He was a major in the Egyptian army, sitting at a table with an open notebook in front of him. He nodded and smiled at Townrow and began writing with a huge fountain pen. Well before noon they had forced Townrow to admit the British had bombed the military airstrips and hangars outside Cairo (they brought in a radio and let him hear the B.B.C. on short wave) and this meant the British and French would be landing any day now. Townrow saw he had been dead wrong about practically everything but the more he confessed the less the Egyptians believed him. They thought he was just pretending to be a crook in order to convince them he wasn't a spy. He couldn't make them understand he had been turned inside out. He was obsessed with Leah. He thought about her all the time, even as he lay on the bed talking to these two Egyptians. This was all part of the reversal. No, not that stuff about being redeemed by the love of a good woman. She happened to be the one good he could think of. If there had been any redemption it had been brought about by the shock of disillusionment; if the ordinary man did not instinctively understand the acts of his government and, indeed, found them bestial he could only respond by taking himself in hand. He must tell the truth. He must be honest. That was the logic of it. Otherwise he lost the right to criticise. Townrow rocked from side to side. These bloody Egyptians couldn't understand the agony he was going through. He just wanted to go on being a bastard, the way he'd always been since they slung him out of college, but, for Christ's sake, how could he if Eden was one too?

He kept thinking about Leah. He could see himself on the lake with her. When the bombing started they would be out on the lake looking for Elie's island. When they found it, Elie would be there, sitting on a pillar, a vague, vast presence like God Almighty. Townrow knew this was all balls, though. The man on the pillar was Leah's husband, and what could they say to him?

Townrow said to Amin and the scribbling major you were really living when you were forced to go back over your tracks and you discovered one of your basic assump- tions had nothing behind it. You were alone. You had been

slung out: of college to begin with, and that was all a misunderstanding. But it was like being shut out of Eden.
And what a sour mockery it was this man's name should
actually *be* Eden. The listening Egyptians seemed to have
all the time in the world. They sipped from glasses of
water. Townrow sipped from a glass of water. Prisoners
could be heard exercising in the yard. Talk. He could hear
his own voice buzzing like a fly. On the previous week the
papers had gone through, putting him legally in possession
of the Khoury apartment block. That was as far as the old
girl would go. The bank deposits, the property in Beirut, the
stock, the house down near the station, all these she hung on
to. But the plum had been signed over and if these two men
thought he was lying he would tell them exactly how it
came about. Like the rest of us she had a bad conscience.
Not espionage. Townrow said he did not have espionage
on his conscience either, he was just an ordinary grafter
and if they didn't believe him would they listen carefully?

Every night at nine-thirty, he said, she went to a certain
spot in town where her husband's body had been found.
Now she sent a message to Townrow saying a Cypriot was
telling her to stop it. He ran a bar opposite and this nightly
ceremony was bad for his trade. In a vague sort of way he
had threatened her and she was frightened. She was always
frightened of Cypriots. Nevertheless she was going to this
same spot that very evening and in case anything happened
to her she wanted Townrow to know about Christou's
threat. That was the man's name. He was a certain John
Christou who ran the Cyprus Bar and Townrow remembered him from way back, when he was here with the army.
He had been in his bar once or twice this trip, too. Come
to think of it, he had been in there with Mrs K herself.

That was his first outing after his convalescence, going
with her again to that strip of pavement in front of the gate
in the high white wall which looked across to the Cyprus
Bar. There was a reason he'd come back to why he was
allowed out.

He wore this same grey linen suit for the first time. It had been tailored while he had been shut up in that bedroom with nothing much to do but read, make passes at Leah and get himself measured for suits. He was not complaining. After all the days were cooler. It was October and he could sit on the balcony wearing nothing but a pair of drawers in the noon sun. He was brown in places he'd never been brown before. All the time he was getting better and Leah could see that for herself.

He called for Mrs K at nine o'clock and they walked into town not saying a great deal until she happened to say she had received a cheque for eighty Egyptian pounds from the insurance company by way of compensation for the damage to her flat and she had sent it straight back. It was absurd. The occasional table with cherubs had cost Elie fifty guineas in Wigmore Street and the grand total, the chairs, that big picture of a cock and hens, would be nearer a thousand. Townrow said she was a fool to send money back to anyone. She ought to have cashed it and said it was without prejudice to her claim for something bigger.

Townrow described this walk to Amin and the major with a kind of wonder they must have found irritating because Amin said, "Where is this getting you?"

All the cigarettes had been smoked and the major went out for some more. When he came back Townrow was explaining he was never going to make clear why he was in Port Said unless he pinned down the detail of what had been happening during October. Nothing was quite so important as what happened the particular night he was talking about. A *farrash* followed the major with coffee and a fly swat with which he despatched perhaps a dozen of the two or three hundred buzzing about the cell and settling on the men's faces and hands. A ship out in the Canal gave a couple of blasts on its siren that made the floor tingle. Once out of the jail, Townrow thought, there would be a run of about two hundred yards to the Canal, a short swim, and then no doubt somebody would throw him a rope.

They arrived so punctually outside the convent gate Christou could have set his watch by it. Unusually he had a light burning outside the Bar. He burst out of his doorway, followed by maybe six other men, and began shouting with a theatrical extravagance that gave the impression he was not serious. "Go away! You get on my nerves. Remorse is a sin. You contaminate my life. The graph of my takings falls. Do you think I'm a rich man? I am an exile. I am poor. You take away my living." He crossed the road alone, watched by his customers, and flashed an electric torch in Townrow's face. "Haven't you had enough? Why don't you go away? The past is dead."

Had enough? Townrow remembered thinking this question had the kind of peculiar comprehensiveness that came from Christou knowing more about him than he had supposed. Yes, he had had enough. How had Christou guessed? And if he had guessed so shrewdly why did he think it was so bloody funny? What was the joke?

"My past is not dead," said Mrs K. "I shall come here if I want to."

"Yes," said Townrow, "why can't she come here if she wants to? What's it got to do with you?"

All the time Christou was talking to them in English he was keeping up a conversation across the street with his customers in Greek who laughed and now and again clapped their hands. Inside the bar the radio was turned up. It was roaring out a pop song from Athens and one of the men on the pavement was singing too. Townrow remembered this encounter with Christou beginning with threats and gaiety and singing. It was like the start of some savage festival. You would never have remembered any of these men in daylight. The electric light over the door of the Bar put masks on their faces.

Christou said this nightly visit was just the old woman's way of getting on his nerves. She had killed Elie, poor bastard, but there was one thing she had forgotten. She wasn't married to him, Christou. "To destroy a man you'd

got first to make him love you. That was what you broke
him with. Love. Now, maybe I'm not worth the full treatment. You're rich. I'm not married. I had two wives, you
know that? Both dead. Why you so modest about yourself?
I'm tight half the time, and I don't know the difference
between a crutch and an armpit."

Honestly, Townrow had never believed the old girl was
frightened of anybody but she had signed over the apartment block, no more, and if she did get hit on the head he
knew there was no will and the rest of the estate would go
to some cousin in England. He objected to this. He still had
hopes of putting her on a boat for the U.K. once she'd made
a decent will. Making sure she wasn't knocked off, then—
that and a certain curiosity—made him tag along to the spot
where Elie had been found; certainly not the idea she
wouldn't have gone by herself if he'd said he was too tired.
She was tough. She had the courage of some half-mad old
pussycat run wild.

Instead of poking Christou with the ferrule of her
umbrella or giving him the edge of her tongue, she said,
composedly, "I shall come as I please. You can't frighten
me. I know your game."

"You killed him, m'dear," said Christou, "you killed him
as surely as if you'd stuffed the poor little man in the John
and pulled the plug."

Why Christou found it necessary to vilify Mrs K was
puzzling. He seemed to think this kind of wit so precious
it had to be translated and tossed across the street to the
customers on the other side. Townrow thought there was
more in the savagery than could be explained by the way
these men were egging him on. It was not just a piece of
brutal theatricality. But because he could not understand
what lay behind it he did not know what to do. He was a
man who liked to act. Quite likely he would do something
to make a fool of himself. At that particular moment this
was what bothered him most. "Haven't you had enough?"
Christou had said, just as though he knew precisely what

Townrow had been through. By implication, it made Townrow some sort of puppet.

"What goes on?"

This was the question when Mrs K stood and faced it out with Christou, even though his behaviour became wilder, even though he threw his hands about and joined in a song that was coming over the radio. She didn't do the obvious thing, turn and clear off. For that matter, you would have thought Christou would have tired and gone to attend to his customers. He was losing money. He had made whatever point he had to make, surely. Mrs K had made hers. Townrow had tried to persuade her to go home. She told him to shut up. He would have liked, himself, to go and have a drink. But he could not leave these two together. It would have been like leaving his identity behind.

He tried to explain it to Amin, in the course of this questioning in Port Said jail, by saying he felt, standing there opposite the Cyprus Bar, pretty much as he felt now, trying to account for himself against some background of information he knew nothing about. A spy? What the hell? Townrow said Amin was playing the same role as Christou. "Haven't you had enough?" Amin would say in a minute. Enough of what? But all his life Townrow had been like this. You honestly did not know who you were or what you were doing. Did Amin ever have the idea *he* was watched and manipulated? Townrow said he used to catch himself wondering about Elie, a man who would have liked to watch and manipulate if ever he had the chance. One day a rat in one of those experimental mazes would suspect he was a rat in an experimental maze. Then he would be as uncertain what to do as Townrow had been, listening to Christou and Mrs K. This particular rat said finally, "Why don't we go and see the scientist?" That was what he meant. What he actually said was, "I've been in Port Said at least two months and I still can't get it clear in my head where Elie is buried."

In view of what happened this must have seemed to Mrs K and the Cypriot a childish thing to bring out, particularly at that moment. Townrow said if the officers wanted evidence of his simple mindedness here it was. To be honest he blurted the statement out without much thought. To be quite honest, he didn't give a damn where Elie was buried, if he really was dead that is. He mentioned the burial (say he *had* been buried at sea, wouldn't there be a plaque in the cathedral? Why hadn't he been shown that?) in the hope it might persuade the old girl to speak up and say something he could understand. They operated on some level that was beyond him. They made him feel stupid. There was a coincidence here. He really *was* stupid though it took the air strike on the Cairo air bases to bring it home to him. He ought to have known how stupid he was the day Leah evaporated at the Greek Club. That was a mystery too. He had never been able to ask Leah about it directly. So he had inhibitions too. Everything was a mystery. Didn't Amin think it was a mystery? Perhaps it was only stupid people who had this idea some pundit might turn up and explain all created things from some totally unexpected point of view, a cancer collector's maybe. And this would be completely convincing. We didn't know it but our sole justification was to provide the raw material in which cancer grew. Townrow knew this was a stupid remark to make. He *was* stupid. That was his alibi.

"What happened then?" said Amin.

The patience of these two Egyptians was extraordinary. They listened, made notes, smoked, drank coffee and all the time the invasion fleet was getting nearer. It was on the cards it was getting nearer. Put the Egyptian Air Force out of action and the chaps could come over on banana leaves. Next thing these two knew would be paratroopers outside the jail. Perhaps they just thought the jail was the safest place in town.

"Didn't you all go into the convent?" asked Amin.

"Yes." What in fact happened when he spoke of Elie's

burial was that Mrs K turned on him and said she didn't believe in expensive funerals; all the paraphernalia of death was superstition. Prayers for the dead were superstition.

Christou, though, said, "You ought to see his grave," and, to Townrow's surprise went to the right of the gate and pulled on a chain which just caught the light from the bar across the street. Inside the building a bell clanged. The effect of this was to make the customers shut up. They stood on the far pavement, silent and expectant.

"Elie was good to the Sisters," said Mrs K. "All his life he gave money. He said it was instead of having children."

A grille opened. Christou spoke in French to whoever was on the other side and Townrow caught Elie's name. The grille was shut, footsteps receded down a gravel path, and in the silence that followed Mrs K said, "Naturally he was brought in here. What would you expect? But they don't speak English and I don't speak French."

When they were waiting it was a time not like any time that had gone before; and afterwards it was different too. It was not joined on to the rest of what Townrow's mind accepted as time. He stood there with Mrs K's bony fingers tightening on his upper arm. She had very long, strong fingers that really could take a grip. And Christou stood on the other side, smelling like a brandy cask. What made this time of waiting different was the confidence. They were expectant, God knows why, and if not cheerful at least calm about what they were expecting. This was unique in Townrow's Port Said experiences, he said. When those footsteps came back and the door opened he would not have been in the slightest surprised if Elie himself had stepped out and shaken hands with him.

Instead it was an old woman in a grey habit carrying an ex-army hurricane lamp. It was only a panel of the great door she had opened. First Mrs K stepped over the threshold. Then Townrow said he went. Christou followed. They were some yards along the path on the other side — they found themselves in a garden — when, hearing a noise,

Townrow looked back and saw the half a dozen men who had stood outside the Cyprus Bar stepping through the doorway, too, scrutinised by the old Sister as they came, her hurricane lamp held up face high. They took their caps off with little flourishes.

Amin and the major must know all about this grave. Townrow was telling the story this way to show the kind of innocence he lived in. The only light in this courtyard was from the swinging lamp. Pillars and open stone door-ways rocked from side to side. They advanced and receded. They might have been blown by some great silent wind pressing out of that star-blasted sky. He remembered how the sound of the night changed as all those footsteps moved off the gravel on to the paving stones. Nobody talked. Even Christou's customers kept their traps shut.

Innocent? He didn't even know there were gardens like this in the middle of town. They had to push along a path whipped by dry leaves to a point where paths radiated be-tween the trunks of palm and great cabbage-like plants stinking of wet earth. And there, between one of these paths and what looked like a giant yucca, was a slab of polished stone with a small wooden cross resting on it. No inscrip-tion. They all stood there, jostling each other, coughing and whispering while the old Sister held the lantern as high as she could.

"I never come here," Mrs K had said in Townrow's ear. She said it sulkily and impatiently. It was too obvious, really, to need saying. "The sisters gave him this plot. The least they could do. He must have given them thousands, one way and another."

That is what she had said. She felt nearer to Elie on the pavement where they had found him. Christou was talking about the small feet Elie had. Elie once gave him some shoes he had finished with but they were too small. Townrow went into this kind of detail because he wanted these Egyptians to know what he saw when he shut his eyes.

UNDER INSPECTION

When you see a stone slab, obviously marking the site of a grave even though it has no inscription, and you stand there in silence with a man's widow and with others who knew the man, the assumption is obvious. This is where he lies. But Townrow could not accept it. Even the Sister with the lamp, which she had now hooked on to the end of a long pole resting on the ground, so that the slab was in shadow from the lamp's own base, even that silent Sister was incredible. Since when did a nun open the door of her convent late at night for a lot of men? Who was she? What was this place? How do you know the slab didn't swing open to show a flight of steps leading down to—well, it might be to some cave, or the seashore, or an airport. Once you knew you'd been misled you naturally grew suspicious. Townrow could just see himself walking into that airport lounge and getting into an argument with a stranger.

"He's buried in Beirut," Townrow would say.

"No, he's not dead," this quarrelsome man in the airport lounge would say. "He's buried at sea. He's on an island."

"You'll be glad to know your passport has been found," said Amin.

Townrow lifted his head and saw there was a blue British passport on the major's desk.

"That my passport?" Townrow asked.

"Yes."

"British?"

"Yes. Christou is a British subject too, isn't he? When did you first meet him?"

Instead of answering, Townrow said he wanted to pee. The major stood up, opened the door so quickly the soldier outside, leaning against a wall, did not have time to stand up. Townrow followed this soldier across the yard with another soldier bringing up the rear. In a whitewashed mud hut was an open sewer sonorous with flies. Townrow paused when he came out and sniffed the dusty air, listening. If the British were bombing Port Said airstrip they were doing it very quietly. The hot noonday sun reeked of

173

disinfectant. The air was motionless between these high walls; it was hot and sickly.

"Thanks," he said, when he was back in front of Amin. "What you've been telling me isn't something to make me talk?"

"You mean the British attack?"

"Cairo."

"You don't understand Arabic? No? We could switch Cairo radio on for you and you would hear the kind of talk the British are putting out for the benefit of Egyptians."

"On Cairo radio?"

"Cairo radio has been put out of action by your Air Force. This is a station in Cyprus broadcasting on the same wavelength."

"How can you tell?"

Amin shrugged. "Tell us what you know about Christou. That's where we'd got to. When did you meet him first? He has already told us you used to go into his bar when you were stationed here with the British Army. What I want to know is when you first made contact with him on your present visit to Port Said."

"Is he arrested too?"

"Yes."

It was so hot in the room that when Townrow shut his eyes it seemed the sockets filled up with sweat. He just could not get it into his head the R. A. F. was bombing Cairo.

"On this visit," Amin repeated patiently, "when did you first see Christou?"

"According to him it was the night before I met you."

"According to you?"

Townrow shrugged.

No doubt he would have discovered, sooner or later, that Elie was buried in the Convent garden. The discovery was made that particular evening because it was the day Leah did as he asked quite unexpectedly. She came back from the bathroom wearing a dark red cotton wrap, locked the door, and then took this wrap off and then lay belly down on the bed quite naked. Her head was plunged in the soft pillow with the face turned away from him. The black, red-shot silky hair flowed forward from the nape of her neck and a white path up the back of her skull. What women did with their hair he did not know. This was so clean, so glistening, so black and yet at the same time so ruddy he guessed she'd been putting it through a rinse that morning. She had deliberately drawn her hair forward so that he couldn't see anything of her face. She would have lain with her face pressed into the pillow; but that would have been harder for breathing and not so provocative. He noticed that her buttocks were slightly mottled. He put his hand on the right buttock and felt what seemed to be discs of hard fat or muscle just under the skin. Otherwise her back was quite white and the legs and arms, being so brown from swimming, hardly seemed to belong to the same figure. Her waist was thicker than he had expected. Once he had paraded in front of her with nothing on while she was fully dressed. Now it was the other way round. He kicked off his sandals, slipped out of his shirt and pants and laid himself face down at her side. He ran his hand across her shoulder-blades.

"That's better," he remembered saying. She must have thought he was better because when he said, later, that he was going round with Mrs K to see Christou she made no objection; and this was the first time he had been let out since she brought him back from the Yacht Club.

So from her point of view it must have been something of a success but frankly, as a lay, it was to begin with too determined; and brutal even. A clock struck five as they gasped in a sweaty lock. She had her eyes closed and she heard no clock striking. That was why she was doing it, not ordinary sex but a deliberate bid for oblivion. He held her tight in his arms but the long glide into a mindlessness where no clocks struck was so unmistakable he felt himself going too. She was going to wherever she had disappeared to that morning at the Greek Club when he had searched in those showers and walked about the garden and ended up drinking with that mat-chested trio. They swore she didn't exist. Maybe she didn't, just at that moment. She had expunged herself. She was doing it again and this time she was expunging him as well. He came to want being expunged. It was like being out on the lake again.

Then he started fighting. He had the idea she was just using him; it might have been just anyone, her husband, or that man Stokes, anyone capable of giving that fundamental massage so that she could slip out of herself and avoid the responsibility of this and that. He just had to struggle back to the land of the living. He had never been a drunk. He had never used alcohol or drugs or sex for return ticket suicide. That was the meaning of her great pelvic lunges. Never before had he felt so sorry for a woman he'd been clapped up. She was *not* taking her with him. That was the whole mad disappointment. She didn't care whether he came. He understood she was the sort of woman who really would kill herself if she ever got in a really bad way. It frightened him, so far as a man can be frightened as he comes up to a sexual climax. He could never do away with himself. All this talk of oblivion and forgetfulness was, so far as he was concerned, just for the birds. If you had to put him in a category he was one of those who wanted to know. He might not have much of a brain but it was one that honestly did try to understand. He wanted to be informed. He hated bad information. He wanted to know the truth. He wanted to know who the hell to believe.

Thoughts like these and there ought to have been a fiasco. Not a bit of it. She yelled first, then he groaned and they both began laughing and straining at each other like mad things, laughing so that he could see the sunlight, reflected from the white ceiling, crimson in her staring throat. She looked at him and he looked at her. He said "My sweety,

sweety," just loving her; and she stuck her tongue out and laughed.

"Jack," she said, with just a little spittle on her lips.

Padding along with Mrs K in the canvas shoes Leah had bought for him, making for the Cyprus Bar on the night he saw Elie's grave in the convent garden, the very *first* night he had been allowed out of his prison, Townrow naturally thought of the weapon he had forced that particular lock with. He had taken a shower but he guessed he still gave off a smell of satiated sex. He was slinky inside and aggressive outwardly. He gloried in it. She's let me out because she knows I'm going back for more. Instead of the cold metal lock and rigid key she had put him on a silky chain.

Of course he'd been gay. He had an aura. Mrs K must have hated this aura but at the time this had made her seem all the funnier. Her pinched Cockney, her umbrella, the walk that became a stumbling trot when she was in a hurry, all these were comical in themselves but when you realised she disapproved of his acknowledged sex-glow to the point of keeping away from him as much as possible, he had to laugh. She wanted to know why.

"Oh, I'm just happy," he had said, which sounded pathetic in the light of what happened. She may not even have noticed anything unusual about him. She might have been keeping away from him simply because it was difficult for two people to make their way along a crowded pavement in any other way. He was so caught up by what Leah and he had discovered about each other that he thought his state must be signalling to anybody he came near; in this dim, hot night, perhaps an actual luminosity of flesh.

When a woman gave up her husband or lover and took a new one she didn't; she didn't, he meant, give up the old one, she took him with her, or as much of him as she wanted. She built him into the new one, like a bird building up its nest again after it has been shattered by a storm. Women were never unfaithful in the way men were.

177

Men were looking for somebody different. Women were after the same man behind the different disguises. They just went on re-modelling the ideal mate, one coupling after another. Women carried forward.

Leah when she took him into bed, took her nutty husband too, and they knew it, Leah and he did, in spite of the "Jack!" which sounded as though a really fresh start was being made. You would have thought he was a new man to her. But he wasn't. He did not mind. He was a realist. This was not an issue to be conceited about. A man had to accept this was the way the female behaved. He accepted it because he would have accepted Leah on any terms. She possessed him. She made him see her as he knew perfectly well she wasn't quite; more beautiful, shining, confident. With a woman like that at your side you would, at desperately long last, know the score. You were plugged in to the mainstream of good sense and right feeling. Even if you were defeated the shining angels were with you.

The shining angels! All that was left of his Bible college and one-time career were religious images like these; others included a cross, a betrayal, a sacrifice.

> Matthew, Mark, Luke and John,
> Went to bed with their trousers on.

That night, and for nights after, Townrow was content to be caught up in whatever view of him Leah might have and it was not until now that it struck him the ease with which he accepted this illusion meant he loved her more than she loved him or ever could. He just knew they were both crazy. What were the Egyptians doing to her now?

"I suppose you are aware," said Christou, "they haven't put us into the same cell because they think we'll commit an indecency or kill each other. There'll be microphones somewhere. Maybe there's one in that grating."

Townrow said he was tired. There was only one bed in the cell and Christou, who was sitting on it, offered to make way but Townrow said he would be just as happy on the earth floor. It was after midnight. The night was quiet. Planes had been over earlier and there had been sound of bombs falling perhaps twenty or thirty miles away. No ack-ack. The barred window was so high they could not see the night sky. It was entirely black in the cell and Townrow would not have known about the bed if Christou had not told him.

"What grating?"

"There's a grating high up, opposite the window. Amin said they were putting you in here because they wanted your room for dancing."

"Dancing?"

"Why not? The night before Waterloo the British had a ball."

"That room's ten feet square."

"They'll keep it select. Perhaps I didn't catch what he said. Maybe it's some other activity. Maybe he said poncing."

It was too hot to sleep, even if Christou had let him. The man talked on and on. The Egyptians had left him his cigarettes and matches. Townrow saw the red glow and, when Christou took a real drag, the dim mask floating in the black. A match struck in cupped hands and the intent face blazed like a spirit before some background too vast to be the wall of a cell; it might have been infinite space. The talking face, with its big, broad, horse-like nose and the white hair streaming back because of the speed it rushed out of this space, drove straight at Townrow. The match went out and he was alone as he had been out on the lake. But for the talk. He dozed and woke up again. He could not be sure he was not talking to himself. Floating among the lake reeds he had certainly talked to himself.

"I hear you went to Elie's island." This must be Christou. The man had the power to disturb him when thought he was beyond being disturbed. Leah was probably locked up in some cell like this being talked to by Mrs K and every word of it being taken down on a tape recorder by that female commissar. It occurred to Townrow that Christou was putting on an act specially for the Egyptians. It was anybody's guess whether he was telling the truth or not, but if it was not the truth it struck at Townrow as though it might have been. It disturbed like the truth. The sensation was like a falling dream—immense speed, a churning of the stomach, a yearning for the fall to stop and a burning for it to go on for ever. I don't want to know all this, he said. He just wanted to know what had happened to Leah.

"So," said Christou, "I dressed up as a woman and took the boat out myself. I had this long white dress, real knickers on underneath, silk stockings, the lot. I had a silk scarf over my head and this little silk jacket. I made up, lipstick, blacked my eyebrows, painted my finger nails. By the time I'd finished I looked more fetching than she'd ever been and there'd have been real trouble with admirers on the way to the waterfront if the two men carrying the coffin hadn't kicked a few arses. I didn't tell you exactly the truth before."

"Before?" said Townrow. "When was that?"

"When you came in first."

"You've told me this story before?"

"No, I'm telling you the truth now, mate."

Even as late as this Townrow thought it could be a tale dreamed up for the Egyptians. But if it was, what point could it have? Perhaps the Egyptians were meant to be pleased when they heard about the arms smuggling. When you remembered what purpose the Greek Cypriots put them to Christou could be right at that. Sometimes the Greeks shot Turks, but sometimes they shot the British.

"It was Elie's last wish. In spite of his wife's attitude he couldn't bear the thought of losing money on all this lovely Russian gunnery. He was a Phoenician. They were great sailors. Bury me at sea, he said, and fill the coffin with rifles."

"How could you if it was full of rifles?"

"You've hit on it, son. Elie was no good in really practical arrangements."

As Townrow understood it, Elie had been engaged in smuggling arms to Cyprus and got caught between the Greeks on the one hand and his wife, when she learned about it, on the other. She said she wasn't going to let him send guns to Cyprus where they might be used to shoot English boys. But he had the boats, he had the international connections, he had the capital. You could imagine Elie talking about the opportunities. This was what Mrs K meant when she had said he had been brought up in the Ottoman Empire and wasn't a politician but a business man. So she put the screw on. And the Greeks put the screw on too and the pressure broke him down. His health deteriorated. He was an old man, of course. He could not have lived for ever. But now he saw his end coming. And it was his idea to fill the coffin with rifles! Can you imagine that? Showed his heart was in the right place in spite of his old woman. He had no children. There was nobody to leave the money to but this old Englishwoman, so it showed he loved her to be so interested in money right up to the last. It wasn't only the coffin. There were other crates on board. For Elie Khoury's estate it represented a clear profit of something over ten thousand pounds sterling. The money had been handed over. They were men of honour.

"If it hadn't been for the patriotism of Mrs Khoury Elie would have been with us today. Not in this cell you understand. He was a brother Arab. But alive! He was just ground down by his wife's disapproval. That's putting it gently."

"Where was I?" said Townrow.

"Where were you? When?"

Townrow remembered the very first time he had met Leah she accused him of being the Englishman on this very boat Christou was talking about; but behind this memory were other memories. He could see, quite clearly, Elie's dead beaked face with the hot sun on it, the coffin open to the briny heat and sailors in white looking down from a rail.

"Silk stockings? Make-up? You must be a pervert to dress like that. Why can't you dry up?"

Christou talked until there was enough light to make out the position of the window. Townrow had been lying for some time holding the bridge of his nose between thumb and forefinger. This steadied him. He felt less dizzy. The moment he could locate the window he felt even better. He was no longer falling through space. The window grew brighter and firmer.

It would have been impossible, Christou said, for him to take that boat out of the harbour in any other way. The Egyptian respected the eccentricities of an Englishwoman regarding the last rites.

"They thought you were Mrs K?"

There were soldiers saluting on the breakwater. At the East Fort they presented arms. An officer in white gloves waved. Naturally there were planes about and when one of them dipped it might have been coincidence but Christou thought there was more in it than that. The Egyptians were a generous people. There was police intimidation, there was a callous bureaucracy, there was almost criminal stupidity among the officials; but the set-up was mitigated by kindnesses and courtesies, like the way this plane dipped overhead as Elie's funeral boat bobbed into the Mediterranean. Christou said he waved at the plane. He wore elbow length black gloves, bought in Simon Artz's store, because he assumed that was the way Englishwomen dressed for a funeral. They had tried to find a black sail but there was no such thing in port and no time to dye one. The coffin was decked with honeysuckle. A boy had been sent to the top of the mast with an enormous bow of black satin. One of the other two Cypriots in the boat was dressed as a priest. He wore a black overcoat buttoned high on his chest and a stiff collar worn back to front. This man, said Christou, made gestures as they sailed out of harbour. He might have been blessing the blue water, the fish that swam in it and the craft that sailed over it. He might have been blessing the strollers on the breakwater. The third man was spinning the chambers in a revolver and squinting down the barrel. It was so hot the spray was left as glittering crystals on his face.

"There were no rifles in that coffin." Townrow dragged this information out of some obscure part of his mind. He would be talking about his life in the womb next. He wondered if he was in a trance. The dead would begin to speak. Having seen that grave in the convent garden he was sure, now, that Elie was dead. So if this was the trance of a medium the next thing would be for him to croak out a message in Elie's prissy English. Elie was there all right, at the back of the consciousness, like a rat in the rafters.

"Right." Christou seemed interested in this remark of Townrow's and turned to look at him in as much of the dawn light as filtered down from the window. "You don't get as many rifles into a coffin as the theoreticians argue. Elie was a good business man but he was a bit academic. We just stacked the crates under the false deck. Hell, it was Elie's funeral, wasn't it? If he'd been alive I could have talked him into coming. I got all the documents out of the undertaker but Madame would not let us borrow the corpse. She had him in one of the chapels of the cathedral, candles at his head, candles at his feet, candles all round. The air was blue. It stank of burning wax. It was a tremendous great blaze of light. Imagine being in a gas cooker with stained glass windows. The old girl kneeled there in the heat. When she got up there was a pool of her liquid fat on the marble floor. She must have lost ten pounds. We borrowed another corpse."

"Another corpse?"

"In this town that's easy," said Christou. "Whoever he was he had a most dignified committal ceremony."

And what a send-off from the harbour! Christou said it was a real peak in his life. The Customs and Excise came aboard. They unscrewed the lid, removed their hats, and looked down at the thin, bearded face of whoever it was, saying, 'Peace be on him!' and 'He's like my own father was,' and 'In the capitalist west they burn them in ovens', which is not what they would have remarked about a lot of rifles. Christou said that he stood at the front of the boat to explain to a launch absolutely full of officers from the battery on the mole why the committal was in the late afternoon. He put on a squeaky voice and spoke in English. The coffin was to slide into the water at sunset. As the western waters turned to blood so Elie would go home. What chiefly amazed them was a woman going to her husband's funeral. How could she support such grief in public? It was pitiable and shocking, they said, like so many other non-Egyptian customs. Where else but in Egypt did you find deep feeling and a way of life that respected the bitterness women had to suffer?

The harbour was alive with small craft. They were all going out with the Englishwoman which was a nuisance and meant the funeral boat was not free from attention until well after midnight; but Christou had lived among the Egyptians long enough to know, he said, how their feelings and sympathies led them at a time like this. No doubt there were men in those small craft actually crying.

"At any moment, of course, I expected to see the real Madame coming after me in one of those launches, shouting and waving. Or running along the breakwater. But the priest was able to tell me she never got up from her knees in that chapel, and she certainly never tried to leave, which was just as well because he had the gate locked. I know what worries you. Sergeant Townrow. This is not the same story I told you before."

"You told me a story before?"

"Sure, I told you a story before."

Townrow sighed. He didn't hold it against Christou he was such a romancer. The fellow spoke with what seemed conviction. Providing what he said was internally consistent and Christou believed it all what more could you ask? This was the nearest Christou would ever get to speaking the truth.

"There was a Jewish gun-boat."

"No, it was a fishing boat out of Larnaca," said Christou.

"What about the storm?"

"There was no storm."

"We were washed overboard. I swam with the coffin. When we fetched up on the rocks," said Townrow, "it split. Then I knew why it was so buoyant. It was empty."

Christou laughed so violently he must have blasted that microphone wherever it was hidden. But what was there to laugh about? Amin had produced what he said was a British passport. If Townrow was in fact British his grip on reality must be so tenuous it was unreasonable to expect an answer to that question about the B.B.C. and the trains to the concentration camps. You couldn't answer for anything outside your own personal experience. And if you remembered your own experiences wrongly you didn't count at all. You weren't human.

"I can't get it out of my head I was on that boat," he said to Christou. "You say there was just you and these two other Cypriots?"

"*You* with us? Well, I didn't notice you. It was a lovely trip. Sweet smell of honeysuckle. Cold, salt, night air."

This talk with Christou made him think differently about the events immediately following the night visit to Elie's grave in the convent garden. As he remembered that night, Townrow would have said it was when he began to wake up to the situation as it really was. But he now saw there was more to the chat between Mrs K and Leah than he had supposed. This took place soon after he had walked Mrs K back to her apartment and Leah had arrived to take him back to *her* place. He had not realised there was so much needle. Nor the significance of Christou's ugly taunting before they went into the convent: "You killed him, m'dear, as sure as if you'd—— " Townrow had heard the words. Otherwise he would not be remembering them now. But they hadn't meant much, for some reason, at the time. Christou said so many extravagant things.

Visiting her husband's grave would have sobered the old girl, you might think, but she never stopped talking. She was excited. She thought she had scored a great victory over Christou. He had told her to stop coming, night after night, to the spot where Elie's body had been discovered. But with Townrow's help she had not only defied him but made him go and pay his respects. Elie would have enjoyed the spectacle of those men standing there with their hats off.

Townrow had argued she ought to snap out of this obsession about Elie's death and do something quickly about her immediate interests.

"You're giving up," she said. "I suppose you've had a rough time of it."

"You began by asking me to look for something that wasn't there."

"Yes, it's there. There is something. I'm utterly alone in this town. When you came I thought at least I'd find someone who'd not treat me like a fool."

Candidly, at that time he still thought she was an old fool, but he denied it and buttered her up. It took this talk with Christou to make him realise that what she had wanted, in all probability, was the obvious follow-through from the insults Christou had shouted at her outside the convent. She wanted to be accused. She sat there, in her brightly lit, newly decorated and furnished apartment— she must have spent hundreds on it, ugly great pieces of furniture with gilt legs and mirrors, a great divan with ivory and ebony inlay and purple, tasselled cushions, and in the middle of it all a cheap, stinking paraffin stove—she sat on this great divan and looked aggressive. He remembered thinking there was something vaguely ecclesiastical, even High Church (but no, more remote and garish— Ethiopian, perhaps) about her appearance. She had removed her coat and sat in a long white dress with a silver buckle. Her hair had been given a blue rinse and piled high. Behind the steel-rimmed spectacles she looked mannish, in a wiry sort of way.

He had gone on buttering her up, saying it was more than ever important to put her real estate in his name. She must have been bitterly disappointed. What she really needed was for him to say, "Yes, you are an old fool. Elie dropped dead of heart failure. There was no murderer. So far as there was one you are the murderer, you made him seize up. You put the screw on him over this arms smuggling." He had an idea she would have taken this from *him*. From Christou, no. She had him, Townrow, fly out from England just to tell her she had finished Elie off with an excess of British patriotism. Obviously she could not accept this from Christou because Christou would have no time for British patriotism. Only Townrow would reassure her and tell her it was all in a good cause. She badly needed sorting out.

Instead of which he had continued this Irish talk. In all fairness, Amin had not at that time produced his British passport. "Put the real estate in my name and it will be protected by my neutral status," was the sort of thing he had kept shouting at her; and all the time she must have been thinking. "These bloody Irish hate us British as much as the bloody Greek-Cypriots, so what kind of support am I to get from him once the idiot realises it was to protect the lads in Cyprus I drove poor Elie into the ground?"

She must have been very angry about it all. He was very angry too, in retrospect, because he had made a great deal out of his Irish citizenship. According to his passport he was dead wrong about his national status and nobody likes being taken for a sucker on a matter as basic as that. It wasn't deceiving the old girl that would, at the time, have upset him; it was deceiving himself. But yet again, now that Christou had put him so fully in the picture concerning Elie's martyrdom, death and burial, and now that the British were bombing the guts out of Egypt, he was both angry and hurt. Amazing how much it hurt, what the British were doing.

The night, though, Mrs K and he came back from the convent he had felt Irish enough to give a concise history of the Troubles if asked. But he was not. Mrs K had sat upright among her purple cushions, a kind of defiance on her face, like some heretical high-priest caught in the middle of a weird and wonderful ceremony; and he ought to have known she was no priest, on the contrary she was the one demanding the kind of absolution only he could give. And all he had been able to think of was swindling her.

"Do you know what the time is?" Leah had arrived in the middle of an argument about Christou. "It's nearly three. This is your first time out. You ought to be in bed."

"You know Christou," Townrow said to her. "Would you say he was a Communist?"

Leah had shrugged. She hadn't taken her eyes off Townrow since entering the room. It may have been the effect of the harsh overhead light but they seemed deep-set, dark. "I wouldn't have thought it mattered one way or the other."

"Of course it matters," Mrs K had said. "Do you know what he was doing? Smuggling guns and ammunition. He'd got Elie involved. Elie was a fool. You know that? He was a fool about politics. *Enosis*. I ask you. The real Cypriots want to be left alone, but the Russians won't let them. That Makarios is a Russian agent. Once Cyprus was united with Greece there would be enough Cypriot Communists to start the civil war again, and win it this time. The last thing the real Cypriots want is for the British to leave. We used to go on holidays before the war. There was a house in the mountains we rented. Five pounds a month, and grapes and lemons thrown in. You could buy very good cigarette lighters for two shillings. It was a real paradise. Wonderful climate, cheap food, scenery. Lots of people retired there, from India and the Malay Civil Service. I had a cousin who married a regular soldier, a batman, and when his officer retired he went to Cyprus and Florrie's husband went with him, and Florrie of course. They had a wonderful house up in the mountains. Wine was that cheap you could have washed in it, though it was nasty stuff to be truthful. And another thing. The Cypriots being British subjects could come and go in the U.K. as freely as you and me. Isn't that enough for them? Of course Christou is a Communist!"

"What happened?" Leah had asked Townrow.

"It was all right. There was no trouble. Christou was there. We all went into the convent. A nun showed us a grave."

"If it hadn't been for that man Christou," Mrs K had said, "Elie would be here today. He killed him, just as he nearly killed you."

Leah had said, "Why *do* you go on?"

"He was a man with his limitation. I don't deny that, all to do with his nationality and his country. I'm not a Roman Catholic, you know. My father was C. of E. It had something to do with his command, conducting religious services on board, marrying people and burying them at sea. You could say it was professional. My first husband was a Congregationalist. I don't believe in God. But I do have this feeling of obligation and duty to my husband," she had said to Leah, "and that is not easy for some of us to understand."

Leah had said nothing.

This was the very moment, Townrow remembered, when a light seemed to come on in his mind and he said, "I just remembered my mother was anti-R.C. She used to talk to me about her family in Ireland. She was a teacher. Crazy old bitch, really."

"What a way to speak about your mother. And your father?"

"He left her. My mother brought me up. He was—I don't know what he was really. He never said."

All the time the two women were talking he was

marvelling about the way his mother had brought him up. Very proud of being Irish and Protestant Irish at that; and patriotic to the point of fanaticism. It was all the odder she'd married an English soldier; and as Leah and Mrs K went for each other he thought about his mother and father. Memories came up, bright and clear. At the age of fifteen he met his father quite by chance in a bookshop, a heavy man in a stained flannel suit who breathed asthmatically and peered at him with his head on one side and his mouth screwed up. "How's the Irishwoman?" he asked in a throaty bleat. "How's the bloody Irishwoman?" He stank of beer. "Here's a quid, and don't spend it on vice, if you know what vice is. Probably you don't, living with that Irishwoman."

Leah was sitting and talking but although individual words registered the general sense escaped him; he was so taken up with this sudden flood of clear recollection. His mother was driving the bull-nose Morris with the canvas roof when she stopped without warning. The white dust rose on the country road behind; and the old man, he remembered, jumped down from the car and climbed a wall, or it might have been a gate and set off across a field towards a line of dark trees. He remembered sitting there with his mother watching his father, in a flapping raincoat make off across the field. "I'm glad it's come this way," his mother said. She put the car in gear and they moved off.

"Aren't we waiting for him?" he had asked.

"He'll get a train at the junction." She had said this quite pleasantly. That must have been the last time he saw his father until he came across him in the bookshop. How had his father recognised him?

"She brainwashed me." Townrow did not know what Leah and Mrs K were talking about, but it was rubbish, that was for sure. "I daresay my old man wasn't as bad as all that. He called her 'the Irishwoman'. Whenever I met him he couldn't bring himself to say anything but 'the Irishwoman'. He got beat up a bit in the Troubles. Funny how it all comes back."

"I'm going." He stood up, yawning and thinking of his mother's Irish voice and the way a little line of hairs on her lip caught the light when she set the car in gear and they chugged off down that lane. It was a rutted lane, rather than a road. There were hard, white ruts; sunbaked chalk as hard as stone.

But what struck, thinking back on the night in the wake of the jail conversation with Christou, was the way he had somehow managed to swallow and could now regurgitate this row between Mrs K and Leah. At the time it was of no importance. He was bored. He was so tired even the sight of Leah, with the blue circles under her eyes, disgusted him.

"Going?" he remembered Mrs K saying. "With her? You're my guest."

He was so naive he did not understand the old girl was jealous until Leah had said "I've never in my life done anything wrong. I've never done anything I feel guilty about."

"Everybody's done something wrong," said Mrs K. "You know the English expression, 'a skeleton in the cupboard'. We've all done bad things." She produced a handkerchief and blew her nose, making a surprising trumpeting. "It's only natural. 'Let him that is without sin cast the first stone.' And you know what happened? Nobody moved. Now, you being Jewish, you wouldn't know that story."

"If somebody dared me to throw a stone I'd throw it," said Leah. "Why not? What harm have I ever done anybody?"

"That's a wicked thing to say." Mrs K stood up and began waving her arms about. "I won't have you in my house. Get out. What would your husband think of you?"

"He's beyond thinking of me or anything but himself. You know very well."

"And is that all a wife has to say? What about the vow?"

"What vow?"

"In sickness or in health. What do you think a vow is for? Or don't you make vows in Jewish marriages?"

"There are limits, if you ask me. I haven't done anything wrong. I've got a clear conscience. Shall we go?" she said to Townrow.

Leah's claim she had no guilt feelings did not weigh with him at the time. This was how a woman talked when she was cornered. He had thought she was lying; but there were times when lying was just part of the game and it did not matter because nobody believed you and you knew they didn't. Now, a fortnight later, he could see she had not been lying, she was dead sincere. She was a nice kid, and she knew it, that's all. She did not deliberately set high standards and torture herself if she could not live up to them. She just struggled on, being nice to people. It was the kind of niceness that went with a general hopelessness about the future. She was tough. She fought to get her old man out of Egypt. Her niceness and hopelessness did not mean she hadn't a mind to make up and keep to. He could see her sticking it out to the last in some hopeless situation. She honestly thought there was nothing really bad about her; and this was one of the reasons why Townrow marvelled. She made him envious. Why couldn't he be nice to himself like she was nice to herself? Could she show him now? She troubled his mind, made him eager and expectant. With her he was like some kid on Christmas morning. He was sure he could no longer walk into any place, lose sight of her, and fail to find her again like that day at the Greek Club. She was in his head and guts.

Christou was still asleep when a soldier brought in tea, some flaps of bread and chunks of soft white cheese. Another soldier with an automatic rifle stood at the open door while this first soldier shook Christou, who cursed, swung his arm round and knocked the tray out of his hand. Some of the hot tea splashed across Townrow's leg. Christou went back to sleep. The soldier left the tray and the scattered food where it lay and walked out. Townrow was so hungry he picked up the bread, wiped the dirt off the cheese, and ate. The food was O.K. It amazed him the Egyptians treated them so well. Perhaps they would come back in a few minutes and shoot them. They were bad organisers. The British might deliberately give a man breakfast before shooting him. The Egyptians would intend not to and then forget to warn the kitchen.

Townrow tried to think about his other women. They were all so different from Leah. None seemed quite so pleased with themselves, if you wanted to put it in a mean sort of way. She honestly didn't consider that life was all her fault. He didn't exactly believe he was the authentic man who pulled the lavatory chain and the house fell down. At some time, though, Leah might, he hoped, let some of her own personality smudge off. He envied her and wanted to feel easy like she did.

Townrow and Christou were allowed to walk about the compound for half an hour or so. There were rumours the Israelis had taken Gaza. They were then given shovels and marched off through a gateway to what looked like open desert. Christou said the latest was that the Israeli army was coming down the old Kantara line in a special train, Pullman coaches mainly, three sittings for lunch and dinner. He and Townrow would now be invited to dig their own graves. It had been established beyond all doubt that he was the Rabbi of Jerusalem. His story about disguising himself as a woman and taking a dead man and a few crates of rifles out into the Med. had not been believed. The only point seized upon had been Townrow's reference to the gunboat and this stamped him as an agent of the C.I.A. It was thought that Townrow's real name was Cohen.

Actually, they were only joining the other prisoners to dig slit trenches in the soft sand. These prisoners wore loose-fitting brown cotton slacks and shirts and seemed cheerful. There must have been over a hundred. They joked among themselves and with the half a dozen or so sentries who smoked, strolled about and shifted their Czech automatic rifles from one shoulder to another. Townrow had an idea the convicts were looking forward to air raids. Anything to break the monotony. Who knew? When the Jews came they might be able to make a break for it in the general confusion. That seemed to be the spirit. The sand shone like a mirror. Overhead the sky was a heavy blue, fading to the horizon. To the north the sun was sucking a lot of haze up out of the Med. A couple of jet fighters went round the town as though whirled round at the end of pieces of string. Christou and Townrow had just succeeded in digging a hole deep enough to provide shade from the sun when Amin arrived with an open truck and said he was taking Townrow into Port Said where a military tribunal was already sitting.

"He doesn't look decent," said Christou to Amin. "The accused ought to be given time to shave. Looking like he does it's a foregone conclusion." He passed a finger across his throat and spat. "Never mind, they'll name a street after him in Tel Aviv."

Townrow climbed up into the back of the truck and sat where indicated, next to a Nubian soldier with scarred cheeks.

"Townrow isn't a Jewish name," he said.

"Townrow? Is that what you're known as now? Be seeing you, then, Cohen." He stood on the edge of his hole grinning and waving an arm. His shirt was open to his waist, revealing hair and tallow. "I don't want you to be anxious on my behalf, Cohen. I know what a one you are for worrying. No need. I daresay Grivas is on the buzzer to Nasser at this very minute. 'What a misunderstanding,' Nasser is saying. 'Mr Christou will be released at once. But as for Cohen, well his name counts against him, don't it, Grivas old chap?' They're real buddies. So whatever you do," Christou shouted as the truck moved off and the dust cloud rose around him, "don't worry on my behalf, Cohen, and think how you'll be immortalised."

"Where's Mrs Strauss?" Townrow turned to Amin. "What's happened to her?"

"At a time like this," he said when Amin did not reply, "I'd have thought you people would have something better to do than hold military tribunals."

"It passes the time." Amin shrugged. "It gives us the illusion we are doing something. What else?"

"Is it true the Jews have reached the Canal?"

West and south of the railway station was a plain dotted with huts, tents, piles of sandbags, a few Sherman tanks, armoured cars and all the other gear of a military camp. The truck paused at the guard room and then trundled over the sand. The light was so brilliant Townrow could at first see nothing when he was ushered through a door into a gloom heavy with cigarette fumes. He heard breathing, coughing and the creaking of chairs. Presently, shuttered windows floated towards him. Men in uniform were, he realised, sitting behind a table on a raised platform and he was standing in front of them. It was a bit like the experience at Cairo airport.

One of these men began speaking in Arabic and Townrow interrupted him.

"I don't understand Arabic. Anyway, I want to see the British Consul."

"Proceedings in language of country," said one of the men on the platform. Townrow could make them out better. They were youngish officers in open shirts bearing a lot of medal ribbons. "In London would you give me proceedings in Arabic? What is sauce for the goose is sauce for the— "

He could not remember.

"Gander," said Townrow. "I must have an interpreter."

"What is your religion?" Amin to Townrow's surprise was standing at his side. "The President of the Court wants to know your religion."

The President must have been the one in the middle with receding hair who was talking away, in Arabic, in the monotonous drone of one quoting some legal enactment. The other officers chatted, leaning back in their chairs so that they could get a sight of each other. There were a lot of other men in the hut, soldiers mainly, sitting on benches. Townrow's eyes were sufficiently adjusted to the light he could even make out the exhausted expression of the old man in gallabieh and skullcap who was going round selling coffee. A long way away, perhaps on the other side of the Canal, an anti-aircraft gun started up. Thirty, forty miles away there was maybe a tank battle in progress.

"Christian." Townrow was trying to remember. "And my next of kin is my mother, Mrs Eileen Townrow, Ely, England."

"They do not want to know your next of kin. Say a Christian credo."

"With or without commitment?"

"Please?"

"What do you want me to say the Creed for?"

"Or Paternoster. Our Father," prompted Amin, en- couragingly.

Townrow said the Lord's Prayer and then asked which of the creeds was required.

"There is a credo of the Egyptian Church.' I believe in one God and in the Logos of one substance with him,' but you would not know this," said Amin sadly. "Say the Apostle's Creed."

"No."

"You mean you don't know it?" Amin prompted, "I believe— "

"I know it but I won't say it."

The tribunal had listened with interest, even inter- rupting the conversation between themselves. The Presi- dent spoke in Arabic at some length and Amin, having waited until he finished, spoke even more sadly than before. "His Excellency says there is much scepticism in this century and he understands your reservations but he would like to hear you speak the words about the Trinity of Christian

Gods—please!" Amin broke off in anguish and addressed the tribunal on what were obviously points of theology.

"He wants to hear you say these words," Amin continued after the President by nodding, frowning and smiling in turn seemed to have conveyed some apology, "purely evidentially. He does not expect a modern European actually to believe them."

"Does he think a Jewish agent wouldn't do a bit of home-work? He'd know a creed. That isn't the test. Look!" Townrow undid the belt of his trousers. He lifted his shirt. "A Jew would be circumcised, wouldn't he?"

The President was about to light a cigarette. He extended the flaring lighter in Townrow's direction, the better to see. The two other members of the tribunal stood up and leaned forward.

"It is never easy," said Amin, helping Townrow to pull his trousers up after this inspection, "to persuade adherents of Islam that Christians are not polytheists and believe in three gods."

"Let us come to the point," said the President, dropping his rule about not speaking English. "It is known you are a British agent investigating the export of arms to Cyprus. The *real* question is whether under cover of being a secret agent you are, in reality, a spy."

Townrow was confused. Who said he was a British agent? "What is the difference between an agent and a spy?"

"It is lucky for you," said the President, "that the respected merchant Mr Elie Khoury died before you arrived in this country. Otherwise you would be under arrest on a charge of murdering him. There still remains the charge of attempting to murder Mr Christou. He has lodged a complaint. All this is trivial. The United Arab Republic is not interested by the British trying to stop arms going to Cyprus. This is not our quarrel. The Canal and Israel is our quarrel. Our information is that you are only pretending to be Townrow with the mission to stop arms smuggling to Cyprus. Your real name is—— "

He searched in vain among the papers on the table and then raised his hands in despair. He and the other members of the tribunal went into conference. There was a pause in the proceedings. What sounded like an old-fashioned Bofors gun started up in the distance. Or it might even have been a steam locomotive. Townrow listened. No, it was some kind of anti-aircraft fire. He guessed the R.A.F. had a reconnaissance plane out. Amin touched Townrow on the shoulder. The coffee seller had arrived. Townrow gave the man a ten piastre note and took a cup.

"Why is it?" said Amin plaintively, "that Britain and the United States made this foreign country in our midst? It is an injustice."

The tribunal had stopped talking between themselves and were listening to Amin with interest.

"Answer the question," said the President sharply. "The answer is that England and France and the United States are all controlled by Jews. You cannot deny this. That is why they made this Jewish state."

Townrow had been counting the military. In addition to the three officers on the platform, there were two majors, a captain and four lieutenants sitting on the first two benches. About a dozen N.C.O. s and men were posted about the hut. But for this absurd tribunal all these men would have been out in the desert. They did not look like men who had heard of the game of bowls, let alone Francis Drake. They were killing time. Why?

"Some Jews," said Townrow, "believe the British could have done more to stop the massacre of Jews in Europe during the war."

"This is propaganda put about by the British. They think they will ingratiate themselves with the Arabs. All empty talk. All lies."

"I'm not a liar. There was a Jew said he was in Hungary when the trains were taking Jews to the death camps and the B.B.C., he said, weren't warning the Jews. That was in 1942."

"Of course they were warning the Jews," said the President in disgust. "Otherwise the British would have been anti-Jewish, like the Germans. No Arab believes that. He spits on the British."

Amin surprised everyone by jumping to his feet and beginning to shout hysterically. "I protest. What the Europeans did to the Jews is a great crime. No Arab rejoices at it. It is infamous to imply Arabs approve what the Germans did. We spit on the Germans. We spit on the Europeans."

The President was on his feet, shouting too, but in Arabic so that Townrow did not get the precise point. Amin, such a mild, sad, even frightened little Copt as Townrow had always thought him, now advanced on the President's table and smacked it with the flat of his hand. One of the other judges was grinning and talking out of the side of his mouth to a clerk. The third judge was smoking and making notes furiously.

The President picked up a glass of water and threw it violently, glass and all, into Amin's face. In the silence that followed he said, with some formality, "This preliminary hearing is now closed. The gravity of the charges are such that the case is referred to the central tribunal in Cairo."

He was about to walk out when Townrow said, "You mean you don't believe the British Government kept quiet about those death camps?"

"It is lying British propaganda," said the President and marched off towards the door, followed by his two fellow officers who seemed delighted the proceedings were over.

Amin was wiping his face with the backs of his hands. He looked as though he might cry. "Why did you bring that subject up?" he said to Townrow piteously, "even if you were trying to curry favour. Stay here. I must go and apologise to Colonel Masry."

That night Townrow lay awake listening to the sound of battle in Sinai. One end of a Nissen hut had been fitted up as a cell. It was a cage, really. He lay on the sand floor listening to the distant thumping of the guns and watching occasional figures pass in front of the open door at the other end of the hut. He could see them outlined against the starlit stack of sandbags and the wall of another hut. If the Israelis were near enough for the fighting to be heard in Port Said they must have been doing pretty well. What had Leah said when they asked her about *her* religion? They probably hadn't bothered. She was Jewish and Egyptian born so they could not have found anybody better to beat hell out of. Her American passport would not count for much. It would add a certain spice.

He woke up when the door of his cage was opened and a hurricane lamp swung in front of his face. He could have been asleep only a few minutes. Maybe they had even waited for his snores. He was dazed by sleep. His legs would not move properly. When the soldiers noticed this they helped him along with what felt like the sharp end of their guns, and he was out in the night, stumbling across the milky sand under clear stars, a slice of moon and an eastern sky that lit up and faded to light up and fade again. A lot of thumping was going on on the other side of the horizon. The concussions bounced up the Canal. Due south there was a steady glow, as it might be from some building on fire at Kantara. Surprisingly, Amin was walking with him.

"You're being put on the train to Cairo."

"You don't mean you still think trains are getting through?"

Amin was very angry. "Traffic is flowing normally. There is no interruption to normal service," he said, as the camp, the railway sidings, the docks, the moored ships, brightened. The fire to the south seemed to be taking hold. The ground underfoot was pinkish in its glow. "The 11 p.m. express for Ismailia and Cairo is leaving at three o'clock sharp."

"Is Mrs Strauss being sent to Cairo?"

"Certainly not."

A clock over the entrance to the platforms said ten past two. Sleeping soldiers sprawled all over the place, in front of the booking office. On the platform, in the carriages, they lay with heads on kitbags and haversacks. Amin had an argument with the clerk about whether Townrow was to travel First Class or Second. Military policemen walked about shouting. From the air it must have looked like a fairground: unshaded lights burned, a bell clanged, and a mad, sighing snarl came from a loaded camel being led between the tracks. Townrow was watching his chance to make a bolt for it. The first thing he did on being pushed into an empty first class compartment was to hop to the opposite door and try the handle. It was locked. He wondered whether Amin, who had a great pistol on his thigh, would have tried a pot shot. Probably, and missed. There were the four of them, two soldiers, Amin and himself, all sitting with the blinds drawn, smoking, a small blue light burning overhead.

"You know, sir," Amin said, "I have never left Egypt. I was born in 1928 in Minuf. My work in Port Said is important but frankly I would accept a secondary appointment in Upper Egypt, in Assiut or Minyah. All this —— " he waved his hand, "trouble. My father, he is dead a long time. I never leave Egypt. Why is that? We are a poor country. Too many people. Either I live in Assiut or I go to Canada when my mother dies."

"Married?"

"I do not care to answer personal questions. You will be better in Cairo. Your case will be properly investigated. Not like here in Port Said. These officers do not understand investigation."

"But the officers run things in Cairo too."

"Yes, but—— " Amin hesitated. "It will be better in Cairo. Cairo is a nice city. Do you know the Zoological Gardens?"

But mostly they sat in silence as the train filled up with troops and peasants with enormous hampers. Townrow supposed it was something that he had not been handcuffed. What corresponded, in his own life, to Amin's notion of settling in Assiut or emigrating to Canada? Nothing. Maybe going to Elie's island for a few days and cutting his throat there, right out in the lake where nobody would know. The very futility of the idea made him laugh with pain.

"What'll happen to Mrs Strauss?" he said, but Amin was asleep. Townrow wondered whether he could prise that pistol out of that holster. Even if he succeeded, what then? You had to be prepared to follow through. Would he have been ready to plug Amin? And what about these other two? They were certainly not asleep. They were talking to each other.

He was reduced to the thought of finding Leah and taking her across the lake to Elie's island. It was crazy but the idea of running away with Leah was the only one he could fix on. He could just see them in that little boat with the outboard motor puttering across the brown water. Once they were there, what then?

He put a hand on Amin's knee and shook it. "Did they believe I wasn't a Jew?"

Amin woke with a snort and put his hand on his pistol. "What?"

"Did they believe I was a Christian? The tribunal?"

Amin yawned and stretched himself. "Excuse me, I slept."

"I was going in for the ministry but I got thrown out of college," said Townrow. "I thought, what the hell after that. If I can't be a minister I'll go to the other extreme and be a bad 'un. But I wasn't really. Hadn't the drive."

"You can be a priest and marry," said Amin sympathetically, when Townrow explained why he had been expelled from that college.

"They like you to qualify before you start getting women pregnant. The irony was, this little girl wasn't. It was a false alarm. That's my life. It's been falsely alarmed. I alarmed myself. I don't alarm myself any more. I disgust myself."

"The reason I want to live in Assiut," said Amin, "is it is more of a Christian town. I am at home there. Jesus takes our sins upon himself."

"He couldn't take Judas's, could he? Judas went out and hanged himself. I don't think I could have done that. I couldn't have hanged myself, I couldn't." Townrow was silent. "Maybe it was a good thing I was thrown out of college."

The train was moving. It moved laboriously, as though the track was just that bit too narrow and the wheels had to take off slivers of steel as they went. The points chinked like dud coins. Townrow had not the slightest doubt they would be shot up from the air before they travelled much farther south. He was going to lie on the floor and pull one of these big soldiers on top of him.

He wanted to see Leah. That was what he was reduced to. Finding Leah and whistling her out of Port Said was the only plan he was capable of formulating, and that was impractical. The Israelis were attacking. O.K. that was their problem. They could always argue it was a fight to exist. The French were an unscrupulous lot. He'd never liked them. Unless he had been childishly ignorant the British, though, did not go in for beating up the wogs any more. Maybe he *was* childishly ignorant. Maybe that Jew on Rome airport was right.

When the first bombs came there probably would not be time or light to see if there were any Union Jacks painted on their sides. If Amin said there were he'd believe him. From now on he would believe any Egyptian, whatever he said.

The train stopped. Another train seemed to be trundling along the roofs of the carriages. Amin flipped up the blind, opened the window and looked out. The sound of aircraft overhead pressed down like a thumb.

"Parachutes," he said.

Townrow stood up and looked out too. It was dawn. Probably the rim of the sun was not quite showing; there were no shadows. Mud huts, trees, a strip of road, and a truck lying on its side, waited in the grey light. Certainly they were waiting. The blank and colourless landscape was as obviously waiting as an old and sightless man on his knees with hands stretched out. Townrow even thought he actually saw such a figure. Nobody on the ground. Nothing moved. Suddenly firing crackled from the ground and he saw that the ground running down to the Raswa bridges was cut up by slit trenches. Infantry were dug in and firing at the paratroops as they swung down.

Overhead there was brilliance and movement. The first wave of planes had gone. There was an impression of light pouring upwards from the hidden sun and racing out to remote space. On the way a few small clouds were touched into pinkish light. Townrow then saw they were not clouds. They were more parachutes. The sun must have been coming up faster than they came down because more and more of them seemed to catch the dawn light. They came down like blossom in a May wind.

"British," said Amin.

Townrow knew the town well enough to guess they were after the twin bridges on the Suez Road. Another wave of planes swept over. By this time the first lot of paratroops were on the ground and in action. Away to the south a machine gun opened up. Townrow saw a big paratrooper in a green beret sling a grenade into a slit trench, lie down, and follow up the explosion by jumping into the trench.

Because the door of the compartment was locked Amin began to climb out of the window as more paratroopers followed grenades into the slit trenches. A certain amount of fire could be heard coming from farther along the train. Amin dropped to the sand and began running crazily out into the open. By now there was a lot of wild shooting. Bullets flew about. In addition to the Egyptian machine guns a heavier weapon seemed to have gone into action, firing small shells into this slit-trench area. Townrow watched as though it might be some game. To begin with he was no more involved than that.

Amin had stopped running. He was walking. Townrow fancied he could hear him shouting. Certainly he was letting fly with his revolver. Townrow was still catching up with his impressions since Amin first shouted "Parachutes" and he now realised that when the fellow had climbed out through the window he had been crying. Townrow knew he had seen his face wet with tears. So many tears so quickly? They must have simply welled out. His cheeks were wet and shining.

Townrow was so disgusted he felt he just had to run after the man and slap him down. The two guards in the compartment seemed stunned by the sight of enemy troops landing, so he was not interfered with when he climbed out of the window and dropped to the ground. He tried shouting after Amin but it had no effect. The fellow was about a hundred yards away and still moving, but more slowly. The paratroops were ignoring the train and clearing the trenches. There were hundreds of them, scattered, running into the rising sun, enfilading the trenches. Townrow could see their main worry was the machine gun fire. They were not interested in the train so Townrow told himself it was not so stupid to run after Amin. He would drop on him and hold him flat in the sand.

He thought he understood why Amin was crying and would have liked to talk to him about it. But just then one of the paratroops turned and gave Amin a burst with his sub machine gun. Townrow threw himself on the ground. This was as well because he was near enough in line with Amin and the soldier for the bullets to go whipping into the train behind him. He guessed Amin was not wrong about these troops being British. This chap with the sub machine gun had a blue beret.

Machine gun fire was now coming from the thickets on the far side of the road. As far as Townrow remembered this was where the waterworks lay. There were basins, wooden huts and a fair amount of cover from trees and bushes. Anyway, these paratroops began scrambling out of the trenches and moving off in that direction. They seemed to have berets of all colours and mottled, mainly brown, uniforms. They were tearing off now in the direction of the waterworks, raising scuffles of fawn dust.

Townrow reached Amin as more planes appeared and strafed the waterworks and bridges. They were slipping rockets into the anti-aircraft sites near the bridges. Townrow now realised the heavier guns were Bofors dipped to fire straight across the area. A lot of men were shouting and howling. Metal drummed in the air.

Amin was lying head well down in a hollow soaked with blood. Parts of his face lay around his skull. Townrow stripped off his shirt, covered the head, weighted it down with stones and walked steadily back towards the train. Nobody shot him.

The diesel engine was on fire. Townrow saw soldiers hopping out of the front part of the train like fleas; then, he crawled under the train. He was wearing those filthy slacks and a singlet. As he walked back towards Port Said planes continued to dive out of the north and plug rockets into the ground with a sound like great strips of canvas being torn. All the time the sun was climbing and warming his back.

He was so frightened he kept stopping to retch. He had never before been under fire without a weapon. So it took him a long time to come out from behind cover when he found any cover.

CHAPTER SIX

A Man should smell Sweet

Midmorning, Townrow was in Gianola's among the plate glass, the mahogany show cases, the stacked boxes of Groppi chocolates, and the trays of French *patisserie*, drinking coffee and eating croissants. He reckoned he looked scruffy, with his stained shirt and two-day beard, but the management was not so particular that morning. Planes buzzed overhead. Whenever there was a respite he could hear remote, desultory machine-gun fire as though somebody was practising up on the front or down in Arab town. Townrow was the only customer. The streets were empty too. Half a dozen waiters talked excitedly in the gloom at the far end of the café.

Townrow phoned Abravanel from the kiosk under the stairs. "Is Leah there?"

"There is an attack. Can't you hear there is an attack?" The old chap was so eaten up with terror for his own safety he had no thought for his daughter.

"They'll leave the town alone. You'll be all right. They'll go for the airfield and the docks and the—— "

"These phones are tapped, you know that?" Abravanel squeaked and Townrow thought he might slam the receiver down.

"Where's Leah? Well, why don't you phone the American Consul if you can't get word of her? She's an American citizen."

"She has double nationality. She is also Egyptian. But I am not anxious for her."

"Why the hell not?"

"You must not come to my apartment. I forbid you. It would be compromising. Leah is not here. She is staying with friends."

This time he did put the receiver down so Townrow rang up Mrs K who was very happy at the turn events had taken. "I only hope they don't just stop in the Canal zone. Well, the boys will be in Cairo. We shall never get peace and quiet until the Union Jack is flying over the Citadel. Everybody knows that, even the Egyptians. It's what they really want themselves you know, once they get rid of this Nasser." She seemed quite uninterested in his own experiences and did not know where Leah was. She took the view that now the British were invading all troubles were at an end. Leah would be quite safe. The Egyptians would be only too glad to ingratiate themselves by handing her back safe and sound; true, she was Jewish and it was not like handing back an English Christian. "We British will be able to hold our heads high again. It's a great pity the French are mixed up in it. Much better if the British had done the job by themselves. Yes, of course I know the phone is tapped. I don't see how they could listen to every phone in Port Said. Why do you keep on about Leah? She'll look after herself. I'm going up on the roof to watch the planes."

The main police station was down by the Commercial Basin. He did not believe this story, about staying with friends. The chances were that Leah was being held down there but the only result of going to find out would in all probability be to get taken in himself. Not being able to think of any better place to go he set off vaguely in that direction. The sun dazzled him as he came out of the café and headed south. Little Egyptian armoured cars were running about the streets like hens. There was a chance he might be picked off from one of these cars but he felt invulnerable or suicidal, he did not know which; he tried to avoid thinking about Amin; that question about the

Zoological Gardens went on echoing between the flat white faces and the verandahs of this long street. He would have liked to convince Amin, even more than the Jew in Rome, that he was not such a bloody innocent. He was a bloody innocent though. Amin and that Jew, they'd be laughing. If he'd been a boy there might have been some excuse. He was—well, what was he? Thirty-two? Forty-two? Honestly, he could not remember. If only he could find Leah he would explain, yes, he might have seemed bloody innocent but that was only because deep down he had the priggish and self-conscious virtue and rectitude and naivety of a newly enlisted Boy Scout and he had fallen into the mistake of assuming this was a piece of information about the British Government. Certainly he was a Boy Scout, a thwarted, green Jack. He was a crook at the same time. That was only out of cussedness. He hated himself. He wanted to get revenged on himself. Now and again other people suffered for what he did, but that was more or less accidental. He saw himself as the main enemy. And when he was explaining to Leah what a Boy Scout he was at heart he would explain Boy Scouts often made the mistake of assuming other people were Boy Scouts too.

Scarcely knowing what he was doing or where he was walking he must have been looking straight into the sun because he was so dazzled enormous patches of black shadow seemed to hang across the brilliant morning. They were so black there might have been annihilation behind what they covered. The city hung in strips and patches. That was how he saw his own life. The clearest strip was the moving picture of his father stepping out of the car, climbing the wall, and setting off across the field to the trees. And that girl, she was seventeen, saying, "I've got news for you, boy," and laughing as though pregnancy was a joke, the foetus actually tickled. He tried to fix his mind on what his life had been. Ma talking on and on about Dublin and the Post Office and his saying, "Why did Uncle Rob hit Dad with a big stick?" Well, what else could an Irishman do when his sister married an English soldier? Photographs taken through some great astronomical telescope revealed gaps in the universe like the gaps he studied in the structure of Port Said, 11.25 hours, November 6; and the gaps in his mind. What seemed black emptiness in some remote part of the universe was a cloud of dust. It was settling on his face. He could feel it withering his skin. Behind the clouds were constellations and galaxies. He guessed.

The ferry to Port Fouad was still running. This part of the city went on functioning. The French must have taken the Raswa bridges so the whole city was now a head cut off from the body of Egypt. The eye winked, then, in the severed head. Two heavy tanks stood in front of the Police Station. Policemen stood on the pavement examining automatic weapons. It looked as though they had just been issued with them and were wondering how they worked. In the first floor windows were soldiers with machine guns. So when the real battle started here was one of the fortresses. On the ferry petty merchants up from Arab Town were lugging huge open baskets of fresh dates and oranges. Silvery fish with pink gills skidded on blocks of ice. A butcher boy carried half a sheep, skinned, dabbed with blue paint, on his head.

From Port Fouad Townrow could look back and see smoke rising to the west and south of Port Said. For about ten minutes there were no planes and no ack-ack. A group of Egyptian soldiers in steel hats sat inside a sandbag-protected emplacement in the middle of the *rond-point*. They smoked and took no notice of him, so he took the lane down to the Greek Sailing Club. He entered the great shed where the boats were stored and walked towards the lavatories. Through an open door he could see, under a palm tree, a table in the shade. It bore empty beer bottles and empty glasses. Chairs were pushed away from the table. It was as though a group of men had been sitting at this table and only just got to their feet and walked away.

Townrow remembered those Greeks in swimming trunks

who had laughed and said, No, they hadn't seen any woman.

But they had seen her. And as Townrow stood outside the swing-door leading to the showers and lavatories, looking out of the building at the abandoned chairs and tables, he remembered very well how Leah had in fact come suddenly face to face with him and said, "Well, where do you think I was?"

"I've been looking everywhere. I just couldn't—— "

"Where do you think I'd be?"

And so far from disappearing into the shadows and brilliance of that particular day she had led him to some other table, far away from the Greeks. She had changed out of her swim suit. She was wearing a dress and had a white silky wrap over her shoulders. She must have been a member and kept a change of clothing in the club. They drank the beer the waiter brought out. There had never been any question of her disappearing. Why should he have thought there was? He remembered perfectly well how they went and sat in a remote part of the garden and talked about her husband. He himself wore nothing but his bathing trunks. He had not known she was changing or he would have changed too. He was just a bit stupefied she should bring up the subject of her husband, just when they were enjoying themselves. She said the reason he had these fits of depression was the way she treated him.

"I thought you said he was sick."

"I treat him badly," she said.

"How do you mean, badly?"

"You know! He's the jealous type."

How could he possibly have so forgotten this talk, right smack against a curtain of banana leaves? He could see them shining in the sun, with lines of fire along the edges. If he now walked out of the boat house and took that path on the other side of the big palm, the banana grove, the table and the two chairs would still be there. Leah too, he reckoned. It was not impossible. He thought she had just disappeared. The bloody vanishing trick was a mystery he'd never got round to clearing up. All he had to do now was walk through the garden, push back a lot of leaves and there she would be. It was worth trying.

"You mean to say," he had asked, "you deliberately work on this jealousy?"

"No, not deliberately," she had said. "I can't help it."

"You make me feel," he had said, "that I've pushed him below the shitty surface of some pond with my big foot."

"When a man is as jealous as that you just can't help it," she said. "I wouldn't say I was too promiscuous. God, he takes it hard. Now why? I suppose he has this natural melancholy and what I do tips the scale."

"A man doesn't get delusions if his wife sleeps around. You said he heard these voices. He felt persecuted."

"Sure he was sick, but I didn't help."

Townrow decided that if he stopped hesitating and walked out of the boat house, past the table with the empty glasses and bottles, and walked down that sandy path he would come on Leah again and be able to take up the conversation at the point it broke off. "I've pushed him below the surface. You know, if I was in his position I wouldn't go gloomy and persecuted. I'd kill you first and then the other man after. I wouldn't accept living on the same planet as either you or me."

"*You* wouldn't accept living on the same planet as—?"

"It would be very natural if he came and shot me down one day."

"I see." She smiled. He saw her lips turn up at the end and the little hollows appear in her cheeks. He knew this trick she had of looking straight ahead with her eyes half closed and then turning her head so that when she fully opened them they blazed in his face. That was the effect. The very calculating way she did it excited him.

"We haven't really given him cause yet, have we?" She half closed her eyes again and stretched a hand in his direction. Why the hell should he forget all this? He had taken that hand.

So he walked past the table and down the sandy path. It was now about noon. The planes were coming in again. They seemed to release their rockets dead overhead to go screaming away south. Somebody might take it into his head to blow up the ferry in which case the Greek Sailing Club would probably stop a few rockets. Townrow turned this possibility over but he continued down the path. He came to a pergola with loofahs hanging down, some of them dead ripe and ready for the bath. Now, that pergola really was something he had forgotten. On the other side of the banana leaves there was a clicking noise. He paused. Perhaps some sort of weapon was being set up. Or it might have been rifle fire from a long way off. Through the leaves he could see hands moving. That must have been the very spot.

A man wearing a brown suit and an open neck shirt was sitting at a table—the very same table at which Leah had talked about her husband—typing on a huge, old-fashioned machine with two fingers. Hearing Townrow's approach he looked up and turned his long nose and worried eyes into the sun. His hair was out of hand. The dirty sideburns were hanging to his face like Spanish moss. He took the cigarette from his mouth and inhaled. A rocket was released about five hundred feet overhead and when words could be heard again, he said, "I thought I gave you twenty four hours to leave."

Townrow was too amazed he was not Leah to say anything at all. He watched Aristides reach under his arm, produce an automatic and slip the safety catch. Until that moment Townrow had not been sure the fellow who was responsible for the note in that café and the man reading the newspaper at a neighbouring table were one and the same.

"Turn round." Aristides gestured with his gun. "I do not like to see the expression on a man's face when I shoot him."

Townrow went and sat down at the table and looked at Aristides across his typewriter. He knew the kind. An Oliver, made in Croydon in the twenties, British army issue. It was comforting to see one again. "You seen a woman about here? Mrs Strauss, you know her? I was expecting to see her."

Aristides looked very annoyed Townrow had not turned round. He stood up. He tried to walk round behind Townrow but Townrow got to his feet and kept facing him. Aristides was so exasperated that he said, "The British and the French are invading Port Said and you look for a woman?"

Townrow kept his eye on the gun. "I'm a friend of Christou. I've just been in jail with him. What's wrong with looking for a woman anyway? What's so absurd about that? I'd rather be looking for a woman than shooting a man down in cold blood when there's a war on. I'd have thought you had other things on your mind. It seems a bit obsessed to me, shooting a man for some private reason in a war. The chances are we'll both be dead in a few hours anyway. So, you're absurd with your gun and your Greek patriotism and your moneymaking. Though you don't look as though you make a hell of a lot out of arms smuggling, not judging by the state of those shoes."

True, they were cracked, both of them, across the toe and bright blue socks could be seen shining through. Both men studied these shoes. Aristides allowed the gun to hang slackly in his hand.

"What did Christou say?"

"He made out to the Egyptians I was a Jew."

"Are you a Jew?"

"No."

Aristides laughed violently. "Did Christou really think you were a Jew?"

"Of course not. It was his sense of humour."

Aristides frowned suddenly. "During the past six months I have exported a hundred and twenty thousand pounds worth of Czech rifles and automatics and grenades. How much have I made? Nothing! I am not a merchant. I am not Elie Khoury."

"What did he die of?"

"Fright."

"I can believe that." Townrow did not think Aristides would bother to shoot him now, but he was so disappointed at not finding Leah that it seemed to matter less than he would have expected. "But was he frightened of you or was he frightened of his wife?"

"Both." Aristides began laughing again. "That was the truth. He wasn't such a rich man. He was just a money grabber but he wasn't so rich. And it didn't matter whether he lived or died. He was old. Now you? You are an English investigator?"

"I was his friend."

This impressed Aristides unfavourably. More creases appeared on his face. "You think I do not understand what friendship means? I too would do anything for my friend. You, for example."

"Am I your friend?"

"Of course you are my friend. Let me tell you what I mean. Have you heard the English radio? The English will be in occupation of Port Said tomorrow. Assume you are still alive. Assume I am still alive. You then go to the English and say,' Here is Aristides who smuggled arms into Cyprus', and then they arrest me."

"If they know where you are."

"I shall keep in touch. Of course they will know where I am. All that is required is word from you. Will you give that word?"

"No."

"You see, we are friends and there is honour between friends, and that is why I did not shoot you two minutes ago. Do you know what I was typing? I will show you. It is an account of the export of arms to Cyprus, with names, prices and dates. It is complete. I sew it into my shirt. We are friends and of course I believe you when you say you will not speak. But it is possible I am arrested? Yes. What do I do? I show this document."

"You mean you'd turn in this evidence so that you get let off?"

"Let off? They would pay me. Of course the information is not accurate. It is plausible, but it is not accurate. It makes no trouble for my friends but it pleases the English."

This was the moment Aristides tucked away his gun. He flexed his shoulders, shot out his chin, rolled his eyes and generally put as many face muscles into movement as possible. He looked as though he was having some kind of fit. But it was only his way of effecting a transition from patriot and assassin to joking friend. "I wouldn't tell you this if I didn't trust you. Look, read this paper. It is addressed to the Commander-in-Chief, British Expeditionary Force, United Arab Republic. That is right, yes?"

Townrow sat down to read this document and Aristides peered over his shoulder. The typing was single spacing, both sides of the paper, the English was grotesque, and it took Townrow some time to work through.

"Nothing about Elie's funeral," he commented.

"What about it?"

"You know, the boat going out to sea, the coffin and the rifles."

Aristides moved round to sit opposite. He looked puzzled. "Coffin and rifles? No, I do not know this story. What is this story?"

So Townrow told him more or less as he remembered Christou rehearsing it back in the jail but Aristides only laughed and shook his head. "The police would not let you move a body out of the basins in this way. And it would be too complicated. There is no need for such stratagems. The Egyptians don't mind guns going to Cyprus. We send them in big boats. How else?"

"Christou's a bit of a comedian."

"Yes?"

"He's got imagination."

"Christou got himself into jail because he knew it would be the safest place in the bombing. When the British troops are back he will make lots of money from his bar."

"And you?"

"When the British come there will be plenty of guns and ammunition. We really will have to smuggle them then. Maybe Christou was telling what would happen in the future."

"Not the way he talked."

"It is in the future."

The two battles, one to the south and one to the west, seemed simultaneously to re-engage. After dropping a load far on the other side of the lighthouse but dead in line with it planes bellied up overhead and flashed in the sun. They winked in the cobalt sky and vanished like stars shooting and scattering in the high, steady brilliance. The bombs burst with a hollow grating as though vast casks partly filled with pebbles were being hammered and rolled. Bursts of fire came from Port Said itself. Perhaps this was the odd tank crew just clearing their guns.

Aristides was talking in this extraordinary unbuttoned way because he was alarmed and confused. When you were with Christou you believed him. When you were with Aristides he was convincing too. On the whole, more convincing. He might even be right about the boat trip with the coffin being still in the future.

"I was looking for somebody." Townrow stood up and began to move off. "You sure you haven't seen her? Straight nose, sort of slightly rounded at the end and a lot of blackish-red hair flounced up and coming untidy. Moves her elbows when she walks. When she's old and fat she'll waddle. I just reckoned she'd be here."

"Give me back my paper." Aristides stretched out his hand.

Townrow looked at the paper once more, then tore it into strips and scattered them on the ground. He walked back under the loofah vine and turned right into a rose garden where the beds were marked out in red brick. The rose bushes were mostly dead and leafless. A spray of water revolved over a small brown lawn.

The fishing boat, the open coffin, and the wooden crucifix were so powerfully rooted in his mind he guessed Aristides was right; and that if it was not an event he was moving away from it was an event he was moving towards. If he jumped across this garden of dead roses and looked behind those flowering bushes who would he see? Leah? Elie? His father? His mother? The tangled garden was weird to him. On the other side of a cactus he might meet himself walking with Leah and carrying on that conversation about the mad husband while the husband himself, a shadow in the air, followed closely with a grin. So Townrow did in fact jump across the garden of dead roses and look behind the flowering bushes. An empty beer crate, a dead cat and orange peel. It made him wonder just whose would be the beaked face in that open coffin. And the woman standing up, dressed as a man. Or was it a man dressed as a woman?

By mid-afternoon Townrow had decided Leah was nowhere in Port Fouad. He had been to the Yacht Club, the *Plage des Enfants* and eaten a bowl of rice, black beans and chopped meat in a dive where servants gathered when off-duty. Troops were everywhere but they took no notice of Townrow who shambled about with a strip of cloth tied round his head now—he had picked it up in the Greek Sailing Club—like some perfunctory turban. It covered his forehead and stopped the sweat from running into his eyes. At the *Plage* he washed his feet in the sea. An Egyptian sentry here gave him bread and cheese.

The French planes came over at 3.30 and Townrow realised he was caught in another drop, this time by the *Paras*. He had surprisingly little trouble making off with a dinghy from the Sailing Club jetty, rowing out into the middle of the Basin and watching the French take Port

Fouad while he rested on his oars. Anti-aircraft fire came from the Eastern Mole, from Port Said itself, from Navy House and other emplacements on the other side of Port Fouad, no doubt near the salt beds. It was entirely in-effective. The *Paras* came out of the low-flying planes so quickly they seemed linked by a thread. It looked like the plane losing its entrails. Then the chutes opened and the men could be seen rocking over the red roof tops apparently using their automatics while they were still in the air, spraying the ground. One man, whose parachute failed to open, fell smack into the water about half a mile from where Townrow was resting. When Townrow arrived at the spot there was no sign of him.

He expected the fishermen's quay to be crawling with troops but it was unguarded and even the gate was wide open. Egyptian tanks patrolled in front of the Casino Palace. He cut along a sidestreet past the old Italian Consulate and struck a square where men in gallabiehs were handing out weapons from a truck to all and sundry. Townrow saw a boy of about sixteen go off with a Bren gun and was tempted to grab a weapon himself. You never knew when you might need a bit of self protection. But he was genuinely scared what he might do if he had a weapon and a French *para* came round the corner letting fly with one of those neat collapsible guns. You could shout at a British soldier. But a Frenchman? If he had a gun he might shoot this Frenchman down, so he thought he had better not have one.

At the Abravanel flat the door was opened by Leah herself and he was so surprised he just stared at her. The first thing he noticed was that she was wearing trousers, navy blue pants. He had never seen her in this getup before. They were men's trousers. She might have taken them off a British bobby. She wore a collar, tie, and a grey woollen cardigan. As if this was not enough she had her hair drawn back tightly. This had the effect of throwing the lines of her face into prominence. It was bonier than he thought.

She had large cheekbones; and, by God, she looked tired. She was pale and there were patches under her eyes. The coldness was what struck him. She did not seem surprised to see him, nor particularly pleased.

"They released you?"

"Of course they released me. They had nothing against me. Anyway, they were afraid because of my American passport."

She stood aside so that he could enter. "They released you too?"

"I rang your father. He said I wasn't to come."

"Oh!" She made an impatient sort of grunt. "Well, he's right. You can't stay."

"Oh no?" He tried to put an arm round her waist but she pushed it away. "I'm going home. I'm getting out of this dreadful country. If my father won't come that's his affair. I am going back to my husband."

"Are you now?" He had thought he was so marshy inside that nothing could churn him up again. Coming through the streets he had felt his guts to be so cold and set they were probably past normal functioning. Inside, he had solidified. No currents flowed. Just seeing her so un-expectedly was enough to show him how wrong he had been. And now when she started talking about her husband the palms of his hands began to sweat.

"Do you mind if I sit down? I had a court martial, you know."

"What happened?"

He gave her the outline until he reached the point where Amin was shot.

"Go on," she said. By this time she was sitting down too. They were both drinking vermouth. Abravanel had shuffled in. They both ignored him so he shuffled out again.

"What are you dressed like that for?" Townrow asked.

He realised that he did not want to tell her about Amin dying. This was a happening he would only want to relate to someone who felt warm towards him. Leah was not warm. She was not exactly hostile but she had changed. He did not think he could tell her about Amin in a way she would understand. So he described the encounter with Aristides and how it had reminded him of the time they were in the Greek Sailing Club together, when he could not find her. And then he *did* find her only to forget he found her.

"Oh, that," she said.

What had happened? Townrow looked at her, biting his lip. He had a feeling he would slap her face hard before long, simply to break this icy façade. Had she received news from her husband?

"You remember the time you told me he was in the loony bin because you kept cuckolding him?" Candidly, this was a fact about life he had not wanted to remember either. He could see this poor bastard's head popping up through the slime and his boot pushing it back again. Nobody normal would want to remember a detail like that. Was it any wonder he forgot he found her? Christ! Now he had made her cry. It was like watching a man cry, the way she was dressed. It was awful. Amin was a man and he had cried.

Townrow thought that if only he had dropped on Amin the moment he left the train he would still be alive. He could talk to Amin. They understood one another. When one spoke the truth the other knew he was speaking the truth; when one lied the other knew he lied. You could not expect much more from a relationship than that. Whole societies could be built on it. Amin, in fact, always told the truth. Anyway, Townrow always believed him and it amounted to the same thing. How could he tell Leah about a man like that dying? He regretted that man. To his surprise Townrow found tears running down his own cheeks. That made three of them.

"Anyway," she said, "I'm leaving this country. When the landings have been made there will be British and French troops here and I shall go. There will be boats."

Townrow saw her standing at the prow. He had a good

view of her from where he was lying in the coffin because, something he had not realised before, the coffin was not lying absolutely flat in the bottom of the boat. There must have been a block of wood under its head. He could see her, simply by looking down his nose.

"I am not afraid for my father any more. When there is a European army here the Jews will be all right. Did I tell you my husband was sick? He needs me more than my father. A woman has to choose."

"Yes, you told me your husband was sick." He could not understand her game but now that he realised she was going to stand up at the front of the boat wearing those policeman's trousers he guessed she was going back to her husband because she knew he, Townrow, was a dead man anyway. If her husband was sane enough to understand rational communication she would be able to tell him about this man she slept with and buried at sea. That way she could put the poor bastard back a couple of cures. He saw the crystal head surfacing and her words hitting it. Momentarily, the head was entire but opaque because of the crackle and then it shattered. A crack and a groan.

It just made Townrow wonder how he would die. It would have to be accidentally. There was nothing he could do about the attack. Or was there? Maybe there was some way of arguing, and he would find it. Then the British would execute him for treason. But honestly no, he could not see himself sniping at British soldiers. The face in the coffin, as he remembered it, was that of an old man. It was old age he would die from. Time enough for Leah to return to the States, divorce her husband, come back to Port Said and marry him. There were years of life in both of them.

"I'm not going out of this flat. I don't care what your old man says. It would be suicide."

She shrugged. He went to the bathroom, took a shower, shaved and put on some clean clothes. Fatigue was what made his mind work in this way, he thought. He was so tired he thought he could foresee his own marine funeral, he was so tired he thought Leah had turned against him, when all the time she had been worrying herself sick what had happened to him. He stretched out on his old bed in the room where she had first put him when he came into the Abravanel household as a patient. Outside was a view of the Italian Consulate and the Cathedral and the light-house. Fatigue did extraordinary things to a man's mind. He could not remember why he had cried. He cry? No, that was incredible. He could actually remember the last time he had wept salt tears. His mother was saying, very bitterly, "It's your birthday and he's forgotten it. Remember at least you're Irish on your mother's side. That's where the honour lies." Or words to that effect. What made him cry was not this talk of honour, or the lack of it, or his father forgetting but being given a mouth organ for his birthday. His own mother ought to have known it was better to give him nothing at all than a sixpenny mouth organ. November 2nd was his birthday.

When he woke it was dark and he could tell by the silence something odd was afoot. Port Said was never silent. But he could hear nothing save his own breathing.

He rolled out of bed and went to the door. A low-powered bulb was burning in the hall and one of the servants, with a shawl completely covering his head, was asleep in front of the door so that it could not have been opened without disturbing him. Townrow went straight to Leah's room. The door was not locked, as he half expected it to be. Closing it behind him he stood for some moments looking across the room to where she lay in bed. The shutters were thrown back. Searchlights played across the night and there was enough reflection for him to make out her form.

"It's me," he said softly. He bent down and touched her bare shoulder. Immediately the deep breathing stopped. "Don't be afraid."

"Who's that?"

"It's me, you fool. Who do you think it is? I'm coming in."

He was already naked. She turned away from him as he slipped in by her side but he caught her in his arms and felt her body thaw his belly and thighs. That was all, just to lie there listening to the breathing and the silence and feel the warmth colour his belly and thighs and head. She never wore clothes in bed. They were naked and the warmth ran out of her. He wanted to laugh, because it was such a marvellous discovery to make, this warmth. She was hissing like a snake.

"No, it's wrong." She went on hissing.

She brought an elbow back smartly and struck him in the paunch. She seemed all elbows, shoulder blades and heels. It was like trying to make love to a dough-mixing machine. She wanted it, didn't she, otherwise why all this hissing and moaning? She was like a machine in heat. Townrow felt a rage so violent the thought sparked he might even be driven to kill her. He was being shut out of all that was left to him of bliss by her stupid resistance. He could not understand why she fought. Her body did not want to fight. The hissing was voluptuous. If only he could push past the barricade of knees and elbows he would fall into a calm tenderness. Her will said no.

"Get out. It's wrong. It's cruel. It's—— " as he waited for the word he could hear her heart thud and the tips of his fingers slip on her greasy skin—"it's, oh it's so selfish and merciless. Rob, poor boy, poor Rob."

The night crackled like a stroked cat. The night was precisely what Townrow wanted to forget. He was not going to wait for whatever hell drove out of the sea. He was so angry he no longer wanted any calm tenderness she had to offer; he just wanted to make his own particular hell now, and if brushing that poor bastard Rob out of the way was how to do it, then out of the way Rob would be brushed, and done down, and his head with a cruel boot shoved beneath the shitty surface.

She switched on the bedside lamp.

"Look! Bed bugs."

Townrow released her and sat up. A mahogany-coloured bead balanced on her naked shoulder. He brought his thumb down on it and striped her skin with blood. He squashed another on his thigh. Leah turned over the pillow. Two huge bed bugs and a crowd of little ones rolled like rusty raindrops only to be killed as they were caught.

The window shook. A violent wind might have sprung up. But no, there was an immediate concussion that rocked the whole building. Judging by the sound of aircraft and the hiss before each explosion Townrow reckoned the R.A.F. was rocketing the beach defences. That was the direction the row was coming from. But he and Leah were concentrating on the bed bugs. They stank like excrement and bled like wounds.

The light went out though neither of them touched it and the window showed how the sky had paled.

"It's horrible. We've never had bugs in this house."

Leah was standing by the bed brushing herself with her hands. "You never saw a bug in the house when my mother was alive."

The town rocked. This was no ordinary bombardment. The pale sky blanched and broke out in a worried pencil-ling of little clouds. The sun pushed up out of Asia to meet this jerky incandescence from the west. Townrow wanted to rush up to the roof as he was, naked, dragging Leah with him, their skin laced with blood.

"What is it? What are they doing?" She was so frightened she came round and hammered him with her knuckles.

"Smashing the town up, I guess."

Townrow was frightened too. They were not just naked man and woman walking about in a top-floor bedroom, stained with crushed bed bugs, and reeking of unassuaged lust. He was slack. She was slack. The bone had gone. They were stripped down to that defencelessness of body and spirit they seemed transparent to one another. They could have walked through each other. They were ghosts. The morning came up and they faded.

Townrow slipped her dressing gown on, not for seemliness but for warmth, and went up to the roof. There seemed to be no planes about but the bombardment was so continuous and violent he could feel the shock waves bursting from the roots of the building and striking at him through the air. Gusts of wind broke in from the north. He could not see the sea. The northern sky opened and shut. He recognised the familiar squeal of shells. Even in the open air the stench of the bed bugs still clung to him. If he lived he would take a bath. Scent I That was something he had never gone for, not even an after-shave. But he would. They produced scent for men now. If he came out of this he would find a good scent and wear it. A man ought to smell nice.

The Fleet must be out there, lobbing shells in from over the horizon. None seemed to be falling in the town. They were sorting out the beach defences. Next thing the troops would be coming ashore. When his particular boat set sail who would see to it he smelled sweet? You could not leave everything to wind and salt water.

There was enough of a parapet to shelter him from the wind. He squatted there, in the red and blue silk that covered him feet and all, with his face turned to the east and south so that the sun would hit him. Very gently, the cold pencillings of cloud began to rust and flake off. There was a steady drizzle of red dust out there. He wanted heat. No woman would ever warm him again, that was sure. If the British bombed Egypt the only heat he was entitled to was from the sun. He could never trust a woman like he could trust the sun.

From the street below came the clatter of boots. There was shouting and small arms fire. Townrow listened intently, telling himself the sounds were caused by not what you might think. Down there were no big insects. There were no huge blackbeetles in mountains of crisp straw.

They were real, frightened men, running in heavily-nailed boots, soldiers. They were running up from the beach, as he would have run had he been in their place. He stood up and looked over the parapet. A self-propelled gun was moving across the square. It charged between the palm trees, crushing ornamental railings, rubbish baskets and a white seat. It turned awkwardly and knocked one wall out of a kiosk where, Townrow remembered, the gardener kept a few tools and lay on a canvas bed smoking hashish.

Townrow imagined Amin coming out to join him on the roof.

"All she wanted to talk about," he found himself saying to Amin, "was her bloody husband. Did she ever tell you what his name was? Poor twit. No, I'm really sorry for him."

He was alone on that roof, of course. Amin ran towards the *paras* and one of them turned and shot him down without giving the matter a lot of thought. Perhaps that was just what Amin wanted. Townrow could not imagine Amin running up from the beach like those soldiers. He would have sat in a beach hut with his little gun waiting for somebody to come along and pick him off.

"Don't sneer at me," Townrow told him, "just because I tell you I'm sorry for her husband. D'you think I've got no feelings. This might happen to any man. You know that? If I was married I reckon it could happen to me, some boozed, fornicating screw having her when my back was turned. And how should I feel?"

Amin was not there and Townrow knew he was dead. "Amin," Townrow imagined himself saying, "the last time we were in bed together I didn't have her. I tried, but she wouldn't let me. I could go to her husband and say with a clear conscience, 'You know what, Rob, the last time I was in bed with your wife we didn't actually do it.' And I'm glad. It's a small thing, but it's a beginning. Can you imagine a man being actually *glad* about a failure like that? Anybody would think fornication was some sort of crime."

A MAN SHOULD SMELL SWEET

Or gunning down a man like Amin, you'd think that was some sort of crime.

The dawn kept on widening in lurid amazement. The pounding of the beaches had been going on so long the silence, when it came, would hurt. Smoke went up. The huts burned. He could not actually see them but what else could it be but the huts?

Bombing the guts out of Egypt, you'd think that was some sort of crime the way he was happy and sickened not to be involved in it. Back home there must be a lot of people who could have been curious to see him vomiting down the front of that blue and red silk dressing gown. No that was too much to expect. They would not have been curious. They would have said vomiting was the way terror took hold of some people.

He wiped the back of his hand across his lips and stood up. He stood quietly looking north. He was steady. His limbs did not tremble. Nothing to be afraid of. This was a precision bombardment. It might be the Royal Tournament at Earl's Court for all the harm it threatened. He had a fine grandstand view. Nothing to make a man puke but the smell of crushed bed bugs. Nevertheless he knew he was climbing up out of some dizzy pit with feelings easily mistaken for terror.

He went down into the flat, found no sign of Leah or her father, so went into the bathroom and took a shower. There was no towel so he tried to dry himself with the dressing gown but it just skidded over him. He found a can of talcum powder and dusted himself. As he came out of the bathroom the bombardment stopped and he put on his socks, his pants, his shirt, in the kind of embarrassed silence that might follow some grotesque vulgarity in the wrong company.

Leah was where he might have expected, in the first place, to find her. She was in her father's room. It was shuttered and the only light came from a weak bulb over the mirror on his dressing table.

The old chap was lying in bed, very still with his eyes closed, and Leah was standing at his side looking down at him. She was wearing slippers and another dressing gown. Her hair was all over the place and Townrow thought she looked pretty savage.

"I've come to apologise," he said. "I looked all over. Where were you?"

Leah made no answer. She drew the sheet over her father's face, so Townrow supposed he was dead. Momentarily he was stopped in what he intended to say. Abravanel's death perplexed him. It came at a moment when it was impossible to give one's mind to it. He would have liked it postponed. In the circumstances the best he could do was to defer making any sort of comment, even expressing sympathy.

"Sorry about what happened in the night." Even Townrow knew this was a ludicrous thing to say at such a moment. But he did not care what impression he made. He was fighting for his life, or what seemed like his life.

"You stopped me from doing something that shouldn't be done. Well, you've got to make a start, haven't you? I mean you've got to start with yourself. That's all you know about. So you've got to start patiently putting one foot right and another foot right. That's what I'm thanking you for."

To Townrow it seemed he had made a statement of such magnificence it was surprising she did not respond with at least a smile. Perhaps she had not understood. True, her father dying like that, he had not timed it well. But it was the only time he had. Odd she did not look at his face more carefully. The expression might have said more than words, but no doubt that single weak bulb threw shadows.

"I'm sorry," he said. "It's terrible for you. But are you sure he's not in some sort of coma? You want a doctor."

She ignored him so he went and removed the sheet from Abravanel's face. She had closed the eyes. The cheek was like cardboard when Townrow touched it. The skin was so blue he must have been dead for hours. Townrow replaced the sheet. Leah went round the room picking up small objects of value, a silver box, a photograph of a woman framed in what looked like gold, a watch, rings, even money, and dropping them into a basket. Abruptly she sat down at the dressing table and studied her face in the mirror, putting her hands up to her cheeks, then lifting and tidying her hair with the tips of her fingers. Her face had sharpened. The expression was wild.

"I love you," he said, "and now I'm trying to break it all up."

She turned in the chair. "You what?"

"Yeah, that's right I mean it. So far as I'm concerned wherever you'll be, that's the centre."

She turned away again and he saw she was watching him in the mirror. She picked up her father's silver-backed hair brushes and handed them to him. "I'd like you to have these. I think my father would have liked you to take something."

"Thank you." He was still holding them and examining the design of bearded faces and leaves when she walked out of the room across the hall and into her own bedroom where, because she had left the door wide open, he could see her drag an enormous black suitcase out from behind a wardrobe. She had it open by the side of the bed and was throwing her clothes into it. The first garment to go in was a fur coat he had not seen before. It was a smoky brown; musquash, he thought, the sort of thing that would set you back eight hundred guineas at Swears and Wells. Then suits, stockings, underclothes. She was just throwing them in. She was a poor packer.

"Would you like me to phone for the doctor?"

"Sure! You do that." She did not stop for a moment. He half expected her to say, "Phone for a doctor in this bombardment?" Because all the time they had been talking, or not talking but reacting silently and trying to catch up with what was going on, the shells had been falling on the beach not much more than half a mile away. "Are you crazy? You expect Catafago to turn out at a time like this?"

Nothing of the sort. Once he had contacted the doctor she would want him to make the funeral arrangements, and as these could be expected to go through quickly in that climate, tomorrow at the latest, Townrow could see them following the hearse through a battlefield. He dialled Catafago's number but although he hung on for five minutes by that French clock supported by a gilt cherub there was no reply. Townrow went and asked Leah whether he could make her some coffee.

"Sure! You do that," she said, still throwing clothes into the black suitcase.

Townrow stood looking at her. He wanted to look at her with the eyes of some unsympathetic stranger, somebody who would notice the lines, and the undeniable tiny hairs she had at the corners of her mouth, all the bad, ugly qualities, the slightly rounded shoulders for example. He wanted to see her as somebody quite ordinary he did not need to love. It was an effort. He had to stick at it.

Townrow was on his way to Mrs K's some time after the shelling stopped when a voice that was unmistakably English hit him from an alley. Bullets whined about the streets. Now and again a man in army boots and one of those nightgown *gallabiehs* clumped past. Townrow had the idea a lot of Egyptian soldiers were disguising themselves as civilians. As genuine civilians, boys of about fifteen or sixteen were running about with old Czech automatic rifles, there was a good chance of a general shoot-up when the British arrived. You would not be able to blame them for potting at anyone in a nightshirt who moved. There was a strong smell of burning rubber. Townrow was on his way to Mrs K partly because there had been no reply when he had phoned her and Elie would have wanted him to check she was all right; and partly, the mood he was in, he wanted to be sure anything Amin would have dared he would dare too. To be out on the streets was not so much dangerous as lunatic.

"Hey! I want a word with you."

Townrow turned his head and saw this Englishman. He was standing in an open doorway. He wore brown boots, a pair of tight cavalry twill trousers held up by a pair of scarlet braces, a lemon-coloured shirt with the sleeves rolled up and a cigar in his right hand. Obviously, he had just taken it out of his mouth to shout. The real abnormality was the eyes. They protruded hideously. Townrow recognised him at once. Faint. Those bulging eyes gave the man an expression of perpetual amazement. Only by gaping, as he did now, could he convey anything approaching incredulity. "You bloody fraud," he said, "giving yourself out as my old friend Captain Ferris. I was in Le Havre three weeks ago. He said he'd never been in Port Said. Andrée confirmed it. What's more, you don't even look like him, not very much anyway."

Somebody had a machine gun at the top of one of the buildings on the other side of the open-air cinema and seemed to be testing it. Sandbags nearly blocked some of the windows. Rifles stuck out through the remaining gaps. During the night the place had been turned into a crude fortress. So far as Townrow could tell the bullets smacking into some large wooden doors about twenty feet away from him came from that top floor.

He stepped into the alley to be out of the line of fire.

"I remember you," he said. "You chose a bad time to turn up again, Faint."

"Got to hand it to you. I was taken in. Captain Ferris, I said, ex-War Graves Commission. You're not half the man." Faint was colouring with anger. "You're just a common, bloody scrounger. You didn't think I'd turn up again, did you? Let me tell you I'm through Port Said three times a year, regular as clockwork. I thought there was something fishy. While the ship was discharging I went over to Le Havre. I went to the Café-Bar de l'Europe and

Captain Ferris laughed, he said, Port Said? No, I haven't been in Port Said. I told him about you and he said I was lucky to get away with losing what I did. That's not the point. "I hate a liar." Faint cut the air with his left hand so vehemently that his heels clicked. He was in a shocking temper. I hate deception. What the hell've I ever done to you you should want to pitch me that bloody yarn?"

"I pitched you no yarn. Anyway, times have changed."

Townrow could not be absolutely sure he had not told this fool he was Captain Ferris of the Café-Bar de l'Europe but he was in no mood for compromise. "You're crazy to wear braces that colour. One of the amateur marksmen will pick you off just for the fun of it. I wonder you're not wearing a Union Jack, Maybe they'll think you *are* wearing a Union Jack. That's fine when the British land but until then you'd be safer in one of these nightshirts."

Small arms fire was breaking out all over. Townrow supposed he was a bit crazy himself. He had not slept. He did not really know what was happening. He was not to cuckold a madman and he was to disbelieve all information received. He would tell the truth. He remembered perfectly well finding Leah again at the Greek Sailing Club. He would not embezzle the Disaster Fund. No, he did not know why the B.B.C. failed to broadcast warnings about those death trains. In future he could only answer for himself and by God he was going to see it was a simple answer.

"What's your name?" Faint put the cigar back in his mouth and waited. Real Havana, Townrow remembered, bought in Bahrein. He had boxes and boxes of them. Faint ignored the battle and cared for nothing but getting to the bottom of this mystery about Townrow's identity. True, he had not seen Amin shot. He had been through no experience like that. But he was tough and you had to admire him. He was concentrating on what really interested him. No, this did not include the shooting.

"I've a bloody good mind to report you to the British

Consul," said Faint." What sort of a layabout are you? Who are you?"

"It's a long story. If you want me to tell it why don't you ask me in? You staying here."

"I've got a friend who puts me up."

Smoke drifted south in such opaque clouds it cast shadows. The sun was high enough for these shadows to be sharp. The smell of burning rubber was stronger. To the north enormous quantities of brittle paper were seemingly being crushed. A grotesque, exaggerated groaning like timbers under strain made the ground tremble. As yet there were no invading troops in view but there was so much shooting going on all round Townrow could only think the Egyptians were settling old scores among themselves.

"You understand Arabic?" he asked Faint.

"Course I bloody don't."

A van with a loudspeaker was touring in the neighbourhood.

"Who are you?" Faint shouted explosively.

"Well, I was born of a patriotic Irishwoman and an Englishman. He was just stupid, I guess. Anyway, she was a schoolteacher but the important thing about her—— "

An explosion followed immediately by the tinkle of breaking glass threw Townrow against the wall. He yelped with pain.

"I'm here on holiday," he said, "in a manner of speaking."

"I don't want to know your life history. Don't be so literal minded."

"I've got to tell you, Faint. Look, my mother wanted me to be a parson. Not surprising for an Irishwoman, eh? I said parson not priest. She was protestant, so you know I actually went to college. At the end of my first year—— "

"Don't want to know this. You owe me fifty quid. I want 'em back. Now."

"Fifty quid?"

"Spun me a yarn. You are not Captain Ferris. You're a bloody fraud. To think I've waited until middle age to be conned by a broken-down ponce. Fifty quid. Now, do you hand it over?"

"I haven't got fifty quid, Faint. I just want to tell you about my life."

"What goes on out there?" Faint spoke with irritation and waved his cigar in the general direction of what now seemed the centre of the battle. "You'd better come in. If you haven't got fifty quid I want some sort of security for it. What the hell goes on?" He came out and stood by Townrow's side. They looked down the street to a cross-roads where a tank had taken up position, and was using its machine gun, firing straight ahead. Townrow recognised a British Centurion. Snipers from windows, parapets and balconies were concentrating their fire on the Centurion which responded by lifting its cannon preparatory, Town-row guessed, to blowing the top off one of those blocks of flats. "They're taking their time," Faint complained. "No sense of urgency. The bloody wogs are filling the Canal with boats loaded with concrete. It'll be years before we get it clear. Just look at that dam' tank! Anybody'd think they were paid by the hour."

Townrow knew he hadn't borrowed fifty quid from Faint. He would surely have had something to show for fifty pounds. Mrs K had kept him going. If it hadn't been for her he would have been spent out long ago. Fifty pounds from Faint? No. He might have lost it, of course. A lot of ways fifty quid could disappear. If you really considered the situation coldly who was he, Townrow, to deny Faint had given him fifty pounds? It came back to this question Faint asked. Who was he? Did he know enough about himself to be sure Faint was the crook and not he? He would play safe. O.K. He would get fifty pounds somehow and hand it all over to Faint without question. It would be the only way of ensuring his own touching, simple-minded, contemptible innocence. Why just fifty quid? Faint ought to get interest.

He'd give the bugger fifty-two pounds ten. Or, in Egyptian currency, fifty-two pounds, fifty piastres. This did not allow for the difference in value between the pound sterling and the Egyptian pound. You had to draw the line short of complete acceptance of what you were responsible for. If Faint had sterling in mind, then sterling he would be paid, or its equivalent; say fifty-two Egyptian pounds, to be on the safe side.

"I've got a friend in the next block. She'll lend it to me."

"I don't care where you get the money from. Next block which way?"

"Midan el Zaher."

"I'm not walking round there with you. Get shot. Tell you what, we can nip over the roof."

"What is this place?" asked Townrow as they climbed the flights of stone stairs. It was one of the older buildings, stinking, and without a lift.

"Sort of whore house." Faint stopped to stub out his cigar on the sole of his boot. A big woman in a dressing gown with sagging cheeks and boot-polish black hair came out of a door as they passed and Faint said, "We'll be back in five minutes. Get some breakfast on, there's a love, I'm peckish."

From the roof they could see over the intervening blocks to the beach. They could not see the whole beach because except due north these intervening blocks were too high. They saw perhaps a hundred yards strip. The beach huts were flaming under a purple and green pall of smoke. Tanks were rolling on to the Corniche road like woodlice on an old plank. To the east there was a glimpse of a Centurion rolling down the waterfront road towards Simon Arzt's.

"That's my ship." Faint pointed to a tanker lying out in the Roads. The sun was at just the angle to set that strip of water alight all the way across to Port Fouad and the various ships hung in the dazzle. "Who is this friend, anyway, who's going to lend you fifty quid? It's not that bloody insulting old woman is it? Captain's daughter, my arse! I've seen that type. That's where we're going to get across. Good jump, isn't it?"

If it had not been for the parapets there would have been no problem. Anybody could clear eight feet if there was room to run at it. The parapets would not permit this. It was a standing jump from one to the other. In between was a drop of perhaps eighty feet.

"Unless I get this money within the next five minutes I'm not going to get it at all." Faint was using the edge of his hand like a meat cleaver. He struck off a portion of air and knocked it in Townrow's direction as representing five minutes. "Fifty quid," he said and struck off another portion to represent that too. The sun shining into his eyes made them seem bigger than ever. They were prominent now, like the eyes of some hunted fish, swivelling back, Townrow could have sworn, to see what monster was in pursuit. His scarlet braces were strips of brilliance. He was breathing heavily from the exertion of struggling up ten flights of stairs. "It's no good you thinking you're going to give me the slip. All this bloody hoo-ha, you think you can give me the slip. If I let you get away I might never see you again. Fifty quid's a lot of money. Wouldn't have lent it to anybody but the Captain. Ought to have seen his face. 'Port Said?' he said, and laughed. Well, go on! Jump, you bugger!"

Townrow shook his head. "I wouldn't make it."

Faint immediately climbed on to the parapet and stood there. It was about a foot wide so there was plenty to stand on. Even so, height could have meant nothing to him. Townrow saw him, brilliantly lit by the sun, so brilliantly that he looked artificial, a dummy, against the billowing back of the northern sky. There was so much shooting going on, there were so many men with guns on other rooftops, Townrow could not know from which direction the shot actually came and plucked Faint off that parapet. All he heard was Faint's skull exploding with a wet plop and feel the hot blood splash across his face. He was amazed there was so much blood immediately available. Faint's body pitched out and down. Townrow saw the braces receding, almost luminous in the gloom down there, a bloody St Andrew's Cross, getting smaller and stopping small.

Townrow lay down behind the parapet and closed his eyes. The blood thickened on his face. He was acquiring a mask.

What he had to do was immediately obvious. Mrs K would cough up the fifty-two Egyptian pounds without question. At the first opportunity he would go down to the alley and load Faint on to that fruit barrow he had noticed out of the corner of his eyes, even as they had been fixed on those red braces. Taking the fifty-two pounds he would then set off with the barrow to the water front. Somehow he would find means of taking Faint out to the tanker. Townrow would then say to the Captain, "I owed this man fifty pounds sterling, so here's fifty-two Egyptian."

And the Captain would say, "You're covered with blood man. Go and wash it off."

"I tell you I owed this man fifty-two Egyptian quid."

"O.K." the Captain would say. "Now you can wash the blood off."

In a manner of speaking he had been washed by this man's blood. It was quite unlike the last time. For one thing he had immediately run down to the street and actually felt where the neck was broken. That was an altogether more confusing death. Did that other man fall or was he pushed? Faint had gone out, perfectly straight-forward, like Amin. They had not been murdered, they had not died accidentally, they had been sacrificed.

And Elie?

He still could not get it out of his head that he was to sail out of Port Said with Elie in one of those fishing boats. Elie would tell him what a fool he was. The fifty quid would mean nothing. You really had to get out of the world, get away, to an island. You couldn't answer for anybody

but yourself and only then if you were alone. Townrow
was speaking to Leah. Even as he ran his hand over her
naked flank he said how sorry he was, sweet, they were
breaking up but seeing what a humped-back trot she was
could anybody blame him. No, he was lying again.

During the battle Townrow and Mrs K were in the
middle of her big sitting room, with the doors and windows
open, drinking coffee and talking about, among other
things, religion. Mrs K said that if she took it up seriously
it would be Spiritualism. It must have been in the 'twenties
her sister, she was dead now, took her to a meeting in
Finsbury Park and when the service was over, quite a nice,
simple service with Bible readings, one of the assistants said
that if she went into the Minister's room he would have a
special message for her. It turned out to be from Mrs K's
first husband, killed in the war.

"What it actually was I won't tell you," said Mrs K, "but
it could have meant nothing to anybody else. Well, to be
frank, he spoke about some snapdragons in Clissold Park.
I remembered them as well as anything. In the summer of
1915 they had lovely beds of yellow snapdragons. Frederick
was in khaki, of course. We looked at them together. That's
all the message was. Looking at the snapdragons was the
peak of his earthly happiness. It made life insignificant, I
thought. Frederick was not a fool. He'd been born, and
grown up and married me, and what was the point of it
all? Snapdragons!"

Mrs K laughed. She was in a good mood because
Abravanel, whom she had never liked, was dead; and now
that the British had landed and the Egyptians were going
to be taught a lesson she was happier than Townrow
remembered seeing her. She talked about religion and
Spiritualism because during the night she had thought Elie
was in the room with her. It was not a dream because she
was not asleep. She had the distinct impression that Elie
was standing at the foot of the bed, talking to her. Soon

after, she got up to quench her thirst. The lights were full on. When she returned from the kitchen she could not see him but she felt he was still there.

"He wanted to be taken out of Port Said altogether," she said, "and buried in Beirut. It's a bit late now. He ought to have put it in his will."

"I suppose the will was just business-like. Elie wouldn't go in for anything, but well, the disposition of . . . He wouldn't say anything about his funeral?"

"He mentioned you."

"Me?"

"Not as a beneficiary, I don't mean. He just wanted you to be informed when he was dead."

For some time a tank down in the square below had been using machine guns on one of the buildings opposite. Now it started to shell the place. A silence was followed by what sounded like the rumble of some edifice squatting on its foundations and the sunlight was dimmed just as though a curtain had been drawn. Townrow went and shut the french windows to keep out the dust. That particular building had been rigged up by the Egyptians as a rough and ready fortress, so what had happened to it was not particularly surprising. Townrow could see palm trees sticking up out of a brown fog. He had Elie's shot gun, ready loaded, in case he had to defend himself against one of these Egyptian guerrilla fighters.

"He said you were to be told before the funeral. That was impossible. Abravanel didn't turn the will out until a week after. Elie liked you. I just imagine he wanted somebody in England to be thinking about him when he was buried. He admired the English."

"And all the time he was shipping arms to Cyprus."

Mrs K wiped her lips with the corner of her handkerchief. "He was just a foreigner when you came to think of it. I told you I would never have married him if he was a Jew. Lebanese are Semites, you know, but they're not Jews. He *was* a foreigner, though, and foreigners don't really think like us. They know right from wrong but they can't act on it. He stood there at the foot of my bed. It was upsetting really. He was on about being moved to Beirut. If I hadn't been so frightened I'd have asked him who was responsible for his death."

"Nobody was responsible for his death," said Townrow. "You can put that out of your mind. He was an old man and he had a bad heart. What d'you expect me to do?" Townrow was alarmed by the way the building was shaking or he would not have talked like this. "Anybody'd think you'd brought me all the way from England to accuse you of murdering him. You couldn't find anybody in Port Said to do it, so you sent for me. For God's sake," he shouted, "it wasn't even your fault. You were a good wife."

Mrs K's face was expressionless. "He liked you."

Townrow shrugged.

"These foreigners are intelligent," said Mrs K, "they know right from wrong as well as you or I do. But they can't act on it and that was Elie's tragedy."

"What do you think he'd say about this invasion?"

"He'd be pleased."

Somebody was coming up in the lift. The door to the landing was wide open so they could hear the whining and rattling in the lift shaft and they could count. Past the first floor. Past the second. Townrow slipped the catch on the gun and sat with it trained on the gates. Anybody getting out at this particular floor was coming to see them or taking the little flight of stone stairs to the roof. When the little mahogany and glass cabin rose into view and stopped nothing happened at all, though. There was no light inside but Townrow could see through the windows that the cabin was empty. He considered this. The only way of bringing the lift up to the fifth floor was by getting inside it and pressing the appropriate button. Either that, or standing on the fifth floor and pressing the call button. Reason told him there must be somebody in the lift, sitting on the floor where he would be hidden by the mahogany panels that made up the lower halves of the two doors. As these panels did not meet by about half an inch somebody was, Townrow guessed, sitting there in the darkness and watching him through that gap. He stared at that vertical black strip but could make out nothing beyond.

Townrow told Mrs K to go and sit in the corner out of harm's way. He himself moved as far to the right as was possible without losing sight of the lift altogether. The main thing was to be out of the line of fire from that gap between the two doors. From his new position Townrow could see the buttons inside the lift. What he was watching for now was a hand coming up to press one of them.

"Fire's getting hold." Mrs K was looking, from her corner, through the double windows and across the square. Townrow realised that what he had thought was shooting could only be the crackling from this fire.

"We ought to be getting down to street level some time. Does this building have a cellar?"

"In Port Said? You'd never keep the water out. That's why Elie had a lead lining."

Anybody coming out of that lift with a rush would be checked. You might not kill a man with a 12-bore shotgun but you could check him. It would provide a breathing space. Maybe there'd be time to talk.

"A lead what?"

"Inside the coffin. It cost over a hundred pounds. I'd no idea lead was so expensive."

"Like gold," said Townrow. He went to the doorway and peeped round. Then he stood on a chair to gain height and peeped round. He could see some way down into the lift but made nothing of it at all. Possibly somebody on the ground floor had been able to get out of the lift after pressing button number five. Townrow asked Mrs K if this was possible but she said she did not know, it was not the sort of game she would play.

Townrow opened the gate to the lift and found himself looking into the eyes of a man who was apparently sitting on its floor. He was bare-headed and in uniform. After staring at Townrow for some moments his eyes switched uneasily from side to side. He was an Egyptian army officer, a lieutenant judging by the two little green crescents on his shoulder. He was a youngish man, certainly no more than thirty.

Getting the lift doors open was not easy because the Egyptian had his legs against them and he was not co-operating. Once his eyes had stopped switching from side to side he just watched with interest.

"You speak English? If you don't get out of this lift somebody's going to press the button and you'll go down to the ground again." This was not true. Townrow had the gate open and that immobilized the lift but he had to say something.

"He's hurt." Mrs K had come out on to the landing and was standing behind Townrow.

"I wouldn't know yet. Let's get him out." Townrow had the door open sufficiently for him to get his foot in and give the man a shove. Then he stepped inside and took him under the arms. The Egyptian was wearing heavy black boots that laced nearly to the knee. No weapons. All the time Townrow was dragging him out he was drumming on the floor with his heels.

"Leave the gate open. Prop the gate open. We don't want anybody else operating this lift."

"He's bleeding."

Townrow looked back into the lift and saw there was a lot of blood on the floor. The landing was wet too where the man had been dragged. For the next hour or so Townhow and Mrs K were busy with this man. They laid him on the floor, put a pillow under his head, removed his boots, cut away his right trouser leg and put a tourniquet on his thigh. The wound was nothing serious. He had lost a lot of blood but no bones were broken. A lot of flesh had been taken away on the lower part of his thigh. Mrs K knew all about this sort of thing. She wrapped him in a blanket and

243

tried to make him drink some coffee. She got Townrow to force his teeth apart with the ivory handle of a paper knife.

He said nothing until an unusually heavy explosion rocked the room and caused a few square feet of ceiling to fall down.

"Russian rocket," he said. His eye fell on the mug of coffee. He lifted it without help and drank. "Russians."

"You speak English." Mrs K sounded reproachful. He might have been a child who had kept a secret from her. "Why didn't you say you spoke English? You're all right now. You won't die. Cheer up."

Mrs K's servant had disappeared so she fried some liver and onions over the primus in the kitchen and they ate out of the pan with flaps of bread. The Egyptian had relapsed into silence but he drank half a glass of milk.

"I can see this boat and you, or somebody like you, sailing it. And this coffin. I've told you about all this?"

"You must have dreamed it."

"Or it's to come. Listen," he said, "that was no dream. I can't remember waking up from a dream like that. I just remember it."

"You dreamed it."

"I can see it so clearly. There was a basket under one of the seats with fishing tackle in it."

"Quiet, isn't it?" said Mrs K. "You can't hear people moving about. They've just shut themselves up. They're lying under the beds. If this building caught fire we'd be roasted, no mistake. An old building like this has the timber in it. I'm going to have a nap."

By mid afternoon the fire opposite had died down. Townrow felt the Egyptian's right leg and slackened the tourniquet slightly.

"You'll be O.K. Would you witness my will if I drew it up? There ought to be two witnesses but I guess one will do at a pinch. I can't ask the lady. She's one of the beneficiaries."

A MAN SHOULD SMELL SWEET

Townrow found a pad of Basildon Bond in Mrs K's roll top desk but there appeared to be no pen or ink.

"You got anything to write with?" he asked the Egyptian. No answer.

He found a ball-point in the man's breast pocket and as the sounds of battle were renewed settled himself down to write. A new development was the air activity. A lot of planes were diving and firing rockets. Townrow could not imagine what they were after. But it was somewhere well away to the south. Perhaps it was the railway station. It could even be Navy House.

He had never written his will, even when he had been on active service, and had only a general recollection of the kind of legal jargon he judged necessary.

"This is the last will and testament," he wrote, "of me, James Farrer Townrow, being thirty-five years of age or thereabouts and sound in mind and body, or reasonably so. All real estate, goods, chattels and other possessions, including the gold ring on my finger, in Port Said, I direct shall be given to Mrs Ethel Khoury, widow of my old friend, Elie, once a merchant of this city. In the event of her predeceasing me—— "

Townrow put the ball-point down, stood up and watched, through the window, an immense column of black smoke rising from a point perhaps a couple of miles away. The explosion sent a red tongue a third of the way up the column which then became a great cliff of smoke. He studied it and wondered who else it made sense to mention.

The telephone service would be out of action, that was for certain. But it was worth making the experiment. He dialled the Abravanel number and was surprised to hear it ringing. At the very least that meant the building was intact. He listened to the ringing and pictured old Abravanel lying there on his bed and Leah maybe still busy with her packing.

"Listen," he said, when she answered the phone, "you'll think this is a crazy sort of request but I want this information for a good purpose. I want you to give it me and not ask any questions. You understand that? This is important. If you ever want to do anything for me this is it. Can I put this question?"

He could hear her breathing. "Where are you?"

"I'm at Mrs K's and she's having a nap. We've an Egyptian soldier with us but he's out of action. He's no trouble. There's nothing to concern yourself about on my behalf."

He tried to make this sarcastic because he wanted to make himself as objectionable to this woman as he reasonably could. He wanted her to react in such a way she would hurt him. Then he might be able to forget her.

"What's the question?" she asked.

"Your husband's name and address. I mean the private address, not the hospital."

"Rob Strauss."

"Did you say Rob? Is that his full name?"

She spelt it. "Rob Maxwell Strauss, Two-forty three West Avenue, Albany, State of New York. What do you want this for?"

"You might as well give me the hospital as well."

She gave it to him. "What are you doing?"

"Writing my will. Stay indoors. You'll be all right. This will soon be finished. You'll be O.K. You can go to the States." He hung up.

Not wanting to be interrupted he waited by the telephone in case she should ring back immediately. After a couple of minutes he sat down to get on with his writing.

". . . In the event of her pre-deceasing me I direct that all these said goods, chattels and real estate should go to Mr Rob Maxwell Strauss, of Two-forty three West Avenue, Albany, State of New York, now a patient in the Jewish Hospital for Nervous Diseases. In any case, I direct that all my property and possessions in the United Kingdom should go to the same Mr Rob Maxwell Strauss."

And if Strauss pre-deceased him? Townrow shrugged.

These cases lived a long time. If he didn't it was too bad, everything would go to Leah, the Zephyr, the bits and pieces of furniture, the I.C.I, shares and the Unit Trusts, say five thousand quid in all. At least she would learn how he felt. He did not think he owed his mother anything. Certainly he owed his father nothing. If that girl really had been pregnant that would have rated a mention. But you could not have been a judas to somebody who did not exist.

"What are you up to?" Mrs K came out of her bedroom in time to catch him persuading the Egyptian to witness his signature. Townrow held the paper against a book to provide a writing surface and, surprisingly, the Egyptian understood and wrote his name in Arabic calligraphy.

"No, damn this," said Townrow, "what's your name?"

"Moustapha el-Habib," breathed the man, and this is what Townrow made him scrawl under his own signature before handing the document over to Mrs K.

"We're still alive. What's all this then?" She looked around for her reading glasses.

Townrow said she was to hang on to this document because it showed the sort of man he now was; and what's more it had legal possibilities, in spite of there being only the one signature. That was not the important aspect of the matter. He went out of the flat and stepped into the lift, intending after this long delay to go in search of Faint and put him on that vegetable cart.

CHAPTER SEVEN

A sea requiem

Two funerals, then, one on a battlefield and the other
at sea. At both Townrow was wary. To begin with
he had the idea that if he pressed on, jaw set, doing
little jobs like picking up Faint and burying Abravanel,
keeping his nose down to the job in hand, certainly not
lifting his head to look in Leah's direction, there would
come a moment when he would know he had passed
through a fire; either he had passed through this fire and
was purified by it, or he was dead. What kept him on edge
was the suspicion that nothing would happen at all. He
would go on living and breathing, Leah would come round
and they would start loving again, the Anglo-French forces
would control the Canal Zone, maybe Cairo too, and
he would come to see, some time in the future, that
invasion and adultery were among the good things in
history.

That was equivalent to nothing happening. The possibility concerned him even more than being shot by a sniper.
All the time he was driving the gharry out to the Jewish
cemetery he was toying with the idea of Egyptian citizenship. How did you qualify? Did you have to learn Arabic?
Did you need to be Moslem? And when he had to negotiate
some crater he would turn and warn Leah so that she and
the rabbi could grab the coffin and stop it sliding out. It
was just resting on the floor of this horse-drawn carriage.
It was not secured. They had been unable to find a rope.
When the gharry went round a crater it tilted. Leah and the

rabbi screamed, and had to grab the coffin by its handles. Townrow prided himself the regular driver could not have handled the gaunt nag any better. He watched the big rump bones rocking backwards and forwards under the loose skin. This was the only transport they had been able to commandeer at short notice. The driver had been hit by something and was lying dead on his box seat.

The sea funeral kept him on the stretch too. There he was, in the fresh air with the sun shining and the blue water racing on either side, but this dream had him by the throat. With him in the boat were Leah in a fur coat with suitcases, Mrs K with her cases and baskets, three nuns in grey habit sitting up at the front, a fresh-faced, boyish army chaplain with a prayer book, and, of course, the brown, stained coffin. *It really was happening.* The funeral was not as he remembered it. The nuns and the army chaplain were an innovation. But essentially it was the same experience, and he sat at the stern, wearing one of Elie's old overcoats buttoned at the throat, handling the crude tiller these rough and ready sailing boats went in for, thinking that having come so far with Leah it would be more than he could bear if she escaped him now. Went to the States, that is to say.

The first funeral had found him thinking exactly the opposite. Life and sanity depended on giving the woman up. The second funeral made it seem life and sanity depended on grabbing her. He realised his desires were running in opposite directions. He had not changed. The explanation was not that the first funeral came before the second—by about three weeks, to be exact—but that he was still torn. What, for the moment, pushed him in the direction of Leah was the feeling only she could get him out of this dazed ritual of boats and death.

Just a boat, water, death. They were facts of nature. He looked astern. What little wake the boat was making flattened the crisp morning waves. He screwed up his eyes and looked at the De Lesseps statue which seemed to be waving its right arm with imperial confidence to indicate the masts and superstructure of the wrecks in the Basin—dredgers, cranes, tugs. But the arm was not actually moving. The fidgeting came from the huge White Ensign and the French Tricolour the troops had tied to it before embarking. Behind the statue was an enormous Union Jack flapping from a pole. Jet fighters toured the morning. Landing craft bobbed out from the beaches.

He shut his eyes and opened them again. Everything was still there. Everything in view was nothing more than a lot of objects and they had no particular meaning. He had to fight against the idea some kind of message was being handed out. Little red clouds became colourless as the sun climbed and he fancied there was real danger of their running together to form a filmy mask, with blank eyes and staring mouth. That really would have been a message. If he had seen that he might have yelled and thrown himself into the water. So he stopped looking at those gauzy clouds. Thank God there were no birds. The ibis and wild duck were scattered in the marshes far on the other side of the blistered town, miles away in safety. Birds came into his mind because, now that he remembered the event more clearly, he could see that as his father walked across the field to the line of trees two huge black birds, they must have been crows, rose so suddenly they might have been let out of a box. It had seemed to mean something at the time. If there had been birds about while the British and French evacuated Port Said that too might have meant something. But all he could see was H.M.S. *Duchess* looking so bright she might have been scoured from funnel to water line with steel wool. Oh, and all the other warships he did not know the names of. The landing craft hit the waves violently and threw up white water.

Townrow had steered so close to a torpedo boat he could shout to a man on the bridge who had been studying the little fishing boat through his glasses.

"We're going to a funeral."

"What's that?" bellowed the fellow through his loud-hailer.

Townrow waved his hand to indicate his passengers and cargo. The chaplain held his prayer book up, as though for inspection, and waved it cheerfully. The three nuns up at the front looked straight ahead. Plainly they were enjoying themselves too. Mrs K sat with her thin grey hair blowing about her face. Townrow knew she was probably the angriest woman in the Eastern Mediterranean. Nobody would have guessed it by looking at her. She stretched out her mouth in what might equally well have been a grin of amusement or a way of coping with the wind. Townrow thought that once they had hurled the coffin over the side she would take off on a broomstick. Leah seemed to be fast asleep, sitting up. She had covered her head tightly with a yellow scarf.

They were not going back. This was the end. What they could not carry with them was lost to Nasser. True, Mrs K had some extraordinary idea of sailing round to Alexandria when they had gone through the committal ceremony. With her Lebanese passport she would then go to Cairo and see a Minister, Nasser himself if need be, ultimately catch a train to Port Said and repossess herself of her property. But this was whistling to keep her courage up. She knew she was beaten. She knew she would never see Egypt again. Nobody was returning. Even the boat would be scuttled once they were safely aboard one of these warships. As an American citizen Leah counted on being put ashore in Cyprus and flown to the States where Townrow supposed she would at once set about trying to realise the value of whatever her father had left. There would be no difficulty over her mother's jewellery. She had shown some of it to him; a string of Bahrein pearls, diamond earrings, rings, brooches. She said she had been unable to have these when her mother died because it had been forbidden to take jewellery out of the country. There was her father's fine gold watch. When sold all these would keep her going for a while. There was stock: Argentine Railways, she said, and the Brazilian Coffee Company. Ironically, there was a bunch of Suez Canal Company shares.

Maybe it would all go on her husband's treatment. He had heard it was expensive over there.

She moved her coat, still without opening her eyes, and revealed a stretch of thigh. It was enough to make him understand he was not the man he supposed he had become as a result of this and that during the past few weeks. Port Said had been an education, and when the Intelligence Branch put the screws on he thought finally he'd seen the light. At long last he had been so placed he could wring some of the sour sweat of deceit and bad faith out of the air. He had counted himself purged of some shame, not a great deal, but it counted. He went through the questioning with such virtue he had felt decency settling into his system, ready for use when the next occasion offered. It only needed a glimpse of the top end of a stocking to know it had all been a lot of bloody self-deception. He had seen no light. He hadn't stumbled across any new wisdom.

He sat watching Leah's face. It was wet with spray. Tiny beads of water were trapped by her eyelashes. Then they ran down her cheeks to the corner of those lips. He had kissed those lips and wanted to kiss them again. He wanted to hold her. He wanted her body warmth around him. He wanted the tight clutch of her flesh and the imagined thrust hurt. It almost made him cry out. He kept his eyes fixed obsessively on her face as a way of isolating her and him from the marine rout and comedy going on all round. He was an unregenerate louse and always had been. Probably he had stuck to his denials over Christou out of conceit or bloody-mindedness. They were drips. He had faced them out. Practically anybody else would too.

Townrow. They had been polite but they didn't go in for much ceremony and they had called him abruptly by his surname, though they were younger than he was. Even the man in the grey thornproof could not have been out of his thirties in spite of the receding hair. Townrow didn't give a damn to begin with. They were British. Being interrogated by the British made a change. It was only after the exchanges grew tense he suggested he had a handle to his name.

"Mr Townrow," said the man in the thornproof. "Of course. Sorry." They had been friendly, shoving packets of cigarettes about and flicking lighters. The little man in the middle smoked a pipe and the atmosphere thickened. The windows were shut. The door was shut. Outside was a paratrooper with a gun.

"What I hate," this man with the pipe and the papers had said, "is giving the impression we do a lot of snooping around. I mean, the ordinary citizen gets a bit shirty. Natural British reaction. But we've got this job to do and after all Port Said was one of the places where arms used to get shipped into Cyprus."

"This invasion must suit you down to the ground."

"So we came over, you see, sort of to look around. We knew about your friend, Mr Khoury, of course. Did you? I mean did you know he was in the gun running business?"

"I had my suspicions."

"We know perfectly well your own relationship to the Khourys was innocent. There is no question about that. It is kind of you to help us. There are a lot of things we *don't* understand. For example, why did Khoury's friend Christou try to kill you?"

"Did he?"

"You see, this is a point we're pretty well briefed about. I don't need to remind you that Christou is a British subject and that what's more he's been wanted back in Cyprus to face certain criminal charges. As a matter of fact he is in Cyprus. He's been back there for ten days or so."

"Christou didn't try to kill me."

"To be frank, it is not important. Officially we don't care whether Christou tried to bump you off or whether he didn't. What *we*— "

"You sure you don't mean a man called Aristides?"

"We'll come to Aristides later. No, I don't mean him. I mean Christou who ran the Cyprus Bar. What *we* are interested in is this business of supplying arms. *If* Christou was concerned, with your friend Khoury, in this traffic it is as well we know about it."

"You mean you don't know whether Christou was in it?"

"We suspect the attack on you is a pointer. We know why you came to Port Said. Now, the theory is that Christou thought you were doing intelligence work."

"If Christou had wanted to kill me he'd have made no mistake about it. I can't help you."

There were two other men in the room, one little more than a boy, in the uniform of a lieutenant in a Rifle regiment; the other was a stooping bird of about thirty in a shiny blue suit. He had a long sallow face and a blue chin. Most of the time he had been writing in a notebook which he supported in his left hand although there were tables. Now and again Townrow had found himself exchanging glances with him. They were not friendly.

The chief inquisitor became as avuncular as his age permitted and Townrow guessed it was what he had been trained to do when interviews reached this stage. "British troops have been killed in Cyprus with arms from Port Said. You may say this is history. Here we are in Port Said and we've bottled up the supply. But *if* Christou was responsible we want to pin it on him. This civilian charge in Cyprus may not come to anything. Before we know where we are he's operating from Beirut. Now, Mr Townrow, you can help us in this. Even after the attack on you it is our information you had conversations with this man, in his bar and in the convent opposite. We also know you were in the same prison cell for a short while. Well, what do you think? Rather, what do you know? We just want you to talk and talk and talk, all about Christou. Please don't think you'll bore us. We've all the time in the world. Even something quite trivial he said might give us a line. Now, when you walked into his bar on that first night—— "

Townrow spoke abruptly. "I don't know anything. The man's a friend of mine."

He could not at this stage remember the names of these three men even though they had introduced themselves politely enough. But he certainly remembered their amusement. Christou, a friend?

The way they looked at him they must have thought him a beat-up, drunken old pug. He knew how the white scar showed up on his cheek. There was a line where the hair did not grow. He had been wearing one of Elie's old shirts without a collar. He felt cold.

"I don't know how you can call a man your friend when he's behaved like Christou. Personally, if I'd been in your shoes I'd have wanted his blood. He's practically confessed to being behind an attempt to do you in. Granted he's amusing. But he's a killer."

"I don't believe it."

A shrug. The man with the notebook went on writing. The boy officer's mouth was slightly open.

"When did you meet Christou first?"

"I've nothing to tell you."

"But damn it all man, surely you can answer questions where your country's interests are concerned?"

"No, to hell with the country," said Townrow. "Christou's a friend of mine. His company's a bloody sight pleasanter than yours is, let me tell you."

"O.K. You've had a pretty upsetting time. I don't want to be tedious. But you've been a soldier in the British Army. This is a business in which the lives of British soldiers have been lost. And will go on being lost. Now, it's rubbish—be honest now—to say Christou is a pal of yours. In any case he won't come to any *more* harm as a result of what you tell us."

"I don't talk about my friends behind their backs."

"Is Aristides a friend?"

"Sure! He could have shot me once and didn't. What better mark of friendship could you wish for than that? I'm

255

not going to talk about any of these people, Christou or Aristides or—— " He stopped because he realised he was on the point of saying Amin. "I'm not going to talk about any of these men for the benefit of you bastards. I don't know you, do I? What do you represent? I don't know you from Adam."

"We're British Intelligence officers. You don't need to know us as people, do you? It's the function that is important."

Townrow remembered looking at them suspiciously. What did they mean by function?

"We don't want to press you." The man looked unbelievably childish; those round, blue eyes, those hands pressed together until the fingers whitened, the clear assumption that everything he did was right and proper, that he was on the right side. "But England expects, you know."

"Bugger England, in that case." He had brought the words out quietly, thoughtfully, as much as to say: if *that's* the conclusion you force me to!

Possibly these men had been right. Possibly Christou was the thug they said. You could not be sure. Christou made him laugh. The man was a card. He was a liar. And now he had been illegally carted off to Cyprus. Egyptian law still operated in the town but the British had extradited him. No doubt they had been cunning enough to get some Egyptian judge to sign a document. Anyway, he was in British custody. Claiming him as a friend was a bit of bravado, perhaps, but in that particular question-and-answer set-up Townrow could not see what other attitude he could have taken than the one he did: I know him and I'm not going to do any dirt on him. He had such a sense of the man's individuality it was mildly surprising to look round this little boat and see that he was not there. Christou had been on other short sea trips. Perhaps he had sailed out and watched innumerable coffins thrown into the sea, once the arms had been taken out that is. The question was whether the idea of exhuming Elie's coffin and taking it out into the Med in precisely the same way would ever have occured to him if Christou hadn't established the routine.

All the time Townrow had been refusing to talk about Christou he might, in reality, have thought it was Amin these Intelligence men were referring to. Possibly there had been a confusion in his mind. He ought to have asked them straight out "You do mean Christou, don't you?" He had done nothing of the sort, so there would always be this slight uncertainty in his mind. But even if he had put such a question and they had replied "Yes, of course we mean Christou. Who else?" he would still have kept his mouth shut.

Mrs K knew nothing of all this. He looked at her. She had removed her glasses and was wiping them. It seemed she was having trouble with the spray. In the keen sunlight her eyes looked tiny and colourless. Poor old girl! She had sailed up and down the oceans, buried two husbands and still had not quite got one of them off her hands. She had no idea why the Allies were pulling out of Port Said. Why hadn't they taken the Canal Zone? Why had they stopped? There was treachery at home, she said. The result was that people like her were ruined. British subjects and Jews of all sorts were ruined. Men and women born and brought up in Port Said, Maltese mainly, were on their way to winter in the U.K.

"I never told you British Intelligence tried to quiz me about Christou."

She was hooking her glasses back over her ears. "It's nice to know they caught up with him."

"I said nothing. They got nothing out of me at all."

"They should have asked me. I could have told them a thing or two."

"I said he was my friend."

Mrs K snorted at this but if he had been hoping for any fiercer reaction he was disappointed. She took a white cotton shawl out of a cloth bag and wrapped it round her shoulders.

"We'll all need winter clothes when we get home. The best place for warm underclothes is Marks and Spencers." She looked about her and addressed the chaplain. "Isn't it time we had the service? We're far enough out."

Approaching the Egyptian coast from, say, Cyprus or the Greek islands you must have been on it, certain times of the year, almost before you could haul down sail. One moment you must have been sliding south with no land in sight; then, a few minutes later, you were running up one of these shallow beaches. There were no headlands, scarcely any rise in the mud and sand beyond the breakers.

Townrow and his boatload were out a couple of miles, three miles maybe and except for the cathedral tower and the lighthouse sticking out of the water to the south they might have been fifty miles out for all the evidence of Egypt they could see. They were far enough out for the boat to be striking a different rhythm, rising and falling on a languorous swell. Townrow spotted the very moment the rhythm changed. The boat stopped, hung in the air, nobody moved; and Townrow thought, yes, why not freeze this moment of time? Mrs K was leaning forward to put one hand on the coffin. Her mouth was slightly open as if she was about to burst into prayer or song. Leah's left hand was keeping her skirt down. Her wedding ring caught the sun and blazed. The nuns might have been carved out of wood. The chaplain had a grin on his face and his left hand flung out, pointing, like the old sailor in that painting *The Boyhood of Raleigh*. And the effect of this arrested motion was to make Townrow think that if time stopped and they hung on that sunny wave through all eternity he ought to have a clearer idea how they had got so far. He must stop mis-remembering. He must clear his mind. What actually *had* happened?

It was not true Mrs K had insisted on bringing Elie with her. She had been all for staying in Port Said, even when the Consul and an officer out of Movement Control called and said all British nationals, French nationals, United States citizens, in fact pretty well everybody without Egyptian papers, were being evacuated. They accepted no responsibility for her safety. And what she said, once she had recovered from her annoyance the evacuation was taking place at all, was, "I am not leaving this town. I'm not afraid of the Egyptians. This building is my husband's property. Was his property. He's buried in this town. I'm too old to quit. Ten years ago I might have quit. There's nothing for me anywhere else. I'm comfortable here. I can't start again. It's come all too late. Elie is in this town and I'll stay with him."

"I'll stay too," Townrow had said.

"You'll what?"

"I'll stay. You'd be the only British citizen in town."

"You clear off out. Nasser won't touch an old woman like me but if they laid hands on you, well, it's God help you. You staying wouldn't do me any good."

"I'll stay," he said. "I reckon that's the right thing to do. People have got to stick together at a time like this."

"But they won't let us stick together. I'm only doing what Elie would do if he'd lived. He'd stay and he'd tell you to go."

"I'll stay," Townrow had said, because he thought she might still need him, though he couldn't guess in what way.

"What's in it for you? Is that girl staying too? Is that why?"

"It's a theory," he agreed, "but it doesn't hold."

"I'm a realist. She's Jewish. Being born here or an American citizen won't make any difference. The Egyptians will jail her if they do nothing worse."

"She's going. She'd have gone before if she could have got transport."

"England too hot for you?"

"Once the Egyptian army has moved back into town and I've seen to it you're all right I'll go."

"No, they'll do for you, and they'll probably do for me

too, but I'm not going. I'm ashamed of being British. Why start an invasion if you don't mean to go through with it? Why stop when you've got as far as this? I'll tell you what, we British have lost our nerve. People of my father's generation wouldn't have lost their nerve. Thank God he's dead and spared the shame. It was bad enough for him me marrying a foreigner but he'd have been really upset at the thought of British troops giving way to the United Nations, black Africans most of them, or yellow men, though I know that for the sake of appearances they sent mostly white troops. But there are Indians. Did you see the Yugoslavs? Now, there's a people I admire, not their politics, but they're independent, you see, and they've got this pride. I was a nurse in Montenegro in the First War and I know. They just never give up, those Balkan people. But there was a lot of tipping. In some ways they had no self-respect. You tipped shop assistants. But they'd never have quit like the British. So that's one reason why I'm staying."

"I'll just hang around and see to it you're all right."

"You don't think I'm afraid of dying? I wouldn't be afraid of dying. There's nothing in it, dying."

"Sometimes I'm afraid and sometimes I'm not."

"No, I've never been afraid," she said. "I don't want you staying in Port Said on my account. I don't mind dying but I hate being thought in any way responsible for other people dying."

"Does that happen often?"

"Not often," she said. "I don't want to see you any more. Have anything you want that was Elie's, or mine for that matter. And look!" She went to her little mahogany writing desk and opened a drawer. He had not been paying close attention because in spite of everything he was still thinking of Leah. How was he going to say goodbye to *her*? Would he kiss her? All the time he had been trying to impress on Mrs K the fact he was not leaving her in the lurch he was holding imaginary conversations with Leah. Even now it was exciting just to think of her. When he was in the same room with her he felt bigger and brighter. Hashish mixed in the tombac of a water pipe did as much for you. Yes, but she was woman. Objectively, she probably was not bright, not too beautiful either, but she changed the chemistry of his blood. A doctor could measure it. There were tests you could make in a laboratory with specimens of his blood. You could classify them. "This one was taken when the subject was in the same room as the woman. This one shows they were a mile apart. This one five miles."

Unconsciously he had been leaning over Mrs K as she wrote. But when she tore the cheque out of the book and handed it to him he realised for the first time what she had been doing.

"You'll find this will be honoured." It was a cheque for ten thousand Swiss francs drawn on a bank in Geneva.

"What's this for?"

"In a manner of speaking I've been employing you."

"No, you take it back." When she refused to accept it he tore the cheque into small pieces and threw them into the waste paper basket. God knows she had made him angry before but he had never let her have it as he did now. "You stubborn old bitch, you've got to get out of this town. They'll drain the blood out of you pint by pint. I don't want your filthy money!"

He saw by the appalled expression on her face she was getting herself up to date fast. Any moment now she would realise he was not the crook she supposed and come out with the final stunning revelation that—oh, Elie was deep in the Mediterranean ooze and his grave in the nunnery garden was plugged with a coffin full of gold bars, or sovereigns! He would shut her up. He was not interested. Didn't she know an honest man when she saw one? He was watching himself so narrowly and censoriously the very words now dragged out of him were legalistic, even punitive.

"You are a racialist bitch." At least, what seemed to him legalistic and punitive. "You despised your husband." He even wondered if he was demonstrating how objectionable she was simply as a way of emphasising how big he was to stay on and look after her. Certainly, he was making the absurd gesture, and the larger the better. He was so incorruptible acid would not touch him, that was certain, but only by convincing her how much he despised her was he going to bring this particular piece of truth home. If he did not bring his almost fanatical altruism home to Mrs K who else was there for him to bring it home to? Now that Elie was dead and Amin was dead and Christou was gone it seemed the only other person he now knew sufficiently well to be impressed by any change in him was Leah, and it was not impossible she would put it down to a spell of sexual impotence, brought on by excess, or the wrong diet, or nervous trouble, or just terror. There had been excuse for being terrified in Port Said the past few weeks.

"I'm staying here in Port Said with you," he had shouted at Mrs K while she looked at him with her little thin mouth pinched up.

"It's something I owe myself. I was a fool to ask you to come. I suppose I lost my nerve. Where Elie is I stay. This is the end of everything."

"I might take you with me yet," he had yelled, and walked out, slamming the door behind him.

That must have been the turning point. Until then he had been busy with an Egyptian army jeep he had commandeered, driving round the streets with crates of flour, tinned milk and corned beef handed out by the British. He signed chits and took the stuff to Arab Town, driving over the rubble and smashed woodwork of the collapsed balconies, out to the Manach district where the shacks had been burned to the ground. Women in black cotton gowns scraped among the wreckage while their men sat in armchairs, smoking, staring, turning their heads and waving. Townrow made for the children. He handed stuff over to the nearest woman and made off to the store for another consignment. The Major i/c Stores wanted him to wear a beret. It would put the official seal on his activities. Town-row said they were not getting him back in the army as easily as that. He used to go out where the troops did not, out to a camp that had sprung up on the edge of the lake.

It was the turning point—going out and slamming the door—because until then the lawlessness of the city had seemed just a phase. Since the Cease Fire the British had shot back only when attacked. They had their own par-ticular order and discipline, intended mainly to keep as many troops alive as possible. Outside the sectors they con-trolled was anarchy. Townrow would drive around, not quite knowing whether he was acting out of bravado, or a genuine wish to be helpful, or whether he had finally turned suicidal. It was even exciting after a while. Any-thing goes. If he had wanted to loot a shop he could have done it. He had the freedom of the tiger in its forest. There was nothing to check him but his own conscience, if a tiger can be said to have a conscience. He was a tiger, he thought, who had picked up inhibitions. The anarchy would con-tinue. Every morning there were new corpses in the streets. It came to seem this condition was not particular to Port Said. Lawlessness was general. It would continue to the end of time. Townrow even acquired a savage grin.

He had found he could not switch it off even when he was talking to Leah. "I'm not going to try and persuade you to stay. You go off. That's fine by me. You buried your father, so there's nothing to keep you."

"What are you going to do?"

"I stay with the old woman and she stays out of cussed-ness."

For a lawyer's daughter Leah was stupid about the for-malities that had to be gone through concerning her father's estate. If it had not been for Townrow she would have left without registering the will or trying to fix some kind of security for the flat and its contents. Townrow made her hire a lawyer who was an Egyptian national and not Jewish nor from any European stock. The best they could manage was a Copt who had known old Abravanel well and, indeed, had worked together in property deals. Townrow saw to it that this man, Awad, was charged to look after Mrs K's bits and pieces too. Once Awad had obtained Abravanel's will from the bank where it had been deposited with all the old man's securities he had it provisionally registered with a magistrate but said the real formalities could only be proceeded with once normal communication with Cairo was started again. He was a big-voiced, brooding, intent, watchful, rather small man who spoke of the care he would take to see that the Abravanel family tomb was looked after. There had been Abravanels in Port Said, he said, since Leah's great-great-grandfather had been presented to the Empress Eugenie in 1869. Awad had the extraordinary idea of locking the flat, then actually sealing the door and windows with lead seals once Leah had finally left. Or was it wax? Awad could not be sure. He would look into the matter. Anyway, seals bearing the municipal device would be affixed to all means of access and the keys deposited with the civil authorities when they returned.

"We are at the end of an era," said Awad. "Let us not deceive ourselves." He looked at Townrow. "What is funny about that?"

Townrow realised he was grinning. "I've been a sick man. I'm O.K. now." Leah even took his arm to walk down the dark passages to the lift. "Everything will be all right now. You can leave with a clear conscience. You've done nothing wrong."

"What's this? The forgiveness of sins? Who do you think you are?"

On the pavement he asked if she had a notebook in which she could write an address. It was his bank in London. If ever she wanted him, he said as he watched her write in her diary with a little gold pencil, that address would find him. He remembered watching her carefully. If he never saw her again he wanted to fix her in his mind. He looked at the large, rather heavy eyes. They were real even if the lashes were not. The firm little cheeks were real too. And the way she breathed through her mouth when she was excited, that was real. He just could not understand what she had that still made life seem gay and full of adventures. Just to touch her was to feel that nothing was impossible, except despair and death, that is.

"What'll your address be?"

She hesitated. He supposed she was wondering whether her husband would get better. Eventually she tore a leaf out of her diary with the address written on it, and walked away without another word or looking back. She picked her way among broken glass. How marvellous to be her. She was wearing very light brown shoes with flat heels. He could hear them slapping on the pavement even when she had turned the corner. Nice to be her, he thought. What fun to be her! She was a curious mixture, a stuck-up bitch at times and a slut at others. The footsteps had died away. If they had come back, if she had reappeared round the corner and stood there, as he imagined her standing there, looking at him with her chin tucked in, as was her way, saying, "Come on, then," he would have gone without a word in spite of his tiger's grin and bitterness. But she did not come and he rolled the little piece of paper between finger and thumb and dropped the pellet in the gutter.

The night of that day he slammed the door on Mrs K and got rid of Leah's address without so much as looking at it he went round the bars. The Eastern Exchange was functioning. It was full of officers. Other Ranks were in the Hotel de la Poste. It was quite like old times. In a bar near Simon Artz's he found a sergeant and three men drinking Cyprus brandy. He advised them to stick to gin and there was a bit of a row, after which they all found themselves standing on the pavement by a parked truck with ropes, picks, shovels and other gear in the back. The driver was sitting at the wheel reading the *Daily Mirror* with the help of an electric torch.

Townrow had drunk enough not to care too precisely

what happened and the sight of this equipment put an idea into his head. He put one hand on the sergeant's shoulder and spoke as intently, as watchfully, as broodingly, as if he had been Awad the Coptic lawyer; but with a sense of excitement, of having turned the last corner and seen some kind of ultimate reward or revelation wobbling before his dazed eyes. He was climbing back into his dream.

"I know where there's loot, sergeant," he had said.

"You English?"

"Ex-sergeant R.A.S.C. It's O.K. I've been about these parts some time. We can pile in your truck and I'll give the directions. Hell, you want to see something, don't you?" He wanted to say that in that city, at that time, the only law was what you decided to do. But there was no need to argue. The party set off with a roar and a cheer.

Townrow had thought there might be some trouble getting into the convent. Surprisingly the great doors were wide open and labourers in white baggy trousers and embroidered waistcoats were stacking enormous baskets in the forecourt under the supervision of a couple of nuns. There were a couple of corded boxes and a line of labelled suitcases. Lights were on in the chapel, half a moon shone, the vast echoing sky poured down a soft radiance that turned into the smell of jasmine as soon as it hit the ground. That was how he understood it. Half way up a palm tree one yellow light burned like the eye of a sick snake. The nuns were leaving. Their voices were excited. The soldiers stood listening to the quick footsteps on the stone flags. The harmonium was, it seemed, being played in the chapel for the last time.

"What's this place then?" said the sergeant.

"We're after something they wouldn't be taking with them anyway." Townrow had led the way into the inner courtyard where the soldiers had to use their torches to see where they were treading. A niche in the cloisters held a Madonna and two circles of lit candles that warmed their faces as they passed. It was not the convent Townrow remembered. It had become a public place. He could see into a lighted room where a bearded man in a broad-brimmed hat and a long black overcoat was sitting in a deck chair reading a small book with delicate pages that made no sound as the man, undoubtedly a priest of some sort, licked his forefinger and turned them over. Townrow remembered wondering if this man had known Elie. Probably. He seemed the boss round there. He was the sort of man who might at any moment look up, see them watching him through the window, and start shouting.

When Townrow showed them the grave and said he wanted it opened up some of the soldiers laughed, the sergeant said, "Bugger this for a lark" and a tall man with a hurricane lamp started singing a plaintive song.

> Some folk, they say, we just fade away
> Out of sight out of mind —

They had brought picks, iron bars, enormous hammers, ropes, two beer mugs and a canvas bag with bottles in it. Townrow had to wait while they stood about drinking beer. At the time, neither he nor these soldiers had thought what they were doing was all that odd. Perhaps they were too drunk to think anything. The tall singer hung the hurricane lamp on the broken frond of a palm tree and said, "Look, they've got graves with zip fasteners."

He had slipped the end of an iron bar into a slot under the end of the stone and was levering it up with ease. In a couple of minutes the gang had removed it altogether and Townrow found himself looking down at packed yellow earth.

"What loot's this, then?" The sergeant put a boot on the grave. "There's a man down there if you ask me."

"Then get him out of it. Start digging. You won't have far to go."

"You joking?"

"Am I bloody joking? This man's a friend of mine."

"You said there was loot?" said one of the men.

"And there might be. I know for a fact he had gold teeth and a platinum plate."

"This is body snatching. That's an offence."

"Not in Egypt. You never seen a mummy?"

Townrow took a shovel and began throwing the earth to one side. It was soft sand. The coffin was lying so close to the surface that he had it entirely exposed to view in a couple of minutes and the sergeant was reading out the name inscribed on the brass plate. "Elly Kowry. There what did I say? There's a bloke in there."

"You don't know until you've opened him up." Townrow leaned on his shovel, sweating in spite of the cool night. "Go on, lift him out and see how heavy he is."

A couple of the men pushed past him. He could see by the ease with which they were slipping ropes under the coffin that it was no great weight. When it had been lugged out Townrow still leaned on his shovel, looking now at a patch of damp in the cavity they had left, the exact form of the coffin but about half the size. Then it faded. He could not be sure of this. The lamp and the torches were throwing an unsteady, deceiving light. He turned and lifted the end of the coffin with one hand. No need to prise open the lid. Sure, Elie was there. And nothing else. He was light. One man could have carried the box on his head. Lead lining? Undertaker's sales talk and Mrs K had fallen for it.

"Is this the loot then?" said the sergeant.

"Sorry, mate. I made a mistake. We'll not be opening this."

"Better put him back then."

"The widow's an Englishwoman. She's going to take him with her."

"You mean this is some bloody prank on your part?"

"She's English. It's natural, isn't it, wanting to take him."

"My father's ashes was sent home," said one of the soldiers.

"That's different. Ashes is different. This is morbid."

"Maybe she'll ask your permission to get him cremated,"

said Townrow. "Come on, let's get him out to the truck."

He had no anxiety. He never questioned the Tightness of what he was doing. Nobody would interfere. Sure enough, the priest in the desk chair reading his Missal did not so much as raise his head when the cortège went past, two soldiers at the head of the coffin, two soldiers at the feet, following the sergeant with his hurricane lamp, who only stopped in the outer courtyard to watch the porters still busy with the baskets and say, "When a man's dead it don't matter whether he's in or out or up or down. He's just a load of stinking crap but you've got to respect the feelings of the next-of-kin. It's a foreign name. But it's O.K. by me if you say she's English."

It had been the first really cold night Townrow remembered since he had arrived. By the time the bearers reached the truck they were laughing so much at some crack that they almost let the coffin slip and Townrow had to put his shoulder under. He remembered the smooth, damp wood against his cheek and the smell of jasmine from the convent. The harmonium droned. The stars were farther away and the night sky was bigger than he remembered it, but he had the same feeling of rolling through a great galactic waste as when he had been out on the lake. If he took the lid off and shook Elie by the hand would it feel like that saint's in the whitewashed tomb? He floated. He was caught in the drift of memory. He was spinning in time. Certain events he had thought in the past were, in fact, yet to come. The difference was he would be prepared for them. In Rome Airport he would have to take the initiative: he would tell that Jew from Budapest that in 1942——

He sat by the driver to give instructions. The streets were all of a sudden full of British trucks, moving down to the embarkation quays. When they arrived at the building where Mrs K's flat was situated Townrow expected an argument with the porter but the hall was deserted. To be accommodated in the lift the coffin had to be stood on end.

That left room for himself, the sergeant and two men. And they were all sober now.

Townrow rang the bell while the coffin was being eased out on to the landing. He expected the boy to come but it was Mrs K herself, wearing a brown tweed suit and holding some knitting in her hands. When she looked past Townrow and saw what was going on her face opened up, mouth, little pig eyes behind those glasses, so that Townrow felt the only way to cope with her was brutally.

"I've got Elie. We're bringing him in. You're taking him out of this town."

She could not understand what was happening, even when the soldiers carried the coffin through and put it on the floor in the hall. She removed her glasses and wiped them. She put them back and immediately saw the name on the brass plate, and from that moment, off and on, she screamed for about half an hour, by which time the soldiers had made themselves scarce and Townrow had stood a lighted candle in her best silver candle sticks at the four corners of the coffin.

When it came to the committal service Townrow shouted to Leah to let down the sail and come over and take his place at the tiller. At the right moment he and the chaplain would have to put Elie over the side and it had just struck Townrow he would float. He did not like to knock a hole in the side while Mrs K was watching. Anyway, that would not have been enough to ensure the coffin went to the bottom. You really needed some great chunk of iron to tie to it, but boats of this sort did not even carry an anchor. Why had nobody thought of this before? They were in for a painful half hour.

The chaplain stood up with his book open. He had to stand with his back to the mast and astride the end of the coffin. It was undignified but there was no alternative. He needed the mast against his back to steady him. The way the boat was rolling Townrow thought it was evens he would pitch over the side before the coffin did. And that was another problem. They would have to drop it over the stern unless they wanted to run the risk of capsizing. Mrs K shivered and turned up the collar of her coat. She seemed to be in a dream. Shock, no doubt, There were plenty of naval craft in the neighbourhood and it occurred to Townrow they might have to ask for help with the funeral if the old girl was not to be even more scandalised and upset. But as he was turning this over in his mind Leah came and sat so close to him their thighs rubbed. He knew this was not deliberate. You could not sit in the stern of that boat very well without rubbing thighs.

But she also said, "We mightn't get taken on board the same boat. So we haven't got much longer. Don't forget no woman likes to be remembered because of the way she behaved in some special situation."

"You've been in a special situation?"

'Don't you think so?"

They had been through it before and he was annoyed she should begin again just when they were starting on this messy, embarrassing, even horrifying funeral. Even knowing it was going to be all of these things did not enable him to do anything to stop it. The experience was too much like a dream. You hated it but you could not wake up. The disgusting nature of what they were committed to became all the more unbearable because Leah had taken it into her head, this moment above all, to remind him she had tried to justify her behaviour. He no longer wanted to know how she justified herself. What they had done together was over and done with. He wanted her to shut up. If she went on talking he would put a hand on her thigh, no matter what the nuns might think. That is to say, she would have got him again.

During the turn-out Leah had found two bottles of G.H. Mumm N.V. champagne in a box. There seemed no sensible alternative to drinking them, particularly as it was the evening of her father's funeral, so she had both bottles in the ice box for a couple of hours. And it was after they had put away the contents of the first bottle she said, "I'm quite different in a normal place, even this place at a normal time. I'd like you to know that. I wouldn't like you to know you've seen the real *me*."

He had said something about being surprised his opinion was of any importance to her.

"You don't understand." Either there never had been any proper glasses, or they were lost, or they had been packed away. But they were drinking the champagne out of tumblers. There was no heating in the flat, it was lateish, and Leah was wearing a fur coat he had not seen before, so long and old-fashioned it was draped over her legs like a blanket when she sat down; dyed squirrel, he guessed, probably her mother's. She was gay. It was the day the two of them had been the only mourners at her father's funeral, and she was gay. Looking closer, he could see it was a brittle gaiety. She had drunk two good tumblers of champagne and her eyes shone as though they had been polished. "I was born in January. I'm a Capricorn subject."

He had forgotten she read books on astrology.

"I know where I'm going," she had said. "I'm ruled by my head. I'm not like you, emotional. No, don't laugh! I'm mature and I never do things on impulse. That make sense? I'm not like you. I take decisions. I took certain decisions over the past few months, but I don't want you to think they are the decisions I'd have taken in a different place and at a different time."

He had asked her what decision she had in mind, particularly.

"Not to crack up," was the reply. "To keep sane."

"You used me."

"I'm not like that."

He opened the second bottle so clumsily the champagne frothed over the dyed squirrel but even this did not stop her talking. "You haven't met people who knew me before I came back from the States, or before I married, or when

I was married—— " She hesitated. "I mean, I still am married. But you don't know anybody who saw me under normal conditions. They just wouldn't believe—— " She stopped. "What makes me sick, you haven't seen me as I really am, and now you'll remember me all wrong. This really upsets me. You know?"

"I think you're fine." He had even tried to pat her arm, because she had seemed to grow more and more excited. "You've been through a rough patch. Things will be all right."

She had actually thrown what was left of her champagne in his face; not much, but enough to startle. "Don't talk like that. What the hell, who d'you think you are to talk to me about my life? You've no call to be so superior. You're not so smart. Being despised by a guy like you, really that's the end! Of course you despise me. Don't lie to me. Be honest with yourself. Relax! Give yourself the benefit of a bit of truth. You know what that is? It's looking at things for what they are. If you want to feel good with yourself, and clean inside, all you've got to say to me is, 'Yes, certainly, an easy lay like you, of course I despise you.'"

He had even wondered whether she would calm down if he said precisely that. "You ought to go to bed. You've had a day. We can talk about this some other time if you want."

"No, we won't say any more about this. It's all finished. I just forbid you to mention the subject again. You understand that. I've certain thoughts of my own and I just want to be left with them. You don't think I'm going to dream about you for the rest of my life, do you? Hell, how cocky can a man get? No, there's only one think I'd ask. I'd like to meet you in the real world."

"Isn't this real?"

"Port Said?" She laughed noisily. "I mean London, or the States, where I'm living an ordinary life. You wouldn't recognise me."

"You mean you wouldn't know me?"

He could not blame her for wanting to think well of

herself. He had come to feel the same sort of need himself. Honestly, though, he thought it went deeper in his case. He wanted to feel clean.

So when she came over to him in the boat and they sat so close their thighs rubbed he patted her on a knee he happened to notice exposed, and said, "You don't have to worry about me. I think you're tops. That's the way I'll always think of you. When you get straightened out you might send me a photo. I'd like a photo of you, you know that?"

"No, look, I want to talk to you. I've got something to tell you. We won't get separated, will we?"

"One thing I've always meant to ask you. About ten years ago were you ever on the beach at Port Said when a soldier fell off a horse?"

"I can't remember. Why?"

"I've always wondered."

"What are you getting at?"

"Go and look after the old girl, that'll be a real kindness."

Leah shrugged.

Mrs K was standing up and the chaplain was actually having to hold her with his right hand. He held the Prayer Book open in his left. The nuns were looking down towards Townrow now, with the sun full on their faces, all pale and pimply. As the boat rose and fell one of the brass handles on the coffin winked like a semaphore, so it could not have been so damp in that earth, Townrow thought.

"We can't go on with it. It'll float," Townrow shouted.

"Eh?" The chaplain lowered his Prayer Book in astonishment.

"It'll float. We put him over the side it'll be like launching a boat."

"Oh, dear. What are we going to do? Are you sure?"

"Put a sail on it and it'd fetch up in Lebanon."

The chaplain was bending his head to hear what Mrs K was saying.

"She says that's his home. He would be going home to Beirut. But no." He turned back to her. "This is out of the question. How would you fix a sail to a coffin? We haven't the materials."

They were lurching about sufficiently near a British destroyer for Townrow to shout, "Funeral party here. You got any old iron we could tie to the coffin?"

An officer on the bridge waved back, obviously thinking it was some sort of joke. Townrow went on shouting until another officer, who seemed more quick-witted, climbed to the bridge and began talking to them in a loud-hailer. "Put her over the side and we'll give her a burst with a machine gun."

Mrs K made her way along, steadying herself by putting one hand on the coffin, while Leah supported her by the other arm. Townrow was still sitting at the tiller and when she stood immediately in front of him she bent down. Her face was no more than six inches from his. Her mouth worked as though she was pushing her dentures about with her tongue. She peered at him. Her rage seemed to make her short-sighted. If she decided to spit at him he was not going to duck. The brilliant sun brought out every line on her face and left it colourless. When eventually she spoke she made her mouth small, she was so bitter. "Don't you think I'd been through enough? I was a fool to agree to this. If you could have brought him back from the dead to outface me you'd have done it. This was the nearest you could get. Are you satisfied now?"

The honest answer was no. Given her determination not to leave Elie and his own decision not to abandon her, the only way he could follow Leah was to dig the old man up and bring him along. To make a real party of it. But the old girl was right. He was not satisfied.

He grabbed her and forced her down to his side where she occupied the seat where Leah had been. "I'm sorry, you old fool. God knows, I'm sorry," he said, and kissed her on the top of her head.

"The Devil could not have thought of anything more awful."

The boat was rolling. The way people seemed to be rushing about in it Townrow thought there was a good chance of their capsizing unless they got under way again. He wanted Leah to go back and haul up the sail but he had only to look at her and see the strained, concentrated manner she was watching him to realise she could have made nothing at all of this escapade. Certainly she did not know that it was all, in a manner of speaking, in her honour.

"No, I'm not satisfied," he said in what he hoped was a comforting tone to Mrs K, "I've made a balls up."

At any other time she might have said he was vulgar. That morning she was past it. Townrow squeezed her. They ought to have stayed in Port Said. Elie ought to have stayed in Port Said. He had been confused.

"We'll make for one of the big ships, and they'll give you a decent funeral, you see if they don't, with weights," he said, and shouted to Leah and the chaplain to hoist the sail.

If ever Townrow reached a place where somebody was ready to sit down and listen he would not have known how to tell this story. How could he tell it without seeming stupid or crazy? He might have blamed the times. When you were caught up in extraordinary events you did extraordinary things, even monstrous things like digging up a dead man and carrying him out to sea. He would never be able to persuade anyone he had done it merely to get Mrs K out of the town. He had only to look at her in her steel-rimmed glasses and her white shawl with her grey, thin hair now beginning at last to escape from its pins and blow about, to know he could never say he had exhumed Elie to save her skin.

It could not have been to impress Leah. She had been appalled when she first realised what was happening. At first she refused to step into the boat. She had looked at the coffin and then turned and looked at Townrow with an expression of real horror on her face. Townrow had to bundle her into the boat but even then she might have climbed out again if the British Military Police hadn't started shouting. She made Townrow feel he had been caught out in some disgusting abnormality, cannibalism or ritual murder. She got used to it. Their situation was so extraordinary. Townrow guessed they had, all of them, Mrs K, Leah, the nuns, the lot, reached a point where they would accept any kind of weird behaviour without too much shock.

So he hadn't dug Elie up and used him like some reeking bait to entice his widow out of her lair and so make a good impression on Leah! She wouldn't have worried if Mrs K had been left behind.

Townrow would not, either, be able to make his behaviour seem reasonable by saying he had once dreamed it all. Or it was a false memory. What sort of reasonableness was that? At best he could say the dream or some obscure recollection put this particular trip in his mind. At that moment it seemed to him just a way to be with Leah, the only way he could honourably be out there, in that rocking boat, protracting the time they had spent together.

And the absurd thing was this great vulgar gesture was all for nothing. He was not able to see more than thirty minutes ahead with any certainty. Beyond was no Leah. They were not to go on together. He needed too much to take a grip on himself and by himself to feel equal to any human company for some time, still less Leah's. And yet he did not want her to forget. One way he might explain himself was in this yearning for her not to forget him. The parting would be spectacular. She would not forget this parting.

He was not even sure whether his deeper yearning was that she would forget. He guessed he had done this absurd thing because when men want to run in opposite directions at the same time they compromise by some idiocy. They were all out in this boat, Mrs K, himself, Elie, because Leah was drawing them after her. She pulled them out to sea because that was the way she was going, like the one wild duck at the tip of some arrow of ducks, flying God knows where.

On the port side the destroyer had a gang ladder lowered so no doubt one of these landing craft was expected. This was one reason why the officer with the load-hailer was angry when Townrow gave signs of bringing his craft alongside. He yelled a warning to keep clear. Townrow took no notice with the result that when he brought up at the ladder a couple of armed sailors with H. M.S. *Spiker* on their hatbands were waiting. What looked like a petty officer with a huge revolver in a canvas holster came out and started shouting.

"What's the game, then? Who are you?" Then he noticed the chaplain. "You'll have to get that boat out of the way. We're taking on men at any moment."

"British subjects," Townrow shouted. "Evacuated from Port Said. We were making for the U.K. But we've got to have a funeral. Besides, I don't think she's going to stay afloat."

The sail had come down and the nuns were holding on to the gang ladder, laughing excitedly. They pointed at their wicker baskets. They had little English—they were Maltese—and cried, "Please, please," looking up at the sailors and laughing and pointing. The morning reeked of oil as much as salt water.

By this time the chaplain had climbed the gang ladder and was standing on the deck talking to yet another officer who had appeared and was now looking down at the boat, and the coffin.

Townrow thought he could scarcely refuse to take British subjects aboard. This would include the Maltese. He would take Leah too. But the chaplain would have to be eloquent to persuade him to accept Elie. Very likely, Townrow thought, he would be told to take his coffin to some other place, and he would. Once he had rid himself of the other passengers he saw himself sailing on until the boat sank or he fetched up on some coast. This was something the old girl would not stand for, if he still had Elie on board. She would want to come too.

The chaplain clambered down the gang ladder.

"The lieutenant says he wants the lid off to see what's inside. I know this is upsetting," he said to Mrs K, "but we're caught up in a war. He asked me if I could swear to what was in the coffin and I had to say no."

"No, no, no, no, for God's sake, no."

"It might be—I don't know what? An explosive. They wouldn't want that risk."

"There's no explosive." Mrs K was weary. She closed her eyes and Townrow watched her face rising and falling against the grey flank of the ship; the expression was of complete repose, she might even have been quite genuinely asleep, but certainly set apart from that particular situation. He wondered where, in her mind, she had floated off to. Himself, he was thinking of the day they first met, when he had fallen off that horse in front of the Khoury beach hut and Elie had given him a glass of fruit juice. There she was, sitting at the back of the hut, looking as though she really wished he had broken his neck. She had never liked or trusted him.

The clacking nuns, showing a length of stocking as white as their faces, were clambering on to the gang ladder, handing baskets and suitcases to the sailors. Leah went too.

"Now what?" Half way up the ladder she was near enough to Townrow to speak without having to lift her voice. "What are you sitting there for? Aren't you coming?"

"Not this trip. You go on. Nice to have known you."

"They could spill some kerosene over the boat. It would burn like a torch, and everything in it." Extraordinary, how quietly Leah was able to talk and yet make herself understood. They were out at sea, surrounded by battleships, men were shouting, planes were scorching overhead, yet she talked with so much intimacy they might have been in bed. "I thought you were mad. I knew you were mad when you came out of Port Said dragging a corpse. It's horrible. You don't seem to understand what you did. It's the most horrible thing I've ever heard of. Anybody would think you wanted to drive Mrs Khoury crazy too. Well, did you? You might have succeeded at that. If anybody digs up my husband when he's dead and tries to tie him to my tail, do you know what I'd do? But it couldn't happen in the States. Are you coming? You could get the Navy pour some oil or something on the boat and the coffin and it would be a real funeral pyre."

"I'm not coming, Leah."

She hesitated. "You know, I sometimes think there's some good reason you didn't go back to England before."

"I cover up pretty well. The police would find it hard to prove."

"Why can't you be serious? You might have said the reason was me, at least. You might never see me again."

She went on up the ladder to the deck, followed by Mrs K, supported by the chaplain and a sailor, just as two other sailors started on the coffin with hammers and chisels.

Townrow yelled at them to stop. They paused and looked at him with their mouths open.

"O.K. You can carry on," he said, as soon as Mrs K had disappeared on board and been led off, presumably, to some cabin. The boat had been tied up to the gang ladder so Townrow could get up now and walk about. "For God's sake! I want to see what's in that box as much as you do. What are you waiting for?"

The nails screamed in the wood as they prised up the lid. Townrow was breaking into his dream. He had been here before. An oil patch slid past, winking green and blue, at a peculiar angle to the horizon. The steel hull, blue water, sky and the brown coffin lay in more planes than a three dimensional world permitted; the coffin, in particular, seemed to stick right out of its background and to grow bigger as he watched it. Faces looked down from the deck. Men stood on the stairs. Townrow held on a rope and inspected the face that was now exposed. It seemed huge. He could not understand how it belonged in the same picture with everything else in sight. It was just as though he had been looking at a trick painting of water and boats and men where the artist had played games with perspective and shown objects in relation to one another in a way not possible in nature; then through the canvas had come thrusting this dead, eyeless, black and grizzle-bearded skull.

"You satisfied?" he shouted up to the officer with the canvas holster.

Townrow did not care, now, how long they all stood there. The experience was not quite as he remembered it. There was no cross and the face was a different colour. The sailors were dressed differently. But essentially it was the same dream he had climbed back into and he did not mind how long they waited, just meditating on the fact. If there were parts of your mind you kept returning to, as he had returned to this, you ought to have a good look at it and make a note of the details. Next time they might be different. Seeing all that hair had been a bit of a shock.

"What was that?" The sailors were on the point of replacing the lid but Townrow stepped forward and looked down at the dead face. He had a crazy idea the lips moved.

The chap with the loud-hailer up on the bridge must have received some message because he said, "You can bring it up. I want that gangway clear in two minutes. We've a landing craft coming up directly. Come on now!"

The lips were as dead and black as leather. The eyes were gummed shut. If any words *had* been uttered that would have been a new twist. Even imagining them was a new twist. Townrow saw himself floating in and out of this dream for the rest of his life, and each time there would be a new twist. Next time there would be no nuns and the warship would be American. There would be times when there was a cross on the dead man's chest and there would be times when there was not. The terrible thing about the form this particular dream took was the longing. Townrow looked up and saw Leah at the rail. That was the real innovation this time. Parting. Goodbye.

If the lips had not actually moved, if words had not really been uttered, at least they had sneered. It's all in aid of nothing. You've been duped. That was the message.

Leah was calling down to him but there was so much noise going on he could not make out what she was saying. He saw how white her knuckles were on the rail.

"Get that boat away," the loud-hailer was saying. The sailors already had the coffin half way up the gang ladder. The lid was lying on top loosely. Townrow supposed they would now put the sneering effigy into a loaded canvas bag and dump it decently over the side while the chaplain said a few words and Mrs K stood by having a cry.

Leah understood for the first time that Townrow himself was not coming on board. She tried to push her way past some sailors and make her way down the gang ladder but they grabbed her. She made a fuss about this. She was not the girl to like restraint at the best of times. Townrow saw how red her face had gone. She was actually hitting at one of these sailors. Everyone was laughing except her, and Townrow.

His mind seemed to be draining away. He could not understand why he had done nothing about that assurance from those sneering lips. You are stupid. They were Elie's lips all right, in spite of the whiskers. Townrow had heard about hair growing after death but it was the first time he had seen it. He took the sneer to be an authentic message. It had authority behind it. But he was not acting on it. He was not going on board that destroyer to be with that woman. Sure, he wanted to be with her. Judging by the way she was fighting off the sailors it was what she wanted too. Nothing rated, nothing cut deep, nothing signified. So, follow your nose. Relax, please yourself, do what you want. That was the message from Elie.

"Hold it," he wanted to shout to her. "I'm coming."

But instead he cut the ropes with a fisherman's knife he had found in a box under his seat and grabbed another rope with the idea of hoisting sail. The sailors cheered ironically. Somebody tossed a tin of corned beaf into the boat. Another man was lowering a bottle of beer on a piece of string. As a landing craft came into view round the stern of the warship a sailor pushed Townrow's boat away from the ladder and, the breeze catching the sail when it was still only half way up the mast, Townrow was ten, twenty, thirty yards away; moving north-east. He was smack in the middle of an enormous fleet, like some dog running on to Horse Guards during the Trooping. H.M.S. *Spiker* was probably telling the whole gathering about him. He could see the light winking away. He set a course between an aircraft carrier and a squat yellow boat flying a Tricolour and opened his bottle of beer which fortunately had a screw top. He was moving fast. The clumsy boat was shipping water. If she kept afloat Townrow reckoned that in a matter of hours he would be over the horizon and what then, he thought, what then?

Point number one: any one of these boats would be prepared to pick him up. He could be dropped in Cyprus or Malta. Within a week he could be in the U.K. If the fund embezzlement still bothered him he could pack the job in. If he was *really* bothered he could call at the nearest police station where they had a service for people with that sort of newly awakened conscience. After he had served his two or three years he would still be saying, as he was saying now, what then? So why, except out of sheer bloody perversity, go through all that?

Point number two: he could not sail about the Eastern Med indefinitely on a bottle of beer, now empty, and a tin of bully. He could not open the tin anyway; he had snapped the little tag that fitted into the key. And if the waves grew really big this boat would duck like a moorhen.

Point number three: give up these long-term objectives.

More immediately, he was setting a course for some point near the heart. He had travelled some of the distance before. On Lake Menzallah he had an outboard motor to help and a dead calm of stagnant water, so shot through with the glancings of sun and star and moon he might have moved naturally and painlessly to some clockless retreat; an island with ruins, a cell, an upturned boat in the rushes, a tomb. You didn't need to go back to England and serve a jail sentence to learn as little as this, that whenever he ran away he was on course and doing what came easily. Like his father running away.

Here he was, then, two months later on a tougher escapade than that lake trip. He knew that much more. He had fewer illusions. He now knew he could not afford to surrender the smallest splinter of judgement to any government, organisation, cause or campaign. He was to trust only the immediate promptings, what the eye saw, the nose smelled, and his hand touched. Nobody again would play him for a sucker about what was right and what was wrong. Nobody but he himself would look after his tender little conscience. This was pride if you like. Arrogance. It was amazing, and ironical, and absurd—he couldn't find the right word—that a lousy crook like himself should creep into middle age thinking of honour. Honour? The word made him incredulous. If it was right for a bastard like him to think of honour no wonder it was a dirty word. Honour? Good men spat at the word. And if she had at all detected this crazy notion taking root in him no wonder Leah was furious. Women did not understand honour. It meant a man had decided, absolutely, to answer for himself. Women did not like that kind of loneliness.

He undid the top button of Elie's old brown overcoat because the breeze had dropped and the December sun was warm. The sea rolled about him like blue, unbroken silk. There was enough haze to confuse the line between sea and sky. Depending how he sat, some of the warships seemed pinned above any reasonable horizon. If he really wanted to reach some point he could call the heart maybe this was as near as he would ever get.

It was almost as though it were some real point in the actual sea he was looking for. This might be it. There was too much dazzle to make out anything below the surface; but down there would be fish and sand. Up here were patches of froth and a floating Tate and Lyle sugar carton. He knew, by the sense of absence, he had arrived. He was away and alone, stark.

The waves battered the side of the boat like the thumping fists of people trying to break into his solitude. For the time being he wanted to keep them out. He wanted to rest in this sense of being absent from whoever or whatever he most profoundly needed. He dreamed, woke and tried to catch up with his dream. Oh! It was everything that had ever happened. The eye specialist assured him there was no permanent injury. The girl screamed with laughter as she said he would have to marry her now. For years he had been going through the same routine without immediately recognising it for what it was. He was always being caught out. Of course he was a fool. A simpleton like him had no option but to hang on and hope the dreaming would stop. Once again, this tattoo of fists. No, keep out! Even Leah, keep out!

He was intent, as though he had finally managed to strike a light with a damp match and was protecting it in the wind.